CHURCH STREET

David

love & best wishes always

Elizabeth Sutherland

Elizabeth Sutherland

Principal Characters in Church Street, Queich, The Kingdom of Fife

Maryam Patel 23, shop assistant, Flat 11c The Old Rectory, Church Street
Sheena Macleod 23, staff nurse, Ninewells Hospital, Dundee, Flat 11c The Old Rectory

Maurice Bruden (Mo) 55, Bruden and Sons, Licensed Grocery, 1 Church Street

Lettice Anderson (Lettie) 91, 16 Church Street
Geordie Burns 76, retired labourer, 18 Church Street

Annie Miller 34, cleaner, 37 Church Street
Hughie Miller 13, paper delivery boy, Queich Academy
Elvis Miller 10, St Serf's Primary School, Church Street
Tamsin Miller 8, St Serf's Primary School, Church Street

Mrs Grace Mair 64, widow, The Rowans Church Street
Colin Mair 41, writer, Levenside Church Street

Agnes Mackenzie 75, widow, Lochview, Church Street
Alastair Mackenzie 40, solicitor, Lochview, Church Street
Rachel Makenzie 25, housewife, Lochview, Church Street
John Jason (Jayjay) 3 months, Lochview, Church Street

Bertie Maclardy 67, teacher (retired) Greenyards, Church Street
Gordon Maclardy 77, teacher (retired) Greenyards, Church Street

Rhoda Mackay 68, shop assistant (retired), Church Street

Bob Foulis 78, retired shepherd, 42 Church Street
Rob Foulis 48, shepherd and hill farmer
Chrissie Foulis 46, Rob's housekeeper and sister

Dr Allan Swinney (Jack) 45, local practitioner, the Old Farmhouse, Church Street

Dr Jill Macauley 45, local practioner, the Old Farmhouse, Church Street

Rev'd Gerald Forbes 59, rector, St Serf's Rectory, Church Street

iv

PART ONE

Chapter One

February 1982

Maryam

'The thing is I can't hear the rain. I see it spattering the window but I can't hear it. I always liked the sound of rain,' Miss Anderson complained in her high, querulous voice as Maryam packed her basket with groceries. 'Oh, and have you got any of those chocolate limes? I can't read the packets. Why don't they print the labels properly?'

While Maryam left the counter to find the sweets, Lettie Anderson turned to the small queue of customers waiting behind her. 'I'm sorry to keep you waiting. I can't hear and I can't see and I forget what I came in for. What am I like?'

The shoppers made appropriate noises. 'Is there anything else?' Maryam asked as she added the sweets to the old woman's basket.

'Probably, I can't remember,' she was quick to reply. Her shadow shrank.

Miss Lettice Anderson, now severely arthritic though still as sharp as a knife, had known better days or so she had told Maryam. 'I've come down in the world. If my father could see me now he'd be somersaulting in his grave.' She insisted that she did not regret the long years spent in the antiquated, stone mansion on the cliff in St Andrews where it was always cold. Her doctor, a much younger colleague of her late father, had suggested that since she could no longer cope with the stairs she move into a residential care home. 'Never,' she had pronounced. Anticipating this reaction, he then suggested he would be willing to recommend her name be put forward to the council housing department for a sheltered cottage. As the lesser of two evils she had eventually agreed. Six months later she had moved into a single bedded, semi-detached, sheltered council-owned cottage in Queich. Squeezed between St Serf's primary school playing field and the Old Rectory in Church Street, it had been built on church glebe sold to the council in the late fifties. Though she would admit it to no one else (Maryam didn't count) she found it not only adequate and convenient but also blessedly warm.

'Sure you can manage?' Maryam asked a little anxiously. Her groceries weighed a ton. 'You could leave your basket here and I'll bring it round at dinner time.'

1

Miss A was very wobbly on her feet. No one, apart from Maryam, knew exactly how old she was. It depended on your attitude to age. Younger customers put her at a hundred which was as old as they could imagine, others had her in her 80s but they were both wrong. Maryam knew she was 91 because she had helped her fill in a form which had DOB. after her name. 'Did you forget your stick?'

'Lost it,' Miss A declared as if it were a matter of pride. Her shadow shook its head.

Clearly she should use a stick but to Maryam's knowledge she had now lost two since the New Year. There was one in the lost property box in the back shop, a smart modern pole, which seemingly had lain unclaimed for months. She would ask Mo if they could give it to Miss A. Meanwhile several customers were waiting for her attention. One of them left his place in the queue to open the shop door for the old woman.

'She should na be oot by hersel' wi' thon heavy bag. I think I'll jist gi'e her a wee haun' up the street. I'll be in later,' he called back as he followed Lettie out of the door. Their shadows merged and retreated.

That was typical of Geordie Burns, Maryam thought as she checked out the next basket. Though only in his early seventies, he was not that spry himself. Not all her customers were so mindful. But then again, some of them were, she believed, as she listened to the chit-chat all around her. Like a café in the shop some days, especially since Mo, her boss, had installed an electric kettle, a tin of cocoa, a packet of tea bags and a jar of Nescafe in the adjoining office-cum-stock room. 'Help yourself if there's no one needs serving,' he told her. That seldom happened. She could do with a coffee right now but no chance of that.

'Did you hear the ambulance last night?'

Maryam nodded her head as she checked the weight of a hand of bananas. She had been asked the same question three times already that morning.

'It was no' an ambulance,' said a voice in the queue. 'It was the polis.'

Every head turned. Maryam's finger paused over the till. Voices hushed as they waited for an explanation. Shadows faded and stilled.

'At one o' they flats in the Old Rectory,' the voice continued. No more needed to be said. The young couple in No 11(a) - well maybe not so young - were known for their volatile relationship. Maryam already knew, had known when the shop opened at eight this morning. Old Bain, the recently retired paper boy - that made her smile, he was over eighty - had been full of it. But it was not the man who had been taken away in the police car, it had been his wife. 'You ken her... what's er name?'

2

'Carly something,' someone supplied.

'Aye, her.' Old Bain had nodded as he picked up a copy of the Courier. 'A right wee madam, so I've heard.'

A right wee madam didn't begin to describe Carly; a proper tartar was nearer the mark, Maryam thought when she had had time to think during a brief break in the back shop at eleven. Hot chocolate this morning to cheer herself on. She had already made up her mind to go up to the police station when her shift in the shop was over and see if she needed anything.

Maryam liked Carly, knew she was in an abusive relationship, but then so, it would seem, was her husband. His tongue versus her fists. Which was worst? A black eye or a bruised psyche. The black eye, alas, was visible. Maryam knew exactly what had happened at No 11(a) because Carly's flat was immediately below hers.

The Old Rectory had been made over into four flats some fifteen years ago. Carly and Andy had been there for almost a year now. Maryam knew exactly how Andy set about destroying his wife. She could hear the supercilious tone of his comments if not the words and her increasingly hysterical responses which were sometimes audible. When she ran out of words she used her fists and Carly was no lightweight. Part of Maryam wanted to exclaim, 'Well done, Carly!' Maybe she should have lashed out a long time ago. The sensible part of her wanted to tell Carly to walk away, in which case her next door neighbour would have had no reason to ring the police. As a result, Carly had been taken off in handcuffs not only for causing her husband's bleeding nose but also for resisting arrest. She would get the blame. She could hear Nasreem's contemptuous voice in her ear, 'that's a love marriage for you.'

Gradually the queue dwindled. The empty shop gave Maryam a moment to tidy the magazine rack. It also gave her a chance to glance at the Radio Times. She liked to read the comments on Coronation Street. The shop seemed very silent apart from the hum and click of the freezers. Without looking up, she was aware that someone was standing in the corner by the fruit and veg. gondola watching her. She looked up directly but there was no one there, at least she could see no one. Whoever it was must have moved behind the central gondola which was stacked high with bakery goods. She looked and she waited but she saw no one. There was no one. Suddenly she felt very cold. This was the first time she had ever seen a shadow by itself.

Maryam had always seen shadows. They belonged to people or maybe people belonged to them. She never knew. First aware of them at the age of five she had taken them entirely for granted, thought everyone saw them

3

and communicated with them inside their heads as she did. It was not for another year that she had realised that she - at least among the children she knew - was unique.

'Everyone has a shadow,' Sheena had told her a little scornfully. 'Look! There's mine. There's yours.' She had danced a little in the school playground and the sun shadow had danced with her.

'Of course I know that,' she had replied equally scornfully. 'I'm not talking about sun shadows.'

'What else is there?' Sheena had asked. A crowd of other children had joined them and were listening.

'I mean your proper shadow, the one you can talk to, the one who lives inside you...sort of. ...' Maryam faltered. The other children's faces had looked blank.

Someone had an idea. 'I know. It's her imaginary friend. I used to have one of those. He was called Seumas and he looked like a rabbit and he was my best friend - ages ago when I was wee,' she added contemptuously.

'What does yours look like?' Sheena had demanded.

'I don't know,' she said truthfully. 'I've never seen it.'

'You must have seen it,' someone insisted.

'I can't. It's sort of behind me and inside me.'

'Can you see mine?' someone else asked curiously.

She nodded.

'What about mine?' They all gathered round her, clamouring for answers.

'What does mine look like?'

She shook her head. How could she explain? If she looked directly at a shadow it turned into a transparent shimmer. It was only visible from the corner of her eye and melted, broke up, and trembled like a heatwave when she focussed on it.

'Does it speak?' someone else asked.

She nodded.

'Tell it to say hello then.'

She shook her head. Shadows spoke in a quiet place somewhere inside her; maybe her head or maybe her heart. She was never sure.

'It's probably a Paki thing,' someone suggested.

'Or else she's making it up,' another voice said dismissively as the children started to drift away.

'I'm not making it up,' she said on the edge of tears.

One of them turned, an older lassie and said, 'Hearing voices? That's seriously daft. Maybe it's the loonie bin you're needing.'

4

Her eyes had filled with tears. Her own shadow tried to comfort her. 'So what if you are a bit daft? Our Mother chose you, daft or not,' it indicated encouragingly. Sheena, who had not gone away with the others, looked at her critically. 'Maybe it's got something to do with your eyes. Perhaps you need specs. You should tell your mam.'

'There's nothing wrong with my eyes and there's nothing wrong with my brain,' she muttered under her breath. She could see perfectly well. By this time she had got used to the shadows.

The only other person who ever mentioned them was Sheena's grandmother. 'I am hearing you have the gift,' she said to her quietly one evening when Sheena was out of the room.

'What gift?' she had asked cautiously. Sheena's Granny was known to be a strange lady.

'The gift of 'seeing'. Use it wisely, a'ghraidh. Some call it the gift that is an affliction.'

That night she consulted her shadow. 'What is an affliction?' she asked.

'You have been chosen,' it replied enigmatically.

'Chosen for what?' she asked her shadow.

'To listen,' the shadow told her.

'Who to?'

Her shadow was silent. It was annoying that way. She had worked out that it never answered what it considered to be foolish questions. Sometimes it would tell her, 'now you are just being stupid.' Other times it would say nothing. This had been one of these times: a big silence in her head. But of course she knew the answer already; Our Mother. Once when she was very young she had confused Our Mother with her own mother and told her about the shadows who talked to her in her head.

Her mother must have been worried because she had discussed it with her teacher. 'She sees things and she hears voices.'

'It's perfectly normal,' Miss Macdonald at Stornoway Primary had reassured her. 'Her imagination is developing. She'll soon learn to discriminate between what is real and what is imaginary.'

Maryam had not grown out of seeing shadows. She had, however, learned to hold her tongue. As she grew older she supposed she might have an abnormality of the brain and sometimes it worried her. Suppose she had a tumour. She ought maybe to see a doctor but what would she say to him? She thought she saw things that looked like what? The shadows were so nebulous, so...shadowy; she was hard put to describe them. Mostly they mirrored the size and sex of the person they shadowed, the younger the brighter; babies were not much more than a blob of light. At a push she would say shadows wore jeans and had darkish hair. Yet that was too concrete an image. She could not swear to the jeans or the hair. Perhaps her eyes were affected, a sort of double vision. But that was not right either. She had been taken to the optician and told she had perfect vision. But she had guessed that all along. It occurred to her that if she had perfect vision then all those people who could not see shadows must have faulty sight. The aberration was in them not her. Even though she could never see individual shadows properly she knew that each was as different as the persons they shadowed. Over the years as she had grown in knowledge and in some sort of understanding, she had come to believe that they were connected in some way to Our Mother, but this she had kept to herself. It sounded pretentious. Not even Sheena knew about Our Mother.

She had not given much thought to the shadows lately, taken them for granted until now. A shadow by itself was strange. All the old worries returned. Perhaps it had been hers and it was leaving her. 'Was it you?' she asked and waited in vain for that inner voice. Another foolish question, she supposed, for the answer did not come. Maybe she should go to the local doctor. There were two of them to choose from and they saw Queich patients locally three days a week in a clinic based in what had once been a flower shop in the High Street.   Doctor Allan Swinney and Doctor Jill Macaulay, partners in every sense of the word, were generally known as Jack and Jill. She knew them a little for they shared the Old Farmhouse at the far end of Church Street and had the Courier delivered daily. Both occasionally came into the shop. Doctor Jack bought cigarettes in a pretend-guilty sort of way when he paid the monthly paper bill and Doctor Jill bought milk and dog food.

She could speak to Sheena again, she supposed. Sheena Macleod was her friend and roommate. They had stayed friends since primary school in Stornoway. Sheena was, unlike herself, a true Celt while Maryam's family, or at least her paternal grandparents, had been immigrants. Twice over immigrants. As Indian shopkeepers who, years before independence, had immigrated to Uganda from whence they had gone to Glasgow in the fifties, opened a general store not unlike the one they had owned in East Africa, though the stock was a little different. Their son, Maryam's father, already an adult, had then married - to the horror of both families - a Glaswegian, Catholic shop-assistant. The black sheep. She smiled a little wryly at the expression because, for an Indian, her father had been very black.   No longer welcome at home after his marriage, he had found work in a grocery hidden away from the rest of the Ugandan Muslim community in Skye. There her parents had created a life for themselves by both giving up the overt practice of their religions. Maryam had been brought up neither a Catholic nor a Muslim but steeped in the Celtic lore of Sheena's grandparents. She knew more about Cuchulin than Christ, Finn MacCoul than Mahomed-may-the-Lord-bless-him. Those were the golden years. She had run free with her friends, loved school, slept over at Sheena's, gossiped in Gaelic, until shortly after her twelfth birthday her golden age abruptly came to an end. Her dad, grudgingly forgiven by his family, had returned to Glasgow to manage his ageing father's business in Baillieston. She spent the next four years at a huge comprehensive school where she was called Paki, teased not so much for her appearance but for her Gaelic accent, intermittently bullied, befriended or ignored. Her free time had been spent mostly around customers, running errands for the assistants in what was now her father's store until shortly after her sixteenth birthday her mother was diagnosed with terminal cancer. As the only child of her parents she was expected to leave school and look after her mother. It was no hardship. She loved her garrulous, good-hearted mam. She would have wanted it no other way.

During those two years while her father worked long hours in the store, her mother had turned back to her old faith with evangelical ardour as if to make up for her years in the wilderness so to speak. As long as she was able, she attended Mass at St Bridget's, made frequent confessions, told her Rosary, welcomed the local assistant priest, Father Bone, a loquacious old soul who loved his sugared tea strong enough, he joked, for the spoon to stand up in. Both of them did their best to convert her and her father to Catholicism, which made them smile. They had a nickname for him which they kept to themselves, but to Maryam, who had come to love the old man for himself, he would always be Father Bonkers.

After her mother's death, her father had married again almost immediately, this time to a devout Muslim, an earnest, pretty woman only seven years older than herself who wore the hijab and expected her to do the same, as did her father who had taken up his faith again as if he had never left it. For the next five years her life had been restricted to long shop hours, a home life that was punctuated by prayers and fasts and visits to the mosque. She dutifully studied the Koran and obeyed the rules of her father's faith. Her home was orderly, meals punctual and plentiful, and she grew to like her stepmother though she was aware that she was constantly watched and her friends quietly vetted, especially potential boyfriends. Sometimes she would compare her three existences, the carefree childhood in Skye, her Catholic adolescence and her Muslim girlhood and wonder at the differences. Her mother's untidy, noisy, bustling household had been always alive with aunties and cousins, their constant chatter, the laughter, the sudden spats of anger. Her stepmother's home, the same four walls now denuded of crucifixes and saints, was orderly and quiet. In the largely silent kitchen, harsh words were never spoken and though there were plenty of smiles there was not much laughter. Nasreem did her best but Maryam had no more been converted to Islam than she had been to Catholicism.

Sometimes she felt stifled. 'It's not that I don't like Nasreem,' she would explain to Sheena, on the fewer occasions that they met for Sheena was now training to be a nurse in the Western General and had a boyfriend. 'It's not that I dislike wearing the hijab, it's just that sometimes I would like to be in charge of my own life.'

'If you had to choose,' Sheena once asked her over a quick coffee one Saturday morning, 'which would you prefer? Catholic or Muslim?' She herself was Presbyterian by birth only and inhabited a much scarier realm, the Kingdom of Freedom.

Maryam had thought. 'I don't know.' It occurred to her, 'they are actually a bit alike.'

'Alike? How?' Sheena who had seldom been in any church and never in a mosque had somewhat distorted views of both. She suspected that all Catholics were bigots and all Muslims fundamentalists.

Maryam thought for a moment. 'They both have unrealistic expectations.'

What does that mean?'

It's not enough just to be good; you have to do it their way.' Maryam sighed. 'They think I should be married.'

She had overheard them one evening talking about her, not realising that the door between the kitchen and the living room was half open. She had gone down to the kitchen to fetch a glass of water and they had not heard her.

'It will be difficult,' her father was saying. 'She is too dark.'

'But she is so beautiful,' Nasreem had protested. 'My cousin will love her.

'Believe me, I know what I'm talking about.'

Maryam knew perfectly well that she was neither black nor white but as they said politely of 'mixed race'. She had not given much attention to her father's comments but Nasreem had called her beautiful. That amazed her. Friends had sometimes said, 'you're gorgeous,' in exaggerated tones but she had thought that was what girls said to each other. It was not necessarily true. That part of the conversation she did not repeat to Sheena.

'So they want to arrange a marriage for you with a complete stranger?' Sheena was in a challenging mood.

'Not completely. He's Nasreem's cousin.'

'Have you met him then?'

Maryam shook her head. 'He's supposed to be coming over from Pakistan soon.'

And you're happy about this?'

Maryam shrugged. 'He might be nice.' She'd know by his shadow.

Suppose he's not. What then?'

The odds were that he would be an elderly widower, stout and devout. She was hardly a catch herself. 'I don't know,' she answered honestly.

Sheena shrugged. Her romance which had been faltering recently had completely stalled. They were silent for a moment, then Sheena said, 'we've got no ties. Why don't we just get out?'

Maryam had not thought her serious. 'That'll be right,' she said lightly.

'I mean it,' said Sheena. 'Why don't we just pack up and go?'

'Where?' said Maryam.

Sheena had her own reasons for wanting to leave home. She had been dumped, as she put it crudely, by the guy she had hoped to marry. She wanted to get out of Glasgow. Why should Maryam not come with her? They would move right away to where Sheena knew no one and Maryam could be free to find her own space in the world.

That evening her father and Nasreem told Maryam officially about the proposed marriage. They showed her a photograph of Nasreem's cousin who looked surprisingly young and handsome. They told her he was a good man who would take care of her. 'But in the end it must be your choice,' her father had said firmly. 'Your decision.'

They were the last words he would ever speak to her. Next morning he had been killed by a lorry driver who had suffered a stroke at the wheel. The lorry, on a slope at the time, gathered momentum, mounted the pavement and crashed into a newsagent's shop window. Her father who happened to be on the pavement had been one of several to be killed outright.

The next few months passed in a fog of misery. Nasreem decided to go back to Pakistan. She fully expected Maryam to go with her and marry her cousin. Meanwhile Sheena had applied for a job in Ninewells Hospital in Dundee. She phoned to say that she had found a flat in a village called Queich. 'It's a bit pricier than I would like. Why not leave Glasgow and come and share it with me? You'd be doing me a huge favour, a ghraidh, and maybe yourself at the same time.' Maryam had hesitated. She had more or less decided to go to Pakistan with Nasreem now that the Baillieston store had been sold and she had no work. Then Sheena had added, 'There's a job going in the local grocer's shop. I can send you the details if you're interested.'

Maryam was and she wasn't. She did not really want to get married nor did she want to upset Nasreem whom she had grown to love. Though she had more or less decided to go to Pakistan, she had not said yes to Nasreem or no to Sheena. That afternoon she filled a paper bag with some stale bread rolls and went for a walk in the local park to feed the ducks - something she had often done with her mother before she became ill - and to make up her mind. A light fall of snow had speckled the grass and a sheet of thin ice had formed on the pond. It was very still, a cold, sunless December day with the threat of further snow.

She stood at the edge of the pond. The ducks were huddled together on the small artificial island. She broke off a piece of roll, threw it and watched it skitter across the ice. The ducks paid no attention. She broke off another piece, threw it nearer but the birds paid no heed. That had never happened before. Ducks were always hungry.

A sudden sweep of wind behind her made her turn her head. Until now she had not noticed the old man sitting on one of the park benches barely two metres behind her. He looked scruffy, cold and homeless. He was watching her.

'They ducks are stupid burds, right enough. I'd no be sae choosy,' he said eyeing the paper bag.

'It's a bit stale,' was all she could think of to reply.

'It's bread isn't it? Bread of life as far as Ah'm concerned.' Without rising from the bench he held out a hand.

Speechless she gave him the bag which he took without glancing at the contents. She noticed his hands. They were surprisingly clean, elegant even. He was still looking at her. 'I ken you, hen. You work in Patel's, am I right?'

She had no memory of him among the customers. 'Not any longer. The business is sold.'

'Is that right?' he answered. 'I'll tell you something for nothing, lassie. You were a sight for sore eyes. You'll be missed.'

'Thanks,' she said and added truthfully, 'and I'll miss it.' As she said it she knew it to be true. She liked working behind the counter, the banter, the fragrance of coffee and fresh bread, the customers, especially the customers. As she lifted her hand in a goodbye gesture, she glanced at his shadow. Strange, she thought. Maybe it was a trick of light on snow or something to do with the wind which was now blowing hard for there was no shadow, only light like the flame of sunset though there was no sun 'Who are you?' she asked with the wind in a swirl around her. She thought he was looking at her but it was hard to see with the fiery light behind him and

10

the busy wind around her. 'Lassie,' he seemed to say though it might have been the wind. 'You need to lisss-ten...'

To what? She wondered, for all she could hear was the wind...the wind? Suddenly she remembered that first time she had heard the wind speak. 'Our Mother,' she asked aloud, 'is that you?' As if in answer a strong gust in her face forced her to turn away. Almost immediately the wind dropped, the park bench was empty and the ducks were scrabbling noisily in the broken ice for the bread crumbs.

That night she told Nasreem that she would not be going with her to Pakistan. There were tears and a few recriminations but not as many as she had expected. 'Your father always said that the choice must be yours. But what will you do?'

Next morning when Sheena's letter arrived enclosing the advert for a shop assistant at Bruden and Sons, Licensed Grocer, Church Street, Queich, she knew exactly what she would do. She replied immediately and was interviewed the following week by Mr Bruden who told her to call him Mo for Maurice, and offered her the job. Then Sheena took her to see the accommodation.

The top flat, number 11(c), the Old Rectory, in the village of Queich on the shores of Loch Leven, population a little over 11,000, was well within commuting distance of Ninewells Hospital in Dundee and a three minute walk from Bruden's. Though Sheena was earning enough to run the second-hand white Mini traveller given to her by her parents on her 21st birthday, it was not sufficient to lease the Old Rectory flat on her own. Sheena had needed Maryam on board but not more than Maryam needed her.

Mo told her later that several local girls had applied for the job but because his life would not have been worth living in Queich if he had appointed one over the others, her application had seemed to him like a godsend. She had started work on the 3rd of January and, if asked, would have owned to being content.

Sheena worked long hours in a stressful job, but she too was happy. Wherever two or three Gaels are gathered together there are ceilidhs ...and there were more than two or three in Ninewells. One of them was a young radiographer called Shamus.

When she first mentioned the lone shadow, Sheena had not laughed at her, which was what she had really wanted. Sheena had taken her all too seriously. 'It might be a ghost,' and had insisted the shop was probably haunted. Sheena's grandmother saw ghosts everywhere, all the time. They were more real to her than human beings.

'Lucky you,' Sheena had added. 'I'd give a week's pay to see a ghost.'

11

'I don't think it's a ghost,' Maryam argued. 'I don't think I believe in ghosts.'

'Of course you do. Don't Muslims have ghosts? Catholics certainly do. Whoo-hoo- oo,' she waved a dish towel suggestively in the air. 'Maybe Mo knifed one of his customers and he came to haunt him and got you instead.'

Maryam laughed reluctantly. The idea that Mo would knife anything other than cheese was ludicrous.

'There you are then,' said Sheena. 'Problem solved. Don't be such a silly moo. Incidentally,' she added, 'why didn't you ask it?'

Maryam shook her head. Sheena had never understood. The shadow at her shoulder spoke to her in her head. In her head she chattered away to it, but she had given up asking it any meaningful questions. It was too much part of her. Would you ask your hand how it managed to peel a potato, or press the right keys on the till? Would you ask your eye how it was able to see?

'No,' she said aloud. The lone shadow had been silent, secretive and cold. For almost the first time in her life she had been afraid, not horror-movie, Hallowe'eny scared, but deeply, inexplicably frightened.

'Then perhaps you should,' said Sheena flicking the TV remote until she came to Eastenders. Sheena loved Eastenders as much as Maryam enjoyed Corrie.

That had been three days ago. So far the lone shadow had not come back.

Mo

Maurice Bruden had never wanted to go into the grocery business. His passion had been - still was - archaeology and his particular interest lay in all things Pictish. He reckoned that he was by descent twice over a Pict, having been born in the Kingdom of Fife not far from the Queich cross-slab and having inherited the name of a Pictish king. 'The name Bruden is not necessarily connected to Brude Mac Maelcon, a doubting pedant had once argued, but Mo was undaunted. In his opinion the tagged-on 'n' denoted a descendent of Brude, High King of the Picts in the 6th century. So he told the pedant for that was what he firmly believed. He attended every lecture and every possible dig - indeed assisted at some - remotely connected to Pictdom and was a devoted member of the Fife Pictish Society. He had his own theories about the symbols which he was always eager to propound; a latter-day Ancient Mariner, to any listener caught unawares. He made his shadow smile.

The only impediment to this theory was the fact that, through his mother, he was Jewish. Yet this had not seriously interfered with his genealogical ambitions. So far he had managed to trace his father's family back to Covenanting times and he had by no means given up on his ancestral search.

His Jewish mother had been working as a pretty, dark-eyed waitress in Perth where Mo's father had met her and that was that. Local criticism, fierce at the time, gradually died down. The plus side of it from his parents' point of view was that Mo's father, desperate to earn a living, finally accepted a job in Mo's grandfather's shop. 'Bruden's' the village grocer thus became 'Bruden and Son'. Mo's father took his German Jewish bride to live in Queich; alas not for long. She died in 1927 giving birth to Mo. His father too had died untimely of a rampant lung cancer. So now there was only Mo, no parents, no son, and at the age of fifty-five, still no wife and no extended family, nor probably ever would be. Fortunately the village partially fulfilled that role for Mo was well liked in Queich and never lacked for invitations to Hogmanay parties, anniversaries of all sorts and, of course, he had his archaeological interest.

Mo was also proud of his Jewish roots. After the war, he had traced his mother's family, what remained of it after the Holocaust, to a second cousin once removed called Inge who lived in Hanover and he had holidayed there several times during the local trades fortnight in July. Inge, several decades older than him and now deceased, had been childless and impoverished so Mo who was comfortably secure in his business supported her financially as he would have cared for his own mother had she lived. He supposed technically having a Jewish mother made him a Jew. On the other hand he had not been circumcised so he was not sure about that and had never asked. He liked to think of himself as a 'Pictish Jew'. Perhaps the only living Pictish Jew, or was he perhaps a Jewish Pict? Now there was a thought to unravel.

It was because of his - to his own way of thinking - exotic descent, he was immediately curious to meet Maryam, whose application under the name of Patel told him she was probably from Pakistan. Though at the time he had no real intention of employing her, he invited her to an interview in the back office behind the store. One glimpse was enough.

They talked through the technicalities of the job, the vagaries of the new till, the hours she would be expected to work. Maryam whose adult years had been spent behind a counter ticked every box.

He tried to tell her that his retiring assistant Rhoda would be a hard act to follow. Miss Rhoda Mackay had been counter staff before his father had died some twenty years past. A bit of a dragon lady, Rhoda, now in her late sixties whose bungalow, The Rowans, she had inherited from her parents, also lived in Church Street. She had her likes and dislikes among the customers but she knew how the shop worked. She had retired because of problems with her knee. She missed the shop for it had been her life. There were a lot of tears and gifts and cards on her last December morning behind the counter. Thereafter once a day, sometimes twice, she turned up ostensibly to buy groceries but mainly to offer advice. Most evenings she rang Mo to remind him of something. She might be hard for a replacement to handle.

He was also truthful in telling this dark, pretty, young woman that hers was not the only application. He did not mention that her employment would save him from the dilemma of having to choose between two local applicants both of whom Rhoda disapproved. He did, however, tell her that her previous experience in the grocery business was an unexpected bonus which indeed it was.

'If I were to offer you the job' - by now he had no doubt in his mind that he would - 'where would you live? I'm afraid I've no accommodation to offer.' He himself lived above the shop.

She explained about the flat in the Old Rectory up the street and that, if she got the job, she would be sharing with a school friend.

'Do you always wear the hijab?' he asked her curiously but not critically. He had more or less expected it from her name but he would have liked to see her hair.

'Only on Fridays,' she said. 'Out of respect for my father, and this always' - she pulled out a tiny silver Celtic cross from behind the folds of her scarf, - 'in memory of my mother.'

'Today is not Friday,' he pointed out somewhat unnecessarily. It was in fact Thursday afternoon, early closing in Queich.

'I wanted you to know the truth about me,' she said. 'My grandfather was an Indian store keeper with a British passport living in Uganda until he and his family chose to come to Scotland. He started his business again in Glasgow. His son, my father, married a Scot so I'm half Scottish, half Pakistani. I have... had family in Glasgow and also in Pakistan.'

'Then you had better know the truth about me. I'm a Pict – a Jewish Pict,' he added a little tentatively. Some people were still funny about Jews, especially Muslims. So he explained about his mother. 'She was a German Jew who died when I was born.'

She was silent for a moment, her eyes downcast. He thought that she was going to walk out. Maybe he shouldn't have told her about his mother.

'What exactly is a Pict?' she asked and now he was in his element.

He told her at length about the Pictish Celts who had ruled Scotland for five hundred years, and his self-appointed ancestor's high role in their history. 'The Picts are the true inhabitants of Alba.'

She listened to him with interest. 'Then who are the Scots?' she asked.

He was in full flow now as he explained in detail the facts of the past. 'The Scots were Irish Celts who did their best to wipe out Pictish civilisation and their language, but we still exist. I promise you we still exist.' He always got a bit heated at this point.

'You won't want me working for you then because my mother was Scottish and my father was a Muslim,' she said with a hint of a smile.

'But I do,' he said, knowing that he did. 'The job is yours, Miss Patel, if you want it.'

'Why me?' she had asked which was not the answer he had expected.

He could not really explain. She was beautiful but that was not the reason. So were the other applicants. All young girls were beautiful in his opinion. She knew the job. A minor consideration because anyone with a bit of brain and an interest in people could learn. He could hardly tell her that the dark little office seemed lighter in her presence, that she made him feel – what? Hopeful. So he dodged the question. 'I prefer not to employ locally,' he answered loftily as if this were some unwritten rule in the grocery business. It had only just occurred to him.

It was true, however, that he would have found it difficult to choose between the local applicants without causing a village rift and, above all things, Mo hated arguments, complaints and bad-mouthing, but that did not explain why he was so determined to hire Maryam. In theory and as a true Pict he felt historically bound to dislike 'the Scots'. Similarly, as technically Jewish, he ought to dislike all Muslims. To a nominal Presbyterian - which he considered himself to be from his Sunday School childhood - Islam was heathen. So why bring a Catholic Muslim into a village in the heart of Presbyterian Queich? He had no real answer then or now to the question that was to come from several of his customers, especially Rhoda and the families of the girls whose applications he had turned down. So he invented a host of reasons if only to silence his critics. 'She already knows the ropes,' he told one persistent customer. 'Her references are impeccable,' he told another. (He had barely looked at them.) 'I felt she needed a bit of support. Not easy to get a job with her background these days.' What a fib, he thought. He knew he was no do-gooder.

The truth, or part of it, lay somewhere deep down in his subconscious. Mo believed himself to be unattractive; too much nose and too little chin. He hated what he saw in the mirror every time he shaved. He was also a bit thin on top; almost 'bald' in fact. The thought of a smart young local girl behind his counter seeing his lack of chin, despising his careful comb-over, was humiliating. He would not have to feel inferior to Maryam Patel with her dark skin and Asian ancestry. 'Racist" he scolded himself. I am a chinless racist, he thought with shame. 'Oh well,' he added aloud. 'Up the Picts!' He saluted himself ironically in the bathroom mirror, made himself a cup of tea, ate a bowl of porridge made from the best local oatmeal soaked overnight and went down the stairs to open the shop for the papers.

He peered up the still dark February street. No snow, thank God. A glistening counterpane of frost covered the roofs of the parked cars and glinted on the black tarmac under the yellow street lamp as he took out the crate of empty milk bottles. In the silence of the dark morning a garden gate clanged and he could hear the clunk of bottles. The milkman and his van were close but the Menzies delivery van was late for it was already after seven.

He glanced round his shop. The freezer and cold cabinets hummed, the heating had come on. Everything was as it should be. Maryam had been on the back shift last night and as usual she had left the counter and the scales spotless. How would he have managed without her? Especially now.

The worry strode from the back of his mind right up to engulf his whole being. Today, February 10, was the day. He allowed his whole frame to shiver, could not prevent it, though the shop was not that cold.

The bell rattled. The Menzies man strode in with two large bundles of newspapers, done up in string, mainly Records and Couriers. 'Morning, Mo.'

'Morning, What's it like?' he asked the retreating back.

'Black ice,' he answered returning with several smaller bundles of Scotsmans, Heralds, Times and weeklies which today included Peoples Friend, a package of D.C.Thomson comics and a couple of glossy monthlies. 'No Guardians sorry. London papers are not in and I'm already behind. Leaves frosted on the bloody railway line. Same old, same old.'

Mo shut the door behind him. He had about thirty minutes to sort the papers for Hughie-the-lad and accept the early bakery delivery. The shop would open to the village at 8 00 am sharp. He knew that by then a small congregation of retired men would be gathered outside, in no particular hurry, gossiping and stamping their feet against the chill of dawn as the sun rose low on the loch.

For the next few minutes he was too busy to think, as he wrote down the street numbers of the twenty-three newspaper deliveries and ticked the orders off in the register. Hughie at thirteen was fairly new to the job, Old Bain having recently retired as a result of falling off his bike and breaking his leg. But it was still there of course, that dank, scratchy, blanket of anxiety that had lain over his shoulders for a fortnight now, the longest fortnight of his life.

At seven-thirty the shop door handle rattled. Mo opened up to let in the delivery man with his trays of bread, morning rolls and butteries. The meat and macaroni pies not forgetting the cream cookies and iced fancies from the Lomond Bakery would come later. The fragrance, usually so satisfying, engulfed him in a sense of nostalgia. I'll miss this, he thought, half of his mind aghast while his mouth automatically moved in reply to the Aberdonian van driver's, 'Fit's like, mon?'

Maryam was hard on his heels with Hughie in her wake. Usually Mo did the early morning shift on his own but now she needed to learn. For the past week she had been coming in from eight to twelve, a split shift for she came on again from four till eight. 'Morning, Sunshine,' he said to her, because it was true. That first morning when she had turned up early he had thought the sun was shining. 'I see it's cleared up,' he had said to her for it had been both taps on when he had taken in the papers. She had looked surprised as she took off her coat. 'Not so's you'd notice,' she had told him and that had been nearly six weeks ago. He had got used to it now, that perception of sunlight that she seemed to create, so mostly he called her Sunshine.

'How's Hughie this morning?' The whey-faced lad yawned and grunted. Mo caught Maryam's eye for a moment of amused recognition and handed the lad a Millionaire's Slice a day past its sell-by date. 'Here, get that down ye, lad.' The boy woke up sufficiently to cram the rich shortbread into his mouth. In a second or two he would come alive again. It had been Maryam's idea to feed the sleepy-head, sometimes with an iced bun or a cream cookie, whatever was left over from the previous day. He salivated a little as he watched Hughie stuff his face. Mo had a sweet tooth and the tastiest of bakery left-overs usually found its way upstairs.

'You watch now, it's black ice out there,' he warned the lad as, still yawning, he stumbled out of the shop with the papers bagged and sorted. Mo watched his assistant as she pushed rolls or butteries into paper bags, ticking the names off in the order book. The scratchy blanket which had loosened while he was busy, enfolded him again. Now he would need to tell her.

The old station clock that Mo had acquired at auction a few years back when the branch line had been axed and now hung on the wall above the door, showed that it was 7.59. Maryam too had noticed. She got to the door first. Five local men, still arguing about the footie on last night's telly, came in and for the next hour they were both too busy to talk. Workmen came in for pies and school kids for Twirly-Wirlies or crisps to stuff in their bags and wifies for fresh bread rolls or butteries. The kids needed an eye kept on them now, and again at break and dinner-time; some kids. He knew the ones to watch.

Just after nine the shop was empty.

Now, he thought. Do it now. But there were other matters more immediately important. Today was Wednesday; there were deliveries from half a dozen food manufacturers. Why did it have to be a Wednesday? But the rest of the week was no better. Come to think of it there were deliveries every day.

'We'll just go through the list one more time,' he said opening the order book. 'Remember, you'll need to check Donaldson's carefully. Their delivery mannie's a bit short of the grey matter.' He tapped his head significantly. 'Needs watching.' Once, only once, Donaldson's of Kirkcaldy had delivered fourteen packets of sausages instead of fifteen so you couldn't be too careful.

'Oh and don't forget that special delivery from Honeyman's. Mrs Mair's son's birthday cake. That's due today. She'll be in for it later.'

Maryam checked over his instructions which he had given her several times already over the past week. 'Oh and mind it's dry-cleaning day,' he added. 'There's that jacket expected back today for Mrs Mackenzie, the one the baby puked on. You know how particular she is. It's already paid for. Was there anything to send?'

'Through the back,' she said.

He glanced at the clock. 9.15. He would need to go. The appointment at Ninewells hospital in Dundee was for 11 30. The distance was about a twenty miles but you never knew with all that traffic on the bridge. The cold thorny blanket threatened to engulf his whole body.

'What's wrong, Mo?' she asked quietly turning her head to look at him.

That sensation of light - was it something to do with the electricity? - seemed to brighten the whole shop but he was aware that she was not quite looking at him. He had noticed this before with Maryam. Sometimes when he thought that she had been speaking to him she had been looking at a spot so nearly him, just over his shoulder, or so it seemed. Once he had shifted his own gaze to where she seemed to be looking but of course there was no one else there. At first he had wondered if perhaps she had a squint. The moment never lasted long enough to analyse it more carefully. Now she was looking at him directly, eye to eye. Hers were a clear dark brown, her gaze straight and steadfast with no hint of damage. Now was his chance to tell her, but once again he chickened. 'Ah'm fine,' he said in his strongest Fife accent. 'Jist fine.'

'No, Mo, pardon me, you are not,' she said in that strange accent of hers that was sing-song Indian overlaid with sing-song Hebridean. All he heard was concern. He was not used to anyone being particularly concerned for him and it paralysed him. To his horror he found his eyes welling up. A weird feeling. He was powerless to stop it. There was a thickness at the back of his throat and suddenly his eyes were so full of water that they spilled over of their own accord. Tears? The shame of it. He turned his whole body abruptly away.

She reached into the pocket of her green overall and pulled out a small packet of tissues. Carefully she opened it and took out one sheet which she handed to him. Then she said, 'Tell me, Mo.'

The shop door clanged open. It still had a bell attached which, being elderly, had a mind of its own. Mostly it clattered. Today it pinged. Loudly. The back of a young mum dragging her baby's stroller appeared in the doorway. Gone were the days when prams were left outside in the street. There could be baby snatchers lurking in every corner even in Queich. Sometimes there were so many push-chairs and strollers and babies strapped to their mothers that there was no room in the shop to move. Today, he remembered, was nursery school morning.

Maryam knew the young wife, Mrs Mackenzie's daughter-in-law whose name Mo had momentarily forgotten. Maryam already knew everyone, he thought with admiration; a good memory for faces was decidedly a bonus in the grocery business. They said 'Hi' to each other and then they both did a bit of baby worship while he surreptitiously wiped his face. Maryam was good at baby worship too. For the umpteenth time he thought how extremely fortunate he had been to find her, which was indeed how he considered it. He had found her. How fortunate. He was no good at baby worship. When he tried, contorting his face into weird shapes, they usually yelled. At that moment another mum came in, her large round-eyed yearling in some contraption strapped to her back. He listened to the banter, heard the laughter and, feeling a little bereft, a little sorry for himself, turned to go into the office.

Maryam noticed. Of course she would. 'Bye Mo,' she told him and the two young women turned to him with smiles. 'Bye! Don't do anything I wouldn't do which gives you plenty scope,' said one of them. Rachel Mackenzie, that was her name. The other mum took her baby's fingers and said, 'wave bye-bye to Uncle Mo.'

He liked that. He liked the fuss. He liked being Uncle Mo. For a moment or two he forgot about the blanket. Maryam would manage the morning, the lunch-time kids, the deliveries, the complaints, the queries and the till. He would have liked to remind her once more about the birthday cake and the fact that he would not be available till after dinner, hopefully 2 pm. But he had told her that over and over; for the past week he had been reminding her that he would be away for most of the day. He left the back office and climbed the narrow staircase that led to his flat.

Ten minutes later he was seated in his red VW Polo and driving towards the slip road to the A92. His body had begun to tremble He could see his hands shake on the steering wheel. The clock on the display panel told him he had plenty of time. He would take the detour round Balqueich to give him luck and a bit of courage.

Five minutes later he parked in a lay-by, got out, crossed the dyke by the new stile, took the hard, rutted path to where the standing stone dominated the field that was green and white with frosted winter wheat. He gazed up at the ringed cross in its frame of carved interlace, then moved behind the stone to look up at the crescent crossed by a floriated V-rod and the double disc below it with its Z rod. He put his two hands on either side of the cold sandstone and waited until the trembling in his fingers ceased. Below the symbols, he gazed at the hunting scene which an art historian had told him probably represented the divine hunt with the warriors and their dogs as the forces of evil chased the fleeing hind which symbolised the human soul. He touched the carved deer. Never had he felt more like that frightened soul.

Rachel

She had no real need to go to the shop that morning. The cupboards had been filled by her mother-in-law the previous day who had trudged up the stairs with two plastic bags stuffed full of Safeway groceries. She should have been grateful. She tried hard to be grateful, but Mrs Mackenzie's martyred manner made it difficult. She wanted to say, 'I didn't ask.'

She pushed the stroller to the far side of the shop and stood in front of the tea and coffee shelf. Earl Grey, she thought to herself. Mrs Mackenzie despised Earl Grey. 'Wishy washy English stuff,' she had said. 'I wouldn't give it cupboard space, but you go your own way. You always do. I'll tell you this for nothing. You won't get Alastair to touch the stuff.'

Al, who had been within hearing distance, had said nothing. That was the trouble. Where his mother was concerned he tended always to agree with her if pushed for an answer, otherwise he said nothing. Good at saying nothing, was her Al. Above all, he hated arguments. She understood why.

He once told her that he had grown up in a maelstrom of controversy; noisy arguments which usually escalated into bitter, door-slamming rows. Once, in the car she had got into an argument with her mother-in-law over something as ridiculous as reincarnation and found herself caught up in its web. 'Let it go,' Al had muttered to her out of the corner of his mouth. 'I'm trying to,' she muttered back as Mrs Mackenzie ranted on and on about the ridiculous concept of a soul reliving a million lives. She had only said mildly that half the world held it to be true but that had been sufficient to start a storm. 'Well,' she would say triumphantly whether her son was present or not, 'Alastair won't agree with you.' She never called him Al and castigated those who did, including Rachel. 'He's got a proper name, hasn't he? A good Scottish name. Why do you want to go calling him after an American gangster?' This time she had kept quiet knowing that her disagreement would provoke another ten minutes at least of aggressive rant.

'Verbal abuse,' she told Al indignantly. 'That's what it is. Verbal abuse.'

He had not disagreed but then neither did he agree. All he said was, 'You need to learn the triggers.'

'I'm not going to shut up about things that matter to me,' she told him, 'if that's what you're suggesting.'

He had pretended not to hear.

It wouldn't of course matter so much if they had lived in different towns or even different streets, but they shared the same house with only a staircase to separate them. Al was a partner in what had been his solicitor father's business in Kirkcaldy and unlike the other two partners, Jerry Macintyre and Hal Foote, lived in Queich away from the office. Lochview was a solidly built Edwardian villa, one of two in Church Street not yet converted into flats. Apart from four brief years at the Edinburgh University, Al had always lived at home and on his marriage had stayed exactly where he was while his mother had moved downstairs. On paper it was a sensible arrangement. For Mrs Mackenzie it should have been heaven if she had had any concept of that state; for Rachel, close to hell. She was unsure of Al's true feelings. Being her senior by some fifteen years and comfortably established in a quietly flourishing family business, he could well afford to buy a property in Bali if he so chose. It was, she realised, partly her own fault that she had landed up more or less living with her mother-in-law. She should have insisted on having her own home before their marriage. Because she had said nothing, Al had taken for granted that she was happy with the arrangement. But then as he had never asked her and at the time she had no proper idea of what living so close to her mother-in-law would be like. Before the baby was born she had tried to broach the subject with her husband. To please her, for she believed he probably loved her, he had fobbed her off with excuses. 'I feel happier knowing that Mother is at hand should anything happen to you. Let's think about it later.'

After Jason was born she had complained about the stairs. 'If we had our own home it would be so much easier.' His excuse then had been, 'Mother's getting very frail. She would hate to move.' In vain she had protested that she had never intended that Mrs Mackenzie should move with them. 'Are you suggesting that we leave her alone in this great barn of a house?' he had answered. 'You aren't thinking this through, my dear.' His tone was placatory. 'After all, I'm responsible for my mother. Unlike your mother, she has no one else.' (Rachel's parents now lived in Australia.) With that remark he left the room as he always did if an argument threatened. She suspected that the courage needed to leave home had always been well beyond him.

The latest row was over Jason's Christening. She and Al had decided, more or less - Al was not much good at family decisions - not to have him 'done'. 'He can choose for himself when he's old enough,' they told each other. Rachel had tried to tell Mrs Mackenzie when she had suggested they hold the ceremony in St Serf's since she was nominally a member (Christmas Eve and sometimes Easter) and Al had once or twice as a young boy gone to their Sunday School. Rachel had expected Al to support her when Mrs Mackenzie had insisted, 'Of course he must be christened. You can have the party downstairs. There's more room.'

Reluctantly she had given in. The groceries yesterday had been some sort of appeasement because Mrs Mackenzie had won. Al had unsurprisingly taken his mother's side. 'For goodness sake, what harm can it do?' he had told her mildly. 'You said yourself that you were in two minds.'

That was before Mrs Mackenzie had interfered.

'I suppose,' she had said reluctantly, 'but I'm not changing his name whatever your mother says.' She knew that Mrs Mackenzie could hardly bring herself to utter the name Jason.

'I suppose we could just add my father's name? That would please her.'

Rachel bit back the words that leapt into her mind. Why would she want to please Mrs Mackenzie?

'After all, she does so much for us.'

This time she retaliated. 'Things I never ask for and I don't need.'

It happened that, unknown to herself, Alastair had added his father's name to the certificate when he had registered the birth.

'I apologise if it's upset you, but I was sure you wouldn't mind. 'John' is not such a bad name, is it? John Jason has a bit of a ring to it don't you think?'

'Jason John,' she corrected him, but when she looked at the birth certificate there it was, John Jason. What about my father, she wanted to scream at him but she held her tongue and changed the subject. 'I'm not having your mother choose his godparents.'

'Of course not,' he agreed. 'Who do you have in mind?'

That was a tough one. Her sister immediately came to mind but Diana lived in Australia. Her school friends lived in Sussex but which of the two to ask? The more she thought about it the more decided she became. 'I'd really like Diana, but she won't be able to come to the service.'

'That's easily solved. Have your sister by all means but choose a local proxy to stand in for her at the service,' said Al who had already consulted his mother on the subject. 'Mother would be happy to do it.'

'No,' she snapped. 'I'll choose my sister's proxy.'

Meanwhile Al chose the godfather, one of his contemporaries at law school and a well-heeled bachelor practising law in Edinburgh who was happy to accept.

Maryam was still serving the other two mums while Rachel bided her time by the tea shelf. She wanted to catch Maryam on her own. The conversation at the counter was about a body that had been found in the loch a few days ago and the latest speculations as to its identity. Rachel thought they would never go. As they were leaving one of the young mums caught sight of her. 'Are you coming, Rachel?' she asked. 'Want us to wait for you?'

'You're all right.' she told them, 'see you later.' She turned to Maryam. 'At last. I was beginning to think they'd be talking till dinnertime.'

Maryam laughed and came round from behind the counter, bent down to speak to Jason who smiled and blew her a bubble of saliva. She stood up and looked at Rachel. 'You okay?' she asked as if she cared.

But she wasn't looking at her. Her eyes seemed to be watching something else. It reminded Rachel of TV when the announcer was speaking to the viewers but reading from the autocue somewhere a fraction above or beyond. Sometimes Rachel would follow the direction of Maryam's eyes but saw no one, nothing out of the ordinary, so she no longer bothered. Almost immediately the focus of her gaze changed and she was looking at her directly. 'Can I help?'

'I was hoping you'd ask.' Rachel told her. She liked to look at Maryam. She was so pretty, radiant really as if she had switched on some internal light bulb. It was probably something to do with her complexion. She had a flawless brown skin. Rachel envied good skin; her own inclined to freckles. It all came out in a rush. 'Jason's getting christened. I didn't really want it but Mrs M. does and Al always sides with her. Diana, my sister's the godmother but she's in Sydney and can't be here. Will you come to the Christening and be proxy?' Suddenly she remembered. Maryam was probably a Muslim. Sometimes she even wore a headscarf. How could she embarrass her like this? 'I'm sorry, I wasn't thinking straight. Maybe I shouldn't have asked?'

Maryam smiled and reached out to touch her hand. 'Of course I'll come to the Christening and I'd be honoured to stand in for your sister. Does that mean I get to hold his lordship?'

'I thought it might be against your religion?' Rachel said anxiously.

'My religion?' she said thoughtfully. 'I kind of respect them all.'

'Do you really?' If asked she would have said that she kind of hated - that was too strong a word - was bored by them all.

Maryam checked the Earl Grey through the till. 'When's the great day?'

'Not till March. I'll send you a proper invite.' The shop bell tinkled. 'I'd better be off, then. Thanks, Maryam.'

'Don't forget this.' Their fingers touched as Maryam handed her the tea. One of the two new customers held open the shop door as she manhandled the stroller outside. She was aware that her hand felt alive and glowing where Maryam had touched her. Weird that.

Nursery school was fun that morning. In fact everything seemed just a smidgeon better.

Bertie Maclardy

'Morning, Maryam. Has my brother been in yet?' Bertie Maclardy was wearing his golfing pullover and brown brogues. He was also in a foul mood.

Gordon had not been home all night. When he woke, the other side of the bed they usually shared was empty and when he looked, the bed in the other room had not been slept in either. Bertie was worried and angry, more worried than angry if he were to be honest. It had happened before. Gordon was getting on, a good ten years his senior and he was becoming forgetful, so forgetful that Bertie was afraid he might let private matters slip.

Gordon and Bertie were not in fact brothers. Although their affair was legal these days (it had started before the Wolfenden Report), they had never bothered to come out. Gordon had been a junior maths teacher in a minor public school in the south of England, Bertie his adoring, eighteen-year old pupil and old enough to know his own mind. The relationship had ended until some decade later they found themselves teaching at adjacent schools in Leicester. Ever careful, there was never a whiff of scandal attached to either man, for, fortunately, neither was in the least attracted to children. Both had experienced short-lived affairs with women, in Gordon's case once, disastrously. These had been enough to inform them that their relationship was the real thing, whatever that might be. They loved each other.

When Bertie was left comfortably well-off by a Hampshire aunt he took early retirement and persuaded Gordon to do the same. Having no close ties in the way of siblings or parents, they decided to move to Scotland, the home of golf, to which they were both addicted and, to save a lot of gossip and speculation, live together as brothers. They had fun bickering mildly over an invented back-story which no one had ever queried. The 'Maclardy brothers' had therefore been born some twenty years previously. A decade ago they had bought Greenyards in Church Street which would have been adjacent to Lochview had the previous owner not sold enough of his garden for a private developer to build two bungalows.

Gordon's seventy-fifth birthday now loomed and though both agreed that this was no age at all these days, there was no doubt in Bertie's mind that Gordon's memory was becoming faulty. Twice to Bertie's knowledge he had forgotten their telephone number when asked. There had been other indications, small ones like leaving the tap in the kitchen running all night and going out to bring in the dust bins and ending up wandering down the High Street. What if he forgot who he now was and only remembered who he had once been? The careful façade that they had built together of golf-daft brothers was in danger of crumbling. Worse still, what if Gordon developed full-blown dementia? How would they manage? How would he cope with a lover who no longer recognised him? 'Whoa, whoa. Stop getting ahead of yourself there, Bert my lad,' he told himself out loud. But where was Gordon? Truth be told Bertie was worried sick.

But it was not just the fear of dementia that scared Bertie, nor the fact that they were lovers not brothers. Gordon had been involved in something possibly criminal in his earlier years; maybe done something very foolish. That one woman he had been involved with - Bertie could only think of her as 'that bitch' - had been blackmailing him. Then one dark October night she had been killed. 'Hit and run' the police had called it. Gordon had been questioned of course, his car examined; so had others for the woman seemingly had several enemies, but nothing had been proved. Gordon had denied that he had had anything to do with it and Bertie professed to believe him. In his heart of hearts he had never been entirely sure and Gordon sometimes woke in the night with hideous nightmares. Nor did he ever drive the Ford Cortina they shared, not since they had come north to Scotland. Made a joke about the Scottish roads. In truth, Bertie did not care. He liked driving. Nor did he really care about the accident. The woman had been a bitch of the first order; she had deserved all she got. Good for Gordon if he had done it. However the case had never been closed. Suppose Gordon, who had genuinely been traumatised by the whole affair, in the throes of dementia, confessed to killing her, whether he had done it by accident, on purpose or not at all. That was what really scared him. Right now Bertie was obsessed with anxiety.

Maryam entered the carton of milk in the till. 'I haven't seen him this morning,' she said. Then she looked at him. He had not intended to be so frank but the shop was empty and Maryam standing there looking at him, well... almost looking at him, unlatched the door to his teeming mind.

'He hasn't been home all night and to tell you the truth I'm worried sick.' The words came tumbling out in spite of himself. 'His memory's not good. He's not that young and I don't know what to do.' How could this girl be of any possible assistance? 'Sorry,' he said. 'I'm being a complete idiot.' He tried to laugh but it came out to his shame as a sob.

'Maybe you're right to be worried,' she said and this time her eyes were fully engaged with his. 'Come.'

She led the way into the back shop. Among the crates of bottles and boxes of groceries stood Mo's desk with an old-fashioned bakelite telephone. A cork notice board covered with lists and reminders hung on the wall. She unpinned one of the bits of paper and put it on the desk in front of him. 'Mo keeps this list of hospitals and local police stations handy in case one of the customers takes ill.' (She did not add 'or shoplifts'.) 'Perhaps you should ring the Queich Police and then try the hospitals.'

'No,' he said firmly. 'Not the police station.' For God's sake, the last people he wanted were the police, but it was a good idea to he ring round the hospitals; Kirkcaldy and Dundee; perhaps the Perth Infirmary.

The shop bell clacked. 'Thanks, Maryam, I'll manage,' he told her more calmly so she left him to it. He tried Kirkcaldy first then Perth. While he was hanging on waiting for the receptionist to make inquires, Maryam came back. She waited until the call was over. 'No joy so far,' he told her.

'I think perhaps you should go home, Mr Maclardy,' she told him standing there in the doorway. The light from the shop seemed to reflect from her.

He misunderstood her. 'Yes of course. I'm sorry,' he said. 'This is Mo's private sanctum. I quite understand.' He stood up immediately and followed her back into the shop. There were two customers still touring the shelves. 'I've made a note of the numbers. I can ring from home.'

'I don't think you'll need them,' she told him quietly.

'How can you possibly know that?' he asked hopefully.

She did not answer. One of the two customers was demanding her attention at the counter. The woman - Mrs Mackenzie - acknowledged him

26

with a brief nod but was far too engaged in her own conversation to speak to him. She was still talking as he left the shop but Maryam saw him. She lifted her hand and gave him a small encouraging wave.

Somehow he knew he would find Gordon at home and of course he did. This time.

Agnes Mackenzie

'Why people don't control their dogs better, I can't understand. I passed precisely two disgusting messes on the pavement this morning. There ought to be a law about it. It's unhygienic and downright dangerous.'

Agnes Mackenzie sounded aggressive. Her hip was bad this morning; something to do with the weather no doubt, but when did her hip ever stop aching? She had complained often enough to the doctor and fair enough she was on the list for a new one but the waiting seemed endless.

Maryam nodded as she rang the brown loaf through the till. She did not always agree with Mrs Mackenzie on one of her rants but this time she did. Twice to her knowledge customers had trodden muck into the shop and the place stank until she had found time to get out the Dettol and a mop. 'Could you write to the papers?' she suggested when the rant was over.

'I could, couldn't I? I could write to the Courier, not that it'll make a bl…ind' - (she had started to say bloody but remembered in time that it was infra dig to swear in front of a shop gel) - 'bit of difference. I don't suppose the guilty dog owners ever read the paper, and even if they do why would they take any notice? The village is going to rack and ruin if you ask me. It's the council I blame. They should have a bye-law or something.'

'You could write to them too.'

'Do you know, Maryam, I think I might just do that. Someone needs to prod them.' She paused. 'By the way, was Alastair's wife in this morning?'

'She was.'

'Buying cakes and biscuits no doubt. I'm really worried about that gel. She eats so badly. We're supposed to be what we eat, aren't we? She eats nothing but fried stuff and chocolate biscuits. It can't be good for the baby's milk. She'll end up with diabetes or cancer. Worse, she'll give the baby a sugar addiction, I shouldn't wonder. I read an article about it in the Telegraph.' Now she had started she couldn't let go.

'Jason looked blooming on his way to nursery,' Maryam said mildly.

'And that's another thing,' Mrs Mackenzie added as she tucked the brown bread into her shopping bag. 'The baby's name; Jason. He'll never forgive her when he's grown up, you know. A man needs a solid strong name if he's to get on in the world.' She paused for breath. 'Fortunately' - she clung on to the thought – 'Alastair has added his father's name to the birth certificate, John. I shall be calling him John,' she added triumphantly.

Sometimes she despaired of her son. Alastair had only done it because she had insisted. 'I can't see why you object so much to Jason,' he had whined. Yes, whined. Alastair had always been a bit of a whiner. 'Because it's common,' she had told him sharply. 'You may be happy to call your son after a so-called pop star, but he won't thank you for it when he's older.'

'Jason was the name of one of the Greek heroes,' he told her defensively.

Was it? She had forgotten. She was pretty darn sure Rachel had not known either.

'How's your hip?' Maryam asked as she crossed the two brown bread rolls off Mo's list of orders. Mo was a list man.

'Awful,' Agnes replied. 'Just awful today.' She was on the brink of tears. It seemed that she was always on the brink of tears these days. She summoned up anger as the only antidote she knew. 'I don't understand what the National Health's playing at. I haven't heard a word from the hospital and it's over three months.'

'What about a sit-down? Would that help?' Maryam suggested.

'For God's sake stop being so nice to me,' Agnes declared. 'Nobody's nice to me these days.' There were tears in her eyes.

Maryam came round from the counter and took her arm. 'There's a chair through the back. Give me a moment and I'll make us a coffee, shall I?'

She fumbled for a handkerchief and couldn't find it. A feeble spark of anger tried to catch fire. She had used her bloody handkerchief on the baby's nose. 'Could you get me a packet of tissues - on my account of course,' she added humbly. The snot was in free fall.

'And that's another thing,' she said frantically fanning the spark of anger as more tears threatened. 'The baby's nose is always running and she does nothing about it. He's always got a dirty face or a runny nose.'

Maryam led her through to the back shop which, thank God, had somewhere to sit. She eased herself carefully on to a bubble-backed chair - rather a good one, she noted, what was it doing in a back shop? - While the gel served the waiting customer and fetched a packet of tissues, Agnes wiped her face. The pain had miraculously eased.

'Tea, Nescaff or chocolate?' Maryam offered. 'Chocolate's the nicest.'

She didn't really want anything except to sit pain free for a few moments but the gel had been so kind she was not inclined to refuse.

'Chocolate then,' she said. For a blissful moment they were both quiet as the kettle thrummed between them. Then she said almost placatingly, 'you don't have to pay any attention to me, you know. I do go on a bit.'

'It's what pain does to you,' the gel said turning her head to look at her; but not at her, Agnes noted, at a spot near her. Was it her eyes? Did she have a squint? The moment passed. The hot chocolate was surprisingly good.

The shop bell clattered. It was an ugly sound. 'I wouldn't put up with that,' she said tartly.

Maryam laughed. 'You're so right. Sometimes, though, it tinkles.'

It tinkled for me, Agnes thought on a ridiculous little surge of pride.

'You're right. So it did,' the gel said. 'That's another customer. I'll need to go.'

'Of course.'

'You stay here as long as you like. There's no rush.'

After a few moments she rose to her feet. So far so good. As, carefully, she walked back up Church Street, she was thinking; she was so sure she had not spoken her silly thought about the shop bell aloud. She supposed she must have done. No matter. Maryam was really a very nice gel, considering...

Considering what? She asked herself as she walked up Lochview's short drive and felt in her coat pocket for the front door key. Considering she's a half-caste. Stop it, she told herself sharply. I am not a racist. Whatever else I might be I am not prejudiced. That gel's a real asset to the village... The front door opened smoothly and she let herself in. What a pity Rachel was not a bit more like her. As quickly as she thought it, another idea took its place. Whatever Rachel might be at least she was not of mixed race. 'I didn't mean it,' she said aloud. 'You know I didn't mean it.' Exactly who she was talking to she had never quite worked out. Herself, she supposed, but wasn't that the first sign of madness? Could she be going mad? Senile dementia? Please God not that. Not on top of everything else. Her hip had started to nag again.

She took off her coat and hung it carefully on a hanger in the cloakroom off the porch. Then taking the paper, she limped through the hall to the drawing room and looked out of the large bay window. The frost had almost gone. The sky looked heavy with un-fallen snow. She began to make plans for the Christening party. She could fit in forty guests without difficulty. She remembered the cocktail parties she and John used to hold from time to time in this very room. Cocktail parties were all the rage when they were first married just after the war. There was a particular knack which she rather enjoyed; circulating, it was called. A few words to one then on to the next, a bit like that dance, the Eightsome Reel. Set to your partner, move to the left, or was it the right? John had never got the hang of drinks' parties. Stuck in the same corner all night with some old bore. She was the one buttering up clients, introducing strangers, filling glasses, handing round canapés and other short eats. Alastair helped when he was old enough to behave himself. She had been so proud of him in his Mackenzie tartan kilt and little bow tie with a plate of nuts and crisps. Orange juice for him; gin and it or a dram for the rest of them. On your feet for two hours without a twinge. She sighed. She couldn't do it now. She would need to ask Annie Miller in to give her some extra hours. Annie was her cleaning lady. Well hardly a lady. Annie was a widow - even that was doubtful - with three children of school age, who cleaned for her twice a week. Not brilliantly. She could probably do with some extra money.

From her perch in the window seat she saw Rachel returning up the drive with the baby in the stroller. She sighed. Would she call in for a moment or two for a little chat? Not her. She turned her thoughts back to the Christening.

Annie Miller

Ten Woodbine she thought as she joined the short line in Bruden's waiting to be served. She deserved that surely. It would have to be baked beans on toast for tea again. If she did without the Woodbine she could manage a bit of bacon. In the past she would have put it on her tab but Mo had got strict lately. No more tick for the likes of her. Okay for posh people such as Ma Mackenzie. She could run an account and buy up the whole shop on tick if she wanted. Mostly she didn't want. Preferred to take the car to Safeway or that posh place in Kirkcaldy. Often she had been tempted to say to the girl - Mo called her Sunshine, heaven knew why, she was as dark as the ace of spades - 'put it down on Mrs Mackenzie's account please.' If she thought she had the least chance of getting away with it she might not have hesitated. Could she get away with half a pound of bacon? If asked she could say that it was for Mrs M. The girl whose name she had never got around to pronouncing (she knew 'Marian' and 'Miriam' but 'Maryam' defeated her) so she too had begun to think of her as 'Sunshine'. She had heard Mo call to her across the shop. 'Any of those broken snaps left, Sunshine?' so Sunshine it would have to be. A pound of bacon, Sunshine, on Mrs M's account. 'You're daft, Ma.' Elvis had laughed at her. 'Her name's Mary- am. Go on say it.' So she did and could in the privacy of their three bed-roomed council home. Saying it aloud in the shop was another matter.

Her turn to be served, the last in the line, so she put the basket with the two tins of beans on the counter without the bacon. She hoped against hope that there was enough bread in the bin. The Family Allowance would be paid the next day but that had to be kept for the rent.

'Good afternoon, Mrs Miller,' the girl said to her, always so perjink. 'Your usual is it?' Cigarettes were behind the counter. You had to ask for them these days.

'I'd better no',' she found herself saying. 'It's that or streaky bacon for the bairns' tea.' (Streaky was cheapest). 'The kitty's empty. I'll be okay tomorrow, here's hoping.'

'How much bacon?' Several packets, labelled streaky and back, sliced the night before by Mo, lay on the far end of the counter.

'Half a pound'll have to do.'

Maryam took one of the packets weighed it on the scales and popped it in Annie's basket. Then she opened the cigarette cabinet and took out ten Woodbine.

Annie opened her purse. There were precisely three shillings and five pence. 'I'll be in tomorrow,' she said hoarsely without looking up. It was not as though she liked owing money and tomorrow was rent day again. 'You could take it out of Hughie's pay,' she added. Why had she said that? Hughie was saving for a pair of them new fangled trainers.

'I'll do no such thing,' the quine said with a wee laugh to show she was not ticking her off.

Annie looked up, but the quine was not looking at her. She glanced over her shoulder to see who was listening but there was no one else in the shop. When she looked back, the quiney was looking straight at her and her brown eyes seemed to sparkle. Suddenly Annie could see why Mo called her Sunshine.

She felt like weeping. Kindnesses did not often come her way these days. When had they ever? 'Ta, Sunshine. I'll be in to pay tomorrow sharp.'

'It'll keep. The rent won't.'

She clutched her shopping bag. Another customer had come into the shop. At the door she paused to look back at the counter. The quine looked up at the same time and caught her eye. She gave her a thumbs-up. Annie did the same. All the way up the street she wondered about the lass. She was absolutely sure she had not mentioned owing rent. The fact remained that it was overdue by two months. How could Sunshine know that? Unless maybe the council had said something... surely they wouldn't?

She had Ma Mackenzie to do-fer tomorrow at nine. That would put £2 in her pocket. Enough to pay the bacon. The packet felt heavy, a lot more that half a pound. She peered down at it and saw the label, Danish best back; tears of gratitude flooded her eyes. It would do for school pieces as well as the bairns' tea.

Back in her kitchenette at Number 27, she filled the kettle and turned on the grill. She hoped the gas would not give out on her; it must be about ready to be cut off. It was a week past since she'd put any money in the meter. She thought of all those unobtainable coins in the meter box, so near and yet so far. They'd never miss a handful. She fantasized about buying the kids chips and cream cookies to go with the best back. Tea made from a used teabag, (you could get at least three cups out of one bag), she spooned in a large sugar - the packet was running low again - Elvis must have made himself and Tammy a sugar piece before school by which time she had already left for her other cleaning job at the pub in the High Street.

She pulled back a chair from the kitchen table and sat down. Then she took out a precious fag and lit up. The first draw made her cough. She was coughing for the kingdom these days. Ma Mackenzie did not like her to cough. 'Are you starting a cold, Annie? I can't have colds brought into the house, not with a baby upstairs.'

No, she was not starting a cold. She had a smoker's hack. She knew she should give up. The papers were always telling her to stop. The doctor told her to stop when she had started barking in the surgery when she had taken wee Tammy in for that sickness bug. She thought of all the money she would save, but it didn't work out like that. That bloke at the Loch Inn said you just spent the money saved on beer or sweeties. Got fat.

Thinking about money drew her eyes to the dresser drawer. There was money there tucked away at the back if she dared to use it. Too soon, she told herself. Someone had dropped a fancy wee paper bag behind one of the padded benches in the pub. She had put it in her pocket meaning to hand it over to the boss when she finished cleaning the floor. Lost property was usually claimed straight off or else went to the police station. The boss was strict about that. She forgot about it in her apron pocket. Truly she had forgotten. Then back at home waiting for the kids she had remembered and found it. There it was all new and shiny in a little square box, a pretty ring with two diamonds and a blue stone in the middle. Looked like an engagement ring; a bit like Princess Di's. They were all the fashion these days. She tried it on her fourth finger, the one that had a Woolworth trinket for a wedding ring. It looked a bit strange on her work-worn hand but good. It felt good. She hadn't wanted to take it off, but then she had heard the bairns at the door and slipped it back into its box and thrust it into the drawer as far in as it would go. There it had stayed.

Next day the boss had asked her if she had cleaned under the benches that morning. 'Why?' she had wondered all innocent like. 'Young bloke said he'd lost a paper poke with an engagement ring in it for his girl friend.'

'I'll keep an eye out,' she mumbled and still not looking at him, added, 'poor lad, eh?' She squirmed at herself for she sounded so false and broke into a fit of coughing.

Nothing more was ever said but she had come to hate the pub job. If she could get somewhere else, maybe the school which would mean more regular work and a good wage, she would give up the pub in a blink.

That was all of three months past and the ring still sat in the drawer. She was not stupid enough to take it to a local jeweller and when did she ever get to Perth or better still Dundee to try to sell it. She knew that the polis counted on jewellers to report anything suspicious and what could look more suspicious than her with that ring. They'd be nee-nawing at her door before you could count ten. Besides did she really want to sell it? Sometimes when she was alone she would take it out and put it on her finger and just admire - no, more than that - just love it.

But the ring was not Annie's only treasure. There was the bird too; a little porcelain blue and golden bird, as pretty as paint. It was after Hal had gone; her first job with an old wifie dead long since. They were in Alloa then. She was pregnant with Tammy so it must have been eight years past. Hal had just gone, left one morning for work (she supposed) and never came back. She never heard from him again and nor had the polis. Reckoned he'd done a bunk. She had got her first job cleaning for this old wifie whose house was full of treasures. Dusting them was an endless job but restful for her as Tammy in her belly weighed a ton. She fell in love with the wee blue bird as soon as she saw it and somehow it ended up in her pocket. No one noticed; certainly not the old wifie who was blind as a bat.

Then Tammy was born and after a while she was re-housed in a three bed-roomed terraced block in Queich. If asked, she could tell the polis that the old wife had given it to her. Just before she left Alloa, the old wifie died so she reckoned it was safe enough. When the kids were older and past breaking stuff she might even display it on the mantelpiece along with the school photos.

Actually the bird was not the only treasure now stored in a cardboard shoe box under her bed. There were a few other things too. A pencil sharpener that had belonged to a girl called after Deanna Durbin in her class at school, a kind lass who had helped her with sums. She treasured that sharpener though she had never tried to use it. She had hidden a green silk scarf with white daisies that someone had left on a bus. She had never worn it in case she met the owner who could be anyone she might pass in the street. Annie did not take things to use, just to possess, to look at sometimes and to treasure. Her treasures. Tammy discovered the shoe box once when she was playing hide-and-seek under her bed. 'Here Ma,' she had said holding up the scarf. 'Why d'ye no' wear this? It's pretty. Did my da give it you?'

She had snatched the box back. 'You leave they alane. Them's mine.'

'I ken it's yours. I'm just asking,' Tammy had retaliated.

'Nane of your business,' Annie told her sharply. After that she had hidden her little treasures in separate places. At the back of the press, in the chest of drawers with the broken handle which took a bit of trouble to open and of course at the back of the kitchen drawer. She loved them, especially the pencil sharpener that looked like a wee gnome sitting on a toadstool with a writing bit at the end of the stalk. It called to mind Deanna and that year after her father died and before her mam walked out. The best year of her life, she reckoned. The ring was more of a burden than a pleasure.

Maybe the time had come to get rid. Take it to a Dundee shop. There must be plenty there. She could wear that posh scarf and her best black coat that had belonged to the kind old wifie and given to her by the daughter after she died. Annie seldom wore it; because of the bird she did not feel entitled. If she dressed up posh no one would question her ownership of the ring. She began in her mind to spend the proceeds. Would it be in the hundreds? Surely. Maybe even a thousand. First thing she'd buy would be Hughie's trainers. In fact she could get them all trainers.

Wrapt up in her dream, the knock on the street door made her jump. The raps came again hard and insistent. She knew immediately who it was that knocked on the door like that. Her body trembled as she opened up to see two police offices in all their intimidating accessories flashing their identity discs. 'Mrs Ann Miller? May we come in for a minute?'

The ring, she thought. They've found out about the ring.... The scarf and the bird and the pencil sharpener flitted through her mind. Her legs turned to jelly and she would have fallen if the polis lassie hadn't caught her arm. 'You need to sit down, Mrs Miller.'

Someone's dead, she thought. Mam? She never saw her mother these days. She was hitched up to some guy in Glasgow. She got a redirected card and ten bob for the bairns one Christmas but no address. Could be her Auntie May. She was not a real auntie but she had fostered her after her mam walked out and her da died. Auntie May was no relation but she had been kind.

The polis lassie sat down beside her on the couch. The man stood in front of them. 'Queich academy asked us to call, Mrs Miller.'

God, god, god, she thought. It's one of the bairns. The ring flashed into her mind again. This was pay back time.

'Hugh's been taken to hospital.'

'No,' she whimpered, 'no my Hughie. Is he ...' but she could not say the word.

'Hughie's got a nasty pain in his tummy. The doctor's with him now. You're not on the phone so the school asked us to inform you. Do you have transport?'

She shook her head dumbly.

'We'll take you up to the Kirkcaldy hospital. Perhaps you'd like to bring him a pair of pyjamas and whatever else you think he'll need.'

Pyjamas? She thought stupidly as she stumbled up the narrow flight of stairs to the bedroom Hughie shared with Elvis. Hughie slept in his vest and underpants like they all did. She looked round the sparse room with the two bunk beds. Two shelves held some of their possessions including their clothes; the rest, odd socks and sweetie papers littered the floor. The curtains were still half drawn and the beds unmade. A plastic bag containing a collection of milk bottle tops hung on a hook behind the door. Elvis was collecting them for some project in school. She emptied them on the lower bed and stuffed in a pair of socks, a grubby pair of jeans and his best T-shirt, the one with King Kong emblazoned on the front. She found a vest without holes and some clean underpants that might have belonged to Elvis. Then she saw the tattered book on the floor with the illustration of the small black boy and the big striped tiger. It was a bit babyish but still she put it into the bag at the top so the polis would see -.what? That Hughie was a clever lad, that he was not the slob she knew she was.

The polis lassie took her right up to the children's ward. In one way she was a bit scunnered to be seen with one of the scum; on the other hand she might never have found Hughie without a bit of help. It was a nice big airy ward but he had screens around his bed and behind them he looked very small and grey and scared.

There was a big lump in her throat and the words when they came out sounded strange. 'See, Hughie, I've brought yon book.'

'Hi, Mam,' he said in a small voice.

The nurse, all smiles, came up and drew her aside. 'Hugh's got himself an appendix which he doesn't need. We require your signature to operate.'

Now she was really scared. 'An operation?'

'It's very straightforward, Mrs Miller, but we need to go ahead quickly. Let's just get your signature and it'll be all over and done with in a blink.'

Her signature she could do. Afterwards she sat beside him and would have held his hand if he had not been so embarrassed. When the porter came to wheel him away, he opened his eyes. 'See and tell Mo I'll no' be in for the papers tomorrow.'

She held back her tears until she was alone in the waiting room. She was desperate for a fag. There was a big clock up on the wall that told her it was getting on for three. The bairns would be out of school in half an hour and she had the house key in her pocket. She'd need to ring the school to keep them but she had no money for the phone. No money for the bus back either. She thought of Tammy's best mate but she had no idea where her ma lived. She picked her lassie up in a car. There was only one number she knew by heart. Mo's. Sunshine had written it on the back of her wrist when Hughie had first started his paper round in case she needed him or he got held up.

She went to the nurses' station and explained about the kids. She was a nice woman, older, friendly. 'Help yourself,' she said handing over the phone.

It was a bit of a palava getting an outside line but she managed it and after several rings she heard Mo's voice, 'Bruden's. Can I help you?'

'It's me, Annie Miller,' she gabbled. It all came out with a rush, Hughie's operation, the children at school, the locked door, and she could hear the tears and the terror in her voice. 'I dinna ha'e the number. Can you tell the school?'

His reassurance was like an arm round her shoulder. 'I can do that,' he told her. 'You stay with Hughie as long as he needs you. We'll see to Tammy and Elvis.'

'Thanks, Mo...thanks a million.'

Suddenly she was calm. She handed the phone back to the nice woman and returned to the waiting room. She had stopped shaking and she could think clearly.

Twenty minutes later the waiting-room door opened. A nurse stood there all bright and shiny. 'Mrs Miller?' she asked.

She got to her feet. Could it be done already? 'That's me,' she said calmly.

'It's all over. He's still sleeping it off but he's absolutely fine.'

Tammy Miller

'Tamsin? Tamsin Miller!' Miss Chambers called out as the school bell clanged.

Tammy put her hand up. The head teacher eye-balled her. She felt her palms go sweaty and her arms prickle with goose-bumps. What had she done this time? Miss Chambers was always at her for something or other, like shouting in the play-ground or fidgeting in assembly. She was a bit scared of Miss Chambers; Potty, the big boys like Elvis called her which had made Mam pretend not to smile. Mam pretending not to smile was a joke in itself. Not that Mam smiled much these days. She had forgotten what Mam's laugh sounded like. Maybe Mam did not know how to laugh. Not like her class teacher, Mrs Thomson. Mrs Thomson laughed a lot which made school loads better.

She pushed through the other kids fast because Miss Chambers did not like to be kept waiting and stood in front of her with her legs straight and her hands clutching each other tightly.

'Tamsin? For goodness sake, child, just look at your hair!' Tammy couldn't look at her hair so she looked down at her feet instead. 'Tell your mother to have it cut or braided. I won't have pupils in my school looking as if they had been dragged through a hedge backwards.' Miss Chambers sounded cross. Tammy knew perfectly well that her hair was a mess. Usually Mam tied it back for her in a pony tail, but she had had to pull Hughie's blanket off him to get him up for his paper round and then she had had to leave for work herself so Tammy had forgotten even to brush it. She had explained to Mrs Thomson who understood but she didn't know how to begin to explain to Miss Chambers.

Luckily she seemed to have got off with it because Miss Chambers was on to something else. 'Your mother has been delayed so you are not to go home. You are to go down to Bruden's and wait for her there. I've told your brother that you will meet him at the school gate and walk with him on the pavement straight down to the corner shop. Is that understood? Your mother will pick you up from there as soon as she can.'

Tammy nodded.

'Repeat to me what I have just said,' Miss Chambers commanded so she did. She would have liked to ask where Mam was but lacked the courage. 'Very well, then. You can go - and see that your hair is tidy tomorrow.'

Again she nodded then darted to the cloakroom to get her jacket. What'd happened to Mam? Mam was always home or else the key was under a stone. Had she gone like her Da? He had been there one morning before she was born and had never come back. She heard Mam telling someone he had just walked out. If Da could just walk out, so could Mam. Now she was shaking.

Elvis was waiting at the school gates with someone else. She could see his animated face. He was talking as usual. Elvis was always at the craic. The only time he was silent was when he was asleep and sometimes not even then. Hughie complained he talked in his dreams. He saw her and waved. The other person turned. It was the lady from the shop. Tammy was surprised or should have been surprised but strangely enough she was not.

'Hi, Tammy,' she said and she was smiling. 'I was just explaining to Elvis that your Mam rang the shop to say she would be late and could you wait with us.' Then she gave them a choice. They could certainly go to the shop and maybe do their homework in the back office, or go to her home which was just down the road and have juice and wait for Mam there. No choice really. Both of them spoke at once. 'Yours!' Tammy added as an afterthought, 'please?'

Out of the school gate she asked them both if they had had a good day. That was all the encouragement Elvis needed. Out it poured all about some boy in the class who had got the strap three times. Tammy, half a pace behind, saw Maryam's hand not so very far from her own untidy head. It was so pretty and brown and the nails were shiny and such a pretty shape and not bitten like hers or encrusted with grime like Elvis'. Somehow her small hand of its own accord reached out and touched those brown fingers and found itself clasped in a warm grasp. The shaking stopped; the worry about Mam vanished as her sweaty little hand was enfolded in those warm brown fingers. She held on tight as they passed the house where yon man stood at the window, but he was not there so she did not have to run. Nor did she have to speak. There was no need. Elvis talked for the two of them and Maryam listened.

It was a big house with two doors. Maryam explained the front door was for the two front apartments and the back door was for the two back flats. She led them up a short drive and through a little gate in a tall dark green prickly hedge round to the back of the house. A long garden of grass sprinkled with snowdrops and wee yellow flowers stretched back behind the house surrounded by big, bare trees. She stared at it as Maryam reached into her bag for her key.

'Is yon gairden all yours?' Elvis asked, impressed.

'Just a wee bit of it,' she said. 'Right at the bottom. Want to see?'

'Yeah,' said Elvis. 'Me too,' said Tammy clutching Maryam's hand again.

Elvis ran ahead down a paved path through the lawn then right at the bottom there were bushes, one of them covered with yellow flowers, and behind the bushes it was magic; almost like a secret garden, Tammy thought. Not too big, just right with a swing seat and a wee bit of grass and a whole patch of blue and white and purple flowers jostling the snowdrops.

'It's braw,' she said. At that moment she felt perfectly happy as she still clutched on to Maryam's hand and watched Elvis in the swing seat pushing himself back and forwards. She felt safe.

'What about some juice?' Maryam suggested.

'Ye-ah!' they both answered together. She let go of Maryam's hand and they both raced up the path towards the back door, Elvis detouring in wide circles with his arms stretched out and making aeroplane noises.

Inside there was a porch to hang up their jackets and school bags and a staircase. Beyond the stairs was a door which opened as they approached; a smart wummin appeared, stuck up, Tammy thought, because she barely glanced at her and Elvis. She spoke to Maryam who touched her arm and replied to her at which she nodded and went back inside the door without another word.

'Who's thon wummin?' She asked clutching Maryam's hand even more tightly.

'A neighbour,' Maryam told her quietly. They followed Elvis who was already half way up the stairs.

The flat had two bedrooms and a kitchen and a living room; like home, Tammy thought, but not like home. It smelled different in that it had no smell, except a faint whiff of perfume which afterwards she found came from a bowl of dark blue flowers on the windowsill. There were three big comfy chairs with a guitar on one of them and best of all, a colour TV set that worked.

The wee kitchenette had a table the same as theirs except all it had on it was a bowl of white flowers with the same faint whiff of scent, and salt and pepper pots that looked like two wee mice.

'They're cute!' Tammy looked at the mice longingly.

'Hold them, if you like,' said Maryam, so she did, very carefully because she could see the salt and pepper holes.

'Orange or red juice?' she asked holding up two bottles.

'Red!' They both replied and Tammy murmured the word 'please' again.

There were biscuits too. Tammy put one of the wee mice, the pepper one, back on the table and kept the other squeezed in her left hand while she drank her juice and ate three ginger snaps. Maryam showed them how to crack them on the elbow and if they broke into three pieces that meant a secret wish. So she put down the salt mouse, and a lot of cracking went on and Tammy's last biscuit broke into three neat pieces. 'I get to have a wish!' she cried.

'So you do, Tammy.'

Tammy was about to tell them her wish, but Maryam held a finger to her lips. It's a secret, remember?' So Tammy kept quiet. Her wishes were usually for a pink fairy bike, the same as some of her school mates had, but not this time.

It did not really surprise her when Maryam told her that Mam was safe and on her way home. That was what she had wished for. Maryam was special. She could hear what people were thinking. She had known that for a long time.

When they'd finished their juice, Maryam told them about Hughie in hospital and how he had had an operation to remove his appendix. He too was fine and maybe they would like to draw him a card and post it so he would get it the next day.

She drew the wee mice. She set them both before her on the kitchen table and drew them on the piece of folded white paper with the felt tip pen that Maryam had provided. Then she had written in her best capital letters, Luv from Tamy with a row of kisses.

Elvis drew a guitar. He was mad about guitars. It was so big and it took so long to finish that there was no room or time for writing. Maryam put them in two envelopes and wrote the hospital address and they stuck on stamps. Then Mam came and told them that Hughie was fine and it was time to go. 'I hope they've been nae bother,' said Mam on the doorstep. She looked sort of grey beside brown Maryam but she smiled a wee bit when Maryam said, 'I hope they can come again.'

On the way home they posted their cards in the pillar box down the road.

'So can I get to go again?' she asked Mam hopefully.

'Mebbe,' said Mam as she unlocked their own back door.

Lettie Anderson

Lettice (she hated her name and Lettie was only minimally better) looked at her watch for the umteenth time. Maryam was now ten minutes late. Why? She lived practically next door, for heaven's sake! She was never late on the days she worked the afternoon shift and the girl always told her when she was going to be working late. Maybe she had forgotten and today of all days when she had some real news. She got up and sat down again, switched on the TV and tried to concentrate on the six o'clock news which was bad as usual. Had the news always been as bad as it was these days? She remembered listening to the news at 9 o'clock on the wireless during the war but never really taking it in because her own private war was raging at the time and it eclipsed the rest. Her father had been taken poorly in the first year of the war. She had nursed him through a long and dreadful cancer until his death in 1943. She reckoned, however, it was not just the cancer that had killed him. Both her brothers, those bright beautiful beloved boys, whose names, Arthur and Alexander, were haloed in her head, had been killed in action, slaughtered in the First World War. He had never been quite the same thereafter.

She remembered her father's funeral in the cemetery outside St Andrews. She had thought seriously of casting herself into the open grave beside him. Might well have done so if Aunt Dorothy had not been clutching her arm. Poor old Dot, her sole remaining relative, was dead and gone too, buried not long after her father. So wartime news was a black smudge on the dark canvas of her life. Summoning up anger, her only weapon against the perpetual sorrows of the past (our Lady of Perpetual Sorrow, she thought suddenly), she allowed the hot rush of rage to obliterate the agony of remembered grief. Anger, on the one hand, had destroyed any happiness she might have found after the war. On the other hand it had kept her alive.

She remembered that last year of the war packing parcels for POWs twice a week in a big hall at Perth. It took an hour to get there by bus. Once she accepted a lift from a neighbour who got petrol coupons for war work. The little buds of friendship that had blossomed as she had stuffed packets of tea and bars of chocolate into cardboard boxes had withered under her sharp tongue. She had been offered that lift only once. She could remember hearing herself go on and on dominating the conversation in the car with her complaints. She knew she was not nice to know, had no friends and deserved none. Had there ever been a time when she had been a nice person? It was all so long ago that she could not remember.

Thinking of that terrible time, she felt the familiar rush of heat to her head. Then the doorbell rang. She stumped into the tiny hall and flung open the door.

'I'm so sorry I'm late,' the girl said. Seeing her pretty brown face, hearing her apologetic words for some unknown reason fuelled her rising rage.

'You'd better come in, then,' she said shortly and left Maryam to follow. She did not offer her the customary glass of sherry which was waiting on the silver salver on a side table in the tiny sitting room. Maryam always refused but it gave herself the excuse to indulge. She much enjoyed her early evening glass of sherry.

Maryam told her about the children's visit. Her soft strangely accented voice was soothing. Gradually Lettie felt the heat in her head cool; the harsh words die away from her tongue. She rose from her chair with her customary difficulty. Waited that moment till the dizziness in her head settled and said, 'A small glass of sherry, my dear? I think you deserve it.'

'Okay,' she said, 'I'd like that.'

Lettie was surprised. She always offered and had always been refused. She hesitated. 'Are you sure? Doesn't your religion forbid alcohol?'

'Only on Fridays,' Maryam explained. 'I'm Muslim on Fridays. Today I'm Catholic and the rest of the week I'm catholic with a small 'c'.'

'I see,' said Lettie, unconscious of the pun, but she didn't. Catholic was catholic was Catholic was it not? However she let the matter pass and poured the sherry for them both. She was bursting to tell her news.

'They came!' she said lifting her glass in a small toast.

Maryam knew immediately what she meant. 'That is good news. Can I see them?'

Lettie reached behind her and took out the blue case with the new spectacles nestling within. 'Lo and behold!' she said, beaming broadly.' I can read again. Thank you my dear.'

'It was a pleasure,' the girl told her. Indeed, Lettie thought, it had been pleasant. Maryam had taken her to the optician in the High Street, stayed with her during her eye test and then they had gone to the Cosy Café for a cup of tea and a cream cake. Things that she could have done without thinking a few years back such as arranging an eye test had become unbelievably hard of late. Without the girl's thoughtfulness she would have just become more blind with every week that passed.

For over a month now Maryam had been coming in to visit her for half an hour or so on the evenings she was free. Lettie was not quite sure how the arrangement had started. She had dropped a glove in the shop and the girl had returned it on her way home from work just after six. She had said, could hear herself saying in a moany voice (she hated her moany voice), 'You're the first person to cross this threshold since ...' She had counted back the weeks. 'Since the doctor visited that time I had 'flu'.'

That had been the start of it and now she had a visitor sitting in her Parker Knoll tapestry-cushioned chair at least three times a week. The difference those visits made to her life was incalculable. 'I've got you a present,' she said reaching behind her for the little parcel wrapped in Christmas paper. She held it out and Maryam took it. 'Go on,' she felt herself beaming now, 'open it.'

It was a pretty necklace that had belonged to her mother; blood red stones interspersed with gold discs. Not real gold of course but the dark red stones, probably glass, glowed prettily. Maryam unwrapped the paper carefully. Lettie liked that. She remembered her brothers tearing open their Christmas parcels while her mother rescued the crumpled paper, ironed it and stored it for the next year. With the same respect, Maryam opened the little cardboard jeweller's box and took out the necklace. The stones glowed in her hand. They looked like precious gems.

'Put it on,' Lettie encouraged her, so she did. She looked beautiful. In a moment of inspiration, Lettie saw that it was not the stones that gleamed on the girl's brown neck. It was Maryam whose inner glow set the stones on fire. 'How nice you look,' she said and she was aware that the ugly moan had entirely gone from her voice.

'They're beautiful,' Maryam told her. She rose from her seat and in one fluid movement bent down and kissed Lettie on the cheek. 'Thank you, Miss Anderson. I'll always cherish it.'

Lettie's face caught fire. The touch on her cheek reminded her of the Book of Revelations where the angel touched the visionary with a burning coal. Why would she think of that? She was not used to kisses. Lettie had not been kissed since - she could not remember.

'I must go,' the girl said after a moment or two.' Sheena will be wondering where I've got to.'

Later that night Lettie looked in the mirror for her cheek was still glowing. There was no visible mark. Not for the first time she wondered about the girl.

Mo

The flat was airless, stuffy with an odour he had never been able to identify, somewhere between stale chips and unmade beds. As he never ate chips and always made his bed and was careful to change the sheets regularly he could not account for it. Now he knew. It was disease. He was diseased. His flat stank of it.

He would have told Sunshine earlier but there had been no opportunity. He had got back to the shop just after three. It could have been sooner but he had needed time to digest the news so he had sat in the hospital car park and tried to assimilate it.

The oncologist had been kind. 'Is there someone at home you can talk to?' he had asked

Mo had nodded. It was not exactly a lie. There was Rhoda of course, but what could Rhoda do? He would not burden her with his woes. There were some friends from the Pictish group but he was not exactly on intimate terms with them. One was a rabid Scot. Nat., always trying to convert him. Best steer clear of him. So it would have to be Sunshine. Suddenly he was desperate to tell her so he had switched on the engine and driven home.

The shop had been busy as he had let himself in by the back door. Almost as soon as he had taken off his coat and hung it in the office the phone had rung. Annie Miller sounded in some distress. He had to get her to repeat her message. Hughie was in hospital, he gathered, and as she had forgotten to leave the key in the usual place the children would be stranded. Could they come down to the shop? Could they please stay there till she got back?

'Don't you worry, Annie. Just tell them to come down to the shop. They'll be fine here,' he had said flatly. Dear God, he thought, what is to become of me? Then he tied on his large green apron and entered the shop. 'Who's next?' he said as heartily as he could manage.

As soon as there was a lull, he had told Sunshine about the children. 'What am I to do with two bairns and a busy shop?' He knew he sounded querulous. 'You're on overtime already.'

She had listened carefully and told him that she would meet the children outside the school and take them home with her. Even as she spoke he felt his worries loosen. He should tell her his own news now but the words would not come. Instead he asked if the various deliveries had arrived, if Mrs Mair had got her cake. No, Mrs Mair had not got her cake but she, Maryam, would deliver it. If she left now there be would be plenty of time to hand it in before the school day ended at 3 30. He could tell her now but instead he found himself worrying about the morning paper round. Had she heard how old Bain was recently? Looked like he might have to do it himself.

She made it easy for him. 'I'll do the paper round. Good to have the exercise and it won't be forever,' she reassured him. She paused and then she asked quietly, 'what's up, Mo?'

For a moment, he thought, if I don't answer, it'll all go away. In the silence the freezers hummed. He turned away to straighten the paper rack. 'It's cancer,' he said and the word which had loomed so large in his head sounded oddly ordinary to his ears. 'A shadow on the lungs.' Like his father, he thought desolated.

'I saw it,' she said quietly or that's what he thought she had said but he must have heard it wrong. She could not have known. 'You'll be ok, Mo.' this time he was sure of what she said.

'You can't know that,' he answered a bit roughly. There was he telling her he might die and all she could do was speak in platitudes.

'You'll be all right,' she had repeated.

For a moment he hated her. 'I've got chemo treatment and after that a big operation, then there's probably radium therapy. I could be dead in six months.'

She did not deny it. Instead she put her hand on his jacket roughly where his heart was. He could feel its warmth through three layers of clothing. 'It'll be tough, yes, but you will be all right.'

There, she had said it again. Damn her. 'I'll have to sell the shop, get it on the market straight away. It'll probably be bought up by one of those supermarkets but no one's going to care. I should have got rid years ago.'

'Do you want to sell the shop?' she had asked.

'Of course I damn well don't want to sell the shop. What choice do I have?'

'Me,' she said still in that calm assured voice. 'Why else do you think I'm here?'

Could she? He must be daft to as much as contemplate the thought. What did she think running a shop entailed? Selling a few groceries and smiling at the customers? 'And can you have a tumour removed, lie in a hospital bed, spend months recuperating without knowing whether or not you'll be dead in six months,' he asked but not quite so harshly.

'No,' she said firmly, 'you have to do that yourself, but I can run your business for you.'

'I beg your pardon, Maryam, but how old are you?'

'Twenty-three past,' she told him and then there was that smile, the reason he called her Sunshine.

'Twenty-three years old,' he repeated. 'You should be out courting, enjoying yourself, having babies. A shop like this takes over your whole life.'

'But it won't,' she told him. 'You'll be back within three months.'

'And if I'm not.'

'You will be.' She was still smiling as she reached out her hand. 'Trust me.' It was not a question but rather a statement.

He found suddenly that he did. He had taken her hand and as he clasped it the shop bell tinkled to announce a customer. At the same time he was aware that the cold dank scratchy blanket of fear that had enveloped his shoulders for so long had lifted a little.

'I'd better be off with that cake,' she had told him. She took the white box and slipped into the office to find her coat.

'Thanks, Sunshine,' he had called after her.

That was this afternoon. Now it was evening. He had shut the shop, disposed reluctantly of the stale bakery, a packet of sausages and a couple of macaroni pies (a waste of bloody good food) into a plastic bag, which he put out in the bin and climbed the stairs on dragging feet. His sitting room was as stuffy as usual but if he opened the window the February cold would seep in and waste the heating from the night storage radiators. Instead he drew the curtains. Misery set in.

On Wednesdays he saved himself a steak pie, rather a big one, from Lomond's Bakery. They did excellent steak pies. All it required was heating.

He made himself switch on the oven. Usually he peeled himself a tattie or two and boiled a large helping of frozen peas. By the time they were ready he was starving, for he tended to snack during the day. Tonight he could not be bothered with vegetables. He poured himself a pint of beer, brewed locally and took out a packet of fags. He looked at the beautiful objects which were no doubt the cause of his disease - no, say it - the cancer. 'What the hell,' he said aloud, lit up and immediately started to cough. Reluctantly he stubbed out the fag and turned on the TV.

Half an hour later he went through to the kitchen to take the pie out of the oven and make himself a cup of tea. Automatically he turned up the volume on the telly as if the sound could drown out the chuntering in his head. In the small lobby the intercom buzzer rang twice. Though he never heard a thing, somehow he felt better. The pie tasted better than usual.

Sheena

'At last!' she called out from the kitchen as Maryam let herself into the flat. 'You're late. Couldn't you get away from the old trout?'

She knew where Maryam went on at least three evenings in the week. Whatever she thought of the arrangement she said nothing. She knew Maryam well enough to realise that nothing she could say would make any difference. Lettie Anderson was an unofficial fixture in Maryam's life, one of several, past and present.

They took it in turns to cook the evening meal, a workable arrangement, not set in stone. On her morning shifts, Maryam prepared tea, as Sheena called it, put it in the oven if need be, set the table then popped down the street to see the old wifie and returned half an hour later to serve the meal by which time Sheena had returned from Dundee. Depending on her shifts, Sheena did the cooking. It worked well because both of them enjoyed it. They were going through a Delia Smith phase at the moment.

The table had been set and a defrosted lamb casserole cooked by Maryam last week was ready to be heated up in the oven. Sheena, exhausted from her day on the ward, was almost prepared to be resentful. After seeing to the food, she went into her room to change out of her uniform. It had been a long day. Back in the sitting room she switched on the telly and decided to pour herself a vodka and coke. Usually they kept alcohol for the weekends but tonight was different. She had news she was longing to share.

At 7 30 or thereabouts she heard Maryam's key in the lock.

'What happened?' she asked and she could hear the resentment in her voice. After all she was the one with the busy commute while all Maryam had to do was amble down the street, stand behind a counter and work a till. One glimpse at her friend and her resentment vanished. 'What's happened?' she asked again. This time she was concerned.

Maryam looked strange somehow. Her brown skin had lost its light. She looked tired and her eyes were dull. She didn't immediately answer.

'What about a G and T? You look like you need it.'

Maryam shook her head.

'What is it? Something's wrong. Is it the old trout?'

'No,' she answered. 'She's fine.'

'What then?'

'It's been a long day,' was all she would say.

'Tell me about it,' Sheena said dryly. 'Let's eat then. I'm starving.'

The lamb casserole was good. Sheena could keep her news no longer to herself. 'You know that doctor I told you about, the Lewis guy from radiography?'

Maryam looked up from her plate. Her gaze shifted slightly. Sheena was so used to it that she thought nothing of it.

'He's asked me out on Saturday.' She paused. 'I think I really, really like him.'

Maryam's focus shifted again. 'Wow,' she said. Sheena could see the effort she was making to sound enthusiastic. 'That's good. Tell me.'

So she did. There wasn't all that much to say. Shamus was not tall, not dark and not particularly handsome, nor was he that young. Maryam smiled. 'So you like him for all the things he isn't,' she said.

'He has amazing eyes,'

'And you're going to marry him,' Maryam told her still smiling.

She had taken the words right out of Sheena's head. 'Am I?' she asked seriously. Like her grandmother, Sheena believed in the second sight and that, on occasions, Maryam could predict the future. Not every future and there were times - though she could not actually recall any - when Maryam got it wrong. 'Seriously?'

'Do you want it to be serious?'

Sheena visualised her new friend and it was his hands she saw. Broad, capable sensitive hands. I love him, she thought. Out loud she said, 'We're going to the Dundee Rep after dinner and I've nothing decent to wear. I'm going to have to get something new.'

'What about that blue top? You look good in that.'

'It's ancient.'

They talked clothes for a while, but when Sheena asked her to go shopping with her the following Monday, she shook her head. 'I'm not sure. Mo's got cancer. He starts his treatment next week.'

'So that's why you're so down! Poor guy... That reminds me. I saw him in the hospital car park today.' She had been in the ward and happened to look out of the broad high window and seen him crossing the car park, his shoulders slumped, his feet dragging, his head bowed. 'I knew there was something wrong.'

'I think I'll just pop round and see if he's okay.'

'What, now? For goodness sake finish your meal first.' Not for the first time Sheena sighed with impatience. Living with Maryam was sometimes hard work. 'I hope he's going to get in some extra help. He can't expect you to manage that shop by yourself.'

'I don't think he's thought that far... which is one of the reasons I need to see if he's okay. I won't be long. Leave the dishes. I'll do them when I get back.'

Sheena watched her rise from the table. She had seen Maryam withdrawn before but not this anxious. 'Tell him all the best,' she called after her as the front door closed.

Maryam

It was only partly because of Mo that Maryam was feeling down, more than down; scared might be too strong a word but it came close.

As she walked down Church Street towards the shop, she pulled the hood of her jacket over her head. The wind was biting and there was sleet in it. Although she had a key to the shop she knew Mo would be upstairs in his flat for she could see that his sitting room light was on. Adjacent to the High Street side of the shop, a narrow walled lane led to another fairly busy road that ran parallel to the High Street. Officially named Mungo Close, this pathway, generally known as Mo's Lane, bordered a strip of garden, part of which had been converted into a gravelled drive where Mo parked his car. She slipped through the gate that led to the private entrance to his flat, pushed the bell and spoke her name.

The intercom crackled a little but Mo did not answer and the door remained firmly shut. She shivered and crouched as close to the door as possible and tried again. While she waited the memory of what had happened earlier in the evening threatened to overwhelm her.

Mrs Mair and her adult son lived in one of the two bungalows built in what had once been the grounds of Lochview and Greenyards. Erected in the early 'fifties, they were both solid, well-designed and comfortable dwellings.

One, The Rowans, belonged to Rhoda Mackay and the other, Levenside, to the Mairs. She had walked up the gravelled path between clumps of snow drops and a few brave crocuses and rung the doorbell which chimed the first bar of By Yon Bonnie Banks. She had never had reason to visit either of the two bungalows in Church Street and could not account for the shivery feeling of dis-ease that prickled her skin as she waited outside the porch door with the white bakery box carefully balanced in the crook of her right arm. She thought perhaps the idea of entertaining Hughie's siblings for an hour or so was worrying her, but why should it? She liked kids with their bright, half-formed shadows. She tried to think of ways to entertain them as she waited at the door.

It was not Mrs Mair who answered, however, it was, she presumed, her son, the one whose birthday seemingly it was. At first glance he was conventionally good-looking, slight with cropped fair hair and pale, ice-blue eyes, not as young as his clothes suggested but with a strength and steeliness that she found intimidating. There was something different about him that she did not immediately recognise.

'I have a delivery from Bruden's for Mrs Mair,' she told him on the doorstep. Best not say too much in case the cake was intended to be a surprise.

'My birthday cake!' he exclaimed with a smile that showed his excellent evenly spaced teeth but did not touch the coldness in his eyes. 'Mother must have forgotten.' He took the box from her. 'No need to go. Come in and help me celebrate.' He was still smiling, but it was no more than a stretch of his mouth. 'You must be the beautiful, dark-eyed maiden I've heard so much about.' His tone was almost but not quite insulting.

Suddenly she saw what was missing. His shadow. Mrs Mair's son had no shadow. Never before in all her twenty-three years to her knowledge had she come across a person with no shadow.

'I have to go,' she said transfixed on the doorstep.

'Oh dear,' he said still in that same not quite insolent tone. 'Mother will be so sorry to have missed you.'

In the second between his shutting the door and her turning she saw Mrs Mair in the passage behind her son. She was very still. Her shadow was still, silent and seemed to have no light in it.

She had hurried down the path and all the way to the school gates. Five minutes later the children streamed out, Tammy with her tousled hair and whey-faced Elvis with his spiky orange-gold hair among the first. She grasped Tammy's warm dry fingers. It was she who clung on to the child's hand not Tammy who had taken hers, or so it had seemed. Its small trustful warmth was comforting, reassuring. Gradually the uneasiness, the premonition of doom faded to the back of her mind.

Later standing on Mo's unlit doorstep she suddenly remembered the lone shadow she had glimpsed behind the shelves in the shop. For weeks now she had not given it much thought. Now she wondered. 'Was it him?' she asked her own shadow, 'Mrs Mair's son?'

'Don't speak his name.' Her shadow's words dropped one by one into her head. 'I don't know his name,' she answered. 'Go home,' the voice in her head told her firmly. But she was not yet willing to give up on Mo. She pushed her finger on the intercom button and left it there. 'He can't hear you,' the voice told her but it might only have been herself commenting on the obvious. Usually she was able to disentangle the voices in her head but on this occasion she was not sure whether it was her own voice speaking or that of her shadow or indeed if they were the same.

Her anxiety for Mo overcame her fear of lone shadows. She hurried round to the shop door and took out her keys. Her hand was shaking as she manipulated the somewhat complicated lock. Inside there was enough light from the freezer cabinets to guide her through the premises into the office where she switched off and reset the burglar alarm before climbing the narrow staircase. If the lone shadow lurked she did not see it, for she kept her eyes guarded.

'Mo?' she called as she climbed the stairs. She could hear the chatter of television. By now she was properly scared. For some reason climbing those narrow steps took all her strength, like running in a nightmare. She knocked on the sitting-room door and went in.

Mo was sitting in his chair with a tray on a small table beside him as the closing theme tune announced the finish of Eastenders. He was eating a pie with a glass of beer. He looked up surprised, leaned forwards and switched off the TV.

'Sunshine?' he exclaimed.

She was so relieved that she started babbling, explaining that she had rung the bell several times, knocked and had been worried about him.

'I never heard a thing,' he said, rising to his feet. 'That was real nice of you.'

Suddenly everything was all right again. She felt extraordinarily tired. When he invited her to 'take the weight off' she almost fell into the other easy chair in Mo's shabby, somewhat Spartan sitting room. She refused a beer but gratefully accepted a cup of coffee. While he was out of the room she looked about her curiously for she had only once briefly visited Mo's flat. Two upholstered leather arm chairs with the sheen long gone stood either side of the old fashioned grate which had been fitted with an electric fire whose imitation hot coals gave out a semblance of heat. A collection of miniature Pictish standing stones made out of some pinkish amalgam decorated the mantelpiece between the array of fading family photographs. Archaeological magazines lay in a scattered heap on a gate-legged table in the window recess and a shelf of books whose titles were for the most part on Pictish art lined the opposite wall. The television set was large and the only concession to luxury in the somewhat cheerless room. She suspected that Mo watched rather a lot of television. There were one or two pictures on the wall, mostly dark oils of Highland scenery that had probably hung there since his father's day.

'I've been thinking,' he said as he came back from the kitchenette carrying a mug of coffee in each hand, his sweet and milky, hers hot and brown, 'maybe I'll ask Rhoda to come in to help out while I'm off. She may be a bit slow these days but her knee's better. Would you manage to work with her?'

'Of course.' She liked Rhoda, an entertaining and dedicated gossip, who knew not only everyone living in Queich but also the names of their parents, children and grandchildren.

'You'll need to help her on the till though and keep an eye on the kiddies. Some'll take advantage.'

With Rhoda? Never, she thought, amused. She had steely vision. 'Could you not do with some help yourself, Mo?' she asked aloud.

'I'll be fine,' he answered a little abruptly.

'It's the shop I'm thinking of.' A woman came in twice a week after hours to scrub the floor otherwise Mo or herself tended to do the rest. 'I think Annie could do with some extra hours. I could ask her if you like?'

'Aye, mebbe,' he replied shortly so she dropped the subject and entertained him with stories of her afternoon with Tammy and Elvis as they drank their coffee, only adding, 'Thankfully Hughie's all right but they'll miss his paper-round money.'

Though Mo said nothing she could see that his shadow was alert. After a moment or two of silence, he changed the subject. 'How did you get on with Mrs Mair? Was she pleased with the cake?'

'I think so. Her son answered the door.' She shivered a little as she told him. Don't let Mo say his name, she told herself, but how could she stop him?

'Colin?' he said and for a moment they were both quiet. I won't ask him, she thought. I don't want to know, but there was no stopping him. 'Strange bloke. Keeps himself to himself. Haven't seen him for a while. She says he's delicate. Delicate my foot! She spoils him, waits on him hand and foot.'

51

When she said nothing, he continued, 'I know I did go on a bit about the cake but here's the scenario, Sunshine. I think she's afraid of him. I had this feeling that if it wasn't delivered he would take it out on her. Did you see her at all?'

She remembered the lurking figure with the shrinking shadow and nodded. 'Doesn't he have a job?' she asked.

'I heard he writes stuff. Works from home.'

'What sort of stuff?' she asked curiously.

He shrugged. 'No idea.'

Her eyes shifted to look at his shadow. Its head was bent. 'What happened to Mr Mair senior?' she asked aloud.

'Died a while ago, so I heard. Some sort of accident before they came here. Insurance seemingly paid for the house or so it's said.' He paused. 'There's rumours about Colin Mair which I'll not repeat.' He frowned. 'There's aye rumours about someone or other in Queich.'

She did not want to talk about the Mairs as if by doing so brought them closer. Instead she stood up, 'I'd better be off then. Thanks for the coffee.'

He came down the stairs with her. 'Want me to walk you home?' he said, ever courteous.

Yes, she thought, please walk home with me but aloud she told him she could manage and said goodnight. When she came to the Mair's bungalow, she feared the lone shadow would be there waiting for her so she crossed the road and kept her eyes to the pavement in front of her. In her mind she implored her own shadow to stay close. As long as she did not look, as long as she did not speak his name, she would be safe. By the time she reached the gravelled drive to the Old Rectory, she was running.

Chapter Two

March

Maryam

She arrived at the church too early. It had been a busy morning. Although the shop opened at nine and closed at noon on a Sunday, she had been there since seven to receive and sort the papers. This had always been Mo's job but with him being so poorly on the chemo treatment and Rhoda so slow in the mornings, she had taken it on. Escaping just after twelve she had hurried home to get dressed up. Sheena, on duty that Sunday had already left for the hospital. There was plenty of time but because she was so nervous she had arrived first for the Christening at three. 'Calm down,' her shadow told her repeatedly but that was easier to hear, harder to obey.

Although she had lived in Queich for nearly three months now Maryam had not yet visited St Serfs. The little church had a single aisle, rather uncomfortable pine wood pews, a stone pulpit, a brass lectern and at the far end an altar draped in purple with a brass bejewelled cross in the middle and two plain brass candlesticks at either end. She was familiar with the lay-out for it was not so different from Father Bonkers' chapel where her mother had worshipped. There were more stained glass windows here. She walked up the aisle and tried to identify the various saints and Bible stories she remembered. A ray of March sun low on the horizon pierced the red robe of a martyr leaving a splash of scarlet on the blue carpet that led from the porch in a straight line to the altar steps. This is a precious place, she thought, but somehow empty. It was her shadow who directed her eyes to what she sought. The baptistry was a small rectangular space cornered off at the west end of the church, surrounded on three sides by a wrought iron tapestry of scrolls and fleur de lys. There she saw what she had been seeking, a statue of Mother Mary standing on a pedestal to the right of the font. An oil lamp glowed above her head. Although she held the Christ Child in her arms, her eyes were, surprisingly, not fixed on her son as was usual in statues of the Madonna. Here the infant's eyes looked steadfastly at his mother while she looked out on to the world. Our Mother?

While she gazed at the image in awe, she was aware that her shadow had prostrated itself behind her. In her heart she spoke to the image, 'You're here too?'

That came as a small revelation that Our Mother was alive in the Madonna. Her shadow murmured, 'Here, there and everywhere.'

'Of course,' she thought in her heart. 'I knew that.'

She moved into the baptistry to be closer. The statue seemed to be speaking to her. She strained every sinew of her body so that she could hear. Suddenly the oil lamp flared up into a tongue of flame. 'My daughter... listen.' was all she heard. It was all she had ever heard from that first time on the Coral Beach in Skye.

She had been five, nearly six years old on her first school picnic and she had been jumping over the wavelets in her new swimsuit on a sunny breezy day. She had gone a little further out into the water than she was allowed. The wind strengthened. They had been calling to her from the shore. 'No further, Maryam. Come back!' Our Mother seemed to grow up in front of her out of the wind and the waves, dazzling, beautiful and at the same time stern, a shimmering whirlwind of water, air, surf and sunlight. 'My daughter,' she had said, maybe aloud, maybe not, 'lisss-ten.'

'Who are you?' she had dared to whisper, her voice no louder than a splash of surf.

The vision had wavered and sparkled and she had listened with every ounce of her flesh. 'Listen... listen... liss-ten,' was all she seemed to hear. It may just have been the shrieking of a gull but she did not think so. In the choppy water she took a step forward and found herself caught up in the whirlwind that was Our Mother. A moment of supreme joy. Unforgettable. Then it was over and she was back on the beach with no recollection of how she had got there.

After that, though, she was conscious of the shadow at her back, always just out of sight and knew it for what it was. She could not swear that this was the first time she had seen the other shadows but certainly it was the first time she was aware of them. Gradually she began to recognise them as reflections of Our Mother, that part of her that was imprinted on every soul.

When, later that night, enfolded in a towel after her bath, she had told her mother what she had experienced, her mother had hugged her and whispered out of hearing of her father, 'It was your guardian angel, pet, sent to you from Our Father in Heaven to keep you safe. Aren't you the lucky one?'

She knew about angels. She had seen them on Christmas cards with their wings and halos. What she had seen had worn no wings and had no halo. It had been sunlight and sea and wind and it had not sounded male, no indeed. To Maryam the vision had become for her 'Our Mother'... Our Mother, which art in Heaven. As for the shadows, she did not think it worth while mentioning them for she believed then and until Sheena had told her differently, that everyone saw them.

Rachel

Getting Jason into the family Christening robe had been a struggle. At a hefty six months he looked as ridiculous in a white, lawn, be-frilled trailing robe intended for an infant as she knew he would. She had already decided on a cute, little sailor suit she had seen in MacEwans in Perth but Alastair had been adamant. 'Mother has ironed the robe. My father and I were both 'done' in it. The least you can do is try it on, Rach.'

'He'll look ridiculous in a dress,' she had replied, emphasising the last word.

Alastair refused to be riled. 'I'd really like him to wear it.' He had sounded so unexpectedly firm that she had not argued.

The tiny mother-of-pearl buttons refused to stretch over his plump little back and the fragile lace-trimmed sleeves barely covered his elbows so she found one of his better matinee jackets to hide the evidence.

'He can't wear that jacket!' Mrs M had exclaimed in horror when they had gone downstairs. 'Surely it's not that cold.'

Without a word, Rachel had showed him the unbuttoned back and straining sleeves.

'What about his shawl, the one I knitted for him?'

In silence Alastair hurried upstairs to fetch it and hand it to Rachel but Jason, who had always hated being swaddled, protested with tears, flinging his arms out and pushing the offending garment off him.

Mrs M sighed loudly. 'If you'd had him done as an infant none of this would have happened,' she complained as Rachel silently buttoned up the offending matinee jacket, but her silence did not necessarily hold her mother-in-law's tongue 'Are you ready? It's nearly three.'

'Plenty of time, Mother,' said Al tensely. 'It's only across the road.'

'It doesn't do to be late,' she retorted sharply. Al said nothing. He knew only too well the unwritten commandment, as Rachel had come to learn, that his mother must always have the last word.

'Where are you meeting the Godparents?' she asked as they left the house.

'At the church, 'Al had answered.

Rachel said nothing. What was there to say?

In fact Mrs M had been surprisingly unfazed by Rachel's choice of proxy. The argument and the hassle had never happened. 'Maryam? The shop gel?' she had said with astonishment. 'Really? I didn't know she was a friend of yours. You do surprise me.' After a moment of thought had added, 'Are you sure Muslims are allowed?'

'She's not a Muslim,' Rachel said shortly.

'Of course she's a Muslim. She even wears a scarf. You'd better have a word with the Rector.'

Rachel said nothing. She refused to go into details of why Maryam wore a scarf on Fridays out of respect for her father.

'Did you hear me, Rachel. I think you should have a word with Mr Forbes.' When Rachel still was silent, she added, 'It's not that I'm against Maryam. I like the gel even though she is not exactly one of us.' She went on and on about the importance of good racial relationships and that was the end of it. No more was said on the matter. Maryam had assured her she could make the promises on behalf of her sister and her son and that was good enough for her.

Most of the guests had arrived by the time they entered the church. Maryam stood a little apart from the other guests looking exotic out of her shop uniform, her shining dark hair, usually drawn up into a tight bun, held loosely by two silver slides and wearing a light green coat. Among the smattering of neighbours there were several strangers, for Mrs M had been liberal with invitations to her own cronies and to Alastair's colleagues and their wives who stood in relaxed groups at the back of the church talking quietly among themselves.

Leaving Alastair and his mother to welcome their friends, Rachel went up to Maryam. 'Hi,' she said 'You look gorgeous.' So she did in a pretty patterned silk scarf over the collar of her close-fitting coat and heels high enough to make her almost as tall as Rachel.

Maryam smiled and immediately the irritation that Rachel had felt over the ill-fitting robe sloughed off her like a shawl. 'Sure you're ready to take on the lump? He's a bit girny this afternoon, I'm afraid - hates his outfit.'

'Quite sure,' said Maryam holding out her arms to take the baby.

To Rachel's surprise Jason leaned away from her towards Maryam and seemed more than content for her to take him.

'What is it with you, Maryam?' she asked, half-laughing. 'You're so good with him.'

'I love him,' she replied pretending to bite the fat little fingers that had begun to probe her face.

Was that it, Rachel wondered? Others professed love for him too, his grandmother for one, and with them he squirmed and grizzled until safely back in her arms.

Mr Forbes, robed in cassock, surplice and white stole, strode down the aisle carrying an electric kettle.

'Good afternoon, everyone. Welcome, welcome!' he called out cheerfully. 'Just want to heat the water a little. Cold water on a bare head can be quite a shock, so just let me add a little of this and we'll be hunky dory.'

Rachel rather liked Mr Forbes. She had of course seen him, gone through the prayer book service with him (one of Al's clients had died so she had been on her own) and told him that Maryam was acting as godmother in place of her sister. 'Maryam Patel?' he had asked 'Do I know her?' She had briefly explained. 'Of course, that Maryam. Lovely girl. Good, good! Knows what she's letting herself in for, I presume? The promises and all that?'

She liked him because he had not queried or criticised her choice. He had trusted her. 'Her father is a Muslim but she was baptised a Catholic. Does that matter?'

'Better and better,' he had said. 'She will know all about 'the devil and his wiles'.'

'Gather round, gather round' he invited the congregation. 'Parents and godparents in the baptistry with the principal boy, if you please.' There was a polite titter as the guests sorted themselves out. 'Have you all got prayer books?'

Alastair found his friend who was to be godfather and the four of them crowded into the small baptistery with the rector around the large font. Rachel held out her arms for Jason but for some reason he was reluctant to leave Maryam. The little boy was chuckling and burbling. He had found one of Maryam's glittery hair slides and was playing with it so she was happy to leave him with her and took her place by Al's side.

'Sure he's not too heavy?' she asked anxiously. 'I know he weighs a ton.'

Maryam was looking at her but not looking at her in that strange way she sometimes had with customers. Then her focus shifted and she looked at her steadfastly in the eye. Immediately Rachel knew what she must do.

'Mr Forbes,' she said, 'would there be room for Mother too?' Where the words came from she never knew. They were not of her choosing. She had never called Mrs M. 'mother' before and might never again. She was astonished at herself.

Mr Forbes replied, 'Quite right. Come in, Granny. Join the happy throng.'

Over her son's head Rachel caught Maryam's eye. 'Did I really do that?' she asked herself. A voice inside her head replied, 'It was well done.'

Maryam was standing directly in front of the plaster statue of the Madonna and Child. At first Rachel thought that it was the light from the oil lamp that lit up her friend but it was not so. The light was inward, suffusing her son with its glow, touching them all with its warmth.

'Please turn to Page 363 in your prayer books,' Mr Forbes continued.

Rachel found the right page and held it up for them both to follow. It was at that moment that she happened to catch Maryam's expression. She was staring at the glass door that led into the porch and she looked different. It took Rachel a moment to recognise that her friend looked scared, more than scared, terrified.

Following her gaze she saw or thought she saw someone standing there watching them, hands pressed up against the glass. Whoever stood there was trying in vain to come in. Instinctively she reached out to place a protective arm on Maryam's shoulder that was stiff and tense. Almost as soon as she saw it, the image vanished. 'You all right?' she whispered but Maryam did not answer.

Agnes Mackenzie

Agnes was so surprised that it took her a moment or two to understand what had happened. Almost immediately Alastair held out his hand. 'Here, Mother. Come and stand with us.'

Of course, she thought, he should have asked her in the first place. Without looking at him and with her head held high, she stepped into the baptistry and stood between her son and Baby John's godfather, Craig, a Perth solicitor whom she had known since his student days. She hardly heard the words that followed for she could not get over the fact that it was Rachel who had asked her. Rachel, who, for the first time in her life, had called her 'mother'. Why? She did not think it was to ingratiate herself with her mother-in-law. Rachel did not know the first thing about manners. It was, she thought, very strange. She was on the cusp of being pleased. For a moment it flashed into her mind that she might give her one of her grandmother's diamond brooches.

She turned her attention back to the event. Mr Forbes who was by now half way through the service had turned to speak directly to the parents and godparents. 'I demand therefore; dost thou in the name of this child renounce the devil...profess the Christian faith... promise obedience to God... ask for baptism,' to which they duly answered. 'I do.' She decided to join in with the others. 'I renounce them all.' She could hear herself, her elderly voice an octave lower than the rest.

The familiar words flowed over her. The painkillers, which she had taken just before they had crossed the road, were beginning to wear off and she could feel the threatening nag in her hip. At least she had got another appointment next week to arrange a date for the operation. She hoped that Annie Miller was coping in her kitchen. The vol au vents she had made with

58

some difficulty the previous evening should be going into the oven to be heated soon.

Suddenly she was jolted back to reality. Mr Forbes had taken the child from the gel. A widower left with three children to raise and recently a grandson, he knew how to handle babies. The child gazed up at his kindly bespectacled face in wonderment.

'Name this child,' Mr Forbes asked looking at each of the parents and god-parents in turn while the baby twisted his head to search for a familiar face.

They all spoke at the same time but they were not in unison. 'Jason John' said Rachel and the gel while Alastair and Craig murmured, 'John Jason.'

A faint titter came from the congregation while Mr Forbes looked quizzical but unfazed. Expertly balancing the child on one arm he reached for the baptismal scallop shell and poured three liberal scoops of tepid water over the downy head. 'John Jason... John' he said with the ghost of a smile in his voice, 'I baptise thee in the Name of the Father, and of the Son, and of the Holy Ghost.'

Agnes was mortified. Was Mr Forbes mocking them? It had sounded very much as if he was, and that titter from their friends confirmed it. She dropped her head and could not watch while little John as she called him in her head was signed with the sign of the Cross and returned to the gel. She could hear him crowing and laughing as if he knew he was the centre of attraction, but she could not raise her head.

Then Mr Forbes presented the parents and godparents with candles. He hesitated then took another candle from a box behind the font and after lighting it, said, 'One for Granny too, I think.' She was forced to look up, take the candle and thank him. Her face felt on fire.

Little John (as she called him) was laughing now, reaching out of the gel's arms to catch his mother's flame. Over his straining head she caught the gel's eye. If she had seen pity she would have cried, but there was not a trace of it. One word flashed into her head. Conspiratorial. One of her brown eyes closed in what could only be described as a wink. Naughty, naughty she thought with a stab of pleasure. She raised one admonitory finger and waggled it in the tiniest of gestures. The gel saw, shifted John to her other arm and lowered her eyes in silent but mock contrition.

Then she saw Tammy. Mr Forbes made a fuss over her which, in Agnes' opinion, was entirely unnecessary, but Rachel had invited her, so that was that. For once she looked almost respectable. Grudgingly it occurred to her that Tamsin was quite a sweet child.

The service over, she turned to the congregation with a beaming smile, accepted their congratulations and compliments on the baby's exemplary behaviour and, her confidence restored, uttered loud invitations to follow her across the road to Lochview in her usual faintly hectoring manner.

Tammy

The service was nearly over when she arrived a little breathless from helping Mam. Ma Mack had told Mam she could come if she behaved herself. Mam was in Ma Mack's kitchen making sandwiches and things. Tammy could go to the party too if she kept quiet.

Unable to see the wee babby from behind the congregation, she climbed up on to a back pew. She did not think Mr Forbes would mind because she sometimes went to his Sunday School and he never minded then. Sometimes at Sunday School the boys negotiated the whole church climbing from pew to pew and he never even told them off. When he called them to listen to his wee stories about Jesus they all knew how to behave themselves.

Mr Forbes saw her. 'Come along in, Tammy,' he said over the heads of everyone. 'Come and give your blessing to Baby John.'

She hesitated for a second. Who was baby John? The baby was called Jason, wasn't he? The guests parted to make way for her, some of them smiling in a sentimental sort of way as she squeezed between them. Suddenly she was in the wee boxy place with the big stone basin and Mr Forbes had her up on the step beside him as he lifted his hand and blessed everyone present. Most of the congregation bowed their heads but not the babby. He was looking at her and with relief she saw that it was Jason after all.

As soon as the service was over Ma Mack caught her by the arm. 'Tamsin,' she whispered, 'Run over to the house, there's a good gel, and remind your mother about the vols-au-vents. Sunshine had handed the baby back to his mum - Mrs Alastair, as Ma Mack called her - and was standing a little apart by herself. She would have liked to say hello to Maryam, but she was in a world of her own, staring in the direction of the porch. Following the line of her eyes Tammy saw, or thought she saw Mr Mair through the glass double door, but it must have been a mistake. There was no one there. Obediently she set out to do as Ma Mack had commanded, weaving a path through the chattering congregation in no hurry to move. Several of them said, 'Hello Tammy'. The double glass swing door to the porch was closed. She pulled one of the handles but what a weird thing, it wouldn't budge. She tugged at both handles and she pushed but she couldn't open it. It was as if someone was the other side of it holding it back.

Suddenly Maryam was by her side. 'We'll go together, shall we?'

'I canna get it open,' she said.

'No,' said Maryam, 'I'm guessing it just wants to keep you safe.'

Tammy laughed. She thought the remark was meant to be a joke, but Maryam wasn't laughing, Under her fingers the door swung open as easily as it always had. The porch felt chilly, colder than the church which was never very warm. Maryam clasped her hand in her brown fingers and together they stepped through the darkish lobby with its notice boards and bookstand. Outside the big oak doors the sun was shining and it was warm for March without a cloud in the sky.

The rest of the congregation led by Ma Mack in her best mood flooded out chattering and shading their eyes from the spring sunlight.

'Off you go, Tammy,' she said not unkindly and turned to Maryam. 'Wasn't the baby good? I do hope you have time to come over and have some cake?'

Tammy ran round to the back door of Lochview.

Mam was bent over the oven door. She looked up as Tammy came in. 'Is that them out of the kirk, then?'

Tammy nodded. 'They're coming.'

'These blooming pastry things! She'll have kittens if they're no' proper.'

Tammy peeped inside the oven. The little pastry cups looked brown and smelled delicious.

'Can I get one?'

'Just the one, mind, for laters.' Annie lifted the trays out and put them carefully on the kitchen table. 'Get them plated while I brew the tea.' She switched on the kettle. 'Quicker than that or we'll be here all night,' she added as Tammy began to arrange them in patterns on the plates.

She could hear the guests in the lobby. They were laughing now and talking loudly to each other as they made their way into the large drawing room. Ma Mack bustled into the kitchen. 'Tea now, please Annie. Two pots should do. Not everyone will want it and Mr Alastair is in charge of the drinks. Just bring it through and Tamsin you can hand round the sandwiches when you've washed your hands.' She looked critically at the spread laid out on the kitchen table and ready to go. 'The vols-au-vents look delicious.' She had made them herself so of course they were good. All Mam had had to do was heat them. 'And I shall, of course, see to the cake myself.'

'Yes, ma'am,' said Annie dutifully as she poured boiling water into the Georgian silver teapot which she had polished for the occasion.

Tammy was longing to see the cake which was already in the drawing-room covered with a muslin cloth awaiting the big moment.

Shyly with a plate of tiny brown bread egg and cress sandwiches carefully clutched between her two newly-washed hands, Tammy entered the drawing room. She went up to a group of three men and stood there without saying a word. They paid her no attention at all. What was she supposed to do? After a while one of the men waved her off without a word.

'Hey there, over here,' someone called out. She turned to see two familiar faces, the Maclardy brothers who lived down the street. 'Tamsin isn't it?' said the younger one, who was called Mr Bertie. At least she presumed he was the younger brother because he had more hair, but he was still old.

'My word! Those look good!' he exclaimed with a big smile, taking one of the small triangles. 'Eh Gordon?'

His brother, who was looking a bit glaiket, noticed the plate of food and brightened up. Without saying a word, he took two of the tiny squares and stuffed them both into his mouth at once, rolled his eyes at Tammy and made her laugh.

'Off you go, Tammy. Give the rest a chance.' Though he spoke jokily, Mr Bertie looked a bit put out, or so she thought as she began to weave a path between the standing guests.

Down to one sandwich on the plate, she looked around the room. Mrs Alastair was handing round the wee pastry things. The noise level was like the school playground at break only deeper. Apart from the Mackenzies, the Maclardys and Maryam of course, Mr Forbes (who had also taken two sandwiches) was the only person she knew until she saw old Lettie seated by herself in an upright chair by the window. She looked lonely.

Tammy wove through the guests. The old lady was looking out of the window. 'Would you like a sandwich, Miss Anderson?' she shouted to make herself heard. Everyone knew that Miss Anderson was not only very old but also very deaf.

Lettie turned. She looked different today. After a moment Tammy knew why. She was wearing a pretty, dark blue, wool dress and a matching jacket and she had pearls round her neck. She had also attempted to put on some lipstick which had run into the little cracks round her mouth.

'Now let me think... no don't interrupt. You're Jeanie! Am I right?'

'Tammy,' she said almost apologetically. She did not like to correct the old lady.

'Tammy? Oh well. You can't help it can you?' She cackled a small laugh 'I'm Lettice. Is it better to be called a hat or a vegetable?' She cackled again. 'Is that for me?' She pointed to the sandwich.

Tammy nodded speechless. Lettie took and nibbled it daintily. 'I'm starving,' she declared.

'Shall us see if there's more?' she asked very loudly.

'No need to shout, dear. It's deafening enough in here. I'll wait for cake. I presume there is a cake?' She peered round the room hopefully. Then she patted the window seat. 'Sit beside me. Talk to me. What's it like to be a child these days?'

Tammy was flummoxed. What was it like? She was a child wasn't she? She ought to know but she didn't. 'Okay,' she said a bit doubtfully, but Lettie was not listening.

'I'll tell you what it was like when I was your age. What is your age, by the way?'

Here was a question she could answer. 'Eight and three quarters. I'll soon be nine,' she answered confidently.

'Eight years old! At eight I lived in the nursery. I was not allowed to go gadding about the way you children do nowadays. Every afternoon I went out with my nurse for a walk in the park. I was not allowed to go the swings for fear of infection from the town children. Nanny Bruce wheeled the pram with my baby brother strapped in and my older brother and I held on to the handle.'

Tammy was fascinated. 'Was it nice?' she asked.

Lettie didn't hear her. 'The swings looked such fun. Once I ran off and had a go but I didn't know how to move.'

Tammy was on surer ground here. 'You push your legs forwards and then you push them back, 'she began but Lettie was lost in a world of her own.

'Nanny was very cross. She smacked me in front of the town children and they laughed.'

Tammy could think of no answer to this. Fortunately at that moment a man called Craig tapped his glass and began to speak. He said a lot of nice things about baby John Jason, complimented Mr and Mrs Alastair and thanked Mrs Mack. Then he proposed a toast and everyone had a drink from their glass or tea-cup including Lettie and Mrs M cut the cake.

'I hope they don't forget me,' said Lettie a little crossly as plates of cake were distributed round the room.

Or me, thought Tammy. At that moment Sunshine appeared in front of them with two plates each with a slice of cake. One of the slices had a little icing rose-bud which she gave to Tammy. Struck dumb with pleasure, she could only nod when Maryam asked if she could sit beside her on the window seat. Mr Forbes, also carrying two plates, one for Maryam and one for himself drew up a chair and joined the little group. 'Thank the good Lord for chairs. I seem to spend most of my life on my feet,' he exclaimed to no one in particular.

After greeting Lettie and asking for her health, he turned to Maryam. 'Settle this question for me if you can,' he said. 'What is the child's name? Jason or John? As godmother you must surely know.'

Maryam laughed. 'Both,' she said. 'You got it right, Mr Forbes. He's John Jason to his father and Jason John to his mother. So John Jason John satisfied everyone.'

Tammy thought for a moment then she said, 'I'm going to call him Jayjay.'

Mr Forbes laughed. 'Well done, Tammy. The art of compromise in one so young.'

'We were talking about childhood, Mr Forbes. Mine was in a nursery. Where did you grow up?' Lettie asked.

'In the streets of Manchester. A two-up, two-down Coronation Street terraced house. We lived on the streets.'

Tammy listened in wonder while he went on to describe his wild boyhood. And then it was Maryam's turn. Lettie asked her whether she was from India or Pakistan but did not wait for an answer. 'My maternal grandfather was in the ICS - Indian Civil Service - for many years and my mother was born in India in the so-called good old days of the Raj.'

'I imagine things are very different now,' said Mr Forbes a little tentatively.

'I wouldn't know,' said Maryam. 'I was brought up in Skye. I have never been to Europe let alone Pakistan.'

At that moment Ma Mack appeared in front of them. Mr Forbes politely got to his feet. 'So here you all are,' she said brightly. 'I was wondering where you'd got to, Rector, I wanted a word.' Then she noticed Tammy and a slight frown appeared on her carefully powdered brow. 'Tamsin,' she said sharply, 'your mother needs you in the kitchen.'

She stood up quickly and the plate with the sugar rosebud, uneaten and precious, slithered down on to the carpet. She bent down to retrieve it. 'Sorry,' she whispered close to tears.

'It can't be helped,' Ma Mack said tartly. 'Please just leave it. Off you go now.'

Mr Forbes came to her rescue. 'Tamsin has just had an excellent idea. Over the baby's name. You could call him Jayjay.'

Ma Mack smiled with her mouth. 'Indeed?' she replied to the rector then turned to Tammy, 'I said, off you go,' she told her icily.

'I'll sort it,' Sunshine whispered as Tammy squeezed past Old Lettie who had heard it all. 'I must go too,' she said rising so awkwardly that her tea cup with the dregs went flying off the small table at her elbow. 'Oh dear,' she said in a loud voice. 'I do apologise. Silly accident. You can't take me anywhere these days.'

But Tammy, as she slipped away, believed it had been no accident.

'I'll walk you home, Miss Anderson,' said Maryam.

Mr Forbes looked at his watch. 'Oh dear! How time flies. I must be off too, alas. Things to do, things to do. Can we have that word another time, Mrs Mackenzie?' he said in a voice that expected no argument.

At the drawing-room door, Tammy turned. Old Lettie was creating confusion as she made her way through the guests with Maryam at her elbow. A glass of red wine went flying. Maryam caught Tammy's eye and wiggled goodbye with her fingers.

'How did it go?' Mam asked as she entered the kitchen. 'I've kept you a wee pastry thingmy.'

'Fine,' she said. 'It was okay. Thanks Mam.'

Bertie

He watched Gordon across the room. He was talking animatedly to one of the partners at Mackenzie, Macintyre and Foote, the Macintyre nephew, he thought, though he couldn't be sure. The property one. His own legal affairs were in Alastair's hands as he specialised in wills. He knew exactly what Gordon would be talking about. And it wouldn't be golf. 'Excuse me,' he said politely to the woman he had been stuck with for the last ten minutes, whose name eluded him 'Good to have talked with you,' and wove his way across the room to find Gordon. As he had guessed the topic was the body in the loch. He had spoken about nothing else for the past few weeks.

'I would have thought the scum would have found out something by now.'

The 'scum?' thought Bertie, appalled. That was a term even the old Gordon would never have used. The interest he had taken in the case verged on paranoia. 'There you are, brother mine,' Bertie interrupted, intending to strike a light note.

Gordon looked at him for a moment without recognition. 'Brother?' he said uncertainly. 'Do I have a brother?'

Thinking it a joke the Macintyre solicitor duly laughed.

Gordon was getting worse. Bertie could no longer put off the inevitable. He would make an appointment with the doctor tomorrow. 'We should be going,' he said a little too heartily.

The Macintyre partner looked relieved, 'I too should be off,' he said, 'and in answer to your concern, the body has been identified. A young lad from Dundee out fishing the loch. Bit of a mystery all round. The empty boat seemingly had drifted on to the opposite shore.'

Another of the partners, this time known to Bertie by the name of Gerald who was ear-wigging the conversation exclaimed. 'Young idiot - sorry to speak ill and all that but these kids from the towns, they 'borrow' the boats for a lark and think they know what they're doing but we all know the loch's damn tricky - sudden squalls and all that and he obviously couldn't swim - wasn't even wearing a life jacket. Sad business.'

'I know - 'Gordon began excitedly but Bertie interrupted. 'Come on Gordon. It's time we were gone.'

'I can't see what all the rush is about,' Gordon said a little crossly.

At that moment the baby who had been so far quiet began to girn. Bertie seized on the excuse. 'The baby's fed up with us all, shouldn't wonder. Look! There's Maryam at the door. You haven't said hello to her yet.'

Gordon was for the moment distracted. 'Wait for us,' he called out to her. She smiled and waved in acknowledgement. Gordon liked Maryam. They both did. Gordon hurried off after her while Bertie found Alastair in the hall. 'Say our goodbyes and thanks to your mother and Rachel, will you? It's been a splendid do.'

He caught up with them at the gate. Inevitably Gordon was talking about the drowning. Bertie was in time to catch the end of his sentence. '...if you ask me it was no accident,' and knew exactly what he had told her; that he believed Colin Mair was mixed up in some shady business because he had seen him more than once in the next door garden in the company of strange young men. Gordon was fixated on Colin Mair because 'the creep' as he called him had been rude to him. Told him he was an 'interfering old faggot' just because Gordon had asked his permission to trim back the laburnum branches which had spilled over from the Mair's strip of garden into the Maclardy's vegetable plot at Greenyards. Gardening, after golf, was Gordon's principal occupation.

'I can't stand the fellow,' Gordon told Maryam in a loud voice as they approached the wrought iron gate of Levenside.

'Who is he talking about,' Bertie heard old Lettie ask querulously as she stumped ahead of them beside Maryam.

What followed seemed strange to Bertie in retrospect. Colin Mair chose that minute to emerge from his bungalow. He stood for a moment at the front door and looked at them.   Bertie who had no quarrel himself with his neighbour and wishing to be neighbourly called out a greeting which Colin ignored.

'There, I told you so, a nasty piece of work,' Gordon muttered to Maryam whose head had been lowered and who had not so far spoken. She looked up deliberately and straight at Colin. Afterwards it seemed to Bertie as if that look had been tangible, a beam which wavered between them, seemingly fragile but unbelievably powerful, chilling. Bertie involuntarily shivered. Colin stared back for an instant then turned on his heel and retreated as if he had not seen any of them and the contact was broken. Of course it was ridiculous. He had seen no such thing but he could not get the image out of his head. He glanced at Maryam. She looked - he groped for the word - diminished, dimmer somehow as if the light that had given her the nickname of 'Sunshine' had dulled. If it had been a battle - and that is almost how it had appeared to him - she had been the loser.

Still cold, Bertie turned to the old woman. 'Did you enjoy the party?' he asked her, changing the subject.

'I suppose I did,' she replied as if she was surprised by the fact. 'I must say Agnes Mackenzie knows how to put on a good spread.'

'And 'John Jason John' obviously approved,' said Bertie as they reached Greenyards, 'and now we must love you and leave you,' he added.

In silence he and Gordon stood for a while outside their gates and watched the two women walk away, Maryam so small and neat, vulnerable somehow, and the old woman who clung on to her right arm. Lettie was perfectly capable of managing with her stick, he thought, but who would not want to touch Maryam? She exuded a strength that for one so young constantly surprised him. Gordon ambled ahead up the short drive, waited until Bertie took out his keys and opened the front door. Thank heavens, he thought, Mair was forgotten at least for the time being, but he was wrong.

'She knew what I was talking about,' Gordon said. 'She knows.'

'Who?' Bertie shut the door behind them.

'Maryam, of course. Did you see her face?'

Bertie said nothing. Indeed he had seen her face.

'At least she takes me seriously. That Mair fellow's a bad lot.'

Though Bertie still said nothing, he was not disinclined to believe him.

April

Mo

He had had no idea that he would feel this bad. The three weeks of treatment had seemed endless. To begin with he had felt okay but as time had gone by the tiredness and nausea had been hard to bear, especially in the shop. He could not tolerate the smell of food, or even the sight of it; especially new bread in the mornings. Even the thought of it sickened him.

The extraordinary thing was he had had no idea that he had so many friends. Cards arrived, he had visitors, offers of transport, little gifts of soup and messages of good will came from so many people, not just customers. The Pictish crowd had rallied round and organised a rota for driving him to hospital now that the nausea had become so bad. 'Queichies' who seldom or never shopped at Bruden's phoned to ask after him. It was a revelation. Tomorrow he would see the consultant about the operation. Although he was dreading the appointment, he felt extraordinarily buoyed up by the unexpected raft of support he had received from the community.

It was 5 30 on Sunday afternoon when the intercom buzzed. Normally at this hour he would be doing the books but Rhoda, bless her, had offered and he had not had the energy to refuse. That would be her now. His heart sank and he hated himself for it. Although Rhoda's knee had more or less recovered, she now had trouble with one of her hips. Her memory for names was still as good as ever and she had taken over the accounts and thus proved herself to be a godsend. Rhoda, he thought, not for the first time, was one of those women who, had she been born into a modern age, would have been to uni and got a degree in accountancy. She could have gone far and would by now be enjoying a fat pension. Bruden's was fortunate to have her, so he kept reminding himself, but as the intercom buzzed again he sighed. Rhoda's company on a quiet Sunday evening was not one he necessarily sought.

He rose reluctantly from his chair and let her in. She took her time on the steep stairs clutching a bag which held the account book and was still panting as she bustled in. Her first words were indignant. Rhoda was often indignant. 'I thought you would be resting.'

'I'm always resting,' he told her with a faint smile. He knew exactly what she was going to say next.

'Did you go?' she demanded.

68

'I wasn't asked,' he said trying to inject some humour into his voice. He had been thankful not to be asked to the Christening.

'Well I call that outrageous,' she declared as she sat down carefully in one of the old leather easy chairs. 'We both know who was there, though, don't we.'

It was not a question so he said nothing. Rhoda, as he had guessed would happen, was ambivalent towards Maryam. War waged in her head. On the one side there was Maryam good at her job, harmless, unexpectedly biddable; on the other side there was Maryam the incomer, too popular, too good at her job, a rival to be challenged on every issue. None was too trivial.

'How has the week gone? Takings up or down?' he asked changing the subject and nodding towards the leather bag containing the day's takings. No cash was ever left in the till overnight. Mo kept it in a safe in his bedroom until it could be safely banked, a task he had, for the time being, consigned to Maryam.

Rhoda ignored the question. 'It's not that I have anything against the girl, you know that, but she still has a lot to learn about customer relationships,' she began.

Mo disagreed but he was not about to tell her that. 'How did those new yoghurts do?' he asked changing the subject.

Rhoda, however, was not about to give up. 'She was godmother, you know. Mrs Mackenzie was not best pleased and no wonder. Wouldn't surprise me if we lost her custom. A shop girl, and black to boot...you should have been asked.'

Which, Mo thought, was as good as saying she too should have been asked. 'Well, well,' he said. 'Never heed. It's all water under the bridge.' It was what he always said in controversial situations.

Rhoda took the hint. 'I was just saying... those new yoghurts did well. I think we should increase the order and vary the flavours.'

She took out the accounts register and handed it to Mo. Her handwriting was meticulous. If anything the profits were slightly up. He complimented her and they talked business for the next ten minutes or so. 'You've done a good job here, Rhoda. I'm grateful.'

She bristled with pleasure as he signed the book and handed it back to her. 'What would we do without you?' he told her.

Still more pleased, she could afford to be generous. 'Maryam helped. We make quite a good team, you know, in spite of...' Noting his expression, she changed tack. 'I've brought you some soup for your supper. You need to keep your strength up.'

'Thank you,' he said and started to rise to his feet. Rhoda's soups were delicious. He told her so, but now he was tired. He looked tired.

Taking the hint, she also rose. 'I'll just put this into the kitchen.' She took a thermos out of her shopping bag and bustled into the kitchenette. 'Right, then. I'll love you and leave you.'

He followed her to the door and closed it behind her.

He looked at his watch. 6.20. There was still time. Perhaps she had seen Rhoda arrive and wisely kept her distance. Maryam popped in most days after work and he had begun not only to look forward to her visits but also to count on them. He had introduced her to the mysteries of Pictdom and she had seemed interested. They had looked at a book with drawings of the recognisable animal symbols and tonight was the turn of the Pictish Beast, that strange creature that had been likened to a swimming elephant, (ridiculous) a dolphin (questionable) or a kelpie, that mythical water-horse of Scottish mythology. It would be interesting to see what she made of it.

Whenever he thought of Maryam a little signal flashed through his head. Be careful, it told himself. Mo's experiences of romantic love had been neither happy nor successful. The first was in his final year at the Perth academy. He could see himself now waiting for hours outside her gate just for a glimpse of Kirsty. He watched her on the playing fields where she excelled at hockey. She excelled at everything she attempted and even gained a scholarship to Cambridge, a rare achievement for one of the academy pupils. If she noticed him among her crowd of admirers both male and female, he was not aware of it. She had excelled in life too; ended up the Conservative candidate for an English constituency and was now an MP and in the shadow cabinet. She had done spectacularly well and he had worshipped her, still did up to a point, as he followed her career with interest.

During his two years of National Service he had lost his virginity, along with a couple of mates, somewhat unsatisfactorily in a German brothel. Best to gloss over that humiliating experience. Then on a holiday dig in Orkney he had fallen in love; at least he supposed it was love. She was Janine, a student archaeologist, who had first introduced him to the Picts. He fell for her golden hair and large green eyes and she, supposedly, for him. They had found every excuse to sift the soil together, and those hidden kisses were sweet. What had gone wrong? He was still not sure. He shouldn't have asked her to marry him. She had laughed at him. 'I'm nowhere near ready to get married,' she teased him. 'Let's just make hay while the sun shines.'

So they did, at every available opportunity. He had never been entirely happy about it and felt embarrassed by the rubber contraption she made him wear. 'The last thing I want is a baby,' she told him firmly. Verbally he had

70

agreed - indeed he was thankful, but there were times when he would have rather just held hands and necked. They parted after that hectic fortnight and never met again or even corresponded. From time to time he saw her name in archaeological magazines. She had gained her doctorate from an English university and switched her allegiance from the Picts to the Anglo Saxons. Whether or not she had married he had no idea. Her legacy to him was his passion for the Picts and for that he would be eternally grateful.

Since then he had enjoyed the odd rare and mild flirtation but nothing serious. He believed that with his lack of chin and nose-dominated looks, which had floored his self-esteem where women were concerned, he was no longer attractive to the opposite sex and actually he didn't mind. Sometimes when he saw a pretty child, he felt a twinge of regret that he had not had children, but he could not imagine himself as a father and that was supported by his dislike of the feral brats that sneaked a chocolate bar from the sweetie shelf and gave him cheek when he caught them at it.

But now there was Sunshine. Though he had fought against his feelings, denied them for long enough even to himself, told himself repeatedly that she was young enough almost to be his grand-daughter, he knew that she would give in her notice if he took a wrong step. She looked in most evenings after she had finished work for the day, brought up the occasional pie or pastry on its sell-by date, had some funny or relevant little anecdote to make him laugh. Although he hoped he might see her tonight, he knew he would not for she had popped in earlier after she had closed the shop at 1 pm on a Sunday bearing a macaroni pie which she knew he enjoyed.

Settling back in his chair he allowed himself the luxury of thinking about her. He visualised her darkness that hid so much inward light and her eyes that shone with such gentleness. That was the word: gentleness. Her voice, her words, her mouth... It struck him as he thought of her mouth that he could never visualise kissing her. Why was that? In his fantasies he would let himself put his arms around her and hold her, but with no physical reaction. The thought of sleeping with her was not exactly repugnant, more like sacrilege, as if she were still a child, or indeed a goddess. He wanted her in his life not to cook his meals, not to iron his clothing, not to lie with at night. So what then? To safeguard, to protect and shield from the assaults of daily life? Yes, that most certainly. To worship? Almost. There was only one word in the whole lexicon to describe adequately how he felt, overused and ambiguous though it might be. He loved her, but he believed he could never tell her.

Since Rhoda had been kind enough to bring it, he had better take the soup. Her soups were delicious. He found a mug and unscrewed the

71

thermos. Chicken broth with lots of rice, just the way he liked it. In passing he glanced out of the small un-curtained kitchen window which looked over the back of the building. The two rubbish bins stood outside the gate under a street lamp on the pavement in readiness for tomorrow's early collection. He had forgotten about the dustbins which had always been one of his jobs. Sunshine must have put them out when she closed the shop that afternoon.

As he watched, a stooped figure in a shabby, unbuttoned raincoat stopped, surreptitiously looked over his shoulder and opened the lid of the nearest bin, peered in, closed it and then moved to the other bin, stealthily peered in and took out a bulging plastic bag which he attempted to hide under the flap of his open raincoat. By the light of the street lamp he knew exactly who it was, but he was not at all sure how he felt about it. Could it be classed as theft? Of course not. He had told Maryam to take what she wanted of the left-overs on Sunday afternoon and Rhoda knew the score. There had been a time when a van used to come from a care home in Kirkcaldy to take what was left of out-of-date perishables, but no longer as the food was considered to be a health risk to vulnerable people. He had not thought of any of his customers as needy.

Tomorrow suddenly stormed into his head. His appointment was for 10 30. He had told no one and he had refused the offer of a lift. This was something he had to do by himself and he was terrified. Waves of chill washed over him. He might well go down to the shop first, not to check on the papers, the orders, the routine. Sunshine was managing well enough. He wanted to see her to take from her what he needed; courage...

Why had he never noticed that Geordie was in need of food?

Geordie

Back in Number 18, Geordie had gone straight into the chilly kitchenette and opened the plastic bag. At the sight of the macaroni pie, the two stale cream cookies, the pint carton of milk and the two browning bananas, he salivated. All he had had to eat that day was a heel of bread and the scrapings of a packet of Stork margarine and three cups of black tea. His own fault. He should know better by now, but Bright Star had been a cert. He had followed its form, made his decision after much care and reassurance from a mate and bet his pension for the week. If it won, his money troubles would be over. He could pay the back rent, stock his cupboards; get in a crate of beer.

He could, of course, give up the nags. Maybe go back to the Pools. He once won £57 on the Pools. That was when he had been in the syndicate. They had dropped him from their cosy little group because he had not paid up. Nobody said anything. The bloke had just stopped coming to the door. It had only been a couple of bob every week but they had mounted up and he was already owing cash to a mate. Not that he had many mates left. 'Never a borrower nor a lender be'. He couldn't remember who said that, but 'struth, was it not a fact? He should give it up, but if he did he would never have enough money to get out of debt. Somebody had to win, why not himself? All he needed was one lucky punt. Then he would never bet another penny.

It was old Lettie who had clyped on him. Sometimes she invited him in for a cup of tea after he had carried her shopping home. (Actually he watched from his window and when he saw her go out with her shopping bag to Bruden's, he followed her discreetly in the hopes of an invitation.) One morning he had been so hungry he had eaten his way through a whole plateful of her chocolate digestives, crammed them down his throat, washed them down with gulps of sweet tea, and she had noticed. Not that he had heard what she said but he could imagine her having to buy a new packet and commenting on the fact. 'Greedy old bugger,' she would have called him. (Maybe not in those words) 'As if biscuits grow on trees.' Someone had heard her, not just anyone. Not Mo. Mo had grown a pair over the years. No tick for the likes of Geordie.

The darkie lass, now, she noticed everything. Once he had caught her staring at him, at least he had thought it was him but maybe not. Sometimes her eyes looked strange, off centre, glaikit. Maybe it was a race thing. He had never known a Paki, at least not to speak to.

He saw her in the evenings coming out of Lettie's door. Sometimes he came out at the same time ostensibly to take a breather but in reality to pass the time of day with her. She always smiled and said, 'Hello Geordie. How are you?' Everyone said 'How are you?' to him like a mantra, but no one waited to find out except Maryam, so he would tell her, 'I'm just fine. Thanks for asking,' even if he felt like the brown stuff owing to the nags.

Once in a blue moon on Saturdays - maybe a bit more often than that - he treated himself to the seaside arcade, a bus ride away. Luckily last week he had remembered to buy a return ticket because he'd come home skint and hungry. There she was at Lettie's gate and there he was at his. They passed the time of day as usual but when he said 'Fine,' she had looked past him in that strange way. Then she asked him a weird question. 'What time do the bin men come on a Monday, Geordie? Do you know?'

'Aye,' he told her. 'Early.' Weird question.

'That's what I thought,' she replied. 'I'll need to get the 'sell-bys' out on Sunday night, then. A big waste of good food really.'

In a moment he knew exactly what she was telling him and sure enough there it was, sitting on the top of a pile of pristine, unsold Sunday Posts, a plastic bag containing a stale-ish loaf, a couple of yoghurts, a mutton pie, a slab of fancy cheese sealed in cellophane with just a squiggle of blue mould at the edge and a couple of not quite wrinkled apples. From then on, every Sunday night he bided in the house until it was late, then sneaked out and found the bag. Did Mo know? He guessed not. Mo had cancer, poor soul. Nobody said a word.

On Monday morning as he munched his way through a slice of un-garnished toasted bread he got a letter from the Council, not a nice letter, reminding him of the consequences of owing rent. What was the worst they could do to him? Put him in jail? At least in the jail he'd get three meals a day and a roof over his head. His mind was whirling with anxiety. His right hand seemed to have developed a shake while he waited in Bruden's for Lettie. While she was still pondering the drinks cabinet (she liked her evening glass of sherry), he found himself alone at the counter with Maryam so he had taken the chance to mutter his thanks. She had looked at him straight and suddenly, unexpected water had filled his eyes. He could not understand himself.

'Maybe,' he began - his voice sounded strange and chokey to himself - 'maybe there's others besides me.' He regretted the words once he had said them. Suppose there were others and they needed that plastic bag more than he did? Why should he care? But he did care. 'It might be kids,' he said. An image of barefoot bairns at the school with him all those years ago flashed into his mind. Sometimes he had shared his 'piece'. Now he was not sure he would do the same. Besides no kids went barefoot these days, did they?

Her eyes slid off and then on him. What was she seeing, he wondered. 'There's enough to go round', she murmured so that only he could hear. Sure enough he had noticed other packets in the bin along side the old newspapers. He was speechless Then she looked him straight in the eye. 'You're kind, Mr Burns,' she said so quietly that he might have misheard.

Lettie was now pondering the bakery goods when he found himself saying, 'I'm owing £147 back rent and there's nothing left in the hoose tae sell.' (He still had his Maisie's's wedding ring, sure enough, but that was sacred.)

At that precise moment the Lomond Bakery delivery man came in with a large tray of goodies that needed her attention and Lettie, having chosen a lemon Madeira cake brought it to the counter. He vanished.

As he waited for Lettie outside the shop, he castigated himself. Why had he been so stupid? One thing was certain he could never go back to Bruden's again. How could he with her knowing he was - what was he? A waster, a pauper. There would be no more sell-bys for him.

'I thought you'd deserted me,' Lettie said emerging from the shop weighed down by the bottle of sherry and whatever else she had in her shopping bag.

'No' me,' he said managing to sound normal. 'Gi'es it over.'

He was quiet on the way home, but that was all right because Lettie was in full flood. '...so I'll have to get the Council in,' she was saying. 'It's driving me mad. Drip, drip, drip all night. Would you ring them for me, Geordie? I can never hear what they're saying on the phone.'

Ring the Council? That would be right. He had a better idea. 'No need to bother the cooncil,' he told her. 'I can fix it for you.'

'Could you really?' She sounded delighted. 'I never thought to ask you.'

'I used to do a bit of plumbing way back in the day.' He had been a scaffie on the bins, a road labourer, a farm hand, but he could manage a dripping tap.

'Come to think of it there's other jobs need doing. The bathroom door's sticking. I'd be so grateful if you'd take a look. I would pay you of course.'

'Forget it,' he found himself saying. Fool, fool that he was. A dripping tap was worth a quid at least. That would feed the meter. He'd have a bit of heat. 'What else are neighbour's for?' he found himself adding. Besides everyone said she'd come down in the world. Probably hadn't a spare bawbee to her name.

'Thanks Geordie. You'll take a cup of tea and I got a nice Lomond's Madeira in fresh this morning.'

'Much obliged,' he told her and indeed he was. A slice of cake would go down very nicely. He felt better. He was almost glad he had told Maryam the truth. He had had to tell someone or bust.

Lettie's sheltered cottage being the mirror image of his own had the stop cock under the sink. There the resemblance ended. The wee place was, pardon the thought, like a junk shop. Crammed so full of knick-knacks you had to be careful where you put your feet. Pictures, wishy-washy water-colours, hung all over the walls and photographs of posh people in big hooses. After he had eaten his cake and swallowed his tea he got up to go.

'Who's them?' he asked stopping in front of a sepia tinted framed photo of an unsmiling couple in ancient gear dandling a be-frilled bairn. Behind them was a hoose with wee turrets that might have been a castle. They looked like royalty.

'Me with my parents,' she told him. Automatically he straightened the picture which hung at an awkward angle. 'There, that's better,' but inwardly he was awed. Who exactly was this Miss Lettie Anderson?

'Thank you, Geordie,' she said graciously at the door. 'I'd offer you a remuneration but I don't want to insult you.'

Insult me? He laughed inwardly. 'Any time,' he told her.

'Do you mean that? Because there's a lot of things I need doing, and can't manage myself. But if you won't take remuneration, I can't ask. We could come to an arrangement.'

'That would suit me fine,' he told her. 'You jist have to ask.' His mind was racing ahead of him. A pound or two extra for the nags and he would be bound to win next time. His luck had to change 'I'll take a look at that door, shall us?'

The first thing he saw when he shut his own door behind him was another letter from the Council. Maisie flashed into his mind. What would she think of him now? She used to take his wage packet every week and pay the rent and top up the meter and give him a couple of quid for beer and the nags. She knew he liked a flutter. O Maisie... He sat down in his shabby old chair and dropped his head on to his arms.

Bertie

Dr Swinney, generally known as 'Jack', though his name was Allan, had asked some elementary questions which Gordon had answered more or less satisfactorily except for when it came to his telephone number which eluded him completely.

'I'd like him to see a consultant', the doctor told Bertie. 'Ninewells will be in touch. You may have a bit of a wait, alas, but that's how things are these days.'

'Who are you talking about?' Gordon asked suspiciously. 'Is Bertie ill?'

'Mr Maclardy's fine,' Dr Swinney said heartily, 'I'm glad to tell you.'

'Then what are we doing here?'

Bertie caught Dr Swinney's eye then turned to Gordon. 'I gather you've been having a spot of bother with your memory?'

'My memory? Nothing wrong with my memory,' Gordon said testily.

'We agreed, Gordon. Twice now you've been gone all night and forgotten your way home,' Bertie reminded him.

'Nonsense,' said Gordon. 'I knew perfectly well what I was doing.'

'What were you doing, Gordon? Your brother has been worried.'

'I was watching the loch. Somebody has to.'

'Why is that, Gordon?' the doctor asked.

'Theere's an old boathouse. That's where he goes,' Gordon answered slyly.

'Who goes?'

'Bertie knows.'

Bertie did know. So that's what he was up to, he thought. This obsession with Colin Mair was becoming dangerous. He was spending more and more time at the spare room window watching his neighbour and the company he occasionally kept.

('He's allowed to have friends surely,' Bertie had argued impatiently.' 'These lads are not friends,' Gordon had flashed back.)

The doctor and Gordon were both looking at him expecting an answer.

'Some rare duck, wasn't it, Gordon?' Bertie ventured. He did not want Gordon naming names. His obsession bordered on slander. 'The loch is of endless interest to twitchers.'

'Is it?' said Gordon surprised. 'I didn't know that?'

'You've forgotten,' Bertie said cruelly. 'That's why you're here, Gordon.'

'Your brother only wants what's best for you.'

'He thinks I'm going doolally.' Gordon was angry. He got up and crossed the room. 'By the way,' he said pausing on the threshold. 'For the record: he's not my brother, never was, never will be.'

He slammed the door behind him.

'I'll make that appointment, immediately, Mr Maclardy. Meanwhile there are some little precautions you can take. See that he carries some form of identification. Put a copy in all his outdoor pockets or better still get him to wear an identity disc.'

Bertie was not listening. He was possessed by an enormous sadness.

He caught Gordon up outside the surgery. 'What say we have a round of golf and then lunch at the Clubhouse?' he suggested as cheerfully as he could manage.

'Why, especially?'

Bertie shrugged. 'It's been a while and it's not raining.'

'Stop trying to run my life. What I choose to do with my time has nothing to do with you.'

'Of course it's to do with me, Gordon.' Bertie could hear the desperation in his own voice. 'Everything you do matters to me.'

Gordon stopped in the middle of the pavement. 'Why?' he asked coldly. 'You're not my brother and you're certainly not my keeper.' He turned abruptly and started to walk off in the opposite direction, then as suddenly turned and came back. 'I thought we were going to the doctor because of you.'

'Me?' said Bertie. 'Why me?'

'You know perfectly well.'

He did know. Of course Gordon had noticed. How could he not notice? In his younger days Bertie had had a problem with drink. His father had been an alcoholic and Gordon had scared him into believing he had probably inherited the same tendency. It had been a hard decision to give up whisky but for some twenty years now he had not taken wine or spirits only beer, his excuse at parties being that he couldn't stand the taste. A few months ago he had grown complacent. An occasional whisky when he was bored, a couple of wines at that christening... surely a small drink occasionally would no longer harm him? Could one grow out of alcoholism, if indeed that was what he had? He blamed that first fall all those years ago on his anxieties over Gordon but he also realised that Gordon, who disliked all alcohol, had been his monitor and his mentor. Once again, riddled with anxiety over Gordon's mental health, he had felt the need for whisky. But Gordon had noticed. Bertie would have to be more careful. He did not think he had the strength or the courage to go through the agonies of withdrawal again. Why should he? What was the point? He felt deeply depressed.

He watched Gordon's retreating back for a few seconds, then turned and walked to the car park. He needed a drink now. Another worry occurred to him as he unlocked the door. Driving. He would have to be careful. The local police were constantly alert for drunk drivers. He dared not risk losing his licence.

Queich High Street was surprisingly spacious, custom built, he had heard, wide enough for a carriage and horses to turn. The Cortina was parked slantwise to the street. He made up his mind not to follow Gordon. Done that, been there. He suspected that Gordon had taken himself off to that dilapidated, fisherman's bothy about half a mile from the pier set back on the shingle that seemingly belonged to no one, where he sat endlessly watching the loch. When Bertie questioned him he was cagey. Once he had been angry. 'Somebody has to watch out for them,' he had exclaimed.

'Who?' Bertie had asked naively.

'You bloody know who,' he had shouted and left the room.

All Bertie knew was that his obsession started with the discovery of a young man's body drowned in the loch. The police had eventually identified him, that lad from Dundee out on a loch for a spree with his mates who had probably swum safely to shore and regrettably, though understandably, gone to ground. Gordon was still convinced that Colin Mair was connected but when Bertie suggested he tell the police, Gordon had flown at him. 'They know,' he yelled at him,' I've told them a dozen times but they don't do a bloody thing.'

These fits of rage were new, connected, he was convinced, to his insipient dementia. Bertie found it exceedingly sad.

He took the car back to Greenyards but could settle to nothing. The round of golf and lunch at the Clubhouse were a distant dream. He went to pour himself a dram and remembered the bottle was empty as was his packet of cigarettes. Bertie had made several attempts also to give up smoking. Sometimes he succeeded for months on end but the desire for nicotine had never entirely left him. Now was one of those times.

He had no other reason to visit the shop. Hughie-the-lad had already delivered the Times so that excuse had gone. Yet he contrived to find a reason to call in most days. He needed to talk to someone about Gordon and who else, apart from the doctor, was there? Although they'd been living in Greenyards for close on ten years, and had dozens of acquaintances mainly at the Golf Clubhouse there was no one he could trust or particularly liked. Maryam somehow was different. He often wondered why that was. Did her opinion really matter in the scheme of his life? Not really. Was it because, in spite of her youth and status, he both liked and trusted her? Partly. More importantly he had the feeling that Maryam liked him. Do we only like those people who appear to like us, he asked himself. Maybe. He didn't know that she did, but he felt it. They had some sort of bond ever since that first time Bertie had disappeared.

The shop was fairly busy. He dawdled at the back over the rows of tinned soups and fruit until he was the only customer left, then, putting on a cheerful face approached the check-out. The cigarettes were kept in a cabinet behind the counter.

Today was Friday. She was wearing a hijab. If anything it made her look even prettier. He liked to rest his eyes on her.

'Twenty Marlboro, if you please, Maryam.' He put the bottle of Grouse on the counter. Then he asked because he genuinely wondered. 'Don't you find those things a bit hot?' He pointed to her head scarf, then added apologetically, 'Sorry. Maybe I shouldn't have asked.' It was a personal question and Bertie in childhood had been taught never to ask personal questions.

She didn't seem to mind. That was the thing about Maryam. You could say what you were thinking and she wouldn't mind; at least so far she hadn't minded.

'Not really,' she told him as she reached behind her for the packet. 'On a cold day it keeps me warm. I love my hijab. Sometimes I think I might wear it all the time.'

'Don't do that,' he said quickly and added without thinking, 'You have such pretty hair.'

'It sort of keeps me safe,' she added as she put the cigarettes on the counter.

Safe? He wondered to himself. What had Maryam to fear? Selfishly burdened with his own anxieties, he had forgotten that the worries of other folk were as real to them as his were for Gordon. But Maryam? So young, so pretty, he had imagined her to be care free. Then he remembered; her parents were dead or so he had heard and she was possibly the only Asian in Queich. How stupid of him.

'How is Mr Gordon?' she asked as he reached for his wallet.

He was silent for a moment. When he glanced up to find her looking straight at him, the words spilled out of him. 'Gordon has dementia,' he told her. 'He's got it into his head that one of our neighbours is responsible for the drowning of that poor lad whose body was found on the far shore. He spends most of his time watching the next door garden from an upstairs window and when he's not there he's down at the shore. I'm seriously worried about him.'

The direction of her gaze shifted minimally. He glanced over his shoulder but saw no-one and when he looked back he saw that she was one again watching him. This time he was aware of her fear. He felt it like a cold hand on his shoulder.

'Has he spoken to the police?' she asked, as if Gordon's fantasies had some substance.

'No... Yes... He says he has, so maybe.'

'Don't you think perhaps he should?'

He was speechless with surprise. Not for one moment had he thought Gordon's obsession had any substance.

'Your brother' - he noted she hesitated over the word brother - 'comes in here most days.' She paused.

'How does he seem to you? His memory?'

'He seems a bit anxious, sort of preoccupied; I suppose, worried, but not about his memory.'

'What then?'

She hesitated. Then she said quietly. 'You.' Her eyes dropped to the bottle of whisky that stood on the counter between them.

Now, he realised with shame, he could not take it. The cigarettes he slipped into his pocket but the whisky remained on the counter.

'You think he's all right mentally, then?' he asked her.

'I don't know.' This time he saw nothing but concern in the dark pools of her eyes. 'Maybe he just needs someone to believe in him.'

He was astonished. His mouth opened and at that moment the shop bell rattled and the young Mackenzie girl backed in pulling her stroller with the oddly named baby. Remembering his manners, Bertie went over to hold the door open for her. With her were several other young mums, so he returned to pay for the fags. The whisky remained on the counter.

On the walk home, he castigated himself for not asking her more about herself and her own anxieties and realised shamefully that all he could think of were his own. Something in her manner had drawn the words out of him. Compulsive? In no way had he been forced to reveal so much. Compassionate? Indeed that was the right word. Her compassion had made him indiscreet. He would never be able to buy whisky at Bruden's again. To his surprise he was not particularly bothered. In fact, strangely enough, he felt lighter than he had done for months.

Rachel

Nursery school had gone well, but Rachel was feeling uneasy. She had made particular friends with four of the other mums who had babies about the same age as Jayjay. Once a month roughly they persuaded their men folk to baby-sit so that they could have a mums' night out. Each took it in turn to organise the evening. Last month they had gone to a restaurant in Perth followed by a film. This Saturday night was up to her and she had booked the five of them into a gig in the Caird Hall in Dundee to see a controversial hypnotist called Arthur Anders who was on tour in Scotland. The other mums had been enthusiastic. They had been excitedly discussing the final arrangements in Bruden's when she had noticed Maryam. She looked tired and no wonder. With Mo unwell she was working all God's hours or so it seemed. When did she ever have any fun?

Outside as they pushed their strollers up Church Street to St Serf's church hall for the afternoon session of nursery school, she found herself saying, 'Do you think we might ask Maryam to join us?'

'Who?' said one of the mums who lived outside Queich.

'The Paki in the shop,' another explained not intending disrespect.

'If you like. There's room for six in the car,' said Lila who took care of the transport. She was a farmer's wife and drove a Range Rover.

'I doubt you'll get a ticket at this late hour,' said the oldest of the group, a plump and chatty Glaswegian called Eva who had a plump and noisy baby, her third child and all of them plump. 'But why not? Great idea. I like Maryam. The more the merrier.'

When Rachel got home that afternoon she rang the ticket office. No problem. A block cancellation meant if they moved their seats forward they could accommodate six. 'Done,' said Rachel. Sounded too good to be true. She had immediately phoned Maryam.

Maryam had hesitated. 'I'm not exactly a mum,' she said doubtfully.

'You're a godmum, though,' said Rachel.' Arthur Anders is said to be a brilliant hypnotist. You'll get a good laugh.'

There was such a long pause that Rachel wondered if they'd been cut off. Then she said doubtfully, 'Are you sure you want me?' She had not sounded brimful of enthusiasm.

'Of course we're sure,' Rachel insisted.

'How is my proxy godson?' she asked, then added, 'If I baby-sit then Alastair could go.'

'No way! Besides Alastair has some lawyer's do. Mother's babysitting. You wouldn't want to deprive her of that now would you?'

They both laughed.

After the Christening it had been surprisingly easy to continue to call Mrs M. Mother. She still interfered. She still refused to call the baby Jason, but was willing to use his new nickname, Jayjay. Rachel would have preferred Jason but for peace she too had accepted the compromise. She loved Alastair. She still kept her distance from her mother-in-law but she was no longer consumed with loathing and she no longer pestered Alastair to move.

'So say you'll come?' she repeated to Maryam. 'I've already got you a ticket.'

'In that case... thanks.'

Her tone was so muted that Rachel was almost sorry she had suggested it. However, she persevered. 'It starts at eight. Can you be at mine for seven sharp? Lila is picking us up.'

Just before seven Maryam had arrived. She was wearing the green coat she had worn at the Christening and her long thick hair was loose.

'How nice you look, Maryam,' Mrs Mackenzie gushed in the same condescending way she spoke to Annie Miller. 'I hope you'll find it an enjoyable evening. Not my sort of thing, I'm afraid.'

Maryam had not replied but Rachel who was watching at the window for Lila's car noticed her guarded look. She doesn't want to go either, she thought in a moment of revelation but it was too late to withdraw. 'There's Lila,' she said. 'We'd better be off.'

The others were duly picked up and the banter started. Everyone made an effort to include Maryam but in fact it was not difficult. Afterwards Rachel could only remember that there was a lot of laughter and that Maryam had not been on the periphery of the group but somehow at the heart of it.

The seats were in the front row. One of them, Eva, Rachel thought, had brought a box of Cadbury's Roses which was passed from hand to hand with a lot of giggling and rustle.

The hypnotist was a cheerful chappy, pleasant looking and no apparent threat to the guarded audience as he worked hard to gain their confidence. Volunteers to go up on to the stage were eventually, and no doubt carefully, weeded down to some dozen willing guinea pigs to whom he was flattering, kindly and persuasive. A delighted extrovert, Eva was one of them. After more banter awash with soft soap and subtle persuasion the dozen dropped their guards.

Nothing so far was distasteful. The volunteers were soon well under the hypnotist's spell. They became what they were told to become, did what they were asked to do, and the audience, who by this time believed they could trust the performer lapped it up. All went well.

Then subtly the act changed. The scene set by Anders was a farmyard. The volunteers were given their animal parts. The rooster, a brash young man with a dyed yellow quiff of hair, strutted the stage. The cow, a big-breasted housewife got down on all fours and mooed to the delight of the audience. An older man with obvious pleasure turned into an idiot goat .One by one the volunteers were awarded their rolls. The stage became a baa-ing, neighing, crowing uproar. By this time Rachel knew, just knew what was to follow. So obviously did Maryam. Eva, by now the star of the volunteers, was sitting quietly, an inane grin on her face awaiting her role. Please not, Rachel prayed, but knew exactly what awaited her friend. So indeed did the audience. Plump Eva, who was so sensitive about her weight, was to be the plump pig. Please God, no. Then she became aware of Maryam.

She was leaning forward. The strength of her stare directed towards the stage was almost visible. Rachel felt it and trembled. On the stage itself there followed an extraordinary turn of events. Someone back stage must have turned on the wind machine. The effect it was to have on the guinea pigs was to waken them from their trance. Self-conscious now, they stopped their capering and turned to each other with questioning faces. Several including Eva actually rubbed their eyes and returned to their seats at the back of the stage, not knowing what exactly had happened. Meanwhile the noisy wind still blew, whipping their hair, shifting their clothes.

Then to the complete astonishment and delight of the audience Arthur Anders got down on four legs and grunted and snuffled his way round the stage. He continued to grunt and snuffle and root around until long after he had become an embarrassment to the audience, who gradually fell silent and shifted uneasily in their seats. One or two walked out, Maryam among them. She rose and without a word left her seat and without a backward glance walked up the side aisle. Watching her, Rachel saw her stop at the first exit and turn round to look back at the stage. The moment she left the theatre, the wind ceased. Turning round, Rachel saw that Anders too had stopped grunting and cavorting. He looked around him speechless and bewildered. Eva and the others silently and to the mild applause of the audience left the stage and returned to their seats.

'What happened?' Eva whispered to Rachel as she sat down on her far side.

'I'm not sure,' Rachel replied.

Anders stood alone on the stage also uncertain of what had happened, knowing though that his control had gone. He opened his mouth to speak and eventually the words came. 'Thank you very much, ladies and gentlemen.' That was it. The curtain was quickly dropped. After some five minutes by which time the audience had begun the familiar chant, 'Why are we waiting?' a manager stepped out in front of the curtain and announced that owing to the sudden illness of Mr Anders, the show for that evening was over. Money would be refunded or the audience was free to rebook without charge.

'What a shame. I was quite enjoying that,' said Lila as they gathered in the foyer.

'It's early. Why don't we go for fish and chips?' someone suggested.

'What's happened to Maryam?' said Eva who had not, of course, seen her leave.

'She's probably in the loo. I'll go and see,' said Rachel.

But she was not there and though they waited till everyone had left the hall, there was no sign of her. 'Maybe she got a bus home,' someone suggested, inclined to be annoyed.

'I hope she's all right,' said Eva.

'She probably needed some fresh air. It was stuffy in there.'

'I bet she's gone to the car,' Rachel suggested. She too was worried. I should never have asked her in the first place, she thought. She had not really wanted to come.

'I still don't understand what happened back there. I don't remember a thing until there was that weird wind.' Eva asked.

Lila attempted to explain. 'It was either a clever twist or the guy really took ill. Anyhow you were brilliant, Eva.'

Rachel said nothing.

Minutes later they reached the car park and found Maryam. She was standing quietly by the passenger door waiting for them.

'What happened to you?' 'Are you all right?' 'Why didn't you wait for us?' The questions bombarded her but all she told them was that she was sorry.

'We thought we'd go for fish and chips. Are you up for it?'

In the dark of the back seat Rachel reached for Maryam's small brown hand. It was burning hot 'Sure you're okay?' she whispered as the others chattered about the show.

Maryam seemed to pull herself together. 'Quite sure,' she said quietly.

To the questions that inevitably followed during the munching of fish and, through the miasma of chips and vinegar all she said was, 'It was so hot I thought I would melt.'

'You know, I reckon that weird wind was not meant to happen. Someone backstage will be in for the chop,' Lila said thoughtfully.

'It certainly broke the spell,' someone else volunteered.

Just in time, Rachel thought to herself. No one else, it seemed, had connected Maryam to the incident. Indeed as the evening continued with increasing banter and laughter, Rachel began to doubt that she had seen anything out of the ordinary.

Agnes Mackenzie

Thank God. There she was. Earlier than expected, though. It was only just after ten and Rachel had said about eleven. Alastair would be home nearer midnight. Baby John, usually such a placid child was teething, restless and bad-tempered. She had given him orange juice and gripe water, walked up and down the room with him until her hip hurt so badly that she had been forced to take more pain killers. Now she was feeling a little woozy but the child was livelier than ever, girning away in his stroller (ridiculous word, what was wrong with 'pram') as she pushed him back and forth, back and forth in the hopes that he would settle.

She made the effort to pick him up when she heard Rachel running up the stairs. At the sight of her, his crying escalated a decibel and ceased the moment Rachel took him up in he arms.

'How's he been?' she asked anxiously.

'He's hungry,' Agnes told her shortly.

'He had a huge helping of Farex as well as me before I went out.'

'Surely he should be weaned by now. Obviously he's not getting enough sustenance,' Agnes told her tartly. All that rubbish stuff his mother ate. Here she was stinking of fish and chips. Hadn't thought to bring her any, though. Not that she much enjoyed fish and chips but she would have liked the chance to refuse them.

John latched himself onto her daughter-in-law's breast and for almost the first time that evening he was quiet.

'Would you like some tea or something stronger?' Rachel asked her.

'No thank you. It's late.' She rose to her feet and reached for her stick. She felt distinctly wobbly.

'Thank you for this evening,' Rachel said meekly over the baby's head. 'I'm sorry Jayjay acted up.'

Agnes winced, but not on purpose. The pain-killers barely touched the agony. Rachel saw and added as sympathetically as she dare. (Agnes did not like sympathy.) 'Let's hope you hear from Ninewells soon.'

'Yes indeed,' she murmured as she eased herself down the stairs, but with little hope. She would have loved a cup of tea. Why had she not accepted Rachel's offer? It was not just that her hip was sore. Although her relationship with Rachel had improved, the gel irritated her beyond words. Why? If she were to be honest with herself - this sometimes happened when she lay sleepless in her bed - she might have admitted to jealousy on several counts. Jealous of Rachel's youth and easy friendships, jealous of her close relationship with her baby. Alastair had had a nanny in those early days and she seldom saw him girny. Jealous, above all, of her closeness to her son. In daylight she would have scorned the suggestion that she might be jealous. Agnes Mackenzie was above such pettiness. So why was it that she could not bring herself to ask about the show? Thank God it had been a short programme because she could not have endured another hour of baby-sitting; and now the house stank of chips.

That was it, she thought next morning as, relying heavily on her stick, she walked down to Bruden's to pick up her fresh brown bread roll. That was why Rachel annoyed her so much. She could not abide the smell of food that still wafted down the stairs and lingered, trapped in the hall. Jealousy had nothing to do with it. She pitied her son having to live in that miasma of smelly food. They should get one of those machines that sucked out bad air. What were they called?

'What are those things which get rid of cooking odours called?' she asked Maryam when it was her turn to be served.

'Air extractor fan?' said Maryam. 'Is that what you mean?'

'Rachel came back last night stinking of fish and chips and the smell sickens me,' she explained 'How do you cope with it?'

'What about Air Freshener?' said Maryam. 'Would that help? We have some in stock.'

Air Freshener? Agnes thought. Another ghastly stink. How common. To be reduced to some cheap scented spray because her daughter-in-law stuffed herself with chips was beyond the pale.

'Thank you, but no. I'll get Alastair to look into acquiring one of those fans.' She looked behind her. A couple of customers were having a gossip by the cold meats cabinet. There was no one waiting to be served.

'Did you enjoy last night?' she asked. 'The baby was grumpy so I didn't have a chance to ask Rachel.'

Maryam looked at her that strange way just for a moment before her eyes focussed again. 'The chips were good,' she said mischievously and smiled that rare beautiful illumination not only of herself but of the whole shop. Sunshine, she thought. How appropriate. She found herself smiling too.

'I think I might have some of that freshener stuff after all,' she said, expansively. Who cared if it was common?

'Of course. I'll find it.' Maryam obligingly left the counter to find the green bottle.

Agnes turned to see Mrs Mair standing just behind her with her basket of groceries ready to be checked out. 'Good morning,' she said graciously. She did not really know Grace Mair even though she lived so close with her reclusive son in the furthermost of the two bungalows that separated Lochview from Greenyards, but the pain had lessened and she was feeling in a better mood.

Having completed her purchase, she decided to wait outside the shop door to walk up the street with Mrs Mair whose little dog fidgeted impatiently waiting for its mistress on the pavement, its leash firmly tied to the short railing intended for the purpose. (Mo quite rightly never allowed dogs on his premises.) It was a noisy little beast, she thought, as they eyed each other carefully. She often heard it yapping for no apparent reason and it was no doubt responsible for some of those disgusting messes on the pavement. Thank heavens Alastair was not a doggy person. Dogs brought their own problems. Because the pain in her hip had miraculously eased, she noticed that it was a lovely morning. Daffodils and grape hyacinths flourished in all the front gardens and the forsythia by the gate of the Old Rectory was at its best.

Mrs Mair emerged. She was a short frail-looking woman with faded mousey hair that framed her lined, somewhat anxious face. She looked surprised to see her.

'I thought we might walk up the street together, that is if you're going home?' Agnes said graciously.

The little woman muttered something that might have been 'fine' and untied the dog's leash. It began immediately to yap.

'We live so close and yet we never seem to see each other,' Agnes continued somewhat gushingly. 'How long have you lived in Church Street? My memory is so bad these days.'

'Three years.'

'That long! You have a son, don't you?'

Mrs Mair nodded.

'I too have a son. He's a solicitor in Kirkcaldy. What does your son do?'

'He's a writer,' she volunteered.

'How nice. Does that mean he works from home? How fortunate for you.' She could hear herself gabbling. This conversation was an uphill struggle. 'What does he write?'

'Fiction,' she said shortly.

'How very interesting.' It was. 'Fiction,' she repeated. 'Do tell me. What is he working on at the moment?'

'He doesn't tell me,' she said shortly, 'and I don't ask.'

Searching for something to say, she asked about the dog who was at one moment straining at the leash, and at the next, stopping to sniff excitedly at hedges or lamp posts.

'She's a shih-tzu,' she explained briefly. They had reached the gate of her bungalow. 'This is me, then,' she said.

They stood outside the wrought iron gate for a moment. 'Do come in and have some coffee. I'm only two doors up,' Agnes said mainly for something to say. She was not usually bested in conversation, nor did she really want this woman and her somewhat unfortunately named animal in her home.

'I'm rather busy,' the other woman said, ducking her head as she turned to unlatch the gate.

'Another time, then.' Looking up at the bungalow she saw the son - Colin - she remembered. He was staring out of the bay window. He smiled at her and raised his hand in greeting. Somehow it was not a friendly wave. As she turned away, she groped for the word; ironic? sardonic? That was it, sardonic.

Suddenly her hip jolted. She gasped in pain as she hobbled up the short drive to her own front door. The post had been. No letter from the NHS as usual.

Maryam

She knew she should not have gone. The prospect had been bleak. She could not cope with large crowds. All those shadows intermingling, all that sadness, sickness and anxiety swamping and crushing her. 'So why did you agree to go?' Sheena had asked her with some asperity. 'You know what you're like in a crowd. All you had to do was say thanks but no thanks. It's not that difficult.'

Sheena who liked labels thought she had a form of claustrophobia. Certainly she had found school assemblies so scary that sometimes she had hidden in the toilets while Sheena had covered for her. She had learned to cope with small groups such as the Christening and a crowded shop, but she still avoided large gatherings.

To begin with all had gone well. The other mums were friendly. She did her best not to let their shadows intervene though she was strongly aware of Eva, who for all her bubble and warmth carried on her shoulders a weeping skeletal shadow. She tried to join in the banter for her heart had expanded in love and warmth to these friendly women who had wanted to include her on their night out. Because they were sitting in the front row she could not see the audience. She deliberately kept her eyes to the front and closed her mind and ears to the clamour behind her.

Arthur Anders had a shadow too. A cocky conceited clone of his outward self. Maryam guarded her eyes but she knew it had spotted her. It was a moment of instant recognition. 'Get out,' it told her in her head. 'We don't want your sort here.'

One by one the volunteers stepped forward to climb the five steps up to the stage. Eva was one of them.

'Don't go,' she had said urgently, half rising herself and holding out her hand.

Eva glanced down at her briefly. 'Why ever not?' she replied brightly. 'It'll be a ball.' Her shadow was completely still, its head wrapt in its hands.

To begin with all was well. The volunteers had succumbed with ease to the persuasive voice of the hypnotist; willing participants to his insistent commands, their shadows seemingly asleep. She dared to look directly at Anders. Immediately aware of her attention, his shadow hissed in her ear. 'Let us alone, bitch, or it will go badly for your mate.' She had known that from the start.

Then came the farmyard scene. Rooster and hen, horse and foal, cow and its calf, a prancing goat, a duck, goose, a sheep and its lamb, one by one the volunteers were awarded their parts and took on their roles with relish. Only Eva, fat Eva, was left sitting quietly with a vacant smile awaiting her orders. When Anders turned to the audience and cried, 'What's missing?' someone from the back shouted out, 'A pig!'

She knew the time for confrontation had come. It was not easy. It required more strength than she thought it was possible to summon because, at the same time, she was sorry that it was necessary, sorry for the humiliation of the man, even sorry for his shadow. 'Our Mother, listen,' she pleaded over and over again.

So the wind rose. That angry shadow did not retreat without a fight. The hideous words and curses that thundered in her head gradually changed to piteous cries. When she saw Anders go down on all fours and grunt his way round the stage she almost relented. Instead she got up and left her seat. At the exit she turned and spoke to the shadow that had suddenly grown meek. 'Go in peace,' she told it. The wind dropped and Anders, himself again, was bewildered and humiliated... She knew she had destroyed a person. It diminished her to destroy. She did not think she could face the others.

The streets were quieter now, the traffic less heavy. Gradually the turmoil in her head grew still. 'You did what you had to do,' her shadow told her sternly. 'Go home.'

She found the car and waited, lifting her head to find the distant stars.

'There you are! What happened to you?' Eva was the first to speak. 'Are you ok?'

She reassured them as they gathered round her. 'What happened back there?' Lila asked. Eva.

'You tell me,' said Eva. She didn't remember anything and listened eagerly as the others told her of the evening. No one mentioned the farmyard or the pig.

'We're early. Let's go for fish and chips,' said one of them.

Only Rachel was quiet. She asked no questions, made no comments until the conversation changed to their children. She whispered to Maryam,' Sure you're all right?'

Maryam nodded. She thought she was. Then she had gone home and Sheena had taken one look at her. 'That bad was it?' she stated briskly.

'You could say.'

'I told you how it would be. Did I not tell you? Those stage hypnotists are dangerous. I remember we had a woman in Glasgow who got a persistent headache from one of those shows. They mess with your mind.'

And I messed with his, she thought bleakly. She continued to be appalled by what she had done for most of that night and next morning in the shop.

Then Mrs Mair had come in. She served her and forced herself to look at her shadow. There were some shadows she loved to see, children like Tammy; others made her sad like Miss Anderson and some who needed help like Mr Bertie. A few she dreaded such as Mrs Mair for they were cloaked in impenetrable misery. One only she feared; the detached shadow that she knew belonged to Colin Mair.

Watching his mother now, she knew that the day would come when she would have to confront her son, that elusive shade that watched her from behind the bakery stand in the shop or through the glass door of St Serf's. 'Please not,' she pleaded with her own shadow. Courage it seemed to say.

Annie Miller

Things were pretty desperate. She had lost the pub job. Nothing to do with the standard of her work, or so they said, nor indeed the lost ring. The boss's cousin, recently widowed, needed a job. She hadn't been forced out, nothing like that. She understood that family comes first so she had agreed to leave meekly without a fuss. The boss gave her an extra ten quid. Ten quid! Truthfully she was quite glad to leave the pub. She had never felt comfortable there knowing what she had done. On the other hand ten quid went nowhere these days especially when she had so many debts. A borrowed fifty pence had to be returned to a neighbour, a pound to Hughie, and of course Bruden's - well Sunshine actually - for all those wee things like washing powder and a big white pan loaf and of course she was still owing for that bacon. Maybe it would be better to go back on to full benefits, but then she couldn't do any work at all and they would be watching her like hawks.

She passed Ma Mackenzie walking with that weirdo, Mistress Mair, up the street. There was no avoiding them. 'Good morning, Annie,' said Ma Mack in that special treacly voice she put on to speak to the likes of herself and Sunshine. The lower orders, she thought with a wee smile. It didn't bother her because she knew she was a lower creature. It wouldn't bother Sunshine either she thought. She rather liked being in the same order as Sunshine.

There was still just over seven pounds left of the tenner. She picked up a big bag of frozen chips from the freezer cabinet, put it in her basket and waited behind the bakery gondola until Sunshine was free. Get on with it, can't you, I've a bus to catch, she thought impatiently as the last customer lingered to chat; finally the shop was empty. She plonked the chips on the counter and in triumph produced a fiver and two coins. 'No change, Sunshine,' she said and could not help the grin that spread across her face. 'I know it's not enough but it's a start.'

Sunshine took it and looked at her in that strange off-centre way that everyone had grown used to. In a second her eyes re-focussed. 'Great,' she said quietly, 'Thank you.'

'How much am I owing now?' Annie dared to ask for she was confident that after her forthcoming trip to Dundee she would be able to pay.

Maryam opened the drawer beneath the counter. Annie couldn't see all the contents but it looked full of odds and ends, paper clips and rubber bands and several pairs of spectacles, oh and a key ring with several keys attached. How could anyone not claim their keys? After a moment Maryam produced an unsealed envelope with Annie's name on it.

'Can I get to see?' she asked boldly.

'Sure,' said Sunshine handing it over.

It was worse than she remembered. The slip of account paper showed dates and purchases amounting to £32.55 pence. With almost five off, the bill would be still in the twenties. If she got £50 for the ring there would still be enough left for Tammy's trainers and Elvis badly needed new school trousers, he was growing like a train.

She returned the sheet to Sunshine and put the chips in her shopping bag. 'I'll be off then,' she said quietly for suddenly she had lost her earlier confidence.

'Wait a minute. You'll need your change,' said Sunshine. 'But' - she began. Sunshine was still speaking, 'for the bus.'

She had completely forgotten about the bus fare. Right enough she still had £2 in her purse from last evening's cleaning stint at the surgery. She had earmarked that for a cup of tea and a trip to Woollies to get some sweeties for the kids.

She held out her hand meekly as Sunshine counted three pound coins into her hand. 'I really meant - 'she began. 'The lassie smiled. It was a sad sort of smile but kind, the sort of smile that had more to do with tears. 'I know you did...do.' she said with that weird off-look.

After Annie had put the chips into the freezing compartment of her fridge, changed into the good coat and was standing in the bus queue, she suddenly remembered. How had Sunshine known she was catching a bus?

The question bothered her for about five minutes as she sat in one of the back seats so that she could have a fag. She supposed she must have mentioned it and forgotten. I'm going daft she thought as she exhaled a lungful of smoke.

Finding the right sort of shop in Dundee was a bit of a problem because she didn't know what she was actually looking for. She paused outside Samuel's for a while gazing at the rings and the watches. Pricy. She even crossed the threshold. In bed over the past few nights she had invented a back story about how a mythical son had changed his mind over an engagement and wanted rid of the ring; no, spurned by his girl friend and broken-hearted would be better. There were several counter staff in the hushed interior, well-dressed, snooty. They would look her up and down. Where was the receipt, would be the first question she would be asked. What? No receipt? One would keep her talking while the other looked up records, police notifications...she fled.

She passed an antique shop. This might be the place. But the ring was not an antique was it? How could you tell? Peering through the window beyond the display of silver salt-cellars and pottery figurines, she could see an elderly gentleman behind the counter; no-one else even browsing. She opened the door. The gentleman looked up, saw her and seemed to frown. Of course he could be short-sighted but Annie didn't think so. Was she so obvious? A woman from the lower orders with an expensive ring to flog? Must be stolen property. She retreated hastily.

She walked for what seemed like miles till she came to the poorer end of the city. Tenements lowered over her, shutting out the sky. Betting shops abounded and then she saw what she wanted. An untidy, second-hand, bric-a-brac store with advertisements for Best Prices Given.

She felt in her coat pocket for the little cube of a box that contained the ring and only then it occurred to her. The box had a jeweller's name on it. Jeez, that was a close thing. She would have to get rid of the box. She continued walking up the street while the fingers of her right hand fumbled for the small catch, found it and managed to extract the ring. Clutching it in her pocket she returned to the shop but still she was reluctant to go in, might not have done if she had not seen the dumpy, middle-aged shop assistant with an untidy straggle of faded ginger hair not indeed all that unlike her own. Not someone to fear. One of the lower orders. The shop bell was startlingly loud.

'I've this ring,' she started to explain. 'My son broke off his engagement...' She faltered at the sound of her own voice.

'Don't bother,' the woman said cheerfully in a strong Dundonian accent. 'I've heard it all before. Just show us the item.'

Silently she took the ring out of her pocket and handed it over. It looked incredibly bright and innocent somehow in comparison with all the other junk. The woman took it and looked at it through one of those wee lenses. 'Thirty quid,' she said dismissively.

Annie was stung. 'Thirty quid? Surely it's worth a bit more than that?'

'Aye, mebbe,' said the woman.' But that's all I'm offering.' She looked up challengingly. 'Take it or leave it.'

Annie saw that she had been mistaken about the woman. In spite of her height, her scrawny hair and her chipped nail varnish she was no push-over.

Worse; Annie was aware that she could see right through her and knew exactly what she had done. Feeling exposed and diminished, Annie nodded.

'Name and address, please,' said the woman taking out a receipt pad, pen poised.

Annie hesitated. She had not thought this through. Why would they be wanting her name and address?

The woman sighed. 'For redemption purposes.'

Redemption purposes? What did that mean?

'You'll' - the woman paused and looked up. 'Your son,' she started again with an emphasis on the word. 'Your son'll mebbe change his mind. Want it back. There'll be interest to pay of course.'

'He'll no' be wanting it back,' said Annie faintly. .

'You're not requiring a receipt then,' said the woman opening the till. It was not a question.

Annie nodded. She could not look at her. She took the three notes, stuffed them into her pocket, and, stumbling over a plastic child's tricycle, left the shop. It was over, done. Except that it wasn't. Sunshine's pretty, unsmiling face suddenly appeared in her mind's eye. She wanted to cry. She was aware of the notes in her pocket together with the empty ring box as if they were living creatures, somehow untouchable. All she wanted was to be rid of them. Tears now blinding her, she hoped she could remember the way back to the bus station. This had been a bad, bad idea.

When the tears had cleared from her eyes she saw on the opposite side of the road a church. That was the answer. She crossed the road, opened the rusty iron gate, walked up the weedy path to the arched door. It was locked. Not so much as a bloody letter box. That figured. Not even God wanted these tainted tenners.

Watchful now, she eyed every passer-by. Women with prams. Pensioners with sticks. Teenagers in torn jeans. No one appeared to be in need as far as she could see. You couldn't just go up to someone and thrust thirty quid into their hands, at least she couldn't. Mind you, if the boot were on the other foot, she would have kissed anyone who came up to her with thirty quid. Probably everyone she saw could do with cash. So why not just keep it?

Sunshine's face loomed up again, her brown face with the strange eyes. What had Sunshine to do with this? Why did she matter so much? Annie needed that thirty quid to buy trainers and trousers for the kids. As she thought it, a Dundee Equitable shoe shop on the far side of the street caught her eye. There was a sale on. Defiantly she pushed open the swing doors and made straight for the children's shoe department...

Half an hour later she stood in the bus queue, her arms burdened with plastic bags. She thought of nothing on the journey home.

Hughie

'Dogs,' Mo had said when he first started on the paper-round. 'You'll need to watch out for the dogs. Mr Bain always carried a biscuit or a bit of sausage to distract them. 'Dogs and papers boys are like chalk and cheese. Best you're warned.'

Old Bain had already alerted him, though he had talked about paperboys as red rags to bulls where dogs were concerned. It was all that talk about dogs that had clinched it for him. Aye, he'd get started at eight no bother. He'd get up at two in the morning if it meant getting to pet a dog. To be on the safe side, he accepted Maryam's packet of Tasty Treats for Pets as she whispered to him that first morning. 'Just to keep handy.'

There were fifteen dogs scattered throughout the village to watch out for on his round. He graded them not according to breed, size or temperament for he loved them all. He graded them according to their conversation. There were the yippers, wee dogs like Ma Mair's Tina in Church Street whose excited greeting verged on the hysterical. There were the deep woofers, big dogs, getting on a bit, mild-tempered on the whole like Gileas, a golden Labrador who condescended to acknowledge him but only after he had gobbled a Tasty Treat. There were the growlers who needed a lot of coaxing and there was Old Podge, the ill-tempered wire-haired terrier who snarled menacingly and bared his yellowing teeth but Hughie was working on him. The rest were mongrels, most of whom had a streak of collie in them. To start with they had arf-arf-arfed menacingly at his approach but lately thanks to the Treats, the tone had mellowed as he approached their doors. His favourite was Moll, a pure-bred collie who lived with his master, a retired shepherd called Mr Foulis, in a cottage on the outskirts of the village, a mate of Old Bain. Mo had offered to take the old codger off his list if it meant him being late for school, but Hughie had shaken his head and muttered something which Mo couldn't hear but Maryam had understood. 'Good for you, Hughie,' she had said and the subject was dropped.

Yes, occasionally he missed Assembly, came into Queich Academy at roll-call or just after but his middle-aged form teacher understood why. In the staff room he had stuck up for him. 'I always had jobs before and after school. It did me no harm. It shows a bit of gumption if you ask me. Besides I happen to know the lad in question comes from a single parent family. They need the money.' (Just as his had done.)

True. Hughie gave half his wages to his mother but the rest he put into a tin with a bulldog on the lid. He had started to save up for a skate-board but had since changed his mind. He now wanted his own puppy. A collie just like Moll. He imagined the little fellow running beside him on his bike as he delivered the papers, lying across his feet on his bed at night, sprawled over his knees as he watched the telly. He had of course asked Mam ages ago for a dog. 'I wouldn't mind a dog,' she had told him. 'I like dogs, but we could never afford to feed it, Hughie. Dogs cost money. Vets are a fortune. Besides what would a puppy do with you in school and me at work? Sorry son, but it's just not on.'

'I'll get the money,' Hughie told her. 'Don't you fret yoursel'.'

'Aye,' she had said disbelievingly, 'that'll be right.'

So that was why he was doing without sweeties and comics. He was saving for a dog. Actually he was not missing out much because at the end of the week there was sometimes an out-of-date Beano or Rover which, as Mo explained, would be returned to Menzies with the other unsold papers, so he might as well have it. All Mo did was tear the date line off it. Sometimes, if there were no left-over buns, Maryam slipped him a Mars Bar and once a Yorkie, his absolute favourite. Maryam was totally ace.

What with his tips and half his wages he had now saved all of seven pounds and fifty-two pence. Would that was enough for a dog?

It was Mr Mair who told him about the Shelter in Kirkcaldy where they gave away lost or abandoned dogs for nothing.

To begin with Hughie had been wary of Mr Mair. He had appeared at the sitting room window on Hughie's first paper round no doubt to find out what all the excitement was about for Tina, put out to wee, had yipped hysterically at the stranger and bounced around him like a ball with teeth. Mr Mair had done nothing. Just stood at the window and watched. Hughie pretended not to notice him as he reached in his pocket for a treat. From thereafter the wee dog still danced around him but the yipping had changed to equally noisy but welcoming yaps.

Now fully recovered from his appendectomy and back on his rounds, Hughie was no longer surprised to find Mr Mair waiting for him on the doorstep for he was there most days now that the April mornings were light.

'Thought any more about that dog?' he asked. He had a weird voice, soft, a bit American and very nasal.

Hughie had thought of nothing else but he still hadn't mentioned it to Mam. He was going to have to pick his moment carefully. Either Mam had come into money, or found a secret stash because last week she had been splashing it about a bit. New stuff all round. Trainers and school trousers for

Elvis, trainers for Tammy, and a blue check shirt and jeans for him. There had been burgers for tea, proper meaty ones with chips, which made a welcome change from beans and cheese toasties and there was Irn Brew to drink. Maybe this was the perfect time to mention a dog, a free dog with himself paying for the tins of Chum.

'Aye,' he said handing the papers - Courier and Times - directly to Mr Mair.

'Here's an idea then,' he said. 'What say you to a trip over to the Animal Shelter near Kirkcaldy to see what's on offer?'

'Me?' he asked a bit bewildered. He still wasn't sure about Mr Mair. The craic in the street was not encouraging. Mr Mair had an uncertain temper, a sarcastic tongue, a scary sort of geezer, unpredictable; best keep your distance. The word 'queer' sometimes qualified his name. It tended to be applied to a whole lot of folk, kids included, and Hughie was not entirely sure what it meant. Yet here he was, thought Hughie, nice as pie, must be OK if he liked dogs.

'I don't see anyone else around,' he said in his sarky voice. 'I thought you were interested in dogs?'

'Aye then,' he muttered.

'Saturday afternoon, two sharp suit you?'

He nodded. 'I'll need to be off,' he managed to mumble.

'Don't let me keep you.' Mr Mair smiled his sarky smile but his eyes were already scanning the Times' headlines as he retreated into his house.

So now what was he to do? He delivered the rest of the papers in a haze of anxiety. What would Mam say about the dog? What would she think of him going off with Mr Mair to Kirkcaldy? Did he want to go to Kirkcaldy with Mr Mair? No of course he didn't, but he did want a dog. Suppose they saw a dog and he got it and brought it back and Mam wouldn't let it in the house? He would have to tell Mam about the dog, but maybe not about the trip to Kirkcaldy, though. Mam was funny about talking to strangers. You couldn't call Mr Mair a stranger, could you? Not exactly. He lived in the street.

Saturday dawned sunny and still he hadn't told Mam. Mostly on Saturdays after he had done his paper round and other chores like clearing the ashes if they'd had a fire on the night before, or once a month washing the windows if it was fine, he was free.

'Get out from under my feet,' Mam would grumble a bit so they all did, Elvis to the park to play footie, Tammy to her mates to play shoppies. Sometimes he and his pals went off on their bikes to fish a burn in the Ochils behind Queich or maybe down to the loch just to skip stones, or to the pictures in Kirkcaldy, but not often because flicks cost money, precious dog money.

He had no plans for this particular Saturday.

He agonised a bit over what to wear. His old stained jeans and a hoodie were out of the question. School uniform would set Mam off with the questions. His new jeans were yet to be tried out. Yes, he would wear his new jeans and it would have to be his hoodie over a T-shirt. He wouldn't wear it pulled over his head. The dog people needed to see he was respectable.

In the end he chose his school blazer with his new jeans. And of course Mam noticed. 'Where are you off to all dressed up like a dog's dinner!' she called from the sitting room.

'Out,' he said reaching the door.

'If it's a lassie!' she cried after him cheerfully. 'Good luck with that.'

He fled.

The journey which lasted about twenty-five minutes was for the most part silent save for the purring of the engine. As they drove out of the village Mr Mair told him to open the glove department of his black Fiat (nice car). There he found a poke of sweeties, black-striped, bull's eyes.

'Help yourself and fish one out for me,' he was instructed. 'I enjoy a good sook in the car.'

Without taking his eyes off the road, he opened his mouth. Hughie could see glistening saliva. He reached in the poke, took out a sweet which stuck to his fingers as he lifted it to Mr Mair's open mouth. For a second he felt the soft wetness of the man's lips on his forefinger and was revolted. Slipping his hand into the pocket of his blazer he scrubbed his finger clean against the cotton lining. Believing himself bound to take one, he felt a little sick.

Help-ma-bob. Suppose he got car sick? He remembered that one time he had got car sick, ages ago, when the social worker had driven them all from the old flat in Alloa to Queich. Tammy had been a baby in Mam's arms. Elvis had been sick on the floor in the back. What would Mr Mair say if he puked?

He didn't talk much, Mr Mair. The silence was broken only by the sweet-sooking, then he said. 'Put on the radio. Find us a bit of music, will you?'

Hughie looked at the array of buttons on the dashboard. He had no idea which to push or what to twist. His hand hovered. 'The one with ON written above it – above the dial.' Mr Mair glanced sideways at him, sighed, then taking his left hand off the steering wheel reached out for Hughie's forefinger and pressed it firmly on the button. Music burst out, a cacophony of unfamiliar sound. Mr Mair held on to his finger just a fraction too long before returning it to his lap.

Every part of Hughie shrank, his ears from the music, his flesh from the chilly dryness of Mr Mair's fingers, his gut from the whole situation from which there was no escape.

The rest of the journey passed without words for which Hughie was thankful. The blaring trumpets (he was almost right. It was in fact an organ playing the Trumpet Voluntary) drowned out the possibility of conversation. It lasted till they reached the Shelter which had once been a farm on the outskirts of the town. He could see donkeys in one of the fields. His spirits rose a little. He liked donkeys too.

Mr Mair parked alongside several other vehicles including an RSPCA van, pulled on the brakes and switched off the radio. 'Great stuff,' he said turning to Hughie. 'Wouldn't you agree?'

Hughie nodded. He sat there rigidly with his hands clasped between his knees unmoving.

'Right then. Let's go pick you a dog,' said Mr Mair.

Still Hughie didn't move.

'What's up, Hugh? I thought you wanted a dog.'

He swallowed and he said the first thing that came into his mind. 'I hev na' tellt ma mither.'

Mr Mair laughed. 'Is that all? You have a lot to unlearn, Hugh, regarding mothers. You don't do what they say. They have to learn to do what you say. You want a dog? You get a dog.' He laughed.

You don't know my mam, Hughie thought but he said nothing. Briefly he visualised Mrs Mair's bent scurrying figure on the street. It had obviously worked with her.

'Hugh?' Mr Mair prodded his arm. 'Wake up, boy.'

He stirred. 'Okay,' he said and tried to open the door. It wouldn't move. He had a moment of panic as he struggled with the handle.

Mr Mair laughed, reached past him brushing his thighs as he did so, and opened the door. 'A bit handless, aren't you? Come on, let's go see those doggies in the window.'

After the preliminaries in the office in which he took no part, a girl in brown overalls and wellies took them out to the kennels. They paused outside each barred cage while she told Mr Mair their history and fondled their eager noses. After a while he stopped listening and tagged behind to make his own assessment.

To begin with he loved them all, their melancholy or beseeching eyes, their pants and yips and woofs but when he saw Jura that was it. He wanted her there and then, a black crossbreed with alert brown collie ears white splodges and enormous paws, so skinny he could count her ribs. Big.

He only half heard the girl explaining that she had been rescued keeping guard over her owner, an elderly man whose body had been found three days after his estimated date of death. She, Jura, had been starving but was responding as well as could be expected to the planned diet and regular exercise. She was estimated to be about six years old.

'She's still mourning,' the girl said fondling the quivering nose pushed through the bars and Hughie could sense her sadness.

Mr Mair had also seen several he thought more suitable, better bred or smaller sized but Hughie had fallen in love and there was no distracting him.

'It often happens that way,' the kennel maid explained knowingly to Mr Mair. 'Want to take her out for a run?'

A beech wood served as the border between two farms. Led by the girl, Jura, securely leashed on an expanding lead, bounded along beside them as they crossed the donkey field and through a barred gate into the woodland, carpeted with beech mast, moss and bluebells. Above them the buds were fat and some had unfurled. It was a magical place.

'You can let her off the lead now,' said the girl to Hughie. She also produced a well-chewed rubber ball and the next half hour passed in a dream... the scent of woodland, the light of a filtered sun, the sounds of a happy dog.

Mr Mair and the girl watched him, the latter with an indulgent smile and the former with an intensity that even as he was romping and calling, 'Here Jura, here girl!' he was well aware of, but now unafraid. With Jura he felt he need never be afraid again.

Then it was over. Jura was returned to her kennel, an arrangement made for the following Saturday and then he was back in the car alone with Mr Mair.

'I'm feeling a bit peckish after all that exercise.' (What exercise thought Hughie? You just watched.) 'Fancy a burger?'

He did and he didn't. He just wanted to get home and out of Mr Mair's car but he was also starving. Hughie was always hungry. 'I don't mind,' he muttered

'I'll take that as a yes, then.' He paused. 'Switch on the radio, will you?'

This time he managed it. Another burst of music that precluded conversation so he was able to think about Jura. How would he tell Mam? But tell her he would. No way was he going to miss out on that dog. It was bad enough not having a dad... but he would not go down that road. I'll just tell her, he told himself.

Eventually they stopped at a Little Chef. As well as a burger butty he chose chips and Mr Mair had a maple syrup pancake. At one point in the meal he was aware that he needed the lavvy. No way, Jose, he told himself. Bad things happened in lavvies, or so he had been told.

He managed a bit of conversation or rather he replied to several questions mainly about the dog but mostly the rest of the day passed in a welter of weird music.

'Same time next Saturday then?' said Mr Mair as he dropped him off in the street.

'Aye,' he said and in time remembered his manners. 'Thanks Mr Mair,' he said as with relief he managed to open the car door.

Watching him drive the few yards up the street he wondered why he had been so scared. Mr Mair was probably an okay geezer. So he told himself but somehow he wasn't entirely convinced.

A much bigger battle lay ahead.

Chapter Three

May

Mo

Somewhere he had read that May was an unlucky month, that the suicide rate rose in May, that in the old days Highlanders starved because their provisions had run out and the new crops not yet ripened. He could believe it.

The convalescent home in the Ochils behind Queich was comfortable. His south-facing room looked out on to a burgeoning garden, bright with yellow and blue and purple flowers. Daffodils he knew by name, but not the others. He had never had a garden, had never learned to tell a weed from a cultivated plant, though he knew that dandelions and daisies were unacceptable. He had never really understood why. He thought them pretty, especially the dandelions that starred the verges of the country roads with gold. As he gazed out of the window, they all looked so fresh and optimistic under a cloudless sky that by contrast he felt tawdry and dull.

Automatically, like a mental tic, his thoughts switched back to the shop. The memory of standing behind the counter for hours on end made him feel tired. He could not imagine himself feeling strong enough ever again to do a day's work. How would he manage? Perhaps the time had come to sell up. The thought depressed him unbearably. He loved his shop. It was his sustenance, his companion, his child. What would he do without it?

'I would be better dead.'

There he had said it aloud. But how? A rope? No. He was no good at knots. Where would he get the strength? A knife in the bath? A possibility but too messy: someone would have to clean up. Pills? That was the answer but where would he get them? How many aspirin would he need?

He dressed himself slowly in time for Sunday lunch, a communal affair with roast beef where people told each other their life stories and grew teary and tired in the telling. He had no desire to go but if he dodged it, someone would come and chase him with kind words into the dining room.

The afternoons were for visitors. Rhoda had organised some sort of rota which meant that his room was not crowded one day and empty the next. Rhoda was there most days herself, like a mother hen clucking over her chick. Come to think of it she had always tried to mother him from the days when she had worked for him full time in the shop. He had not been bothered then and he was not bothered now. She was old enough, well no, not quite, to be his mother. A war widow, she had been married for only a few months in 1943, not long enough to have children and he had never known a mother. It made some sort of sense.

She would be here again this afternoon if no one else had volunteered. No days were allowed to go by without at least one visitor. He was grateful to her, of course he was, but mostly he couldn't be bothered. Visitors depressed him with their busy lives, their rude good health, their endless cheerfulness... The shop, that nervous tic, resurfaced in his mind. Rhoda had said one of the freezer cabinets was faulty.

The roast beef was tough and the Yorkshire pud flabby. As soon as possible he made his excuses and returned to his room. After a while his eyes closed. The vision of the shop dissolved. He dozed a little in his chair and woke with a start to find the sun full in his face, but when he opened his eyes it was not the sun, it was Maryam.

She came when she could which was not often as she was kept busy in the shop most afternoons. He guessed, maybe unkindly, that Rhoda saw to that. Sunday afternoon visitors were usually other acquaintances who were working during the week and busy with their families on a Saturday. When he opened his eyes to see Sunshine in the room - literally - his heart leapt.

After the usual preliminaries he asked her how she had got there for he knew that unlike Rhoda and his other visitors she had no car.

'I cycled,' she told him.

He was overwhelmed, hadn't known she had a bicycle, (she hadn't but had borrowed one from Rachel) told her to sit, rose to make her tea from the facilities in his room, exclaimed at her hardiness.

'Mo,' she said laughing, 'it's only seven miles.'

He was still fussing when she interrupted. 'It's such a lovely day. They told me I could take you out for a wee walk. There's a wheelchair waiting.'

'Aye, I'd like that.' Suddenly he would. 'But I'll not be needing a wheelchair,' he told her firmly. He felt he could run a marathon.

It was harder than he thought. Outside in the naked air his breathing grew difficult, his body sweated and his legs felt like rubber. Fortunately there were benches and chairs strategically placed on the lawns and in the shrubbery, many of them already occupied on this lovely afternoon.

'Let's sit,' she said leading him to the nearest. It took him a few moments to get his breath back as she chattered to him about Hughie-the-lad who had got himself a dog.

'A dog?' He could hear the weakness in his voice.

'A big dog called Jura. You should see her paws, like big soft plates they are.'

'Not in the shop I hope?' he asked a little anxiously. Animals in his shop were taboo.

She looked at him and her eyes shifted for a second or two in that weird way that made him want to look over his shoulder. Then they turned back on him with her full gaze, so penetrating that he had to look away.

'Hughie keeps him tethered to the rail outside. He knows the rules. We both do. Rhoda sees to that.' She smiled at him so mischievously that he found himself smiling too. She paused. 'Don't worry, Mo. The shop is doing just fine.'

'What about the freezer cabinet? Rhoda was saying.'

'Sorted,' she assured him. 'Geordie Burns did it. I bet you didn't know he was such a handyman.'

He hadn't and it surprised him. Geordie was one of the few - be honest now - the many that had forced him to refuse them credit.

It was as if she could read his mind. 'He doesn't ask,' she told him. 'He's got a wee job now doing stuff for our Lettie. He does her garden and we've asked him to mow the Old Rectory grass over the summer months.'

The news did not particularly inspire him. Even Geordie with his gambling problem was doing well while he...he felt diminished. 'I was thinking,' he began. He was about to tell her that he was thinking of selling up. A little wind had risen. It blew strands of her long, loose hair across her face

'I know what you're thinking, Mo,' she told him, brushing aside her hair. 'It's May. The dead month they called it in Skye. Come June and you will think differently. You'll be strong again, back in the shop behind that counter sorting us all out.'

'How do you know?' he tasked her wretchedly. 'I might be dead.' There, he had said it. He had thought it often enough over these past few weeks, how he would do it, where he would do it, even when and that was soon.

'I know,' she said quietly and reached out to cover his hands that were clasped and twisting in his lap.

Afterwards when he thought about it he likened it to a shot of coke - not that he had ever experienced cocaine - no, it was more like a shot of life itself. It coursed through his veins invigorating, encouraging and warming him. There was nothing that he could compare with that touch. He was to remember it for the rest of his life. He lifted his right hand and covered hers that was spread over his left. Nor did they move or speak for several moments. The wind stirred in all the surrounding trees.

The sun had disappeared behind a billowy cloud. 'We should go back,' she said gently disengaging his grasp.

He rose easily and together they walked back to the house. 'Stay and have a cup of tea,' he asked her when they reached the door of his room.

She might have agreed if two members of the Pictish Society, a husband and wife, had not turned up bearing a basket of fruit and the latest copy of a history magazine which carried an article on a recent find in Fife, a Class One undressed slab with the faintest outline of a single disc.

'What is that?' Maryam asked.

Eager to explain they all spoke at once. 'Possibly a cauldron,' said the woman. 'I see it representing a dwelling place,' said her husband, but Mo's voice was the loudest. 'It's the symbol for the sun,' he told her.

'No one really knows,' said the woman diplomatically, 'but it's exciting. It's the third Pictish Stone to be identified in Scotland this year.'

He didn't want her to go but he could not persuade her to stay. He went outside the door with her to say goodbye. 'Take it from me, it's the sun symbol, Sunshine,' he said firmly, 'and when I get out of here, I'll take you to see it.'

'Is that a promise?' she asked him seriously.

I'm better, he thought with wonder. 'It's a promise,' he told her and knew he would keep it.

Bertie

Gordon was changing. Life was no longer a laugh. Had it ever been, he wondered. Not all the time obviously. They had squabbled from time to time over trivialities but without aggression. Now it seemed Gordon was perpetually angry.

'I know you think I'm mad', he would shout, 'but I'm not daft. You're drinking again and I can smell the nicotine on you. Meanwhile we have a murdering psychopath living next door and you don't give a damn.'

'I don't think you're mad, Gordon, but you can't deny you're a bit forgetful and I'm allowed to be worried,' he would reply placatingly.

'And you're addicted to – to' - (he had lost the word) – 'and nicotine. That doesn't worry me?'

Normally at this point in a row one of them, usually Gordon, if Bertie were to be honest, would touch the other, hug and apologise. That no longer happened. The days became more silent, the absences longer and the rows harsher. Did Gordon even notice? Hurt and anxious, Bertie was chain-smoking. If he had so much as one dram Gordon would smell it on him and swear, 'Christ! Not this again,' and slam out of the room.

Bertie no longer visited Bruden's if he could help it for he was ashamed. He got his Marlboro and whisky supply at an off-license in the High Street where no one noticed or cared, and picked up the bulk of the groceries from Safeway. He had not seen Maryam, Mo or Rhoda for a couple of weeks now. He half believed that Maryam would somehow shame him into confronting his own problem and he was not ready for that. Even thinking of Maryam shamed him. Why should she bother him so much? She was only a young girl, someone of no importance to him or anyone else, a brown-skinned, shop assistant, he lashed out in his mind, but such racist arguments only made him feel worse.

He was washing the kitchen floor - a chore he hated above all others - and considering yet again whether the time had come to employ a cleaner. When they had first come to Greenyards, they had made a conscious decision not to employ help in the house. However carefully they had constructed their relationship, cleaners could be nosy, see more than necessary, put two and two together and possibly make four. It was a risk neither of them was prepared to take. Now, however, with Gordon the way he was and the prognosis depressing, Bertie wondered if the risk were not after all worth taking. He did not feel like discussing it with Gordon for they were temporarily 'not speaking'. How childish that sounded, but Gordon had never forgiven him for that difficult hospital visit and of course too much nicotine and alcohol. A spasm of anger shook Bertie. For Christ's sake, he had to have something to look forward to. A dram at night was permissible, was it not? One dram. Last night, though, it had been nearly half a bottle. No bloody wonder he felt so wretched today. Far from cheering him up, it depressed him beyond words afterwards. At the time, though, it was as near to heaven as he was ever likely to get these days.

He was emptying the bucket of dirty water into the sink when he heard Gordon shouting. What in heaven's name was it now? He pretended not to hear and, turning on both taps, rinsed the squeezy mop.

Within seconds Gordon was at the kitchen door. His eyes were wild and his thin thatch of hair awry. Bertie's first thought was that he had completely flipped his lid.

'Did you not hear me calling you?' Gordon was shouting. 'You've got to come and see this. Please, Bert, this time it's important.'

'Okay, okay, get a grip,' he said drying his hands on the kitchen towel and following him out of the kitchen, into the narrow back passage and up the steep flight of the back stairs, a short cut through the old servants' quarters to the front bedrooms.

Though most nights they shared Gordon's room, for obvious reasons they each had their own front bedroom for show, both large spacious places with comfortable double beds and sinks big enough to shave in. One of the three somewhat sparsely furnished spare room windows looked out over the Mairs' back garden. Gordon had pulled a chair under the window where he chose to sit and keep watch. His obsession with Colin Mair had not diminished over the weeks. Today it reached a new level.

'Look,' he demanded. 'Tell me who that is and then tell me not to worry.'

Bertie peered through the window into the next door back yard, grassed over with a tool shed at the far end. The lawn, liberally sprinkled with daisies and dandelions, badly needed its first cut of the season but the shed looked in a good condition. Come to think of it he had never noticed the shed.

'That's a new shed, isn't it?' he said after a moment. 'Oh and they must have got another dog.' A cross-breed about the size of a collie with strange ears and large paws bounded down the lawn, picked up a ball, shook it excitedly then bounded back.

'The shed's where Mair does his writing,' Gordon told him, 'but I don't think that dog is theirs.'

At that moment a boy ran down the length of the lawn, tumbled onto his knees and embraced the endearing animal who licked his face, woofed excitedly and bounced around him.

'I know that boy,' said Bertie, surprised to say the least. The Mairs had not struck him as child friendly. 'It's Hughie-the-lad, isn't it? What's he doing in the Mairs' back garden?'

'That's who he is!' Gordon exclaimed 'I thought I recognised him. He shouldn't be there at all. It's not safe. We have to stop him.'

Bertie said nothing. What could they do? For the first time he began to see that Gordon maybe had a point. What was the lad doing there?

'I tell you, something will happen to that boy. He's in danger. Colin Mair is a – a thingamy.'

'You don't know that, Gordon,' he said but without conviction. Gordon's constant condemnation of his neighbour was beginning to affect his own judgement.

'His family needs to know where he is. Do we know them?'

'Of course we do. Annie Miller's his mother. She lives up the street. Don't you remember? She's a cleaner, I believe.' As he spoke the words he knew exactly what he would do. No more bloody kitchen floors.

'She needs to know - now,' said Gordon frantically.

'Well then, let's tell her,' Bertie agreed, looking at his watch. It was half ten on a Saturday morning. Annie could well be at home. They could get her house number from Bruden's.

'You go,' said Gordon decisively. 'I'll keep watch.'

There was no help for it. He would have to go to Bruden's. With any luck Maryam might not be there.

She was, of course, but as soon as he saw her he was relieved. She might well know what Hughie was up to. He hoped that it was all above board.

The shop was busy with several customers stoking up on groceries for the weekend.The drinks cabinet was firmly locked, no alcohol on sale till midday. That was both a relief and a drawback. He knew he would have to visit the off-license that afternoon. He picked up a packet of sausages, not his favourite food but Gordon enjoyed sausage and mash with lashings of onions. He could freeze the remains of last night's steak casserole for another day. Bertie did all the cooking these days.

Eventually it was his turn to be served. He plonked his basket on the counter. 'Morning, Maryam.' After the usual pleasantries he launched out. 'How's Hughie-the-lad these days?'

She looked up in her usual way, not at him but near enough. 'He's got a dog,' she told him as she rang the sausages through the till. 'He takes him on his paper round and he's training him to deliver the papers to the door.'

Bertie was almost amused. 'Good luck with that, eh?' They both laughed and suddenly she was looking at him properly but her eyes were clouded. Since there was no one else waiting to be served he felt compelled to tell her.' I only ask because Gordon - we both - saw him next door in the Mairs' back garden.'

'Yes,' she said. 'Mrs Miller can't keep her - Jura, the dog, I mean.'

'Can't or won't?' he asked

'Can't. Big dogs eat a lot, and Annie has three kids to feed. Hughie was telling us that Mr Mair is kindly keeping him in his shed, and Hughie can see him there any time he wants.'

'That's a shame,' Bertie said.

'Yes, it is,' she replied quietly. Then she turned the full force of her dark eyes on to him.

'It's possible we could help,' he found himself saying. 'Is Annie - Mrs Miller - looking for more work?'

'You would need to ask her.' She had such astonishing eyes. He could not take his own off hers. 'Number 37, opposite the school.'

So dangling his shopping bag with the sausages and a packet of frozen mixed vegetables he walked purposefully up the street. A child was sitting on the step outside the half-open door of the three-up two-down, semi-detached, council house playing with a battered teddy, a one-armed doll and a toy tea-set.

'Hullo, young lady. Is your mother in?' he asked.

'Mam!' She yelled over her shoulder so loudly that he jumped. Then she grinned at him. "I'm Tammy,' she said. 'Would you like a cuppa tea?'

'I would,' he replied seriously, remembering how much he had enjoyed children in those long ago days when he was a young teacher.

She handed him a minute cup without a saucer. 'Milk and sugar?'

'Yes please.' He held out his cup. She poured imaginary milk and handed him a miniature empty sugar bowl.

By the time Annie got there they were fast friends.

Lettie

It was gout, the doctor had said. Gout on one sherry an evening? Surely not.

'Nothing to do with your diet, Miss Anderson,' she told her. 'I'm afraid it's one of your medications. I could take you off it but the real question is this. Which would you rather have, gout or a stroke?'

What sort of question was that?

Geordie must have seen Doctor Jill leaving. He was at the door the moment she left. 'What's up, Miss A?' he asked when eventually she answered the door, hobbling on two sticks. The pain was excruciating whether she sat, lay down or walked. She told him.

'You jist sit yersel' doon, hen. Will I mak' ye a cuppa?'

'Please and one for yourself, of course. Oh, and Geordie there's a prescription the doctor left. Could you possibly pick it up?'

Though Geordie's tea-making skills were questionable; he liked it very strong and very sweet with a handful of biscuits whereas she preferred brown dishwater, she was glad of the company. Geordie had become her rock these days. Jobs in the garden or in the house, shopping, nothing was too much trouble.

'How much should I pay him?' she asked Maryam on one of her evening visits. 'I don't want him to offend him. What do you think?'

Maryam was quiet for a moment. Then she said, 'What if you were to put by a wee bit for him every week and then after a month, say, give him a present.'

That sounded sensible. It would save the embarrassment of fumbling for coins after every little obligement. She sometimes wondered about Geordie. He was looking so unkempt these days and there were times when he crammed the biscuits into his mouth as if he were starving.

'Do you think he needs the money?' she asked searching Maryam's face or an answer. Maryam was not looking at her. That odd intense stare that she sometimes had was both at her and beyond her. 'Maryam?' she said a little sharply to recall her attention.

Her eyes refocused. 'I think he relies a lot on your friendship too,' she said quietly.

But Lettie knew. A voice in her head said as clearly as if it had spoken aloud; he's desperate. She was so unaccustomed to voices in her head that she could think of nothing to say. She also knew about desperation. Most of her life she had been desperate, desperately lonely, aggrieved...angry. Her perspective shifted. For a moment, it was as if she had become Geordie. She felt his desperation, not her own. It was a strange sensation. For the first time she knew what desperation truly felt like and she was astonished.

'Poor Geordie. I wonder if he's got any relatives?'

Even as she asked, Lettie knew he hadn't. She was aware that her mouth was open and her hands were shaking. Her sherry spilt a little as she lifted the glass, so she put it down again quickly.

'How's the gout today?' Maryam asked in that soft, sing-songy voice of hers, after a pause.

She had forgotten about the gout. Suddenly she asked, not knowing where the question came from. 'Do you believe in your God?'

'My God?' Maryam asked.

'Allah, do you call him?' Lettie was embarrassed now and wished she had not asked. It was inappropriate... rude. It was always a mistake to talk about religion. She had spent so many years blaming God that she had grown to resent his very name. Maybe Allah was nicer. Then she said, the words pulled out of her as if by forceps. 'I think...I think I hate the Christian God. He is so - condemnatory, if that's a word.' She looked up anxiously. 'I hope I haven't shocked you, dear?'

Maryam got up from her chair and came over and knelt down at Lettie's feet. She touched her hand and its warmth spread like fire though her body. She stopped shaking. 'I don't think you do,' she said. 'I just think maybe you've got her wrong.'

'Her?' said Lettie, mesmerised by the closeness of the young girl's person. Such glowing skin, such glossy hair.'I thought you believed in Allah.'

Maryam shook her head. 'I see her sometimes,' she said.

'Who dear?'

'Our Mother.'

'You mean the Virgin Mary?' Lettie asked in a low voice. The Virgin Mary was not a term that came easily to her Protestant tongue.

'She was a very special daughter.'

'Are you telling me that God - your God - is a woman?' Lettie was more surprised than shocked.

Maryam smiled. 'Do you find the idea that we are all sons and daughters of Our Mother strange?'

'Frankly yes,' said Lettie. 'Exceedingly strange.' And possibly blasphemous, she thought. The God she had encouraged herself to hate was male to the tips of his white flowing beard. She wished she hadn't asked. Quickly she changed the subject. 'How are things in the shop without Mo?'

'Okay,' she said and thankfully the subject of God was dropped.

After a moment Maryam withdrew her hand and rose to her feet in one graceful fluid movement. (Oh to be able to move like that.)

'I must go. Sheena will be home soon and it's my turn to cook.'

Lettie looked at her anxiously. 'You will come again?' she pleaded 'You're not offended, I hope?'

'Of course I'll come again. We have Geordie to sort out, don't we?'

Lettie had for the moment forgotten about Geordie. She sat back in her chair, and thought about the girl. What a beautiful daughter she must be to someone. She wished...she wished, but no, she would not go down that path. The idea of a Mother God...Goddess was intriguing, exotic even. Hindus had lots of goddesses, didn't they? Maybe Maryam was Hindu... a lady god? No, that sounded twee. Goddess sounded Dark Age, heathen. But a mother god... Our Mother, not Our Father? Was the concept really so very strange? Perhaps if she had believed in her, Arthur and Alex would not have been killed in the First World War. Perhaps if the world believed in her, life would have been different. Lord Jesus might not have died that dreadful, shocking death. No mother would have permitted it...

But then mothers need men to impregnate them with daughters. Maybe not, though. Mary had not needed a man. The Virgin Birth they called it, though she had never in her heart of hearts gone along with that theory. Thought it just another Bible story. But if it were true and Mary had not needed a man, then 'Our Mother' as Maryam had called her, would not have needed a man either. Maybe Our Mother not Our Father had created the universe. Maybe Our Mother had created Eve first and placed her before Adam in that metaphorical Garden of Eden. The clues were there. Eve was surely the stronger of the two, the bolder, the more curious, the leader. Maybe Our Mother created Adam from Eve's rib... or womb.

Stop it, she told herself; this way madness lies.... but how intensely interesting. The idea that she - and the rest of humankind - had got it badly wrong over the centuries was decidedly intriguing. How could that have happened? Very easily, she thought, as she remembered her brothers, how her mother had nurtured and encouraged them and yes, idolised them, like most mothers do their sons. She gave her head a little shake but could not stem the incoming tide of her thoughts.

Who was this half-black, part-Muslim, (or possibly Hindu) shop girl then that she, Lettice, should listen to her talk of a mother god? She wanted to think it ridiculous, she wanted to dismiss it all as feminist nonsense, but then she remembered the strangeness of Maryam. If, as her father always insisted the proof of the pudding is in the eating, Mo's little shop assistant surely tasted like ambrosia.

Whatever the truth of it, one fact had emerged clearly from Maryam's visit, a truth that could not be queried; Geordie was in need. I'll start a little fund for him, she thought. She would put away a few shillings (she still thought of money in LSD) every time he did something for her and then give him a present as Maryam had suggested - say once a month. She still had that little money box shaped like an elephant that you had to smash to get into. When it was full she would present it to him as a sort of joke gift and then he could do what he liked with it. Calculating how much she already owed him, she found six pound-coins in her purse and pushed them in, one by one. It felt good, and guess what? Her gout was distinctly better.

That had been yesterday. She was still thinking about the possibility of Our Mother instead of - or maybe as well as - Our Father, when she saw that nice Mr Maclardy passing by her window. She waved but he had not noticed her. He looked preoccupied. Oh well, everyone had their worries.

Annie Miller

Annie, just home from Ma Mackenzie, had been sitting on the settee for a moment of peace with a cup of tea in her hand. When the knock had come. Before answering she had a quick peep out of the window and saw Mr Bertie Maclardy standing there talking to Tammy. Her mind flew to her children. The Maclardy brothers had both been teachers, therefore critical and tight-lipped. Not Tammy surely. Maybe Elvis had given him cheek; he had a bad habit of answering back. Why else would one of them call round on a Saturday morning?

'Mr Maclardy?' She said answered defensively behind the half-open door.

'Mrs Miller,' he had said friendly like 'Can you spare me a moment or two? Won't keep you long, I promise. Just wanted a word.'

She opened the door to let him in. Nice looking man, she thought automatically re-arranging her face from anxious to curious. 'Take a seat,' she said. Luckily the sitting room was tidy-ish.

He thanked her and chose the armchair with the polyester tiger throw to hide the stains. It was a while since she'd had a gentleman caller; years in fact, so long that she had forgotten the rules. She noticed her half-drunk mug with 'Super Mum' in black letters sprawled round it and dredged up her manners. 'Would you care for a cuppa?' and immediately wished the words unsaid. Supposing he asked for Nescaff? There was none in the house.

'Thank you, but no. Tammy has already given me a cup of tea.' He laughed so she had laughed too. 'I realise you are a very busy lady. In fact...' He paused long enough for her to preen a little (her a lady!). 'I shouldn't perhaps even ask, but if you could spare a couple of hours in the week to clean for us, we would be most grateful. My brother and I have reached the age when we would welcome a bit of help in the house.'

More work. She beamed. At this rate she would be able to afford Nescaff. In five minutes the deal had been done. Four hours a week on Tues and Friday afternoons at £2 50 a session starting the following week. An hour meant an extra fiver in her purse.

'Sure you would nae like a cuppa tea?' she asked with more confidence when he stood up.

'You're very kind but I really must go.' He paused at the sitting room door. 'By the way, Mrs Miller...'

'Annie,' she interrupted. 'Call me Annie.'

'Thank you Annie. As I was about a to say - I didn't know Hughie had a dog.'

'He does nae.' She'd told him over and over. 'We canna keep a dog. I've tellt him a dozen times.'

'I beg your pardon. It's just that my brother Gordon saw him with a dog and assumed...'

'He assumed wrong then. Where did he see him?'

'In the garden next door to Greenyards - the Mairs' bungalow. It probably belongs to Mr Mair.'

'That'll be right,' she said shortly.

'It's just that Hughie's goes there a lot, every day after school. Oh and he takes it on his paper round first thing. We assumed that the dog was his.' Again he paused.

Annie said nothing. Her head was whirling.

'I'm sorry if I've spoken out of turn. Hughie's a good lad and I wouldn't want him to get into trouble. He and the dog seemed very close.'

'He likes dogs right enough,' Annie said reluctantly. She liked dogs too, but if she found it hard to feed three hungry bairns how could she feed a dog? There were no left over scraps.

Mr Maclardy looked as if he wanted to say more. 'Well then... we'll see you on Tuesday at 2 pm?'

She nodded. Her head was still full of Hughie and the dog. She held open the front door. 'Is it a big dog?' she asked.

'It is,' he told her with a smile. 'Enormous paws.'

It would be, she thought.

'Look Mrs Miller – Annie. Let me speak frankly. I've seen Hughie with the dog. They said in the shop that Hughie had got a dog. My brother gets notions - .' He stopped abruptly and shook his head. 'Is there no way you could let Hughie keep the dog here? I realise that feeding a big dog is an expensive undertaking... If we were to offer you three pounds an afternoon, would that help?'

She was bewildered. Six pounds a week! What sort of notions? Was Hughie bothering them? Why did it matter to the Maclardy brothers? What was he getting at? 'Is it Hughie?' she asked anxiously, 'Is he bothering you or is it the dog?'

'Nothing like that,' he said awkwardly. 'You must do what you think right, Annie, of course, but the offer is on the table. Think about it.'

What was that all about, she wondered as she watched him go. Then she thought about her son. That Hughie. Do anything to get this own way. Come to think of it, he was more out than in these days. Off sometimes before she was up, back late for tea. As for the weekends, he was never at home. She assumed he was with his mates, but maybe he wasn't. Maybe he was at the Mairs' house with a dog... his dog.

She went through to the kitchenette to get the dinner. Sugar sandwiches for the bairns on a Saturday. She slathered the sliced white bread with Stork, layered it with grnulated sugar and got out the bottle of ginger. Why ginger, she often wondered, for it was just lemonade, opened yesterday so a little flat. Could be Irn Brew with all that extra cash coming in... not if they had a dog, though.

Tammy was the first in. 'Mam,' she shouted as she came in the back door. 'Can I get to go to the pictures with Jayne? It's in Kirkcaldy but her mam'll pay. It's at two, so I'll need my dinner now.

She was already half way through her sugar sandwich when Elvis came in filthy as usual. 'Where ha'e you been? Just look at the state of you,' she exclaimed and turned on the kitchen tap. He held his hands under the running water for a second and rubbed most of the mud off on the roller towel on the back of the door. He and his pals had been playing at the loch. Starving as usual, he fell on his piece.

'Where's Hughie?' she asked. 'Did you see him?'

Elvis nodded, his mouth full, but he avoided her eye.

'Where?'

The lad shrugged.

'Was he wi' a dog? You'll answer me now, son.'

'How div ye ken aboot the dog?'

So that was how Annie came to know about Hughie's dog. When Hughie eventually turned up for his dinner he admitted defensively that Colin was keeping it - 'her name's Jura by the way' - and feeding her for her son.'

'Colin?' she asked sharply.

'Mr Mair then,' he answered sulkily. 'He likes dogs.'

Annie was not just angry - he should have told her, at least - she was also worried. The word 'paedo' headlined in her mind. She had read in the papers about men who befriended kids for the worst of reasons. There had been that old geezer in Alloa who had behaved unspeakably...

'He had no right. Who does he think he is?' she could hear her voice rising.

Hughie was quick to defend him. 'He's okay. Jura likes him,' he declared defiantly.

'Well, I don't want you bothering him or Mistress Mair any longer. You're not to go there again, do you hear?' Colin indeed! Count ten, she told herself feeling hot with rage.

'I'll go where I fucking like,' he shouted back, knocking over his chair and storming out of the house. 'You canna stop me.'

'You come back here at once, Hugh Miller. You're not too big for a hiding,' she shouted at the door but it was too late. He had gone.

Now she was more anxious than angry.

She could settle to nothing. Her first thought was to find Mr Maclardy. What did he mean by his brother's 'notions'? She grabbed her coat and stormed out of the house. But by the time she reached Greenyards she was having second thoughts. She paused outside the fancy gate to the Mairs' bungalow. His mother was standing in the window staring out. Annie was embarrassed. She raised her hand in an awkward gesture but Mistress Mair chose not to notice.

By this time she had lost her nerve and found herself hurrying past and before she knew it there was the shop, a refuge from whatever it was that she feared. From a corner of the window she could catch a glimpse of the counter. Thank God it was not Rhoda on duty, or Mo. To her relief she saw Maryam standing there and knew instantly that this was why she had come.

She skulked behind the bakery gondola, chose a jammy doughnut as a peace offering for Hughie, waited until the other customers, a group of bairns with their Saturday pocket money, had gone.

Maryam's smile of welcome calmed her as it always did.

'I'm glad it's you,' she whispered. 'I thought it might be Rhoda.'

'She's got a bad back,' said Maryam and went right to the heart of the matter. 'Hughie okay?'

'No,' she said and in a quick gabble poured out the whole story. Fortunately the shop stayed empty.

Maryam listened. The faint frown in the space between her dark eyebrows faded when she mentioned Mr Maclardy's generous offer.

'Then you can keep Jura,' she said. 'That's good news. Hughie loves her so much. You should see them together with the papers.'

'Hughie's gone. I don't know if he's coming back. I think I've blown it.'

'Of course he'll be back. That doughnut's for him, isn't it?'

She nodded.

'Hughie loves his doughnuts.' She smiled. 'A home for his dog and a doughnut for his tea. What more would he want?'

Maryam was not looking at her but Annie was used to that.

'I could go and thank Mistress Mair right enough. It was dead nice of her really.' The words came from somewhere outside of herself.

So she did. Mrs Mair came to the door and Annie explained at great length. 'About time,' she said a bit sharpish. Then she added, 'my wee boy's bent over backwards for that dog.' Mr Mair – her wee boy? Somewhere inside her Annie wanted to laugh. 'And this wee girl will miss her big bootiful Jura, won't she, then?' The woman continued in doggy speak as she picked up and cuddled her own little pet who had pushed his way through her legs and begun to yap. 'I'll tell my son when he gets in.'

Hughie came back at tea time with Jura, a blanket and a couple of tins of Chum. It was a huge dog right enough. He saw the doughnut sitting by itself on the kitchen table.

'Thanks Mam,' he told her but she knew it was not just for the doughnut.

Rachel

'Hello Annie. You okay?' Rachel asked, meeting her on the way out as she entered the shop. 'See you on Monday as usual?'

'Aye,' said Annie. 'How's Mistress Mackenzie?'

'Sore and having to learn how to walk again. Jayjay may even beat her to it.' Her mother-in-law had had her hip operation and was now recuperating in a nursing home. Alastair was visiting her now, or so she supposed.

'Tell her I was asking for her,' said Annie.

Rachel manoeuvred the stroller into the shop.

'Hi gorgeous!' said Maryam coming round from behind the counter to speak to her godson while Rachel eyed the wine shelves. Surely Jayjay couldn't be affected by just one glass of red on a Saturday night. After all he was practically weaned. On this occasion, however, Al wouldn't be there to scold her because he would be out. Not scold her exactly. She wished he would scold her. It was the sulking she could not stand. 'If you've something to say, then say it,' she would storm at him but the more she ranted the quieter he became and the silences could stretch into days. It had not been a problem between them when she was pregnant. She laid off all alcohol during those nine months and for Jayjay's first three months when she was feeding him full time, but somehow over the past month or so she had needed a bit of comfort. Partly of course it was Alastair's own fault. So many nights in the week he worked overtime in the office thus leaving her alone. Boredom and loneliness had driven her so, like so many other women (or so she had read in one of the glossies) to gin or, as in her case, red wine, medium dry, the dearer the better.

She had a few friends of course, but they were busy were their own families in the evenings and now that Carly Drummond and her dreadful husband had suddenly upped sticks and left Queich after that scandal when Carly had been arrested, she had no one to gossip with over a glass of red...

'I don't really want you going there anymore,' Alastair had told her, understandably, she supposed, since his firm were handling her case. Anyhow they had left for Dundee last month and there were new tenants expected any day now in No 11(a).

'Why don't you see more of mother?' Alastair had suggested when she had complained that he was never in these days. How she hated those three little words 'why don't you'. He had inherited them straight from his mother and usually implied criticism of some sort. As for his mother, they could be polite to each other but fundamentally they were incompatible. At least that was the kindest word she could think of.

'I think she's probably lonely.' he had added.

'And I'm not?' She retaliated on the edge of anger.

'You at least have Jayjay.'

'You can't gossip or have a coffee or enjoy dinner with a baby.'

She had banged out of the room.

Later, it occurred to her, that this was probably the longest conversation they had had for a while. Certainly he had not suggested it again. So she remained bored and lonely until she had had a glass of wine or three starting in the late afternoon. Jayjay still clung greedily to his evening top-up and as a surprising bonus slept the night through as a result of the wine, or so she had convinced herself.

On one occasion recently Alastair had come home unexpectedly early to find her half tipsy. She had served dinner through a stumbling, apologetic fog. Alastair's silence had taken him into the chilly spare bedroom for a couple of nights.

Since then and to show she was repentant she had cut the wine out of their menu. Alastair hadn't appeared to notice. Their relationship, however, had not noticeably improved. She was almost glad when Jayjay girned or demanded attention. At least it broke the silence.

Waiting to be served, she lingered for a while at the wine shelves. Well why not? Alastair had some men-only golfing dinner in St Andrews. Would it be Merlot or Sauvignon? Abandoned, or so it seemed to him, Jayjay began to yell. She left the shelf quickly to pop his pacifier into his mouth. Mother would be appalled. 'Such a common habit,' she would complain but who cared if it did the trick. She and her son with his moods and sulks could go hang for all she cared.

She turned to take her place in the small queue that had gathered while she was contemplating the wines. As she waited, a bottle of Californian red defiantly in her basket, she watched Maryam, 'Sunshine' as Mo called her, and it was not hard to see why. Something about her glowing skin and her brown eyes seemed to emit light. She would have liked to see more of Maryam. Especially tonight when Alastair was out presumably enjoying himself. She couldn't fairly fault him for that. He worked hard and had little fun. Why shouldn't he have an occasional dinner with his cronies? So she told herself as she tried to stifle her resentment.

The queue had gone. 'Maryam,' she began but without much hope. 'I don't suppose you'd care to share this with me tonight?' She put the wine on the counter. 'Alastair's out, Mother's in hospital and Jayjay and I would love your company for dinner. I've got some halibut.' (She had been saving it in the freezer for their anniversary next week)

Maryam looked up. That strange squint of hers was so much a part of her that Rachel hardly noticed. She braced herself for the refusal she fully anticipated.

'I've a better idea,' Maryam said, and this time her eyes were focussed. 'Why don't you come to mine? That is if you like curry? I took it out of the freezer this morning. It's a family recipe which I made last week. Sheena's on night duty and will have had her share by the time I get home from work. There'll be plenty left for us.'

'I'd really like that.' Rachel was delighted by the invitation. 'I'll bring this.' She waved the bottle of wine.

Seven hours later with Jayjay fed and half asleep in the stroller and a bag with a change of nappies, a bottle of boiled water and of course the all-important wine she rang the bell of number 11(c).

With much giggling, Maryam helped her bump the stroller up the stairs to the flat. In jeans and a pale yellow top she looked so young and pretty in her matching Friday head scarf or perhaps because of it, that Rachel exclaimed enviously, 'How do you keep so slim?' She herself had put on an alarming amount since Jayjay's birth.

'It's weird,' said Maryam. 'Being surrounded by food all day puts you right off eating.'

'An original way to diet then; surround yourself with food. Let me know when there's a job going in the shop.' Rachael stopped laughing. 'By the way, how is Mo?'

'Finding it hard.'

The smell of curry wafted through the flat. Mother would not approve, Rachel thought, but she rather liked it. It was ages since she had enjoyed a curry. Same with fish and chips. If she and Alastair indulged, it had to be a takeaway eaten in the car. That hadn't happened for a long while, though.

'How is Mrs Mackenzie?' Maryam asked with real concern in her voice.

'Coming home next week.'

Maryam had accepted the wine but that was not what was offered. Rachel had forgotten that, as part Muslim, Maryam was probably teetotal, at least on a Friday. How stupid of her.

The alternative offered looked like wine but was in fact grape juice and delicious.

'This is nice,' she said surprised to find herself liking it.

'It belongs to Sheena. She daren't drink and drive to Dundee let alone nurse her patients on alcohol. It's great with curry.'

It was. The meal was the best she had tasted for months. Jayjay slept blissfully on while they chatted and laughed and relaxed. Or at least Rachel did. She was aware that she was talking too much. The urge to pour out her thoughts and feelings had become more powerful than the need for wine.

'Maryam,' she began once the dishes were cleared and washed and they were sitting in the window recess watching the red and gold dusk. 'Can I ask you something?'

'Mm hmm?'

'That night at the hypnotist...Did you do something weird to make that wretched man lose the plot?'

Maryam was silent for a moment then she looked up, her eyes intent and serious. 'Why do you ask?'

'The girls talk about it a lot. Something happened and then you walked out and disappeared. Some of us think – I think - that maybe you ...Sorry, perhaps I shouldn't have said anything.' Her voice tailed off. She wished now she had held her tongue. What could Maryam have done anyhow?

Maryam's glance slid sideways.

'Sorry. Forget I asked.'

Her eyes re-focussed. 'It's not altogether me,' Maryam said slowly. 'I saw his soul shadow.'

'Soul shadow?' Rachel was part curious, part fearful that the girl had lost the plot.

Maryam smiled. 'You think I'm crazy, don't you?'

She had, but only briefly. 'No,' she said seriously. 'Of course I don't think you're crazy. I just don't understand.'

'I used to think everyone saw shadows and I still think everyone could - well most people,' she amended.

Rachel felt her mouth opening in astonishment. 'Go on,' she said. 'What did his shadow look like?'

'A cruel man,' she said simply.

'So you did do something to him?'

'My shadow did.'

Rachel was quiet for a moment as her mind re-imagined the scene in the theatre.

'You have to admit, it was quite funny.' She said.

Maryam shook her head. 'No, it wasn't,' she said. 'Truly it wasn't.'

'He deserved it, don't you think?'

'It made me vomit.'

'Really? Is that where you went afterwards, to the loo? We looked but obviously not carefully enough.' Although Maryam said nothing, Rachel could not let the subject go. 'Do I have a shadow?' she persisted.

Maryam nodded. 'My shadow can see your shadow and they tell me things.'

'What sort of things?'

Maryam hesitated. Rachel sighed and answered for her. 'I drink too much. I still resent living with my mother-in-law and I'm losing my husband. A spoiled cow. Something like that?'

Maryam shook her head. 'You're so wrong.'

'Tell me then.'

'My shadow sees someone who's not having a lot of fun at the moment.'

The kindness of the words spoken so gently touched Rachel's heart and she began quietly to cry. Tears poured from her eyes and her throat contracted in sobs. 'I'm sorry,' she managed to gasp. 'I'm really sorry.'

Maryam reached out her hand to cover hers. The touch calmed her and though the tears still fell, the sobs subsided. 'Sorry,' she said more calmly. 'It's just that I'm bloody miserable these days. I don't think Alastair even likes me anymore let alone loves me. Everything at home is a mess.'

Maryam handed her a tissue. 'I know,' she said gently.

'Don't be so bloody nice to me or I'll never stop.' But she had stopped as quickly as she had started. She wiped her eyes. 'How do you know all that stuff?'

Maryam answered, 'It's not something specially to be envied.'

'What do shadows look like?'

'Just shadows. I can't explain. Some are brighter than others, though.'

'That hypnotist. What was his like?'

Maryam leaned forwards, a small frown between her eyes. 'Sort of... without light.'

'Was it... is it scary, seeing shadows?'

She was silent for a while. Then she said quietly, 'Our Mother protects me.'

Rachel felt her mouth fall open. 'Our Mother?' she asked quietly. Maryam rose and moved towards the uncurtained window. The last rays of the sun wrapped her in an aura of fiery light.

'I suppose,' she said so softly that afterwards Rachel wondered if she had properly heard.' I suppose you could call her God.'

'Our Mother as opposed to Our Father which art in Heaven? Is that what you mean?'

At that precise moment Jayjay let out a cry, startling them both back into the reality of the moment. Rachel got up to go to him in his stroller in a corner of the living room. She felt light-footed, light-headed, almost light-hearted. It was a weird feeling as though she had cried away a hard skin. Jayjay too was fine, not crying or angry but awake and alert. 'Hey, you!' she said picking him up and cuddling him. 'Did you think we had forgotten you, gorgeous boy?'

She carried him over to the window recess where he laughed and held out his arms instinctively to Maryam. Unquestioningly Rachel handed him over to his godmother. 'Does he have a shadow?' she asked tentatively. She was not sure if their conversation had been real.

121

'Of course.' Maryam was laughing with the child. 'Dazzling and beautiful.'

Afterwards when Rachel was laying in bed, sober and thoughtful and still elated - how could she not be? - she remembered that moment. If Our Mother was God, and at that moment it did not seem at all impossible, then Maryam was undoubtedly her Daughter.

Hughie

He believed he had to let Mr Mair - Colin - drive him and Jura up into the foothills of the Ochils.

To Hughie's surprise, Colin had been bafflingly annoyed when Mam had told Mrs Mair that she had decided to let him keep Jura. He had thought both Mairs would have been relieved.

'We had a deliberate arrangement,' Colin said sharply. 'What will the poor beast do when you're at school all day?'

Hughie had thought of that. If Mam was working, Elvis, in exchange for a share of his paper-round money, would go home at dinner-time and take her our for a quick run and he could be back from school by four. 'It's sorted,' he explained.

Colin said surprisingly, 'I'll miss the creature. What about a romp in the hills on Saturday?' Hughie had shaken his head. Just to prevent such invitations, he had arranged with a mate to do stuff with Jura on Saturdays. When Colin then suggested Sunday afternoon instead, he had no excuse ready. He could hardly say that his mother disapproved, so all he did was nod. 'Two o'clock then sharp at my gate.'

It was a perfect day. The loch was a shiny blue tablecloth, the hills green and gold with whin and broom, the flinty road verges green and gold with dandelions and the fields green and gold with buttercups as Colin drove up into the hills. Jura in the back of the car woofed excitedly at the sight of sheep.

'She'll have to be kept on the lead,' Colin said as he parked on the grass where the narrowing road petered out in a wooden gate. 'It's the lambing season.'

'Fine,' he answered. He was beginning to relax a little as they crossed one field and then another. Jura strained at his long leash but the sheep were not bothered. The lambs were enchanting. It was nice up here.

The third fence up took them up high onto the hill. There were no sheep here, nothing but sun and sky and green heather tufts until a curlew, startled by their presence, suddenly soared above them crying its mournful dirge. Hughie's mouth fell open. He had never before heard a curlew call. At

Colin's bidding, he let Jura off the lead and she bounded ahead of them, happy and free. He wished he could run after her, but he felt trapped, imprisoned by the presence of this stranger whose breathing grew heavier beside him.

As if he could read his mind, Colin told him to run on ahead. 'Don't let an old man like me hold you back.' So he did. Springing from heather clump to grassy tussock, gulping the clear cool air, he shaded his eyes from time to time to follow Jura. He ran until he was breathless then flung himself down on the turf in the lea of a great lichened boulder, and, shading his eyes against the white glare of the sun, decided he had been mean to Colin. He had been ace to get him Jura and brilliant to bring them here to this magic place. To think he hadn't wanted to come!

'This'll do,' Colin said some minutes later choosing to sit down with his back to the boulder and closer than Hughie would have chosen. 'Tea-time, I think.' He took his rucksack off his back and opened its straps.

Jura came up panting to see what was happening, squatted and looked from one to the other questioningly. 'I haven't forgotten you, greedy beast.' Colin raked through his backpack and produced a plastic bowl and a bottle of water. Hughie found himself almost liking the man for his thoughtfulness. Jura lapped the bowl dry and Hughie relaxed.

There were filled rolls and a can of ginger for Hugh. 'Such perverted taste' Colin remarked tossing it over to him, and a flask of coffee for himself. Hughie devoured his roll ravenously. There was ham and cheese inside. His favourite. Jura was nowhere to be seen. He started up anxiously.

'She'll be fine,' said Colin and sure enough she was. Her nose was down a rabbit burrow a few metres above them. All he could see was her wagging tail.

When they had eaten Colin felt in his jacket pocket and pulled out a packet of cigarettes. He took one out, hesitated, then handed the pack to Hughie. 'Go on,' he encouraged him in his nasal sardonic voice. 'Promise I won't tell your mother.'

It was not the way to Hughie's heart. He thought he hated fags because of the stink that clung to his mother, and the threats she thundered at him a while ago when he had picked up one of her dud ends, left smoking in the ashtray. On the other hand he was curious. What harm would one do? So while he shook his head vigorously, his eyes told a different story.

Colin dropped the pack between them and fished in another pocket for his lighter, lit his own, and inhaled deeply. He poked the pack against Hugh's thigh. 'Sure you won't?' he asked lazily and Hughie fell. He picked up the packet, selected one and pushed it between his lips just to get the feel of it. He had not made up his mind to smoke it.

Before he knew it the lighter was flicked on in his face. Colin's fingers were stained with nicotine. Because he could hardly help himself he drew in a mouthful of smoke. Whether it was the proximity of those thin stained fingers or the smoke he was never quite sure, but the next moment he was on his knees retching up his ham rolls on to the heather. In an instant Colin's hand, both hands, were on his brow and that nasal voice so close that his nicotine breath was hot on his ear. 'That'll teach you,' he said and then he laughed, not a scornful laugh but intimate, excited, terrifying. Then his mouth touched his neck. It felt like a warm slug.

'Let me alane!' Hughie thrust out his elbow and caught the older man painfully in the ribs. The spasm of vomiting over, he flung away the cigarette, sprang to his feet and shouting for Jura ran downhill as if for his life.

Not sure if the dog would follow him, he stopped and turned once to call him in the words he had been practising ever since he had got him home. 'Jura tae me. Now.'

Colin was standing where he had left him. He was also shouting whether for himself or for the dog, Hughie was not sure. 'Come back here, you ungrateful little shit.' Neither paid him any attention. Hughie turned away and ran on. Jura was already ahead bounding down the hill, woofing excitedly. To him it was all a splendid game.

Hughie did not stop running until he tripped over a tussock and sprawled within inches of a stone dyke. In trepidation he looked back but there was no sign of Colin. Jura licked his face and he put his arms round the dog and sobbed, not with tears, not from exhaustion but out of sheer terror.

Unhurt apart from scraped knees he found himself facing a crumbling mossy wall topped with a barbed wire fence. Beyond was a field full of sheep and he had no lead. Keeping to the side of the wall he began to run again, more slowly this time till he came to a gate that opened out into a lane that led to a farm cottage which he had never seen before. There were other dogs.

A cacophony of barking led by an excited Jura kept him one side of the gate. Before long there were three collies at the other side soon to be joined by their owner, a middle-aged man in a cloth cap, overalls and a long stick with a crooked handle.

'Whit the hell dae yer think ye'r dae-ing?' he shouted striding up the lane and brandishing his stick.

Hughie was speechless, partly from running and partly because no words would come from his restricted throat.

'Are you deaf? I'm speaking to ye,' the man shouted as he approached his side of the gate. 'Get that bloody dog on a lead.'

Still speechless, Hughie could only shake his head.

'Well?' said the man, whose face was stubbled and lined, but had astonishingly blue eyes.

It was the eyes that gave Hughie courage. 'It's lost.' he muttered.

Eyeing him less angrily the man said roughly, 'The lead's lost or you're lost?'

'Aye,' whispered Hughie hanging his head.

'You wait there,' said the man who turned on his heel, strode off to a shed and emerged seconds later with a length of rope. With clumsy fingers Hughie fastened it to Jura's collar while the man opened the gate just wide enough for them to enter. Through and safe, Hughie felt the shackles that had bound his body with fear loosen and waited for the telling-off that he expected, that was normal and deserved. Sure enough it came as the man marched him down the weedy rutted path to the cottage.

'Just what the so-and-so do ye think ye were dae-ing oot on the hill wi' a dog and all they lambs?'

What could he say? 'Sorry,' was all that came out.

'Aye ye'll no' half be sorry by the time Ah've feenished wi' ye. Whaur dae ye come frae?' By this time they had reached the cottage.

'Queich.'

He opened the door and without going in shouted, 'Chrissy!'

A sturdy middle-aged woman emerged wiping her hands on her apron. 'Aye Rob?'

'Ah found this lad on the hill. Frae Queich, he says. Trespassing wi' a dog. Ye'll need to deal wi' him. I've a yow in labour.'

Abruptly he called his dogs to heel, strode off and disappeared into one of the sheds.

Chrissie looked at him. 'Do I know you?' she said cocking her head on one side and looking from him to the dog. Her eyes, almost as blue as her brother's were re-assuring.

'I'm the paper-boy,' he squeaked. He had been doing a lot of that recently. His voice was beginning to break.

'Hughie-the-lad! I've seen you at my faither's hoose.'

When Hugh looked blank she smiled, 'Mr Foulis. Moll's maister? I heard you'd got a dog of yer ain.'

That established, she took them both in, gave Jura a bowl of water and made him a cup of tea. He thought he was not hungry. The sickness still lingered but he accepted a toffee from a poke she kept in her pocket and felt better. She was nice. He would have liked to answer her questions but he had no words to describe what had happened or rather what had not happened on the hillside. She did not press him but she was kind and then she drove them home. He had not asked for a lift but he was grateful. 'I'm off to see ma dad anyways and make him his tea. It's no skin off my nose, 'she joked.

The more he thought of it, the less he believed that Colin had been anything more than decent to him. He felt ashamed, babyish even, for puking and for running away. How would he ever face him again? Chrissie chatted away to him in the car and took him right to his own door.

Mam never knew. He certainly wasn't going to tell her. What was there, after all, to tell? But Hughie still felt ill at ease with himself and his family, at his school and in his head. He could not understand himself.

Maryam

Monday morning at six-thirty was loud with bird song. She stopped to listen to a thrush singing its heart out in a white lilac bush close to the Old Rectory gate. His little throat trembled with the power of his song. She could just see his shadow, a beautiful shining wraith that sheathed his little body. He saw her and burst into a hosanna of welcome.

It amazed her all over again that so many people doubted that creatures had souls. If they had shadows they also had souls, she told Sheena. Her friend was silent for a while but afterwards she nodded. 'If you say so,' she said peacefully but unconvinced.

'If they are created they must have souls. Surely you don't doubt that?' Maryam had argued with some passion. (Yet the word 'soul' had other connotations. 'Shadow' was not right either, for shadow implied darkness and these were reflections of light. Halo? Aura? She had pondered them all. There was no satisfactory word to describe these reflections of Our Mother that lingered in her creations. None, at least, that she knew, so she called them shadows and thought of them as souls. 'From the moment Our Mother gives life to a single cell, it belongs to her. It's a reflection of her. Life comes from her, belongs to her, and shows itself in shadows of light.'

'What about Darwin?' Sheena asked, provocatively.

'He got it right; from a single cell to a butterfly or...' she groped on her mind for an analogy' ...a chimp to a man. It took millennia in our time but Our Mother exists in her own time and shadows exist in Our Mother's time.'

'Your Mother must be busy,' Sheena had once said, 'like a great queen bee churning out boys and bugs.'

The analogy was laughable, so Maryam had laughed. Did Sheena believe anything she said? She knew from her shadow that she did not, that she was puzzled, doubting but loyal. One day hopefully she would understand. She would learn just as Maryam herself was still learning. Our Mother put herself into all her creations. Why Maryam had been given this gift of perception bewildered her when she stopped to think about it. Mostly, though, she took it for granted. She remembered that first vision of her as wave, water, weed and wind. Over the years she had sometimes seen her again, fleeting glimpses only, once at a music festival where she had risen like the wind out of a sea of faces raised in twilight as the music throbbed, an amalgam of them all. Another time high on the Campsie Hills outside Glasgow in a soaring windy rainbow of colour, cloud and sun, and again, more briefly at the beginning of the month.

The flats had needed a gardener and Geordie, at her suggestion, had accepted the job. She had come home one sunny evening from visiting Lettie to find him mowing the front lawn for the first cut of the year. As she breathed in the fresh clean scent of cut grass, she had seen something beyond him, indescribable, awesome, a whirlwind of shimmering green rising from the ground, made of grass and daisies and dandelions and eyebright and clover, beautiful and joyous beyond measure and she had once again recognised Our Mother. Once again the same words rang through her head. 'My daughter ...listen.' Overwhelmed by her vision, she had sunk to her knees. At the same moment Geordie had looked up, seen her, thought she had fallen and hurried to her rescue. The vision had vanished but it had taught her yet another lesson, that even the grass had its shadow.

Parting with difficulty from the singing thrush, she hurried to the shop a little late. The papers had already arrived and lay in bundles tied with string on the pavement. She unlocked the door, disconnected the burglar alarm and stacked the papers on the counter. Within seconds of her arrival, Annie arrived to scrub the floor and wipe down the gondolas. One of the two regular cleaners had recently retired. When Maryam suggested that Annie be offered the job, both Mo and Rhoda had been doubtful. 'She's owing cash,' Mo said shortly and Rhoda had been more explicit. 'I wouldn't trust that woman as far as I can fly.'

Maryam had persisted. 'She's paid off most of what she owes. She's lost her job in the pub and needs the money.'

When determined, Maryam usually got her own way. Sometimes the power of her own will scared her, so she used it only rarely. On this occasion she had had no doubts. Rhoda had sniffed but Mo had nodded so Annie had started work last month three mornings a week from seven till eight when the shop was empty of customers. Mo paid her a pound over the minimum wage for unsocial hours, so now Annie had no need to ask for credit.

They didn't talk much for both were too busy but Maryam, aware of Annie's shadow, knew that she was troubled. 'Something bothering you, Annie?'

Annie looked up from the mop. 'Aye. It's Hughie. I dinna ken whit's got into the loon. He disappeared wi' the dog all day yesterday and he would'na touch his tea. He's off his vittals, off wi' the bairns, off wi' me. Shut hissel into his room and not even the Two Ronnies could tempt him oot.'

Maryam suddenly felt cold. 'Maybe he's sickening for something?'

'Mebbe. He'll no tell me whit's wrang.'

'What about his paper round?'

Annie shrugged. 'He kens he needs the money if he's to keep his dog.'

Her hour up, she was putting her coat on over her overall to get Elvis and Tammy off to school, when Hughie showed up having tethered Jura to the rail outside. He was more whey-faced than usual.

Maryam looked at his shadow and what she saw scared her.

He barely glanced at his mother, let alone answer when she asked him if he'd taken the bowl of cornflakes she had left out for his breakfast, and only grunted with his back turned to her when she told him to 'see and behave hissel'. Thus he never saw the look and despairing shrug that Annie gave Maryam as she left the shop.

'I saved this for you,' Maryam said casually and pushed forward a jam doughnut wrapped in cling film left over from Saturday's delivery.

'Ta,' he said briefly stuffing the cake into his anorak pocket. Maryam began to pack the newspapers for delivery into the satchel. He watched her and listened to the particular Monday requirements.

'Jura okay?' she asked casually.

He did not answer her but when she came to the Mairs' order, he stopped her. 'I'm no' doin' they,' he said firmly.

She glanced up at his shadow. It seemed to have its head in its arms.

'Any reason?' she asked as she slipped it out of the bundle.

'I hate him,' he muttered.

'Why would that be, Hughie?' she asked. Pretending not to hear her, he picked up the satchel and ambled out of the shop. She looked up and there it was, that strange disconnected shadow that had nothing to do with light watching her from the bakery gondola. The shadow, almost unrecognisable as such, was an ugly smudge, rather than a pool of light and she was afraid not just for Hughie but also for herself.

For a moment they were alone together in the empty shop. She forced herself to face it. Cold waves of discomfort washed over her, similar to how she felt on that night in the Caird Hall. The hypnotist had been cruel. This shadow was altogether different, more powerful, terrifying. It seemed to be smiling. The word that flashed into her mind was evil.

At that moment the Lomond bakery man backed in with his tray of goodies and morning chat. The shadow vanished. For the next half-hour she was too busy to think and soon it was eight o clock and time to open the shop for the usual early birds.

By half-nine when the morning rush had quietened, old Mr Foulis' daughter came in. She liked Chrissie. Indeed if she were to think about it there were few customers that she could admit to disliking though some were a bit more likeable than others. Colin Mair strode into her mind, but she refused to spoil the morning by thinking about the Mairs. Nevertheless she could not get rid of them entirely with their two daily papers sitting there on the edge of the counter, undelivered.

Chrissie Foulis was not a regular customer, but turned up religiously on the first Monday of the month to pay her father's paper bill. As it was only the last week in May, Maryam's first thought was that Hughie must have forgotten to deliver the old man's Courier.

But it was not that. They spent a few moments on weather and health chat. Chrissie bought a couple of packets of Lomond oatcakes. 'I'm that busy helping Rob wi' the lambing I've nae time to bake,' she explained. After a pause she came out with the reason for her visit. 'I saw yon paper-boy, Hughie, is it? Yesterday.'

'Where was that?' Maryam was instantly curious.

'He was oot on the hill wi' his dog.' She explained. 'He'd no' say why. What me and Rob's wonderin' is this. What would induce a laddie to walk a' they miles up to oor place in the lambing season wi' an unleashed dog?'

Maryam looked up. She sensed that the lone shadow was still there lurking behind the gondolas. She could almost smell it, a feral, primaeval whisper of a smell.

'Was he by himself?'

'I'm no' sure. Bob said he acted scared and kept looking ower his shoulder when he caught him on the hill. There was something funny going on, right enough, so I took him back in the motor. Ha'e you seen him the day?'

Maryam nodded. 'He was a bit quiet, right enough,' she said but she did not tell him about his refusal to deliver the Mairs' papers.

'Rob and I were worried, you hear of a' they bad things that happen to bairns,' she said. 'Do ye ken his mam?'

129

Maryam nodded. 'I'll tell her.'

Reassured, Chrissie hurried away.

Annie certainly needed to know. She had mentioned that Colin Mair had got him the dog and had been looking after it which had been 'dead nice of him really' but as she'd told Hughie he had no need to go bothering the Mairs anymore. This morning Hughie had refused to deliver his papers. But she also knew that Colin Mair would be hard to resist, impossible perhaps for a thirteen year-old boy.

At ten o clock Mo came down to let her off for a coffee break.

The first thing he noticed were the Mairs' papers lying on the counter. In spite of his illness, Mo still noticed everything. Unbuttoning her overall, she explained. Mo was inclined to be judgmental. 'He canna just pick and choose,' he began but she interrupted him, 'He knows that, Mo. We'll sort it. Meanwhile I'll just run up with them myself. Won't take me five minutes.' It was the last thing she wanted to do but the first she knew she must.

It was so warm and sunny that she left the shop dressed only in jeans and a short sleeved top. The laburnum tree in the Mairs' garden shimmered a dazzling yellow and the shadows of the tulips shimmered red, and purple and gold. Stay with me, she told her soul shadow.

She opened the Mairs'wrought iron gate. She could see the car in the open garage so she reckoned he was in but it was his mother who came to the door.

'Hughie forgot these this morning,' she said handing her the papers. 'Sorry they're late.'

'That boy!' Mrs Mair exclaimed. 'What's he like? Here all day and everyday when we had the dog. Now we never see him. There's gratitude for you.'

'He's a teenager,' she said lamely.

'That's no excuse. Children these days… of course it's his background. As I said to my Colin, what do you expect from a single parent family?' The irony of that remark escaped her as her little dog pushed its nose through her legs and yapped menacingly. She picked it up and cuddled it. 'Poor wee Tina-wina misses her big old Jura, doesn't she? Never mind, diddums, you've still got your mummy.' She turned her attention back to Maryam. 'It's my son I'm sorry for. He really put himself out for that boy and now he's got what he wants, he's off without a word of thanks. What's the world coming to full of blacks and beggars and spoilt brats.' Suddenly realising what she had said she added a bit grudgingly. 'Present company excepted, of course.'

Maryam would have liked to tell the unpleasant woman to make other arrangements for her papers but instead she looked at both shadows, mistress and dog and saw behind the aggression in both, a tragic lack of light.

She put her hand on the yapping dog's head. She calmed immediately and when she tried to lick her fingers, she let it. Her abrasive little tongue was warm. Mrs Mair attempted a smile. 'She likes you,' she said with some surprise, but she was pleased. Not many people took to Tina or herself for that matter.

After a moment, Maryam withdrew her hand from the little creature's head, and after stroking her glossy coat again explained that she would have to run.

'Say goodbye to the nice girl.' Mrs Mair shook the little dog's not unwilling paw. 'Thank you,' she called out belatedly after her. At the gate, Maryam looked back to wave and saw Colin standing in the window watching her, expressionless.

'Not now,' she implored her own shadow and, half running, returned to the shop. She was suddenly tired.

Chapter Five

June

Mo

The first Monday in June was a local holiday. Bruden's closed at mid-day after the paper and milk orders were sorted. Mo, feeling almost well again, had decided this was the day to take Maryam to see the new Pictish find but there was a slight problem. Maryam had already promised to spend the afternoon with Lettie and Geordie sorting out the old lady's kitchen.

'Perhaps they could come too?' Mo found himself saying. It was the last thing he wanted. In his head he had planned a pleasant lunch at Rusacks Hotel in St Andrews, just the two of them as a way of thanking her for her support over the past four months.

The oldies had both been surprised by the invitation. Geordie had also been doubtful. 'What do you want wi' two old codgers spoiling your fun?' But he had been over-ruled by Lettie who was delighted. 'It'll be a chance to dress up,' she said. 'I have a nice summer dress if it hasn't been eaten by moths. I can't remember the last time it had an airing.'

Right enough, there was a strong smell of camphor when Lettie got into the car. There had been a bit of polite argy-bargy about who was to sit where. In the end Lettie had taken the front seat with Geordie and Maryam in the back. It was not how Mo had planned it but, apart from the odour of camphor, he found it enjoyable from the start.

Lettie was in a chatty mood, regaling them with tales of a royal garden party she and her father had once attended at Holyrood. Then they all had a friendly argument about the monarchy which Lettie supported up to the remotest princess and Geordie clearly did not. Mo found himself drifting off into fantasy. He and Maryam married and taking her elderly parents for a spin. Ridiculous he knew, but oddly comforting.

It was a glorious day. When the argument ended Lettie commented on the countryside, the different shades of green, from the emerald of baby beech to the bottle green of pine. The word 'bottle' set Geordie off. 'Div ye ken that wee song I learnt in the war aboot bottles?' Mo and Lettie knew it so they spent the next ten minutes teaching Maryam Ten green bottles hanging on the wall, which made them all laugh. It was something Mo had noticed before. Folk laughed more around Maryam. Today the laughter was longer and, outside the car in the countryside, the myriad shades of nature were brighter and stronger than on any other early summer day he could recall. He was conscious of feeling well now that the radium treatment was over, yes, and contented, but something more. He was aware of feeling cherished.

As the new Pictish stone was built into the wall of a field necessitating a fairly long trek uphill, Lettie decided to stay in the car. 'I'll be perfectly happy here. You two will be quicker on your own. Geordie will stay with me.'

Poor Geordie who so obviously had wanted to go with them, now had no choice, but he put on a good face. 'Aye,' he agreed. 'Off ye go, yous two. Take your time. I'll keep Miss A company.'

The first field was full of Ayrshire cattle, amiably chewing the cud. One of them, heavily pregnant, looked up, saw them and seemed somehow to communicate to the herd for, as if to some hidden command, they all lifted their heads, stared at them and together moved as one, purposefully towards them.

For a moment Mo was alarmed. 'Best step back,' he warned Maryam but she was already walking towards them, both hands outstretched. 'Be careful, Sunshine,' he urged keeping close to her side, but she paid no attention to him. The cows were all round her pushing their heads towards her and she touched each one of them. Not a word was spoken but the communication between them that he could not understand spoke more clearly than words. He moved away, watched and wondered.

After a while she came back to him and, followed closely by the herd, they continued to walk uphill towards the gate that led into the walled field with the Pictish Stone. He was awestruck. Who was this girl he had employed to serve in his shop? What was she doing here with him? After a few moments he dared to ask her, 'How did you do that, Sunshine?'

'Do what?'

He could not rightly describe what he'd seen. 'That thing with the cows.'

'They belong to Our Mother,' she told him quietly.

'Our Mother. Who's she?' He thought she was talking about some local farmer.

'Maybe I should have said God.'

He was shocked into silence. What was she talking about? God? He was also embarrassed for her. She sounded like a nutcase.

She turned her head to look at him but in that strange squinting way of hers, not seeing him. Then suddenly she was. She laughed. 'I know,' she said as if answering his thoughts. 'I sound daft, but Mo, you asked me a question so I answered you.'

He could think of nothing to say. They walked in silence while he thought about what she had told him. He opened the gate for her, closing it carefully against the cows. This field was a great green stretch of wheat. Almost before he expected it, he saw the stone. Set upright into the dyke, lichen free, the incised outline of a simple circle was clear to see. 'There it is,' he said. 'Granite, hard to carve and equally hard to interpret. An old dead stone.'

She knelt down and placed her two hands flat on its surface. 'Dead?' She looked up at him. 'Very much alive, I'm glad to say. It's beautiful.'

'That circle is said to represent the sun.'

'No, Mo. It's not the sun. It represents a little grave,' she told him firmly.

'How on earth do you know that?'

'He was only a wee lad. He was buried up there on the hill. His father placed the stone above him but it was moved when the wall was built.'

'Maybe you're right,' he said doubtfully. Fantasy, he thought. She lives in a world of fantasy. But at the same time he realised that it didn't matter. He loved her for loving the Stone. He loved her in spite of her weird thoughts and beliefs. He reached out his hand to help her up. 'How do you know all this stuff, Sunshine?'

'I listen,' she told him simply.

Part of him wished he hadn't asked; part of him wanted to know more. 'What exactly do you hear?' This was no light question. He was serious. He wanted to know who she was, what she was, why the world seemed different when she was around.

So she answered him 'I know that I'm Our Mother's daughter.'

'And the rest of us, me, Geordie, Old Lettie in the car, these cows?'

'We are all Children of Our Mother. So is this wheat and the buttercups and the thistles and the baby nettles against the wall.'

It was beyond him. She was well beyond him. Maybe it all came from her darkie religion. That would be it. Suddenly he looked at his watch. 'We'd better go. I've booked us tea at five and the oldies will be getting hungry.' So, he realised was he. It was a long time since he had felt really hungry.

'I'll need to take you to see the Queich Stone. You can tell me all about it,' he said adding to himself the proviso, I might not believe you.

'That's up to you,' she told him once again answering his thought. At the time they both laughed. Later he remembered.

The cows accompanied them down to the first gate.

Geordie

It had been a smashing day out. Miss A had chosen a half portion of something unpronounceable but not him. Mo had told him in the toilets that it was his treat and he was to choose whatever he liked from the menu. So he had fish and chips and mushy peas and three wee packets of tomato sauce, a huge plateful and a huge price on the menu. Mo took the same, all washed down with cups of strong tea and followed by trifle. What a feast and he got to tell some of his old army stories which no one had heard for decades.

Next morning he was at Miss A.'s bright and early to make a start on the annuals. Miss A had ordered them from the local garden centre and they had been delivered last Friday. Two dozen blue lobelia, two dozen impatiens, and a dozen petunias sat in their little pots, ready to be planted at carefully measured seven inch intervals in the prepared borders that ran either side of the gravel path from the doorstep to the gate.

After a couple of hours with the trowel and the watering can he was happy with the result. Eyeing the front garden with proprietary pride, he was quite pleased with himself. Now, though, he would have to tidy his own plot next door for the contrast was a bit shame-making. He hadn't been able to summon up the enthusiasm to dig his own border in the autumn partly because he couldn't be bothered, mostly because he had no cash to buy plants but also because he had expected to be evicted. But now he was so busy with the mower and wee jobs for the neighbours that he had been able to pay back the council some of his overdue rent so he was keeping his fingers crossed. Also he had been too busy to take a trip to the arcade. He might go this afternoon after he had cut the back lawn at Lochview... He was expecting a few bob from Miss A sometime soon and his larder was comfortably stacked with two macaroni pies. Okay, the sell-by date was passed, but macaroni lasted weeks, didn't it?

At that moment Miss A opened the front door. Her face beamed when she saw the neat rows. 'It looks wonderful, Geordie. What a show they'll make.'

'There's a few left over. Will I put them in the back garden?'

'I don't think so. There's no sun there and no room what with the washing line and the shrubs.' She paused. 'I don't suppose they'd be any use to you?'

Geordie demurred. Now he would have to do something about his front patch of ground and soonest. The plants would die else. In time he remembered his manners. 'Aye, weel... If you're no' needin' them, I'd no' like to see them wasted.'

'Good. That's settled then. Meanwhile it's time for elevenses. Tea or would you prefer coffee for a change?'

He nodded. 'Tea if you please. Ye ken me! Ah'll jist tak' me boots aff.'

They chatted happily about the outing. 'Do you think they'll get together, they twa?' Geordie asked, his mouth full of buttered scone.

'Which two are you talking about?' Miss A asked a little nippily.

'Mo and the darkie.'

'Geordie! What a thing to say. Her name is Maryam and he's old enough to be her father.'

'Come off it, Miss A. It'd be a grand match for the two of them. She'll get the business and he a bonnie lass.' Not to mention a housekeeper and a nurse if he gets the cancer back, but he kept that thought to himself.

She got all huffy but he could see she was putting it on. 'Maryam is a very pretty girl. She's also very young. She's plenty of time before she settles down.'

'Aye, but there's no many o' her lot around here to chose frae.'

'Geordie!' She declared still pretending to be miffed. 'I do believe you're a racist.'

He thought about that while chewing the last of his scone. He had never before considered the idea of racism in himself. If he had had a bairn would he let it marry a Paki? That was the test wasn't it? Would he have ever married a Paki? Damn right he would if she had looked like Sunshine.

'Mebbe I am,' he said aloud, 'I still say it would be a step-up in the world for her and a great match for him.'

Miss A. gave an exasperated sigh but she offered him another cup of tea and changed the subject.

They chatted a bit about the weather and she had a little moan about the increase of dog shit in the street (only she didn't call it that) and they decided it must be Hughie-the-lad's new pet that accompanied him on his paper round. 'Annie needs to be told,' she said. 'For once I'm in full agreement with Agnes Mackenzie. Did you see her letter in the paper? The street's perfectly disgusting.'

'Aye,' he agreed but truth be told he wasn't bothered. There had always been dog-shit in the street and no doubt there always would be.

After he had swallowed the last of his tea he stood up to go.

She reached for her bag. 'Before you go, Geordie, I've something to give you.' She opened in her wallet. 'I've thought long and hard about this,' she said, 'and taken advice.' (From whom? he wondered) 'The worker is worthy of his hire and though you haven't asked for it, I have decided to remunerate you for all your hard work over the past few months.' His mind leapt forward to the arcade and his eyes settled on her somewhat shabby purse-wallet. How much would it be? His heart sank a bit when he saw her take out a bit of paper instead of a good old bank note.

'I don't carry much cash around with me so I've written you a cheque.'

He didn't own a bank account but he reckoned the Clydesdale would still be open if he hurried. 'Ta, Miss A. Much appreciated I'm sure.' He unfolded the bit of paper/ and stared disbelievingly at the sum Fifty pounds. Then he looked closer. The cheque was not made out to him. It was crossed and made out to the Fife Council Housing Department.

His jaw dropped literally. 'Now Geordie, I don't want you to be offended. I know what your rent is because I pay the same so I thought this would cover a couple of months and free you to use your pension on other necessities.'

How did she know that he was still owing for the last three months? When it dawned on him that now he was safe from eviction, he looked up at her. 'It's far too much,' he said gratefully.

'You've earned it,' she told him.

Somehow now that his wee house was safe, the anticipation of a visit to the arcade faded. Maybe he would spend Mrs Mackenzie's couple of quid for doing her grass on a beer and another fish supper. Aye that's just what he would do.

He rose to his feet. He felt taller somehow, lighter 'I'll be for the off, then. Ta for the tea and all.'

'A pleasure, Geordie. See you tomorrow, then?'

'Aye, ye will,' he called from the lobby where he was tying his boot laces.

Tammy

I like the dog. I like Jura. I wish he was sleeping on my bed. Hughie's dead lucky getting that dog from Mr Mair. Mam says he's not to go to the Mairs' hoosie any more; he's nae to bother them but I dinna see why the no. I'd like it fine if Mister Mair was to gi'e me a wee kitty. Mam says I'm no' to get a kitten. One pet's enough to keep, but it could stay in my wee room and be nae bother to her or to Jura. I bet Jura'd like it anyway. They'd be pals. I could share my ain food wi' her. Now that Mam's got all they wee jobbies the food's great, specially the fish suppers on Saturdays. I could keep some o' the fish for her. Kitties like fish. I'd called her Mopsy. That's a good name for a cat.

So Tammy thought as she walked back from school. She'd been kept back by the teacher to practise her writing: I must learn to control myself in class twelve times with no mistakes. She tried to explain that it wasn't her fault but when the teacher asked her whose fault was it, she couldna clype on the laddie who'd furtively shown her a beetle in a match box and she had screamed.

She dawdled a bit as she passed the Mairs' bungalow. As luck would have it, Mr Mair was in the front garden planting pansies in the bed by the gate. She knew they were pansies because last Saturday she had helped Maryam plant them in the Old Rectory garden; she liked their bonnie wee faces. 'And they like yours,' Maryam had told her. That was dead nice.

'I like pansies,' she said to Mr Mair as she lingered by his gate, 'and they like me.'

Mr Mair stood up and regarded her speculatively for a minute. 'What's not to like?' he said in that funny voice of his that came through his nose and was sort of American.

'And I like kittens,' she said a bit shyly. She felt her cheeks go hot. It was a bit like asking outright but now she had started, she persisted. 'Do you ken where I could get a kitten?'

'What does your mother think?' He stared at her in a knowing way as if he could see right through her.

She couldn't lie so she hedged. 'She likes Jura okay.'

He was still looking at her a bit weirdly. 'What's your name?' he asked.

'Tamsin,' she told him. It sounded better than Tammy which was, after all, the name of a hat.

'Well Tamsin, I don't keep cats in my kitchen, but I do keep chocolate biscuits. How about it?'

She had a moment of doubt. She didn't really take to Mr Mair but a chocolate biscuit was tempting. 'Tunnoch's?' she asked. (Her favourite.)

'Blue Riband,' he replied shortly. (They were okay too.)

What harm could it do? Hughie came here often so why not her? 'Okay,' she said

She noticed that he looked up and down the street before opening the gate for her. She looked too .Mam would not be pleased with her for bothering Mister Mair. She made up her mind not to stay for more than a minute.

He led the way round to the back of the bungalow and into the kitchen. As soon as they got inside a dog started to yap and scrabble at the closed kitchen door. 'That's Tina,' he explained. 'My mother's dog. Drop a pin and she starts up. Pay no attention.' He looked at her and then suddenly his hands were round her waist as he lifted her up on to the draining board beside the sink. His hands felt hot through the cotton of her white school shirt. She was about to protest indignantly when he turned away to open a cupboard door. 'Now where are those biscuits?'

There were no biscuits, not even plain ones but there was fruit cake, rich and dark and, in her opinion, disgusting. She shook her head and tried to say 'no thanks' but he paid no attention. He cut them both a slice and put them on a plate beside her on the draining board. Then he poured her a glass of milk. She lifted it and took a tentative sip, but the cake was a step too far.

'I might have an idea where to find you a cat.'

'Is it that place where you got Jura?'

'Leave it to me,' he said putting his finger to his nose. 'No blabbing to your mother, now. It'll be our secret.'

'Thanks Mister!'

The kitchen door opened, Tina burst in closely followed by Mistress Mair who starred at her and demanded to know, 'Who's this, then?' She sounded disapproving.

'This is Tamsin, Mother, Hugh's sister. You remember Hugh?'

'Of course I remember Hugh. I'm not entirely senile.' She looked Tammy up and down as if she was dirt. 'Tamsin, is it? What sort of a name is that?' She sniffed contemptuously. 'Well Tamsin you tell that brother of yours that he had better learn some manners. All Mr Mair has done for him and not a word of thanks. What do you want?'

Tammy's cheeks fired up again this time with shame. Had Hugh really not said thanks for Jura? And now here was she more or less asking Mr Mair for a kitten. She hung her head and no words would come.

Mister Mair turned to his mother to protest sharply. 'That's enough, Mother. Tamsin's my guest. I'll bring you some tea in a minute or two.'

He held the kitchen door open for her and with another sniff she picked up the little dog and left the room.

Poor Mister Mair. What a horrid mam. She couldn't wait to get out of the house. She decided it was not too far to slip off the draining board on to the floor. 'I'll need to be off now,' she told him. 'My mam'll be looking for me.'

'Mothers, eh?' he said and winked at her.

She said nothing. Mam was nothing like Mistress Mair, thank goodness. She suddenly wanted to see her. She felt like running out of the back door but stopped on the threshold. 'Thanks for the cake, Mister Mair.'

'Which you didn't eat.' He laughed. Then he felt in his pocket and pulled out a fifty pence piece. 'Sorry about the biscuits,' he said. 'Get yourself one with this.'

She hesitated, knew she ought to refuse but fifty pence was a wee fortune. She could get herself a big poke of jelly babies with that, so she took it.

'I'll think about that cat,' he called out after her.

Poor Mister Mair, she thought again as she ran down towards the shop. She supposed he was quite nice really.

Maryam was there when she presented her with the money and the jelly babies. 'Mister Mair gave it me,' she said because she told Maryam everything. 'He's going to get me a wee cat. He's dead nice,' she added on a note of defiance.

Maryam's funny eyes suddenly switched on to hers. 'I didn't know you wanted a cat.'

'Aye', she said confidentially. 'A wee kitty wi' a black face and white paws. I'm going to call it Mopsy.' She paused. Now that she'd started she needed to tell her the whole story. 'Only Mam does nae want another animal in the hoose. It's no' fair. Hughie can have Jura but Elvis and me's got naething.'

Maryam put twenty-five pence change into her hand. She leaned down a little to speak to her. Her eyes were soft and brown and her face so pretty that Tammy wanted to put her arms round her and hug her. 'Would you like me to speak to your mam, Tammy?'

She nodded, inarticulate with gratitude.

'And if she says yes, we'll answer that notice on the board.'

'What notice?'

Mo kept a notice board hanging on the end of one of the gondolas which Tammy never read. Maryam came round from the counter and, putting one arm round Tammy's shoulder, pointed to the handwritten note pinned above the adverts for bicycles and buggies, SWRI meetings and St Serf's summer fete. Tammy read: good home wanted for two kittens and a phone number.

'No need to bother Mr Mair, is there?' Maryam told her.

Thank the pope, she thought. That was what Mam said when something good happened. 'Thank the pope' whoever he was. 'Can you tell Mr Mair?' she asked aloud.

'I'll tell him.'

Agnes Mackenzie

She sat in the window recess and watched for her son.

Only two days home from ten days in Ninewells and a fortnight's rehabilitation in Kirkcaldy, she had been disappointed by Rachel's behaviour. She had not seen her properly for a while because, of the two, Alastair had been her main visitor. Rachel had brought Jayjay in to see her twice but only briefly at Agnes' request. Jayjay was inclined to be so fidgety and girny these days that he disturbed the ward; also it was pleasant to have her son to herself. He had called in most days; bless him, if only for a brief ten minutes. Mr Forbes from St Serfs had looked in which was of course his job but nice of him all the same. She was not exactly a regular worshipper. The pews were so uncomfortable. Maybe she would go a bit more often now that her hip was sorted. To her surprise, Sheena whatever-her-name-was, who shared a flat in the Old Rectory with the coloured gel from the shop, also visited her when she was in Ninewells. Easy enough for her, she supposed, as she worked there as a nurse but kind all the same. She had had fifteen cards which surprised her pleasantly. One of the nurses had strung them up over a string along the curtain rail. One card had come from the shop staff and Maryam had asked Sheena to bring it in. Agnes reckoned that in spite of Maryam's - no she ought not to go down that path, the gel was not responsible for the colour of her skin or her faith - faiths, she could not fault her manners. Agnes could not decide which was worst, Roman Christian or Muslim, but inclined to the former. Nevertheless she was a nice gel. She must remember to thank her when she was able to walk as far as Bruden's.

Her thoughts veered back to her daughter-in-law. She had expected a little consideration, a daily visit at least; a bit of pampering. She ought to realise that, housebound, she needed a little TLC, as they called it these days. She had watched her that very morning coming up the path with two heavy Safeway shopping bags. When she had dumped them in the porch Agnes had distinctly heard the clink of bottles. After she had fetched Jayjay from his car seat, Agnes had called out to her from her chair so she had poked her head round the drawing room door and asked, 'What is it, Mother?' so impatiently that she hadn't like to suggest they have a cup of coffee together. Her short temper, her unsmiling appearance, the clinking bottles suggested as clearly as words that Rachel was drinking too much. How completely and totally irresponsible with a baby to look after: She would have to speak to her son.

Was Alastair always this late? It was nearly eight o'clock. As far as she knew Rachel had not been out since morning, but she could have missed her. She had gone to bed herself for a rest that afternoon after Annie had left, fallen asleep and not wakened till after four. She had heard Jayjay crying on and off but nothing else. If she had been more able on her pins she would have gone up to see for herself what was going on, but stairs were still out of the question.

At twenty past eight precisely - she had kept half an eye on the grandfather clock since six o'clock - Alastair's car drew in to the double garage. She watched him walk past the window and waved but he never noticed her. Nobody noticed her these days, she thought on a surge of self-pity. Her daughter-in-law seldom bothered, no-one had rung or called on her (Annie didn't count) and now her son was ignoring her. A small puff of anger propelled her on her crutches to the drawing-room door.

'Alastair?' she called out to him. He was hanging his hat up in the porch.

'Mother,' he replied dully and looked up.

What she saw shocked her into silence. He looked like an old man. His skin was grey, his eyes dull and his shoulders stooped. It flashed into her mind that he knew exactly what his wife was doing and that was why he stayed on at the office, why he looked so dreich. The anger that had taken her to the door, engulfed her again. 'I need to speak to you,' she told him sharply.

Suddenly he recollected himself. 'It's late. I should go up. I hope you've had a better day?' he said flatly.

'No, I have not,' she replied shortly. 'I've had a wretched day. No one to speak to, no one to care whether I'm alive or dead, least of all my son...or his wife.'

'I'm sorry,' he said wearily following her into the drawing room. 'Did Annie Miller not turn up?'

'I don't count the cleaning woman as a friend or family', she snapped. It was not at all what she wanted to say. She wanted to touch him, comfort him, rally him, but somehow she could not shake off the mantle of anger. 'You know she's drinking?' she snapped.

'Annie?' he said.

'Of course not Annie. Rachel. Your wife.'

He looked at her for a moment then dropped his head in his hands and began to shake.

Her anger receded leaving her frightened. 'Alastair? What's wrong with you? Are you ill?'

A moment later he lifted his head. His drawn face was wet with - could they be tears? She had not seen Alastair cry since ... His father had done his best to beat such unmanliness out of him. Literally.

He seemed to pull himself together. 'Yes,' he said wearily. 'She sometimes overdoes it a little.'

'You need to put a stop to it. It's not safe or fair to Jayjay'

'Yes Mother,' he agreed flatly.

The words had such little conviction that Agnes felt her temper stirring again.

'I mean it, Alastair. Whatever has got into her? I can't understand it. She has everything. A nice home, no money worries, a beautiful child and a good husband. What's the matter with the gel?'

He said nothing. In silence he moved to the door and opened it.

'Alastair.'

'Good night, Mother.' He closed the door firmly behind him.

She was too cross, too anxious to sit down again. In pain, she manoeuvred her crutches back and forth across the room. Was he ill? This would not the first time after all...She shook her head as if to get rid of the thought. If she could only manage the stairs she would go straight up and give them both a piece of her mind. Gradually anxiety overcame the crossness. Was it something she'd done, said, not done that caused Rachel to drink? But things had been better between them lately had they not? Mother and daughter-in-law would never exactly be friends but surely they were not enemies? Perhaps it was not Rachel's drinking that had made Alastair so dour. Maybe it was something she had done. She always assumed they had been close but deep down she knew that she had been too controlling. In retrospect, expecting them all to live together under the same roof might have been a mistake. On the other hand surely she had the right to be cared for in her old age? There were residential homes of course. Maybe she should apply to that place in Perth. Sell the house to pay for it. That would soon make them sit up and think. Anger and anxiety yielded again into self-pity.

After a while she sat down again, and looked up at the ceiling. Upstairs all was quiet but she knew all was not well. Self-pity, anger and anxiety melted into unhappiness. Then she remembered. There was a box of chocolates in the escritoire across the room; Milk Tray. The Maclardy brothers had brought it into Ninewells when they had visited her and she had not yet opened it. Painfully she got to her feet again, opened the cupboard door and there it was, the purple box still in its cellophane skin. Her favourite was orange cream so she ate them both and then the fudge and finally the toffee in little bites to protect her teeth. She might ask the Maclardy's in for afternoon tea as a gesture of thanks. Annie could prepare it and Bertie could boil the kettle. Thus was she comforted. She reached for the telephone.

Bertie

Since Annie's arrival Gordon's obsession with watching the Mairs' garden had lessened or possibly, so Bertie hoped, was forgotten. Annie had assured them both that Hughie was no longer visiting the bungalow. Jura had settled down happily and was already part of the family.

Privately she had told Bertie while having a well-earned cup of tea after scrubbing the kitchen floor that Mo had told her that Hughie now refused to deliver the Mairs' daily papers. 'I dinna ken whit's got into the laddie,' she said, 'so Mr Gordon needna fash hissel'. Hughie'd no' go back there if ye paid him.'

That remark did nothing to reassure Bertie. On the contrary, it told him that perhaps Gordon had been right to concern himself with Colin Mair's habits. 'Probably that's a good thing,' he said evenly.

'Seemingly he's got a sharp tongue, that Mr Mair. He probably showed Hughie the pointed end o' it,' Annie confided. 'Hughie doesna like to be tellt off by no one. Mr Mair seemingly was no' pleased to lose the dog.'

She got to her feet. 'I'll be off then. Ta for the tea, Mr Maclardy. See you Monday.'

He paid her for the hours, looked critically at the kitchen floor, found it satisfactory if not perfect and went to find Gordon who was sitting in the garden reading the Courier. He did a lot of that these sunny days. Sometimes when Bertie went to fetch him to go shopping or to the dentist (his teeth had been giving him trouble) he would say earnestly, 'I need to read the paper, Bertie. It's terrible some of the things that are happening. What's the world coming to?'

When he wasn't poring over the paper he would go out on his own, mostly down to the loch. Bertie had twice trailed him and the route had always been the same. Down the High Street, through Struther Lane and down to Queich Quay where a wooden pier harboured a small fleet of assorted boats, private or for hire, then turned left along the shore as far as the dilapidated green hut which belonged, he presumed, to the Queich estate. There he would force open the weather-beaten door which was never locked, peer into the cobwebby, murky interior, inspect the back, listen, sit on a near-by convenient bench for a while and then return home. He refused to wear the neck cord with an identity disc attached to it, so Bertie had pinned a label to the inside of his weatherproof jacket. The police knew the situation and so far he had only been brought back once wandering and clearly lost on the road up into the Ochils.

Today they had been asked to afternoon tea by Agnes Mackenzie, not an invitation to be relished but more of a chore to be endured. Poor woman, Bertie thought. A new hip was a major operation and she was having to learn to walk again but there were just so many complaints and criticisms that he could stand in a very long hour and a half.

He glanced at his watch. Gordon would have to change his shirt. Time to call him in. For once he did not argue. 'Where are we going?' he asked not for the first time that day.

'A tea-party,' Bertie did not mention where. No point really. Gordon would probably have forgotten before they got there.

'Good. I like tea parties,' he replied good-temperedly, as he gathered up the scatter of newsprint around his deck chair and followed Bertie indoors.

It was a quarter to four. Bertie paused on the upstairs landing and looked out. The street was full of children ambling home from St Serf's Primary. He watched them for a moment and then he saw his next-door neighbour. He was standing at the gate of the bungalow with a pair of shears in his hand, supposedly trimming his cotoneaster hedge, in reality watching the children.

None of them paid him any attention. Bertie thought nothing of it and was about to turn away when he saw two little girls in their navy skirts and short-sleeved, pale blue, Aertex summer tops. Mair was speaking to them. Bertie looked more closely and saw that he recognised one of the children, Annie's girl, Tammy, wasn't it? The child who had been playing outside her home that time he had called to ask her mother to work for them. What on earth was she doing talking to Mr Mair? He remembered Hughie and the dog and supposed it was all above board. He must stop being so suspicious. He was getting as bad as Gordon. After all what harm was Mair doing? He knew the family. Why should he not speak to the child?

He found Gordon in their bedroom with a pile of laundered shirts on the bed. (Bertie did all the ironing.) 'What am I doing here?' he asked with an air of desperation.

'Choosing a shirt for the tea-party,' he said as patiently as he could. 'What about the green check?'

He chose the maroon with grey stripes and ten minutes later they were ringing the bell at Lochview.

'This looks nice,' Bertie said heartily. An occasional table set with tea things on an embroidered white linen cloth laden with buttered scones and fruitcake had been laid in the window recess.

'All Annie's doing,' she told them.' I gather you employ our Annie too?'

'We do indeed,' Bertie replied taking the proffered arm chair which had been drawn up to the table opposite Mrs M. Gordon sat between them in the window seat. Well, well,' Bertie said rubbing his hands together 'this is nice.' He could hear the false bonhomie in his tone.

An electric kettle had been installed in the fireplace. At her request he filled the teapot and handed round the cups. The ensuing conversation covered her progress, slow, the baby who was teething, fretful, Alastair, working too hard for little thanks (Rachel was never mentioned), Annie, who needed to be watched, and then inevitably the dog shit. Had the pavements improved since she had published that letter to the Courier?

The scones having been polished off by a silent Gordon, Mrs M then turned her attention to the neighbours. 'Do you see much of the Mairs?' she asked handing round the cake.

Bertie was determined not to be drawn. 'Surprisingly little considering we live next door.'

'It's that dog I can't stand,' she said.

'Oh, I don't know,' Bertie responded reluctantly. 'I suppose it does yap a bit.'

'That too, but worse.' She was not finished with the pavement. 'They let the creature do its business in the street. Deliberately. I've seen it. The pavement is still disgusting. I've written to two papers and I've rung the council umpteen times but they're not interested. I tell you it's a health hazard. Can you not speak to him, Bertie? After all you live next door.'

Bertie was about to answer when Gordon suddenly entered the conversation. 'He's a paedophile,' he said so loudly that no one could pretend not to have heard. 'Of course he should be stopped.'

In the shocked silence that followed this revelation, Bertie said placatingly, 'Now Gordon, you don't know that for certain.'

'I do,' he said his voice rising. 'I've been to the Police Station but no one pays a blind bit of attention to me. Who cares about a bit of dog mess on the pavement? The man's a murderer and a paedophile.'

Bertie was more embarrassed than angry. 'You must forgive my brother, Mrs Mackenzie. Gordon has a bit of a bee in his bonnet about our neighbour.'

'Nothing would surprise me where that man is concerned,' she said. 'Oh, must you go?' she added as Bertie rose to his feet. She was visibly disappointed.

'It's been very pleasant,' Bertie said in as light a voice as he could manage. 'Delightful. Thank you so much. Come, Gordon. We'll see ourselves out.'

Gordon, silent again, rose to follow him while Mrs M struggled with the aid of crutches to her feet. 'You must come again,' she told them. 'I have really enjoyed your company. I get so little intelligent conversation these days.'

At the door, Gordon turned. 'It's true you know. Just ask the paper boy. I saw them.'

With deprecating shrugs and waves and half smiles, Bertie tried to convey Gordon's condition to their hostess, but it was clear whom Mrs Mackenzie chose to believe. Now it would be all over the village that Colin Mair was not to be trusted, worse, a criminal and not just because he allowed his mother's dog to foul the pavement.

Maryam

She had not forgotten about the kitten. Sadly, when she phoned the advertiser, the one kitten that still remained unsold of the two advertised, cost a massive three hundred pounds. Seemingly it was pure-bred, seal-point Siamese.

'That's a pity,' the owner said when Maryam explained the situation. 'He's a real beauty, feisty and strong.'

146

'Sure but I have my orders,' Maryam told her humorously. 'We're looking for a black kitten with white paws. Nothing else will do.'

The owner laughed. 'I'll keep an eye out,' she said.

Colin Mair was not so easy to contact. He rarely came into the shop. She tried to explain to his mother but she would not listen. Her eyes slewed off her Friday headscarf in disapproval and her shadow shrank into mist as she spoke. 'I have nothing to do with Colin's arrangements but I doubt very much he'll do anything again for that family. The boy behaved atrociously. Not a word of thanks for obtaining the dog and keeping him at great inconvenience to me and my Tina. Now he's refusing to deliver our papers. I wonder at Mo. I'd have sacked him on the spot.'

'I'm sure Hughie is very grateful for Jura. He's a lovely dog but Mr Mair has no need to find a cat for Tammy. She already has one in mind.' It was not exactly a lie. Chrissie Foulis had a farm. All farms had cats. She would see Chrissie tomorrow afternoon at the Queich Fayre. She might know of a kitten.

Queich Fayre happened on the last Saturday in June, a week before the school broke up and everyone disappeared on holiday. The local recreation park - a large grassy field that included the scant ruins of an early medieval chapel dedicated to St Serf, several small groves of colourful shrubs good for hide-and-seek, a trio of magnificent copper beeches, a duck pond dominated by two swans with uneven tempers and a swing park - turned itself into a fair ground. Colourful booths sold anything and everything from candy floss to hand-made jewellery. In the morning local farmers competed for best of breed animals and the Pony Club organised races for tots. The SWRI (Scottish Women's Rural Institute) ran an all-day tea tent with home-made soup, cheese scones and cakes to die for. Charities ran raffles. St John's Ambulance kept a watch out for accidents and people who had not seen each other for months socialised in (for once) warm sunlight.

The main attraction for the youngsters was 'the shows', which ran from early afternoon till midnight. These included dodgems, rides, merry-go-rounds, shooting galleries and a fortune teller.

Sheena who had taken this Saturday off duty brought her boy friend, Shamus, and Maryam wore her prettiest summer dress. Mo had attached himself to them, a strangely unfamiliar Mo in an open-neck blue and white check shirt, new chinos and sandals. This was a Mo determined to put the horrors of the past six months behind him and enjoy himself. He knew almost everyone by face if not by name and was soon hustled off to the beer tent for a pint with a couple of retired farmers.

Maryam too found herself greeted on all sides by friendly faces. It was a day for laughter and reminiscence. Eventually, leaving Sheena and Shamus in the tea tent with a couple of hospital friends, she went off on a serious quest to find Chrissie.

Shading her eyes against the strong summer sun, she scanned the sales tables under their coloured awnings and saw old Bob Foulis, Chrissie and Rob's father, making his way towards her. He had his ageing dog, Moll, tightly leashed at his heel. He touched his cap courteously. 'Aye,' he replied to her question. 'Chrissie's at the produce stall selling eggs. but she'll no be there the noo. She'll be at the Trials wi' her brother. He's putting Bess into the field. Are ye comin'?'

The tannoy was announcing the event as he spoke. A sheep-herding competition at the far end of the field was due to start in ten minutes.

They made slow progress through the crowds for Bob was greeted by several acquaintances and so indeed was she. His dog, now white around her muzzle pushed a patient path through the throng until they reached the far end of the playing field where the sheepdog trials were to be held. A goodly throng of shepherds, their families, friends and fans of the sport were gathered round the cordoned-off area where the sheep pen with its little flock of patient ewes awaited. Hand-picked, these dozen ewes knew what was expected of them. They had done this before and quite enjoyed it. Maryam knew this instinctively. They performed obediently but they had their own favourites among the dogs. She smiled a little. The shepherds believed that they and their dogs were in control. Not so. Those sheep chose the winner. She could feel Our Mother's smile.

There was Chrissie. She bustled over to greet her father and she had Hughie in tow. 'See who I found!' she exclaimed. Hughie grinned shyly. He had Jura with him, straining at the leash. 'They've come to see our Bess. Hughie here reckons she'll win hands down.'

'That's right, lad.' The old man clapped him on the back then turned his attention to Jura. 'How's this lass o' yours?'

While they were talking Maryam turned to Chrissie. 'Hughie's looking great these days. I was hearing he's got a wee Saturday job up at the farm?'

'Aye,' said Chrissie. 'Rob took a shine to him and he does wee jobs around the place. He's talking about taking up shepherding as a career, but he's yet to thole a lambing. That'll likely finish him for good.' She laughed.

'Maybe not.' As Maryam spoke she knew that Hughie would spend the rest of his life with Chrissie and Rob Foulis and remain on their farm long after they had gone.

'Did you ever find out why he was on the hill that day?' Chrissie asked.

At the same moment old Bob turned to her with some remark that demanded her attention and the question was left unanswered. But she already knew what Hughie's shadow had told her, the awfulness of it, if not the details.

The trials began with old Bob talking knowledgeably about each dog that took part. Bess did well but was not the winner. 'Give her another two years and she'll walk it,' the old man told them.

'I'll need to go,' said Chrissie. 'Those eggs'll no' sell themselves.'

Before she left, Maryam asked her about a kitten. 'There're tortoise-shell kittens at the farm over the hill. Would that do?'

Maryam told her she'd find out, then turned to Hugh. 'Do you know if Tammy's here?'

He frowned. 'I dinna ken. Maybe she's at the shows. I tellt her to stay wi' me Mam and I'd take her later.' His shadow hid its head. She could feel its fearfulness.

'I'll find her,' she reassured him.

The music, which had been a backdrop to the other events, grew louder as she approached the conglomeration of caravans surrounding the entrance to the fairground. She recognised Elvis, the Beatles, Rolling Stones and Pink Floyd recordings as they blared out drowning the whine and crash of dodgems and the shrieks of children as they whirled dizzily past her on a walzer. She soon spotted Tammy with three of her friends whizzing past and above her on the Flying Saucers.

She watched and waited till the gaudy aliens slowed and lowered, then Tammy saw her. 'Maryam!' she shrieked. 'Stay. Wait for me. It's Maryam,' she shouted to her three companions who saw her and waved excitedly.

Off they clambered, all four of them, dizzy from the ride and high with excitement as they crowded round her. She knew them all and they knew her. 'Do the dodgems with me, plee-ase Maryam,' Tammy cried. 'And me!' They all clamoured. At eight years old they were too young to go by themselves.

'I can pay,' boasted Tammy. 'I've got money.' The others looked crestfallen. One of them, Jayne, was annoyed. 'And we all know where you got that from.' She began to chant, 'Tammy's got a sugar daddy!'

'I have not,' Tammy snapped back.

'You have sot.'

The argument would have exploded if Maryam had not said, 'I just passed the candy-floss man. Who likes candy-floss?'

'Me!'

'I do! Then can we go on the dodgems?' Tammy persisted.

'Let's do something we can all do together,' she suggested. 'What about the Haunted House?' She knew it was important, necessary to stay close. She had not seen him yet but she had sensed his shadow. It felt as if the sun had gone in but she could see it was still shining.

So they got their huge sticks of candy-floss which she paid for. Her resources were limited and the prices were high. She could afford one more ride apiece.

It was while they were in line for the Haunted House ride that she saw him. He was watching them, half-hidden behind the coconut shy.

'Tammy,' she said. more urgently that she intended,' sit beside me?'
She looked at her with big round eyes. 'Are you scared?'

'Maybe, a bit.' She was terrified but not of the luminous skulls and dangling spiders.

The children screamed at the tops of their voices, scared but safe so that they could enjoy not only the sound of their own voices but also the tingle of fear. Maryam was silent because, though Tammy held fast to her fingers, she was truly afraid.

The ride ended all too soon and there he was, waiting for them. His mouth smiled under speculative eyes.

Ignoring the children, he greeted Maryam as if she were a close friend. 'Well hullo, there, Maryam!' he said in his soft faux American drawl. 'I could hear you all screaming your heads off.'

Tammy was the only one who greeted him. 'Hullo Mr Mair,' she said moving towards him. 'We're going on the dodgems.'

'I'm up for that,' he said with his eyes on Maryam. 'My treat.' It was not even a question.

'Thanks Mr Mair,' they all cried excitedly and, led by Tammy, ran ahead weaving their way through the sauntering crowd.

Maryam turned to follow them with Colin Mair at her side. Aloud she said evenly, 'You'll be glad to hear we've got a kitten in mind for Tammy.'

He laughed. 'Best of luck with that', he said aloud. Suddenly his shadow appeared on her other side, cold, menacing, detached. She was trapped between them. In her head she heard it speak. 'You'll get no thanks from that ungrateful bunch.'

Emboldened by her own shadow she challenged him. 'Leave the child alone.'

'Why tell me? Tell the little minx to stay away,' it sneered, and vanished. She knew it was there somewhere among them but she could no longer see it.

They reached the dodgem arena. The children were high with excitement.

'Who's gonna drive me?' Mr Mair drawled. He looked at them briefly then turned his eyes on Maryam.

'I will! I will!' Three of them shouted, bouncing around him like puppies.

It was, to Tammy's obvious disappointment, that he picked her best friend.

'Jayne, I'll trust you to keep me alive,' he said ignoring Tammy who was outraged. At that moment Maryam realised that Tammy was not the only endangered child.

But Jayne had a mind of her own. She had not offered. 'I'm going with Maryam,' she said coolly.

'No I am.' Tammy, still annoyed by Colin's request, had firmly commandeered Maryam's hand.

In the end he rode with one of the other children, Ellen by name, a timid child who rarely spoke. Maryam let Tammy steer, a bad decision, she was soon to realise. After a few harmless rounds suddenly Tammy, eyes glittering and mouth stretched in a mirthless grimace, steered straight for an unsuspecting Ellen and crashed into her friend's side of the car. Then she did it again. Colin Mair sat there beside her, half-smiling, seemingly encouraging her, seemingly amused, while Ellen took the brunt of the impact. So taken by shock and surprise was Maryam that she had neither the time nor the strength to control the changed child. It took the lad responsible for safety to weave through the other drivers and steer her car off the course.

Afterwards Tammy was as upset and shaken as Ellen, not understanding - how could she? - what had happened. 'I want my Mam,' she wailed and Maryam would have been happy to take her home but not without Ellen. The other two girls had long gone off in a huff by themselves.

Maryam took both their hands. Ellen was crying quietly. Her little shadow was shivering and bewildered.

'I'm sorry, Ell,' Tammy told her over and over again. 'I didna mean it Whit did I dae?' She too was crying.

When Maryam looked up, Colin Mair and his shadow had gone.

Chapter Six

July

Rachel

She needed to talk to Maryam. Talk properly not just for a few snatched moments in Bruden's between customers. After that strange yet elating evening at the Old Rectory she had not been sure at all of what she thought about the dark girl who had been so odd. She could of course be schizo, hearing voices, seeing shadows but what if she were not? She remembered the hypnotist.

At the time she had tried to tell Alastair what had happened but as soon as she had started to talk he had switched off. Since then she had come to the conclusion that it was not her drinking that peeved him. After that evening with Maryam she had laid off wine but it had made no difference. Alastair was more distant than ever, still as silent and moody. However hard she tried to please him with tastier recipes, a tidier house, a smarter appearance, nothing changed. His absences at meetings with colleagues or working late happened more frequently. His interest in Jayjay seemed feigned. It was nothing to do with his mother for his visits downstairs too were curtailed. So if it were none of these things, then what was it? Another woman? She thought of the women she knew in his office, mostly middle-aged, respectable and married. Love was supposed to brighten your eyes, lighten your step, energise your body, wasn't it? He looked grey, acted withdrawn and appeared unhappy. Was he ill, then? Some secret unspeakable disease that he was ashamed to share? STD? AIDS? Could that account for the lack of sex within their marriage? If not, it occurred to her that the something wrong must be herself.

She had tried talking to him. 'Is everything all right?' she asked one night as they toyed with the cinnamon rice pudding she knew he liked (but she hated). It was no use waiting until they had finished eating for if he were home he tended to disappear into his study as soon as they had risen from the table leaving her to watch television and feed Jayjay alone.

He hesitated before answering her and she realised he had not been listening when he asked, belatedly, 'What did you say?'

'Are you worried about Mother?'

'Mother?' he said obviously surprised by the question. 'Should I be worried about Mother?'

'Not particularly.' She'd just had a hip operation and found walking hard, but that's what he had said.

152

'It's just that you seem a bit down these days. 'I was thinking' - she was determined to broach the subject - 'isn't it time we thought about a holiday?' When he made no reply she carried on, 'We could go to somewhere warm with facilities for children. Eva's going to the Costa del Sol after the harvest and the other girls are all off somewhere later in the month. Jayjay's old enough to travel so what about it?'

He was so quiet that she thought he had gone into one of his sulks again. A seed of anger stirred in her head.

'You can at least answer me, Alastair, or am I not allowed to speak any more?'

'Don't be ridiculous,' he said wearily. 'You know we can't leave Mother on her own.'

'She could go on holiday too. A week in Crieff Hydro or somewhere nice. She'd enjoy that.'

He stood up. 'She'd hate it on her own. Besides it's out of the question for me at the moment.' He pushed in his chair.

'But why?' she protested hotly. 'Just tell me why?'

He stopped at the door. 'There's nothing to stop you from going. Take the baby and find somewhere nice. You don't need me.'

'Of course I need you,' she cried. 'You're my husband, God damn it!'

He stopped with his back to her. 'I'm sorry, Rach,' he said quietly. 'I can't do this any more.'

'Do what?' she called out after him but he had already gone. That night he slept in the spare room again. That had been happening a lot lately. As for sex, twice, she reckoned since Jason's birth. There was something badly wrong but if he wouldn't talk to her what was she to do?

She had two glasses of wine and a restless night. Next morning he was apologetic, almost. You should book that holiday,' he told her as she was feeding Jayjay his oatmeal and banana. 'No need to take Mother unless you want to.'

He still looked grey and tired and unhappy. She was filled with a sudden pity for him. Something was wrong somewhere and she had no idea how to fix it. 'It won't be any fun without you,' she said, 'and Alastair, it's you that needs the break.'

He sighed. 'Possibly,' he told her with a faint smile. 'Maybe later in the year.'

'I can wait.'

'No,' he said more firmly. 'You should go soon. Of course you should. I want you to go.'

He kissed her cheek briefly and left for work.

Later that morning she went downstairs and found her mother-in-law ensconced in her window seat reading the Courier.

'What a surprise,' she said dryly looking up from her paper over the rim of her glasses. For a moment Rachel thought of turning her back and leaving. You see? She argued with her better herself. This is exactly why I hate visiting. You have more important things to worry about, her better self replied, so she stuck it.

'I'm going down to Bruden's. Anything I can get you?'

Obviously her mother-in-law's better self had kicked in too for she replied quite graciously. 'Thank you, Rachel. Annie forgot to pick up my prescription yesterday. I would be grateful – and I'd like one or two things from Bruden's...what about some coffee first?'

So Rachel put Jayjay down on the floor to let him crawl while she switched on the electric kettle. Not a good idea. The drawing room, as Agnes called it, was full of knick-knacks, some of them precious. Jayjay already had a small porcelain robin in his grasp. 'Sorry about that,' Rachel apologised as she tried to wrest it from him. 'I usually keep him in his playpen.'

The older woman laughed. A pretty laugh. Rachel realised she had seldom, if ever, heard Al's mother laugh. 'Alastair was exactly the same. A healthy curiosity, his nanny called it.'

Rachel tried to hold him on her knee but he would have none of it. He began to girn. Agnes held out her arms. 'Let me have him. You drink your coffee.'

He was quiet for a moment staring up at her face with curious eyes, but only for a moment. At his grandmother's suggestion, Rachel pulled the furniture about and made a little den. As directed she found a box of alphabet bricks in a cupboard by the fireplace and Jayjay was happy. 'I keep meaning to give them to you,' Agnes explained. 'They belonged to Alastair.' She took a sip of her coffee. 'What a long time ago that seems.'

Now was her chance to speak to his mother about Al, the reason for her visit, so she took it. 'What was Al – Alastair like as a child?' she asked in a rush before her courage deserted her.

Agnes' expression softened. She took another sip of coffee. 'This is nice, by the way, just the right amount of granules. Annie puts in too much. What were you saying? Oh yes, Alastair.' She was quiet for a moment remembering. 'A nice little boy,' she said firmly. 'Very well-behaved. He always did as he was told.'

He would be, Rachel thought spikily but then Agnes continued, 'I take no credit for it. His nanny saw to that. A bit of a gorgon for discipline, I suppose, but it did the trick. That's what children need nowadays. A bit of discipline. Spare the rod etc.'

Rachel was interested. She had said it with such pride as if she knew all the answers but then she repeated, 'As I said, nanny was the one. To tell you the truth I was rather afraid of her myself.' She smiled.

Am I supposed to laugh, Rachel asked herself. 'She though of Al, cowed, silent, obedient because he had to be. 'Did she smack him?' She could hear the disapproval in her tone.

'Of course she smacked him,' Agnes replied feistily. 'I was smacked when I disobeyed my parents. Weren't you?'

No, she thought, not that I remember. 'Poor wee boy,' she said aloud.

Agnes leaned forwards. 'Poor wee boy?' she echoed sharply. 'What are you talking about? You have a good husband, haven't you? Jayjay has a good father, hasn't he? It made him the man he is.'

'But was he happy?'

'Happy? Of course he was happy. He had everything. A secure home, a good education...'

Rachel shook her head. She had experienced little of those things but she at least had been happy. There was no point in carrying on this conversation. They would never agree. 'We should go,' she said beginning to rise. 'Thanks for the coffee.'

Agnes held out her hand. 'No Rachel. If you have something to say to me, say it. Is something wrong?'.

All right, Rachel thought, I will. She won't like it but who cares. 'Everything,' she said shortly. 'Al's not himself. He doesn't speak, he's hardly ever at home and when he is, he disappears into his study. I've tried everything, new recipes, a nice home, but he doesn't even notice. I'm really worried about him.'

Agnes was silent for a long moment. 'Are you sure it's not your imagination?' She paused. 'I have to ask, Rachel, but are you perhaps drinking too much? His father had a bit of a problem with drink from time to time...'

'No,' Rachel interrupted, 'I admit that I overdid it for a while when I first started to wean Jayjay but not any longer.'

'I've seen you coming in laden with bottles.'

'It's grape juice or elderflower cordial. I rarely have wine these days.' She'd had a couple of glasses last night right enough. Maybe that was it.

'Then I beg your pardon, Rachel. It's just that Alastair hates drunkenness.'

'I know he does,' she said but she had not known about his father.

They were both silent for a while. Jason chattered in his den. Then Agnes said shortly. 'This has happened before. I really thought he was over it.'

'What has happened before? Tell me.'

There wasn't much to tell. His first depression had come in his last year at school and then again at university. He had had to repeat his final year. He had got over it eventually. The doctor had suggested complete rest. He had been studying too hard.

'So that's it, is it? Overwork? What do you think?'

Agnes lifted her shoulders. 'I've hardly seen him lately. I do think he looks tired and he was quite short with me last time I spoke to him which is so unlike him. I think maybe he should have a holiday. You both should,' she added graciously.

Rachel was now really worried. At Bruden's she arranged to meet Maryam after work in the Cosy Café in the High Street for a late lunch. Jayjay, exhausted by his morning's excitement and a hefty lunch fell asleep in his stroller.

Maryam listened carefully. Rachel now paid no attention to her weird off-centre gaze. 'I honestly don't think I'm exaggerating. I could see that Mother was worried too.' (She was able to call her 'mother' quite easily now.) 'Seemingly it's happened before.'

Maryam did not dismiss her fears as unnecessary which Rachel had half hoped she would do. She was desperate for some reassurance but it did not come. 'Before? When?' Maryam asked.

'Years ago when he was a student. Overwork apparently. I didn't say much to his mother but now I'm really worried.'

Maryam was quiet for a moment, her eyes unfocussed, distant. Then she looked directly at Rachel. 'Maybe he should see his doctor.'

'He'll never agree' she said wretchedly. 'He'll just shut me out as usual and disappear into his study.'

'Make an appointment for him, then,' she urged.

Jayjay had now woken and was demanding attention which Maryam was happy to give him while Rachel paid the bill.

'Thanks Maryam. You've been such a help,' she said later outside the chemist as they prepared to go their different ways.

'I mean it, Rachel. Your Alastair needs all the help he can get.' Her dark eyes were serious and compelling.

'How do you know?' she asked impulsively.

Maryam shook her head. 'I just listen,' she said.

Lettie

July the seventh was never a good day.

Geordie had been in that morning but she had not been good company. In the end she told him she had a headache so he left her in peace. Then she had cleaned the two brass candlesticks that had been left to her by her godmother. She possessed good Edinburgh silver ones that she could have used but they had belonged to her parents and on this one day of the year she found it hard to like, let alone love, her parents.

That afternoon she had found the two new candles, pink, slightly scented of roses, which she had bought in that gift shop in St Andrews on the day Mo had taken them out for tea. (What a happy occasion that had been; a memory to cling on to.) At about four o'clock when it had stopped raining she had found her secateurs and gone out into the garden and picked three pink roses. They were particularly abundant this year after Geordie had pruned them back hard in the spring. She chose the best and arranged them in a crystal vase which she placed between the candlesticks on the occasional table by her chair. Then she had taken off the locket she always wore next to her skin which contained a tiny precious photograph and put it in front of the roses. In her bedroom she had found under her hankies in her bedside drawer a little tissue paper parcel. She unfolded it and placed the single white bootee threaded with ribbon beside the locket. She lit the candles. These were all she had, one fast fading tiny sepia photograph and one small hand-knitted baby sock threaded with pink ribbon that had lost its shine. Tears - so much harder to cry these days - stung her eyes...

Once a year on the anniversary she allowed herself to remember. Not that the memory ever really left her, but this one day in the year she allowed herself to relive it all, painful though it was. She gave herself permission to mourn.

And then the doorbell rang. No, not now, she thought with her face wet with tears and her mouth trembling. Who on earth could it be at this hour? They'll go away, she told herself. She thought they had until she heard the tap on the sitting room door and Maryam stood there.

It was lovely to see her of course but not now, not like this. Lettie had been taught that tears were an indulgence. She turned her head, hastily wiped her eyes on a damp handkerchief and attempted to put on her society voice. 'My dear child, how lovely to see you. What are you doing here at this time of day? I thought you were working late.' The words were all right but the tone was strange, broken and harsh.

'I heard you,' she said from the door.

'Heard me? Good gracious me!' But how, she thought, how on earth could she have heard me?

'I was listening,' the girl replied as if she had spoken aloud.

'You must have the ears of a lynx then. I wish you'd tell me your secret. I'm as deaf as two posts.'

'Are you busy?'

Unexpectedly, Lettie laughed. The idea that she was ever busy these days both amused and saddened her. She laughed but she was crying too. She fumbled for her handkerchief. 'I know it's early, sun not over the yard-arm and all that but let's have a glass of sherry. You know where it is.'

While Maryam was busy finding and filling the tiny glasses, she attempted to pull herself together. Her first instinct was to protect her locket. She closed it but she had mislaid her spectacles and the clasp was too small to see.

'Can I help?' the girl asked. Silently, because the tears were ready to fall again, Lettie handed it to her. Maryam did not ask or comment but Lettie felt some explanation for the tears and the shrine was due.

'Someone I once loved,' she said. Let her think what she liked.

'I know,' Maryam said so quietly that Lettie was not sure she had heard properly.

'You can't know, dear,' she said a little sharply. No one else knew. It occurred to her how sad that was. When she popped her clogs no one would know. How unbearably sad. She reached up for her locket now round her neck. The chain was long enough for her to open it but not to see it herself. 'My child,' she said, holding it out so that Maryam could see. 'She was my child.'

Maryam reached forward to touch the image. 'She's beautiful.'

'Is she? Lettie sighed. 'How can you tell? She was so young. Today would have been her birthday.' She took a gulp of sherry and told herself sternly, no more tears.

'What was her name?' Maryam asked as if she really wanted to know.

Lettie took a deep breath to stifle the tears. 'I called her Rosemary. I don't know what they called her. She was given another birth certificate. I know nothing about her, not even her name.'

The old familiar feelings of guilt and inadequacy and helplessness that had dogged her for so many years threatened to return. 'Do you know something, Maryam?' she said apropos of nothing, 'I think I'm happier now in my nineties than I have ever been in my whole life. Don't you find that rather sad?'

'Perhaps,' the girl said, 'but maybe you made other people happy.'

Lettie shook her head. 'No,' she said firmly. 'My mother died of cancer probably because of me. She told me I had broken my father's heart.' She took another gulp of sherry, put down the empty glass and made up her mind.

She had been twenty-three when the First World War broke out, young and inexperienced. She had become a VAD, a sort of junior nurse looking after the wounded a few miles out of St Andrews. When both her brothers, one older and one younger, had been killed in the trenches she had gone home to care for her stricken parents. Her father, a doctor, smothered his grief in his work. She nursed her mother through influenza. They were emotionally tough years. After the war she had longed to escape, take up nursing properly, leave her silent grief-struck home but how could she be so heartless... It had happened in the dunes with a student not long out of school. He was lonely, she was desperate. The affair lasted about a week. Then he left in a hurry, sent down from university for some misdemeanour; he had been a bit wild and rebellious, she remembered, but when he left she had missed those trysts in the dunes.

Then she discovered she was pregnant. Her parents now added anger and disappointment to their grief and she, guilt to hers. Her father sent her up to a croft in the Highlands to have the child. The crofter's wife was known to him for hers was not the only unwanted pregnancy he had helped to conceal. The adoption was arranged for her. She was not given an option.

'That was what I wanted too,' she said. 'I made no attempt to keep my child. I was thirty years old and deeply ashamed. That's what I find so sad. I was given this beautiful gift and I threw it away. My mother died of cancer a year later and I was blamed. Indeed I blamed myself. I became my father's assistant in his surgery until he died during the last war but he never really forgave me. Why should he?'

'Would you like to find her, your daughter?' Maryam asked.

'Is such a thing even possible?' Lettie asked sadly, but before Maryam could answer she added, 'I admit I've thought about it, but no, she's no longer the child I gave birth to, she's a woman of over sixty. Why would I want to disrupt her life all over again even supposing she is still alive? My regrets are not for now, they are for the girl I used to be.'

'Can you not forgive her?'

Lettie reached out her hand to touch Maryam. 'Most of the time, yes. Just this one day in the year I get guilty and angry. The anger never really goes.'

'If I were to tell you that she is alive and well and happy, what would you say?'

'That you are kind, always kind, my dear, but how could you possibly know?'

'I told you... I listen.'

To your Mother, yes I know, she thought, but she said nothing. She could not believe it was that easy, but at the same time she was deeply and inexplicably comforted as if a burden had shifted.

Mo

His appointment with the consultant oncologist was at 12.15. This time he made no secret of it. Both Rhoda and Sunshine knew. He had hoped that Sunshine would offer to come with him but he was not going to ask. Besides she was on the till that morning with Rhoda due in at two o'clock. Not even Sunshine could be in two places at once. All day yesterday it had been on the tip of his tongue to ask. He would even have been willing to shut the shop for a few hours though the thought was sacrilegious. In his head he planned another day out for just the two of them with a late lunch in Dundee followed by that promised visit to the Queich cross-slab in the afternoon. It was all too complicated. Forget it, mate, he told himself. But it was hard. Supposing the cancer was still there? Supposing it had spread? He considered asking Sunshine her opinion but thought better of it. How could she possibly know?

He had thought a lot about that strange behaviour of the cows on their day out and the still stranger conversation about God. A lot of superstitious rubbish he reckoned, tried to reckon, but watching her in the shop with the customers, he could not be sure. Whatever it was she believed she was clearly unlike other girls of her age. She was not really like anyone else. From the practical point of view he blessed the day he had hired her. New customers now came in, sales were up. She even got on with Rhoda. Strange too, the way he had come to employ her. Though plenty of locals would have liked the job, he had hesitated not for one moment in offering it to her. Almost as if he had been brain-washed.

He looked at his watch and checked the flat for switches. He was a bit paranoid about leaving them on, especially the television, told himself to stop being such a numptie and went downstairs to let Sunshine know he was off.

He heard the laughter. There was always laughter and banter when Sunshine was on duty. He could not quite make out what the joke was but he found himself smiling. 'That's me for the offsky,' he announced jocularly from the office entrance when he could get a word in.

160

She turned to look at him, those dark eyes that saw so much. She knows already, a voice spoke clearly in his head, but all she said was. 'Bye, Mo.' For a moment he felt bereft.

He locked the back door behind him and took out his car keys.

'Cutting it a bit fine, aren't you?'

Rhoda stood by the passenger door smartly dressed in a navy blazer over a summer dress, consulting her wristwatch, her hair newly permed and quite an odd colour. Auburn, he reckoned. 'Come to see the condemned man off then?' he joked.

'I'm coming with you,' she said firmly.

He was surprised. 'You don't have to do that.'

'I know I don't, but you're stuck with me all the same. Did you think we'd let you do this by yourself?'

'What about the shop? We'll not be back in time.'

'Stuff the shop,' she said firmly. 'Maryam will cope...actually it was her idea.'

Of course, he thought, that figured. 'Hop in then,' he told her, opening the passenger door for her.

Seat belt fixed, she opened her handbag and took out a poke of barley sugars. 'I always take one when travelling. Calms the nerves,' she told him. 'We should start stocking them in the shop.'

In fact he took three on the journey to Dundee and the conversation flowed.

She came into the hospital with him, sat beside him in the oncology waiting room until he was called in and was there when he came out, so she was the first to hear that the news was good. 'I won't want to see you for three months,' the consultant told him. 'Plenty of room for optimism.'

She did not seem overly surprised. 'We knew you'd get the all clear,' she told him in the restaurant at lunch.

'We?' he queried though he had guessed her answer.

'Maryam, then. She had a hunch.'

Of course, he thought, but why of course? 'Rhoda,' he asked over coffee, 'what do you make of Maryam?'

'To be honest I had my doubts about her to begin with; a black in Bruden's and all that colour nonsense, but I'm well and truly converted. She's' a nice lassie.'

'Aye she is,' he agreed quickly, 'but do you not think she has some weird notions?'

'That's because she listens to her inner voice,' Rhoda said dismissively.

He was surprised. 'Inner voice?' he echoed.

'Aye. I read a bit about it in the Courier. If we all listened to our inner voices a bit more the world would be a better place. Something like that.'

'Right,' he said but not understanding what she was talking about. 'Right... the inner voice it is, then.'

'I wouldn't worry about it,' she told him. 'It's probably a foreign, religious thing where Maryam's concerned. She's allowed.'

'Of course. Absolutely,' he agreed and they changed the subject.

In fact he was enjoying himself. Heady over the cancer all-clear, he had not wanted the day to end so he suggested taking her to see the Queich cross-slab. Not perhaps his brightest idea because she was wearing the wrong shoes, black patent leather town pumps with heels that found the rough path over the field hard going. He offered her his arm which she was happy to accept so all was well and though she had no idea what he was talking about as he launched into a description of the stone, she did not look bored either.

When they got back, Rhoda asked him in for a cup of tea. Well, why not, he told himself. Rhoda's bungalow was comfortable and there was a home-made cake which made a pleasant change from the Lomond bakery. Altogether it had been an enjoyable afternoon.

At four o'clock he was beginning to feel guilty. He should not be sitting here enjoying the comforts of Rhoda's bungalow while Sunshine was still on her feet at the counter. It had been a long day for her. 'I should go.' he said reluctantly. Rhoda's tea, Rhoda's armchair, Rhoda's possessions all seemed pleasanter now that he had to leave. They talked business for a few more moments as she walked him to her gate.

The next door dog was yapping excitedly at him from the dividing fence as he said his thank-you. 'Does that not bother you?' he asked curiously.

'What? Tina?' She looked surprised. 'I've got used to it, I suppose. To tell you the truth I hardly notice.'

'I'm thinking of giving Sunshine the day off tomorrow. I think she deserves it,' he added as the little dog's yapping subsided.

'Are you sure you'll manage a whole morning?' she asked a little fussily.

'No sweat,' he told her. 'See you at two tomorrow then?'

'You surely will,' she said happily.

'Thinking it over that night he reckoned it had been a very good day. He wondered if his results had been different would he still have enjoyed it so much. Silly hypothesis. He had got the all-clear and that was what mattered. Rhoda was a good egg, but then he had always known that. He felt strong and positive. For some obscure reason, he believed that he had Maryam to thank for it.

Elvis

It was no' fair. Hughie had Jura and now Tammy had Mopsy. Why should he not get a pet too? And it was his birthday on Friday. He glared at his mother who was peeling a pile of tatties at the sink. Surely she hadn't forgotten? It was not as if he hadn't reminded her often enough. Every day for the past week, maybe longer. 'I want a rabbit,' he decided, 'or maybe a wee white moosie.' His pal had a wee broon moose which he once took into school squashed into his pocket. When it was discovered the teacher had a fit and climbed on to a chair. That had been rare.

'I want never gets,' his mother told him sharply. 'Ye canna get a rabbit with a big dog in the hoose and ye canna get a moose wi' a cat.'

'I'd watch it,' he said sulkily, but truthfully deep down inside him he didn't want either a rabbit or a mouse. It was just that he got nothing. Hughie was the oldest and he got everything he asked for - well nearly everything - and Tammy was spoiled rotten. What did he ever get but his brother's cast-offs. 'It's jist no fair,' he added but the fire had gone out of him.

'Och away oot wi' ye from under ma feet. The sun's shining, ye'r on holiday. What more do ye want?' she said crossly. He mooched towards the kitchen door. 'Oh and yet can get me a pinta frae Bruden's seeing ye've naethin' better to do with yer time.'

She gave him the money. 'See and bring me the change.'

'Aw Maa-am' he protested. There would be little change. She relented. 'Ye can keep it this once.'

He didn't mind going to Bruden's. It was a braw day right enough. He ambled down the street, kicked at a stone and made a face at the Mairs' dog when it yapped at him as he passed its gate. Bruden's was quite busy. He picked up the carton of milk, chose a ball of bubble gum with the scant change and joined the queue at the check-out counter.

Sunshine was with a customer and had her nose in a big book like his teacher's register. Why they cried her Sunshine, he would never understand. She was as dark as the ace of spades, wasn't she? Moonshine would be more like it, but come to think of it that wasn't right either. Starlight then? She looked up at that moment and seemed to catch his eye for a fleeting second. Aye, he thought, Starlight would be better for her eyes shone, but maybe not Starlight for stars twinkled and glittered, didn't they? Planetshine, then. (They'd been doing planets in class lately.)

Then it was his turn at the counter and the shop was empty. 'You okay, then?' she asked as she rang through the milk.

He shrugged.

'What does that mean?' she asked, with that weird squinty look of hers.

So he let it all come out, the resentment, the hurt, the total unfairness of being the middle child, the fact that it was his birthday next week, but who cared. She leaned her bare brown arms on the counter and listened. Nobody ever listened to him. She had nice arms he thought.

'Elvis' she said,' what would you really like?'

'I said,' he prevaricated. 'A wee moose in a wee cage, or maybe a canary.' A canary? Where had that come from? A canary would be fine, yellow like proper sunshine and it could tweet.

She was still looking at him. Waiting for him to answer. Suddenly there flashed into his head a memory of the afternoon he and Tammy had spent in her home, that time Hughie got his operation. It had been on a chair in the corner of the room and he had gone over and touched it, made it sing.

Before he could answer, Rhoda came bustling into the shop through the back entrance buttoning her overall and Sunshine's attention was distracted. He waited for a moment while the two grown-ups nattered but it was obvious she had forgotten about him so when a group of older girls clattered into the shop, he slipped out.

He didn't mind too much because his head was bursting with the knowledge of what it was he wanted above everything else in all the world. A guitar. Made sense, so it did. Him with a name like that. He never knew a time when he hadn't worshipped his namesake. Got that from his Mam so he did and he was proud of it. It seemed to him that Hughie and Tammy were content with lesser objects. He took after his Mam. He thought of her screeching 'Blue Suede Shoes' at the top of her voice when she thought the hoose was empty. All he needed was a guitar.

So how to get one? Guitars cost real money, didn't they? He thought of the one he had seen in Maryam's house. It had a beaded strap all colours of the rainbow. Sunshine had said it was no' hers. It had belonged to the wumman in her flat, the nurse one who had seen Hughie in the hospital. He remembered the deep resounding twang it had made when he tweaked it and for moment he had felt giddy with desire.

If only he could get a job like Hughie who not only had his paper round but was working during the school holidays out at the Foulis' farm. Rakin' it in, Hughie was, though he couldna spend it as he was putting most of it by in a wee saving book for boots and new winter claes. Tammy was after money too for a wee harness and lead for Mopsy. When Mam told her it was right at the bottom of a very long list, Tammy had muttered under her breath. 'Mr Mair 'll soon gi'e me it.' Mam had not heard but he had. 'In yer dreams,' he had sneered. But Tammy had insisted. 'He gave me fifty pence the other day.'

'He never. Whit for?'

'For sweeties - and he paid me on to the dodgems - so there!' She had stuck out her tongue and run away laughing.

Maybe there was some truth in it. Mr Mair had got Hughie his dog...some folk said Mr Mair was queer. Must be right queer to get Hughie a dog and give Tammy fifty pence. Off his heid more like. The question was could he, Elvis, put up wi' a bit of queerness for the sake of a guitar? What was queerness any road? Was it the same as daftness? If so, the answer overwhelmingly was aye, he could.

So he dawdled up the street. When he saw Tina still yapping at her gate, the great idea came to him. The wee creature had its nose through the iron spars. 'Yap yap yap yap yap,' it snapped at him. Elvis looked carefully up and down the street, then eyed the Mairs' front garden. No one to be seen so he lifted the wrought-iron latch and opened the gate sufficiently to let the wee creature out. For a second he thought it wasn't going to move. Then suddenly it stopped barking and slunk out. Then it sat down on the pavement, cocked its little head to one side and looked up at him expectantly.

Now what to do? They stared at each other, then he said encouragingly, 'Come on, boy!' He needed it to run away for him to catch it, bring it back and claim to have rescued it.

Then the door of the bungalow opened and there was Mistress Mair, all flappy and shouty with her arms waving wildly. 'Tina? Where's my wee Tina? Did you open the gate? What have you done, you naughty boy?'

He was rooted to the spot. Tina started to yap again. Mistress Mair pushed past him and scooped her up into her arms. 'Oh my poor baby. What was the nasty boy doing to you?'

The more he tried to explain the louder she shouted. He wanted to run away but he didn't dare. Then Mr Mair came strolling down the path. 'What's all the fuss about?' he asked calmly enough. Mrs Mair blustered and shouted and told him to call the police. The polis? Cripes.

Mr Mair was okay. He told his mother to calm down. The dog was all right, wasn't it? He listened to her rants for another moment then told her to go back indoors and take the dog with her. He'd deal with the matter. He listened to Elvis' garbled explanation, such as it was, and then he looked bored. 'Save it,' he said. 'I don't really care.' Then he asked all casual like as if it didn't matter, 'So what do they call you?'

'Ah'm Elvis,' he replied which was maybe a mistake but it was oot before he could think twice.

'So - Elvis - are you all shook up, then?' He had a weird voice, all twangy through his nose. Not knowing what the older man was talking about he could think of no answer. 'Off you go, Elvis. I don't know what you're up to but I'll bet it was no good. Run along now.'

He turned to shut the gate. It was now or never. 'I'm Hughie's brother.'

That stopped him. Dead. 'So?' he said coldly without turning round. 'What do you want?'

'A guitar,' he said boldly. Afterwards he wondered at himself for speaking so cheekily. There was something about Mr Mair that drew it out of him. He could not rightly put it into words. It was almost as if Mr Mair wanted him as much as he wanted a guitar, but that didn't make sense either.

He turned then and eyeballed him but he was not angry. 'A guitar is it?' he said speculatively. 'What makes you think I've got a guitar?'

He shrugged. It was like he was playing some strange sort of game and, whatever he did or said, he would still be the winner. Mr Mair grinned. 'It so happens you're right.' He paused the added casually, 'Want to see it?' Mr Mair held open the gate.

He nodded. Without hesitating he went in. 'Shut the gate behind you,' Mr Mair told him, without looking round, so he did. He still thought he was winning.

Bertie

It was a perfect day for golf, sunny but with a cool breeze. St Andrews would be at its best, the turf springy under his two-toned golfing brogues, the bunkers dry and the greens like velvet. He could not help his feelings of regret but it was no use to attempt to take Gordon. If he agreed to come he would wander off at the first opportunity, drop his clubs or putt with a driver. Sadly he knew they would never play golf together again, and not just golf. He tried not to think too deeply about the future, but knew the day would come when arrangements would have to be made. Indeed he had gone so far as to identify two care homes at opposite ends of the neighbourhood, both vastly expensive. They might well have to sell Greenyards to make ends meet, and then where would he go? What would he do? But it hadn't come to that yet. That problem was for another day.

Meanwhile what to do this afternoon? What else was there to do? Without golf to fill these long endless summer afternoons he was bored. It was all right for Gordon to sit in his deck chair endlessly scuffling through the newspaper, reading and re-reading the same paragraph that was forever new to him. He wandered less these days which was something to be thankful for, he supposed. That gnawing anxiety of not knowing where he was, what he was doing or if he would ever come home had diminished, thank God. Occasionally he wondered if he might take the Cortina and spend an hour knocking a ball about on the local course. Gordon would certainly not notice his absence but then suppose something were to happen to him. He could even set the house on fire, perish the thought. No. He would have to ditch that idea. Lately he was giving a lot more thought to one in particular of the two residential care homes. Montgomery House was its name, five miles door to door.

He had just decided to mow the back lawn when the doorbell rang. Who on earth? Probably Jehovah's Witnesses; they were about due for another visit he thought as he went to answer. Two police officers stood there. His heart sank.

Mr Maclardy? Mr Bertram Maclardy?' the girl spoke. She was young with her blond hair escaping in wisps under her uniform cap. 'Good afternoon. We're from Queich Police Station. I'm P.C. Shirley and this is my colleague, P.C. Turner'

Constable Turner, he recognised from previous encounters in the police station. The girl was new to him. What on earth did they want?

'Good day, sir. Might we have a word with Mr Gordon Maclardy?' PC Turner asked politely.

Not if he could avoid it. Inwardly he felt sick. 'Anything I can help with?'

'Nothing to worry about, sir.'

'You'd better come in, then,' he said reluctantly. 'I'll fetch him. He's in the garden.'

'The garden will do fine,' the girl said, stepping purposefully over the threshold.

'How is your brother these days?' Constable Turner, who knew the situation, asked quietly. He had dealt several times before with Bertie's anxious telephone calls or visits to the police station.

How to answer him. Truthfully, he decided. 'He sometimes gets notions - ideas into his head - and, as you know, he wanders.'

'That's why we're here, sir.'

'He was concerned about that the young man who drowned some months ago. As soon as the lad was identified and the matter finalised by the police, he lost interest.'

'Perhaps we could speak to Mr Gordon himself?' The girl intervened.

'Of course,' Bertie told her brusquely. He was inclined to be angry. 'My brother has dementia. Constable Turner knows that.'

Neither commented as Bertie led them out into the back garden. Gordon was seated in his deck chair as close to the partition fence as was possible;

the papers had fallen from his lap and he lay with his mouth open snoring faintly. Not a good sign. He usually awoke more confused after a cat nap.

Bertie touched him lightly on the shoulder. 'Gordon? Wake up. These two officers would like to have a word with you.'

His eyes shot open. For a moment he looked terrified.

Bertie wondered if he was remembering that accident all those years ago which had never properly been explained. He gripped Gordon's shoulder reassuringly. 'Nothing to worry about, old chap. You remember Constable Turner?' Of course he didn't.

Gordon's look of terror changed to conspiratorial. 'You've come!' he exclaimed in a hushed voice. 'Thank God. Bert said you'd never believe me.'

'Please don't upset yourself, sir,' the girl said calmly. 'We would like to ask you a few questions, if that would be convenient?'

'Of course, of course', said Gordon. 'Just don't speak too loudly. Walls have ears, have ears.' he repeated in a low voice, indicating the boundary fence behind him with his thumb.

'We understand, sir,' Turner said soothingly.' Nothing for you to worry about,' He then explained as succinctly as possible that the shore hut had been vandalised recently. 'We have our suspicions as to the identity of the culprits but no positive proof. You have been seen several times in the vicinity and we wondered if you had seen anyone or anything untoward?'

Gordon looked confused then suddenly he understood. 'Yes,' he said. 'That's the place. They use it. Get up to all sorts.'

'They, sir? Could you be a bit more specific?' the girl asked, notebook poised.

Gordon beckoned to her so that he could whisper. She leaned closer. 'The people next door. They're wicked... evil. It's them you should be speaking to.' Then pointing to Bertie he added, 'He knows. He'll tell you.'

Bertie shook his head. 'Please, Gordon, you have no proof.'

'Don't look at me like that,' he said angrily to Bertie. 'It's high time the police did something about it.'

'Tell us what exactly, Mr Maclardy?'

'Those devils next door. He takes his victims to that hut on the shore and he does unspeakable things. They both do' he whispered. 'They're paedophiles.'

Bertie was in despair. Gordon looked as demented as he sounded.

Doubt flickered in the police officers' eyes. They both looked questioningly at Bertie who murmured, 'I did warn you. My brother sometimes gets ideas into his head.'

Gordon heard him. He was possessed by rage. 'It's God's truth,' he shouted. 'You know it as well as I do.'

'We understand, sir,' Turner told him in a soothing voice, the tone that one would use to a child or an idiot. 'Please don't upset yourself. You can safely leave the matter in our hands. You and your brother have been most helpful.' He turned to Bertie. 'I think we have all we need here. We won't disturb you any further.'

Gordon, who still had rare flashes of insight, was aware of the officers' disbelief. As they turned to leave he shouted after them angrily, 'By the way, he's not my brother.'

Bertie said nothing. What was the point? The two officers would do nothing, believe nothing. Why should he worry? But of course he did. The burden of anxiety had not lessened. It was sodden through with sadness.

After he had seen the officers to the door, he returned to the garden. Gordon was shuffling through the paper seemingly oblivious to what had happened.

'Just going down to the shop for milk,' he called out. Without taking his eyes off the paper, Gordon waved in acknowledgement.

He hoped Maryam would be on the counter.

Annie

She had more work than she had dreamed possible since the New Year and she was managing, just. Four hours a week at the Maclardy's, five hours in the shop, four hours at Mistress Mackenzie's, a couple of hours at Rhoda's to do the rough work, two mornings at the Rectory, three evenings a week at the surgery, oh and two hours a week at Miss Anderson. 'My regulars' as she called them. So many now that she had to mark the Courier free calendar to keep herself right.

Didn't leave much time for the kids on holiday but they managed, didn't they? And the dog fitted in fine and so far there had been no ructions with the kitten. What a wee spitfire he was, but it was nice to have two animals about the house. Made the place more homely. Bit of a stink in the kitchenette from the litter tray but the wee thing would learn. That litter tray had been given to Tammy by Chrissie Foulis, not new but fine for the job. Chrissie was a real nice woman, sent down a dozen eggs wi' Hughie most weeks. Great that Hughie had a wee holiday job up there. Play his cards right and he could land a job for life. Her granny, so she'd been told, had come from a farm and it had done her no harm. She was right proud of Hughie with his two wee jobs.

Tammy too was happy enough with her kitty cat. Poor wee thing had a time of it forced into a dolly's crib, dressed up in a dolly's clothes, but she could take care of herself. Tammy's arms were proof of that.

It was Elvis that was the worry. She never knew where he was these days, not since she'd told him off for pestering those Mairs. It was Mr Bert who had warned her. Told her that he'd seen him from the back room window next door with Mr Mair. 'I'm sure there's no harm in it. The Mairs often have kids in their garden,' he told her apologetically, 'but best you know.'

So she had told Elvis off good and proper. He had said nothing, just glowered at her. Tammy had heard it all. 'He gave me fifty pence,' she crowed, 'and he paid me on to the dodgems.'

'Why would he give ye money? What did you hae to dae?' she asked angrily.

Tammy shrugged. 'He likes kids, I guess.'

'Well I don't want you going there either of you. You're no' to speak to strange men. Do you hear me?'

Tammy turned her attention to her kitten. 'It's no snot off my nose. He's a creep anyways.'

Elvis could keep quiet no longer, 'He is not,' he shouted. 'He's nice. He got Hughie Jura and he gave you fifty pence and he's going to get me a guitar.'

'He is not,' Annie declared sharply. 'You can put that idea right out of your heid.'

'Why?' Elvis whined. 'Why should I? Hughie got what he wanted and Tammy's got Topsy. It's no fair.'

'What's this aboot a guitar? You never said.'

'You never asked.'

'You should have said.' She had been planning on buying him new trainers for his birthday. How would she ever afford a guitar?

'You canna play a guitar,' Tammy said scornfully.

'Mr Mair'll learn me. He said.'

Annie made up her mind. It would mean another trip to Dundee. Maybe that second hand place had guitars cheap. You could get wee guitars, kiddies' size. Might not cost the earth. 'If it's a guitar ye want, it's a guitar ye'll get,' she said firmly,' but no' frae they Mairs. Are you listening?'

He said nothing.

'I'll have no more talk o' rabbits and rats, mind.'

After a moment he nodded.

She decided to take the bus to Dundee that Saturday. By the time she was ready to go Hughie was back from the farm and slumped on the settee with a packet of wine gums watching motor racing on the telly with Jura sprawled across him. He'd been up since seven so he deserved a rest. Tammy was playing on the doorstep with Mopsy and two of her pals but there no sign of Elvis. Where was the lad? She had half thought of taking him with her as a pre-birthday treat, but changed her mind in case he wanted what was beyond her means. She put on her cotton skirt with the roses on it and her best cardie and told them goodbye with dire threats as to their behaviour while she was gone. The sun was shining.

Finding a child's guitar was not that difficult and not that expensive. Good old Woolworth. She was not entirely convinced that Elvis would be satisfied but Maryam had told her that Sheena was good on the guitar and would be okay about showing him what to do. When he had mastered the toy instrument he could maybe start saving up for something better. It was probably just a fad anyhow. He'd be bored of it before long, but better that than another animal.

At Maryam's suggestion, she left the bulky parcel in Mo's office at Bruden's. She could pick it up on the morning of his birthday so that it would come as a big surprise. Mo had been real nice about it and told her that Bruden's would provide a Lomond Bakery cake for his tea with eleven candles. Best thing she ever did was getting that job in the shop. Okay it was hard work and unsocial hours but the perks were great. 'Don't thank me,' Mo had said smiling. (He was in a great mood these days.) 'It was Maryam's idea.'

So life was on the up and up, she thought as she walked along Church Street with a giant pack of frozen chips in her shopping bag. It would be chip butties and ham for their tea.

Still no sign of Elvis.

Maryam

She woke suddenly and glanced at her alarm clock. Five minutes past one. Moonlight streaked through the bedroom window and lay in a pool in the middle of her room. Then she heard the telephone. It occasionally rang in the middle of the night calling Sheena in for an emergency so she paid no attention. Then she remembered that Sheena was on night duty. In the same moment she was aware that her room was full of wind. The pool of moonlight had quietly become a shimmering swirl of movement. Our Mother? She was immediately awake and alert. The words were the same as always clear as music in her head, urgent, demanding. 'My Daughter listen... lisss...ten,' and then it had gone and there was only moonlight, the curtains still astir, and the persistent ring of the telephone.

She rose obediently and hurried into the little hallway and lifted the receiver.

'Maryam? Thank God. I'm sorry to ring you so late but you're my last resort.' It was Rachel and she sounded frantic.

'I'm listening,' she said, automatically echoing the words of Our Mother.

'It's Al's mother,' she explained.' She's fallen and knocked herself out. She's refusing to go to hospital but I'm really worried about her and I can't get hold of Alastair. He's not at home or in the office and the Golf Club's closed. What if he's had an accident or been taken ill? To tell you the truth I'm worried sick. I've a bad feeling about this. I think something's wrong. I'm so sorry to bother you but there's no one else I can think of to ask.'

Maryam knew she was right to be worried. Why else had Our Mother come? 'Give me your phone number and I'll go over to the house and check,' she said more calmly than she felt.

As she pulled on her clothes she remembered how happy Rachel had seemed on Monday. She had come into Bruden's all smiles and chatter to cancel Mrs Mackenzie's bread and paper orders. Alastair seemingly was back to his old self, friendly, relaxed as if some huge burden had dropped off his shoulders. It had been a happy weekend so when he told her he had booked her and Jayjay into Peebles Hydro for the coming week and promised to join her at the weekend she had accepted without argument. Indeed she was so relieved and grateful for his change of mood that she had offered to take his mother with her. That had pleased him. They had gone downstairs together to invite the old lady and she had been pathetically delighted. He had made the extra booking and planned to drive down the A 701 together on Tuesday - yesterday - morning. Rachel had seemed so happy. Now this.

Outside the moon was full and the garden bathed in light and the scent of flowers, some of whom were sleeping, others very much awake. Pulling her cardigan closer for the fussy wind was like a hand in the small of her back nudging her forward with an extraordinary urgency, she let herself out of the Old Rectory gate crossed the road and half ran the short distance to Lochview. The front gates were closed and the drive darkened in the shadow of rhododendrons.

The first thing she noticed was Alastair's Mercedes parked in the open garage, so, she thought, he must surely be at home.

There were two door bells, one for each flat so she pressed the top one, but there was no answer. She tried it again and then the bottom one which she could distinctly hear echoing through the empty lower flat.

After a few seconds she stepped back to look up at the top windows, which were all closed. There was no sign of life, no indication that Alastair was there. The disquiet which had been growing in her head since the first shrill call of the telephone increased. First she tried the front door but it was locked, impenetrable. Indeed the whole house had a locked-in, forbidding aspect with not a window open that she could see. She could go and get help, but by the time she had gone home to telephone for the police, it might be too late.

She hurried round to the back of the house. A kitchen wing had been added some years ago and though the back door was locked and all the main windows closed she noticed a small scullery window that was just within reach. She did not hesitate. Driven by that inner urgency that assured her that all was not well, she found a stone in the garden and smashed the frosted glass, knocked the jagged edges away, found the latch and opened the window wide. Even though she was small, it was not easy to lever herself through the narrow space and she scraped her hand in trying. Once inside, she groped her way through the moonlit kitchen to the foot of the stairs.

'Mr Mackenzie?' she called out, 'Alastair, are you there?' The only answer was silence. Then she noticed the smell, faint but unmistakeable. She had been brought up with that particular smell.

She had no time to search for light switches nor would she have dared to use them but fortunately the moon was guide enough. The stink grew stronger as she reached the upper landing. Holding her cardigan to her nose she went straight to the closed kitchen door, opened it and saw with horror the gaping oven and the man's body sprawled on the floor, his head inside resting on an incongruously gaudy cushion. Finding all the gas cooker switches, she turned them off, then ran to the window and wrenched it open, gulping in a gust of fresh air as she did so. Pulling his inert body clear of the oven she dragged him to the window.

'Our Mother help him.' She urged then turned and vomited into the sink.

The wind that had prodded her back had now reached gale force and with a roar rushed through the open window. A vase of marigolds on the kitchen table crashed to the floor and the door slammed. There was something unreal and sentient in its intensity as it filled the room with fresh clean air, dominating and dispersing the noxious, nauseating fumes. She knelt by the still body, leaned over him and, opening his mouth with her fingers, pressed hers to his not to breathe but to draw out the fumes into her own lungs.

Overcome by nausea again she lifted her head and saw in a shaft of moonlight the faint rise and fall of his heart beat.

The nausea passed. 'Mr Mackenzie - Alastair?' she took his hand. 'Wake up. It's over.'

She reached for the plastic bowl in the sink and had it ready. She held his head while he vomited. The wind played round them both but now it was caressing, refreshing, a friend. She lifted her head to receive its caress and breathed it deeply into her lungs.

Then he opened his eyes and saw her. 'Maryam?' he croaked for his throat was raw and painful. 'What are you doing here?'

'The wind brought me,' she told him, knowing that it was true. Our Mother's wind.

'He looked surprised. 'Wind?' he croaked.

She looked up. There was no wind. The curtains were still. Only the moon shone.

'Rachel rang,' she told him.' She was worried about you.'

'Rachel rang you in the middle of the night?'

He closed his eyes and she saw glinting beneath his lids the shine of tears.

She helped him up into a chair. 'I should ring for an ambulance,' she said.

'No.' He caught her wrist. 'No need. No ambulance.'

'Mr Mackenzie,' which was what she usually called him. 'You nearly died. You need proper help.'

He looked at her strangely. 'I thought I was dead. When I opened my eyes and saw you, I thought I was dead.'

She did not argue for she too had thought him dead. Then she saw his shadow and knew that indeed he had been on the cusp of death but that now he was well and had no need of medical help. She was awe-struck. They were both silent, unable to find words to express what had happened.

'Will you ring Rachel and tell her you're okay?' she asked him eventually. 'Can you do that?'

He did not answer. Instead he glanced down at his watch. It was now two hours since he had turned on the oven. 'What did you do to me?' he asked hoarsely but without anger. He was as awestruck as she was.

'I told you. It was the wind.' She knew he was safe. Our Mother's healing was complete.

'Why? How did you know?'

'I listened,' was all she told him.

'Will you tell my wife?' he asked after a moment.

'No,' she told him quietly, 'because you will. Everything you remember.'

She did not need to know why he had done it, yet she did. It was there written on his shadow's face. Those feelings of hopelessness, despair and failure that had overwhelmed him from time to time throughout his life. He had convinced himself that his wife, his son and his mother and his business would all be better off without him cluttering up their lives, that no one would miss him, that he was unloved, unnecessary.

'Rachel loves you, Mr Mackenzie. She and your mother and your baby, they love the very bones of you.'

He turned away his head and to hide his tears. These were penitent tears, healing tears. His shadow's arms were wrapped around him consolingly. 'Thank you,' it told her in her head. Her own eyes filled. Presently she let herself out through the front door. The night was still, not a breath of wind to stir the sleeping world.

Suddenly she felt very tired.

Geordie

Miss A's mower was finally kaput. He had done his best, taken it apart and put it together again but somehow he had spare nuts and bolts and it was worse than before. He would have to tell her.

'I could tak' it doon tae the garage,' he said doubtfully, forgetting she was deaf.

'What's that? Speak up, Geordie.'

So he repeated himself. 'They mend mowers, so I've heard, or mebbe I could get a loan of the Maclardy's.' They had a big petrol machine which he had often eyed enviously.

'No, no,' she said firmly. 'Neither a borrower nor a lender be, as my father would say. It's decades old. It's done its turn. If you're kind enough to mow the grass, Geordie, you deserve the proper tools. I think we should buy another one.'

'Aye, that would be best. Maybe second hand? There's sometimes adverts in the Courier for old mowers.'

'No thank you, Geordie. I'd like something new, a decent machine that'll see me out.'

The discussion lasted happily through a cup of tea and a Penguin biscuit and it was decided that Geordie should find the nearest supplier and choose an electric machine with enough cable to reach from the kitchen to the far end of the back garden. Neither of them had an idea of what it would cost, so she gave him fifty pounds and hoped it would be enough.

With the notes carefully stowed into his trouser pocket, he called in at Bruden's. Mo or Rhoda would probably know where to go, but he hoped it would be Sunshine.

It was Mo himself at the counter. 'Perth,' he said decisively, picked up an old envelope and wrote down the name and address of an ironmonger, a private business same as Bruden's. 'Tell the boss I sent you and you'll maybe get a discount. He's a mate of mine, treasurer of the Fife Pictish Society.'

So at two-thirty that afternoon Geordie found himself on the Perth bus with fifty pounds plus a couple of quid of his own in his pocket and an afternoon on the razzle, or so he told himself. He could go for a pint and maybe - just maybe - put a tenner on the nags; depending on how much the mower cost, of course. He tried to put the thought to the back of his mind, but like a weed in a nurtured flower bed, it kept pushing through the fertile soil.

He found the ironmonger no bother, was served by the boss himself who was pleased to have news of Mo and gave him a ten percent discount on a spanking new Flymo which was light, easy to use and, he was assured, efficient. It cost him thirty-seven pounds and fifty pence which included the price of delivery. So he had that spare tenner. Miss A would never know and if he won he would pay for the mower himself. He had already identified two bookies. He had that choice. First though, he would treat himself to a bite to eat. Miss A had told him to get himself a bit of dinner and here he was in an Eyetie café, not too posh. It wouldna cost an arm and a leg.

He chose a window seat and ordered the works. Sausage, egg and bacon, tomato, black pudding and chips. He could even get a pint to wash it all down for the café was licensed. By the time he had shovelled it all away, the next bus would be due. The bookies still lingered at the back of his mind. He could always get a later bus.

Between mouthfuls and gulps he kept an eye on the sunny street. Shoppers, business folk with brief cases, kids on scooters, toddlers clinging on to harassed mums, pensioners all shapes and sizes, passed.

He had just finished his last mouthful and laid down his knife and fork when he saw a face he knew. That Mair fellow who lived in the street. There he was on the pavement the other side of the road. Geordie watched him curiously between the passing vans and cars and buses. Wait a minute. He was not on his own. He had a kid with him. He knew that kid; one of Annie Miller's bairns, the middle one with the outlandish name which he could not for the moment recall. Not Hughie. He was the paper boy and he had a dog and there was a wee lassie who once nearly knocked him over as he came out of his own gate. 'Look whaur ye're goin,' he had told her crossly but she could have said the same thing to him. Instead she shouted back,' Sorry, mister!' so he had forgiven her. This was the middle one, with the ginger hair and the freckles and the big new teeth that were just a wee bit crooked. Elvis, that was it. Fancy saddling a kid with a name like that.

There was Elvis across the street walking along beside Mr Mair. He watched them till they disappeared out of his vision but he was curious. What was Mr Mair doing in Perth with a street bairn? Och well, it was no business of his and it was the school holidays. Must be family friends. Come to think of it he'd heard in the shop that Mr Mair had got that dog for Hughie. Perhaps they were related. Perhaps Annie worked for the Mairs. There could be dozens of reasons why middle-aged, middle-class Mr Mair should be walking up the road with a wee scrote from a cooncil hoose. There were rumours though. The craic was that Mr Mair was overly fond of bairns.

He paid the bill and asked the waitress for the time - he had long ago sold his watch. He had fifteen minutes till the next bus and a wait of two hours if he missed it. He could pass the time by trying out the bookies. There would be slot machines somewhere, though the idea no longer excited him. It would take him about ten minutes to reach the bus station so if he decided to go straight back to Queich he would need to step on it. Without ever making a firm decision he found himself at the bus station. He climbed on board.

Chapter Seven

Hughie

Jura was sick. He had found her on the morning of Elvis' birthday curled up under the kitchenette table panting, hot and dull-eyed. There was vomit and shit everywhere. 'Oh Jura, poor lass, what's up wi' ye?' he was on his knees caressing her head. Now she was shivering. He covered her with a tea towel.

It was Saturday morning, so Mam was having a bit of a lie-in which gave him ten minutes to clean up before his paper round. If it had been anyone else's poo he would have retched his guts out, but Mam came down anyway. To his surprise she was not angry.

'Poor beastie. She's taken something bad. What did she hae to eat last night?'

He thought back again. She had licked her plate right enough and had half a tin of Chum and some biscuit. 'Just the usual.'

'Did you let her oot last night? Maybe it was something in the gairden.' He thought back again. He had let her out as usual but for once he had not gone with her. He'd been watching Top of the Pops on the telly. Half an hour later he had gone out to call her in. She'd come to bed with him as usual but she had been restless. Sometime in the night she must have gone down the stair, maybe to get a drink of water. Maybe it was the water. Guiltily he remembered he hadn't washed the bowl for a wee while.

'Oh Jura pet, what have I done to you?' he muttered into her ear. Two tears rolled down his cheeks. Her panting was frantic and the shivering worse. 'Dinna die, Jura, dinna die.'

'She's no' going to die. She needs the vet.' Mam told him to run down to Bruden's and get Maryam or Mo, whoever was behind the counter to ring the vet. 'Get a move on, son,' she urged him, 'I'll mind the dog.'

'I canna do the papers,' he told her brokenly from the door. 'Oh Mam is she gonna die?'

'Dinna fret, Hughie. Ah'll no let her die. Maybe Elvis'll do the papers. After all he's eleven now.' They both remembered it was his birthday. 'Stir your stumps!' she told him impatiently.

Great! Sunshine was there. She listened carefully as he explained as best he could what had happened. She rang Mo who was down in two minutes. What she said to him he never knew for she spoke to him privately in the wee room at the back. Anyhow Mo called him through and told him. 'Best we take the car,' so minutes later they were at the hoose. By this time poor Jura was all floppy and scarcely breathing so Mo wrapped her in a blanket and carried her out to the car. Hughie sat in the back with her, cradling her head, watering her with tears. 'The vet's expecting us,' Mo told him. 'Sunshine rang. Rod Grant's a good mate.'

It was some seven miles to Mr Grant's dispensary. Mo tried to keep him cheerful but Hughie was convinced Jura was dying and he was somehow to blame He felt a wee bit ashamed of himself for crying but he could not help it. Jura was his pal, his other self, and he loved her.

The vet who was a wee baldie guy took her away. Meanwhile he and Mo sat in the waiting room. Mo was kind and told him to cry all he liked. He didn't say Jura would be all right and he didn't say anything about the paper round.

After what seemed like forever the wee guy came back. 'She'll be all right,' he told Hughie. 'The worst is past but she's badly dehydrated. We'll keep her here for the weekend just to be certain, but Jura's one tough lady.'

'Can I get to see her?' he asked as the tears of anxiety fell afresh as tears of relief.

She was lying in a wee cage on a blanket and she looked fast asleep. While he stroked her, he heard the vet talking to Mo. 'We'll send a specimen off to the lab but it looks like food poisoning. 'I'm not saying anything definite until the tests come back. Meanwhile I'll need the lad's address and phone number.'

That would be for the bill. Hughie knew that vets cost mega cash which Mam didn't have, but all Mo said was, 'Best deal through me. Hughie's my employee.' He could take the cash out of his wages however long it took.

Suddenly he remembered Bob and Chrissie. He was supposed to be at the farm and unless Elvis had stepped in, the papers would be waiting.

'Come along, lad. Mr Grant's got work to do and so have we. Those papers won't deliver themselves.'

'We'll take good care of her', the vet reassured him.

Reluctantly Hughie followed Mo back to the car.

Sunshine had already rung Chrissie who gave him the morning off. 'I hope it was naething he picked up on the fairm,' she had said anxiously. 'Rob's aye careful but it's a possibeelity.'

Elvis had never turned up so he had the papers to deliver. 'We'll ring the vet later,' Sunshine reassured him as he picked up the satchel. 'She'll be fine, Hughie.'

It was weird doing the round without Jura bounding along by his wheels. Those customers who were quick to grumble about his lateness changed their tune when he explained that his dog was ill. Old Bob Foulis, who was Rob and Chrissie's da even asked him in for a cup of tea which he declined. He was too worried to stop.

Before he went home Sunshine rang Mr Grant for him. 'She's still sleeping but there's no need to worry,' she reported, but he got the vet's number off her so he could ring himself. There was a handy phone box in the street.

He got home about twelve. Mam asked him about Jura but he could tell she wasn't really listening. She was more concerned about Elvis who had refused to do the papers because it was his birthday and anyway he was going out 'Whaur was he going that was so important that he couldn't gi'e his brother a hand, that's whit I'd like to ken,' she declared. 'He'd better be back soon or I'll skelp his backside, birthday or no birthday.'

She'd picked up Elvis' present from the shop. Tammy had drawn him a card and got money off Mam to buy him a bar of Toblerone. Hughie had still his card to write and the Superman comic book to wrap that he'd bought off his own money.

'Put them in the room wi' the rest,' Mama told him. 'It's burgers for dinner.' Mam's parcel lay on the settee. It was big and wrapped in shiny red paper with a red balloon tied to it.

At twelve-thirty the burgers were ready. The house reeked of them and suddenly he was hungry. He hadn't eaten all morning, but there was still no sign of Elvis. Mam was getting cross.

'Awa' oot and see if you can find him,' she told Hughie. 'He'll likely be in the pairk wi' his pals. Whit they get up tae, God alane kens. He's never at home these days.'

But there was no sign of him in the park or in the street. One of his school mates was twisting himself around on the swings. He shrugged. 'Ah dinna ken whaur he is and ah dinna care,' he said. He had not seen him for days.

Back home Mam was angry. Tammy came in from the door step where she'd been playing. 'Ah'm stairving,' she complained.

'We're waiting on Elvis,' she snapped. 'Whaur the hell is he, on his birthday too.'

'Ah ken whaur he'll be,' Tammy began but Mam never heard because just at that moment Elvis pitched up.

'Finally,' said Mam swallowing down her anger. 'Whaur in the name o' the wee man ha'e you been?' But she never waited for an answer. 'Sit in at the table. It's burger butties for your dinner.'

Nobody spoke much for everyone's mouth was full of roll and burger, two each for the boys washed down with Irn Brew. Then Elvis asked, 'Whaur's Jura?'

'If you'd been here ye'd have kent,' Mam said tartly but she told him all the same.

'The vet says she'd been poisoned,' Hughie said. 'Did you give her anything bad to eat?'

'Me?' said Elvis. 'I never.' As he spoke colour flooded into his cheeks and Hughie wondered was he was lying. He pushed back his chair.

'What did you give her?' He was livid with rage. 'Go on. What was it you gave her?'

'I never!' he blustered. 'Mam tell him I never.'

'Of course he didn't!' Mam declared. 'Why would he? Where would he get poison? Stop bullying yer brother, Hughie.'

Hughie was about to protest but she was having none of it. 'Hud yer wheesht the both o' yous. Who's for ice cream?'

'Me me me!' cried Tammy. Hughie glared but said nothing while Elvis just looked his usual self, shifty. Meanwhile the choc ices went down a treat.

After dinner Mam shooed them into the room. She was dead excited and so was Tammy who bounced round them with the kitten in her arms. Hughie knew about the guitar. He kinda understood when Elvis moaned about Hughie getting the dog and Tammy the kitten. He was pleased that Elvis was to get what he wanted and Mam was probably right. Why would he ever want to hurt Jura?

Elvis tore open the parcel.

'Well?' said Mam expectantly, 'do you like it, then?'

'It's for kids. It's a kid's toy,' Elvis said flatly.

'But it'll still play,' she said hopefully.

He picked it up and twanged it. The sound was discordant and tinny so he discarded it on the settee and turned to Tammy's chocolate. His face visibly brightened. 'Thanks Tam,' he told her. Then he unwrapped the Superman book. 'Ace,' he said.

'Can I get a read of it when you've done?' Tammy asked.

'Sure,' he said. 'Take it.' He paused and looked round as if he expected more. 'If that's it, then, I'll be off.'

'Me too,' said Tammy but Mam was having none of it.

'You'll bide whaur ye are. None of yous move. See and watch them, Hughie.'

They all knew she was off to get the cake, Lomond Bakery's best and so it was. It had a wee net and a wee figure of a footballer and a sticker with Happy Birthday stuck on top with eleven blue candles.

'Right then,' said Mam starting the song in a quavery throaty voice. 'Happy birthday to you...' Tammy and Hughie joined in. Hughie watched

Elvis bend to blow out the candles. For a moment his face was all lit up and naked somehow. He's my wee brother, Hughie thought with a pang, this is his big day and he's no' happy.

As soon as the cake was cut and eaten, Elvis said. 'I'll need to be off, then.'

'Need to be off?' Mam said sharply. 'Why? Whaur are ye going?'

But Elvis was already gone. 'Whaur the hell? Would you credit that? What's he up to then?' said Mam, fed up.

'I know,' said Tammy, 'but it's a secret.'

Mam gripped her shoulders. 'You've no business keeping secrets from me,' she said grimly, so Tammy clyped.

'He's off to Mr Mair. He's learning him to play the guitar, a proper guitar.'

They all looked at the discarded toy on the settee.

Agnes Mackenzie

She thought about the fall. She had not done anything stupid like forget her stick or trip over her slippers. She had switched on the bedside light, crossed the room, clear-headed, stick in hand, to go to the loo at about midnight when the window had been blown open by a sudden gust of wind so strong that, like a fist in the small of her back, it had blown her over, or so, in retrospect, it had seemed. She had cut her head on the edge of a chair and there had been rather a lot of blood. The next thing she remembered was Rachel bending over her, calling her back to consciousness. In her adjoining room Rachel had heard a bang that had woken her up.

'It was the wind,' Agnes had explained after Rachel had helped her up and staunched the bleeding with a towel.

'What wind?' Rachel had asked, and immediately gone on to suggest she ring for an ambulance.

'Good gracious me, why?' Agnes had exclaimed. 'I'm perfectly all right,' and she was. Her hip ached a little but that was nothing new. She had not been damaged as far as she could tell, except for that small cut above her left eyebrow. 'Don't you dare put me back in hospital,' she declared. 'I've had enough of hospitals.'

Instead Rachel had sent for the night manager who brought along a first-aid box. While Rachel dressed the wound, he examined the window carefully, but could find nothing wrong with it, apart from a loose catch. He and Rachel reluctantly agreed that, as the bleeding had stopped, they would wait till morning before calling for medical aid. Rachel had added not quite threateningly as he left the room, 'We'll let Alastair make the decision.'

Agnes had thereafter enjoyed an excellent night's sleep and awakened better than she expected; well, in fact.

She was aware that neither Rachel nor the manager had believed her story about the wind. They obviously thought she was going gaga, but she knew what she had heard, remembered clearly what she had felt. That fist in her back.

As a result there had been two bonuses, the lesser reflected in the bill. She had not been charged for the room. The main bonus however was Alastair. He had driven down from Queich the following afternoon and stayed with them for the next three days. He and Rachel had spent time together leaving Jayjay in the hotel nursery in the care of an excellent young woman while she sat in the sun or ambled around the extensive garden with several other retired guests whose company she found congenial. Alastair seemed more like himself, thank heavens.

They had got back the previous evening and this morning she felt the better for the break. She glanced at the carriage clock on the mantelpiece. Nearly ten and Annie was still clattering about in the kitchen. The windows were wide open, the August sun was warm. She felt surprisingly contented.

'That's me done,' said Annie poking her head round the drawing room door.

'Come in, Annie.' The woman looked tired, she thought, in need of a holiday herself. That would probably be out of the question with three children. 'What about a sit down and a cup of coffee?' she found herself saying. 'Have you time?'

Annie looked surprised but she didn't say no. At Agnes' bidding, she sat down gingerly on the edge of a high-backed, beaded chair.

Agnes bent down carefully to switch on the electric kettle. She had all the ingredients at hand. 'How do you like it?' she asked, 'sugar and milk?'

'Aye,' said Annie accepting the proffered cup and saucer. (Agnes didn't approve of mugs which she associated with builders' tea-breaks.) 'Thanks,' she added accepting a rich tea biscuit on a matching plate. 'Did you have a good time away, then?' she asked a little awkwardly.

'I did, indeed,' said Agnes who was beginning almost to enjoy herself. 'The weather was wonderful. I got quite brown.' She held out her hands for inspection.

That's nice,' said Anne, taking a tentative sip of her coffee.

'What about you?' Agnes asked graciously. 'How are the children? Are they enjoying the school holidays?'

'Och well,' she shrugged 'Ye ken how it is wi' kids. There's aye something.'

'Like what, Annie? Remind me.'

It all came pouring out. Hughie's dog had been poisoned. It had nearly died. 'The vet let her home yesterday but she's no' hersel' yet and Hughie's worried sick.'

'What a shame,' Agnes commiserated. 'At least it wasn't one of the children.'

'Try telling Hughie that,' Annie retorted. 'Jura's means more to him than a' the rest o' us put together.'

'What about little ... Tamsin, isn't it?'

'Tammy's fine. She's got her cat to keep. Daft on him, she is. He's a bonny wee creature right enough.'

'Quite a menagerie at home, then,' said Agnes.' What about your other boy?' Agnes could not bring herself to say 'Elvis'. It was on a par with 'Jason' as a name. Totally unsuitable. 'Does he have a pet too?'

Annie frowned. 'Elvis? If only,' she said leaning forward to put down the coffee cup. Agnes tried to follow the garbled tale. She gathered that he had had a birthday, got a new guitar which was rubbish. He preferred spending his time with 'they Mairs doon the street even on his birthday. I'm at my wits end wi' the laddie, so I am. He'll no' do a thing I tell 'im.'

The Mairs? She hardly knew them. 'What's the appeal, I wonder?'

'Seemingly he's learning him the guitar, a proper guitar no' a toy from Woollies,' she explained bitterly.

'I don't really know the Mairs,' said Agnes, 'but maybe, if you're worried you should have a word with Mrs Mair?'

'Elvis'd kill me. The sun shines out of their...them both.'

Agnes was tempted to tell her not to worry but she was remembering Gordon Maclardy's somewhat outspoken remarks about his next door neighbour and felt uneasy. Instead she said, 'School starts again soon, doesn't it?'

'I wish. Two weeks today.' She rose to her feet. 'Ta, Mrs Mackenzie. I'll need to be off. Do you want any messages frae the shop?'

Agnes thanked her and shook her head.

With Annie gone and Rachel at nursery with Jayjay, she decided it was high time she ventured out by herself. She went to the loo, put on a jacket though there was no need for the sun was warm, grasped her stick and set off.

Outside it was so bright that she took a moment to adjust to the daylight. She felt strong and confident as she opened the front gate and ventured on to the street. Good! No dog mess so far. She passed Rhoda's bungalow and then the Mairs. Strange really how they did not know each other better considering they lived only two doors apart. At three years the Mairs were

184

virtual newcomers, though. She glanced curiously into their garden as she passed but there was no one around. Then she came to Greenyards. She wondered how Gordon was. It was obvious that he was going behind, not quite past it yet but she could see that Bertie was worried. Should she call in?

She was aware that a wind had risen, not cold but lively enough to coax her gently down the street. It really was a glorious day.

Maryam was on the counter. Good. Since Jayjay's christening she had grown to like the dark gel. She never seemed to get bored like so many young folk these days nor was she impatient as Rhoda could sometimes be. Agnes put a pint of milk, a macaroni cheese for supper and a packet of Tiny Tots for the baby in her basket and waited in the short queue for her turn.

With no one else waiting behind her, she found herself telling the gel all about the holiday. 'The weather was kind and the food exceptional. I feel so much better in spite of - .' She paused not wanting to bore the gel who was checking her purchases through the till, but Maryam looked up, her eyes dark and soft and above all interested so she told her. 'I think I had a little turn.'

There she had said it, the words she had not allowed herself to contemplate, something she would have denied strongly to anyone else if challenged.

'I'm listening,' the gel said quietly.

So she told her about how the wind had blown the window open, how it had felt like a fist in the small of her back and pushed her over so that she knocked herself out and cut her head.

'That must have been scary,' Maryam said.

'The truth is that there was no wind that night. Rachel and the hotel manager both looked at me as if I had lost the plot. And there was nothing much wrong with the window.'

'Wind sometimes has a mind of its own.'

Agnes hardly heard her. Her own mind had a will of its own and now it was focussed. Something about the gel's dark eyes drew the next words out of her. 'I think I might have had a TIA.' There she had said it, the words that she did not want to think.

'Why don't you tell your doctor just to make sure?'

She thought about Maryam's advice as she walked home. The last thing she wanted to do was go to the doctor and if Rachel or Alastair had made the suggestion she would have told them not to fuss. But the gel was right. She should go and see Doctor Jill.

She noticed that the wind had changed again. It had blown her down the street and now it was enabling her home and yet the leaves on the lime trees that lined the street never so much as quivered. Yes indeed, the wind had a mind of its own.

Outside the Mairs' bungalow it dropped. Now there was no enabling breeze about her shoulders, no more pressure on her back but she hardly noticed. Well, why not? She asked herself. She remembered when the last time she had tried without success to be friendly to Mrs Mair, she had promised to renew her invitation. She had always meant to keep that promise but what with her hip and everything she had never got round to it. She glanced at her watch. It was not too late, only half past eleven. She unlatched the front gate, walked past the flowering annuals that made a pretty show. She rang the bell. That ridiculous chime echoed through the house to be followed by a furious yapping. She had forgotten about the dog. After a few seconds Mrs Mair opened the door carrying the little creature.

'Good morning,' Agnes began brightly. 'What a beautiful day, isn't it?'

She was confidently expecting her little gingery haired neighbour to reply in like manner and issue an invitation to come in, sit down, have some coffee. It never happened, so she tried again. 'It's quite ridiculous how close we live and yet we never see each other. I was wondering if you and your son - Colin isn't it? - would care to come in for a drink one evening? I'll ask my son and his wife to join us.'

'I'm not sure...' she began. Agnes could see she was groping for an excuse to say no. 'He's so busy with his book these days. I'd need to ask him.'

'Do,' she said peering over the woman's shoulder but the house seemed empty. 'If he's too busy why not come yourself? Tea perhaps one afternoon?'

Her reply was to the dog. 'Be quiet Tina!' The little creature had started to yap excitedly at someone passing on the street. 'Tina keeps me so busy.'

Agnes was damned if she was going to include the dog in her invitation. She had done her best. She felt surprisingly angry.

'I understand,' she said but she didn't. Mrs Mair was about to shut the door but Agnes had not finished.

'By the way,' she said loudly. 'Annie Miller who works for me is worried about her son, the one with the odd name.' She forced herself to say it and smile, 'Elvis, would you believe? Seemingly he spends a lot of his time here. She hopes he isn't being a nuisance.

Mrs Mair suddenly came alive. 'Those Miller brats! Ungrateful little so-and-so's, if you ask me. My Colin, at great inconvenience to himself, found one of them a dog, took care of it too would you believe, but does he get any thanks? They're just ignorant, no manners, badly brought up. My Colin has done his best to support them. He likes children, but really the Millers are impossible.'

Her vehemence was upsetting but Agnes too was angry. 'I've always found them to be delightful children.' (That was perhaps going a bit far.) 'Annie has her difficulties but she does a splendid job on the whole.'

'I speak as I find,' Mrs Mair replied coolly.

'I won't keep you then.' Agnes too could do cool. 'Good day to you, Mrs Mair.'

The wind had risen again, slamming the front gate shut behind her. This time it frazzled the lime leaves. In spite of her jacket she was chilled.

She looked back once and sighed. I've done my best, she argued defensively. She was well aware that her best had not been enough.

Mo

'I'll see you for your tea, then? Six o'clock sharp.' Earlier that morning Rhoda had poked her head into the shop to remind him. (She always reminded him.) Her startling auburn head with its smart new bob that curved a little inwards just below her chin was immaculate. He would have liked to compliment her on her hair but you never knew with Rhoda. She might see it as too personal a remark, so he admired her in silence.

He glanced at the clock above the counter and saw that it was ten to two, near the end of his shift. He hoped Maryam would be prompt because he had a committee meeting of the Fife Pictish Society in Kirkcaldy at three and he disliked being late.

With no customers to serve, he crossed the shop to sort the tins. Someone had been playing silly beggars with the soups, Heinz Vegetable stuck in among the Baxter's Chicken Broths. Good old Heinz, he thought. For a time when he had been poorly he had eaten rather a lot of it. Now no longer. Rhoda had seen to that. First, when he had been more or less fit again, it had been Sunday tea, a splendid collation of cold meats, salad, cole slaw (which to be honest he could have done without) and tomatoes with home-made scones and jam to follow. Sunday tea was now a fixture and he was going round on Thursdays which was half-day, too. There was usually a gammon steak or pork chops with veggies and chips or roast tatties. The thought of Rhoda's home-made Victoria sponge for afters made him salivate. What a treat.

Mo was aware that Rhoda liked him. They had always got on well though never at a personal level because before she had had her knee done she had entertained a bidie-in. He was never mentioned but if Rhoda thought no one knew, how wrong she had been. True, no one knew his name. He was a commercial traveller in ladies hosiery who came and went like a rat in the larder, as he had once overheard two of his more gossipy customers repeat. Few saw him as he arrived late in the evening and left early next morning but his car, a black Rover, had been fairly regularly spotted in the street and duly noted and discussed behind the gondolas in the shop. He sometimes wondered if customers thought he had no ears, for they seldom lowered their voices.

That was a good few years ago. Then Rhoda had been forced by her crippling knee problems to retire from her job. With her new knee and re-employment, she had changed and he knew why. She had switched her energies from the traveller and her own health to himself. Did he mind? Not a bit. Though he had found her good intentions more than a little overpowering when he was so poorly himself, recently he had begun distinctly to enjoy the attention, not to mention the food. If the way to a man's heart was through his belly, bring it on.

But did he love her? How could he when all his emotions were centred elsewhere? Sunshine was the light of his life, his reason for getting up in the morning, for, or so he believed, his recovery from cancer. But his love for Sunshine had an aura of mystery about it. Sometimes he fantasised about asking her to be his wife, but his imagination baulked at the idea of all that marriage implied. Though he adored her, he did not want to sleep with her. That was a thought too far, almost sacrilege

The door opened and he turned his attention to his customers. The usual craic about the weather, state of health, local news followed as he worked the till and found the right change. He was mildly aware that one of Annie's children had joined the short line of customers waiting to be served and was eyeing the sweetie shelf which stood in full sight of the counter staff for obvious reasons. Over the years Mo had learned to keep a close eye on the penny tray.

At three minutes to two Maryam appeared through the office door and his eyes rested and stayed on her. How pretty she looked, he thought with an ache of yearning. Her mane of hair held back by combs was like a dark waterfall down her back and even clad in her simple green uniform overall she looked to him more like an exotic goddess than a shop assistant. He was only dimly aware of the child at the counter. He had a bag of toffees in his hand.

'Hi, Elvis,' Maryam said, stepping forward to take Mo's place at the counter. 'Is it just the toffees today?'

Mo was about to slip away when to his surprise he saw Elvis leave the counter with the packet of toffees clutched in his hand and make for the door. The boy looked wretched he thought, scared, so what was he playing at?

'Hey, son,' he called out. 'I think you've forgotten something.'

Elvis stopped and turned round. He had a strange grin on his face and Mo could see he was trembling.

'No,' he said defiantly.' Ah' takin' them. Ye canna stop me.'

'Funny ha-ha,' Mo called out. 'Joke's over, son. If you've got twenty-five pence we'll say no more. If not, you'll need to put them back pronto.'

'The lad stood his ground... 'I'm no payin' a penny and I'm no' putting them back either. You'll need to get the polis,' he shouted.

Mo was about to get angry when Maryam whispered, 'Leave him to me. You get off.'

Mo was torn. Part of him wanted to control the situation even if it meant calling in the police, part of him wanted to see how Maryam would deal with the lad but mostly he wanted to get changed and off to his meeting. He hesitated.

As she eased her way past him he was aware that somewhere a wind had arisen, too warm to have come from the freezing cabinets. The shop door can't have been closed properly, perhaps a summer storm.

Maryam had reached the lad. Instead of holding out her hand for the sweets, to Mo's surprise she put her arms around him and held him close. He buried his head in her breast and burst into tears.

Over the sobbing child's head she told Mo, 'I'll manage fine. Your meeting won't wait.'

Nor it would and of course she could manage. He waited to see if all was well and listened as the lad sobbed, 'Jist get me the polis. I dinna want to go back there.'

With her arm still round his shoulder she reassured him. You don't need the police, Elvis. Will you stay with me? Mr Bruden's got to go out and I could do with a hand.'

He nodded. She led him back to the counter where she quietly replaced the toffees.

It was not something he really approved of, a child behind the counter but he found himself saying, 'If you want the job, lad, there's a spare apron in the back.'

Elvis wiped his eyes on the sleeve of his T-shirt and nodded.

Mo left them to it. Outside he noticed there was no wind whatsoever. It was as still as a landscape.

Maryam

She did not have to ask Elvis what was wrong. His little shadow, usually so bright, crouched behind his back, dull, scared and silent. She set him to tidy the sweetie counter which was maybe a mistake but clearly pleased both him and his shadow.

'I'll no' tak' ony,' he assured her. 'Trust me.'

She smiled. 'I know you won't. If you make a good go of it, maybe I'll buy you the toffees.'

'I can get them masel',' he said proudly pulling a paper pound note out of the pocket of his jeans.

She was not going to ask him how he got it for she already guessed but he told her all the same. 'I got it for my birthday.'

She knew it was not exactly the truth. They both looked at it clutched in his hot little hand. Suddenly he pushed it into hers. 'Keep it,' he told her, not looking at her. 'I dinna want it.'

Maryam tucked it back into his pocket. 'It's yours, Elvis. Maybe you'll need it.'

The shop door opened and Lettie came in with Geordie at her side.

'I see you've got a new assistant,' Lettie said looking kindly at Elvis' small figure swathed in a green cotton apron. 'Maybe you could give Mr Burns a hand while I settle my account?'

Elvis nodded so he and Geordie armed with a wire basket and Lettie's shopping list did the round of the shelves.

Lettie's appearance told her all. The bowed shoulders had straightened a little, her expression had brightened. Her shadow exuded a new and strange contentment as if she had cast away the carapace of grief and anger.

'Will I get out the sherry decanter this evening?' Lettie asked after the usual chit-chat about the weather and her health.

'That would be nice,' Maryam said a little wistfully. Lately she had come to enjoy her visits to Miss Anderson but as to that evening, she could not be sure. Her own shadow was silent.

Geordie set the basket on the counter and turned to thank Elvis. 'One good deed deserves another,' he said. 'Am I no' correct?' He appealed first to Lettie and then to Maryam. 'What aboot a sweetie then?'

Elvis nodded and chose a sherbet sucker which he put into his pocket. Geordie reached into his trousers and pulled out a handful of change. Meanwhile his shadow lifted its head and grew taller. It was a while since Geordie had been able to buy sweeties for himself let alone anyone else.

Lettie put her purse away and Geordie lifted her shopping bag.

It was a busy afternoon as customers came and left. In the ice cream cabinet, the ice lollies had sold out. Elvis arranged then rearranged the confectionary, fetched and carried, took the banter and accumulated a hoard of pennies from kindly locals.

Rachel blew in. 'Can't stop,' She plonked milk and a packet of chocolate fingers on the counter. 'Don't know who likes them most, mother or Jayjay.' She laughed. 'I've got them both in the car. We're picking up Alastair from his office and going to St Andrews for a picnic. See you soon. Loads to tell you.' At the door she turned. 'Love you,' she called and blew her a kiss.

As Rachel left, Maryam felt the warm summer air turn cold. Colin Mair had come in. Elvis had seen him first. He darted round to the safe side of the counter and stood beside Maryam who put a protective hand on his small, trembling shoulder. Colin Mair's shadow followed him but it was not like the others. Detached it stayed by the door, a dark and watchful sentinel.

Colin came straight to the counter. 'My papers please,' he said with his eyes on Elvis. Usually he had some snide comment to make on their non-delivery, the need for Bruden's to find proper staff, but today his attention was on the child. 'So this is where you've got to,' he said in that weird nasal American twang. 'Do you realise I've been waiting for - he looked at his watch – 'exactly one hour and seventeen minutes.'

Elvis muttered something unintelligible that might have been 'sorry' and pressed closer to Maryam.

'Well, well, we'll say no more about it.' He picked up his papers. 'Coming?' he spoke directly to the child.

To her surprise Elvis detached himself from her arm and was about to obey.

'Take off that ridiculous apron then,' he told him impatiently.

Elvis did not look at her as he fumbled with the ties.

'Elvis is helping me this afternoon,' she said but the words sounded lame to her own ears.

Colin paused with his back to her. 'It's entirely up to him. He's the one who wants to learn guitar.' Without turning round he left the shop.

Elvis handed her the apron. 'I'll need to go,' he said without looking at her.

'You don't have to do anything you don't want, Elvis,' she told him quietly, her hand on his shoulder.

'Aye, I do,' he said pulling away from her. 'He's got me a proper grown-up guitar,' he shouted back at her from the door. 'We're going on a picnic.'

'Wait!' she called out after him. 'You forgot your toffees.'

Picking up a packet from the sweet stand she left the counter to catch him but he had already gone. She called out but there was no sign of him in

Church Street. She turned to go back to the counter and there in front of her stood the lone shadow immoveable as a brick wall, unsmiling, cold as sin. She remembered the first time she had seen it, alone and watchful behind the carousel, then again outside the glass door of St Serf's and she was scared, not so much for herself but for the child. Our Mother listen.

She was still standing there, rooted by fear and indecision when the door behind her opened and Dr Jill came in. 'God, it's cold in here!' she exclaimed. 'How do you stand it, Maryam?'

The shadow vanished. As if Our Mother had spoken, Maryam knew what she had to do. 'Please take what you want,' she told her customer. Meanwhile she adjusted the Yale snib. 'Can you close the door behind you? I have to go.'

She did not wait for Doctor Jill's reaction. Outside there was no sign of either Elvis or Mr Mair or indeed his shadow in the street.

She needed to find the child.

Annie

When Elvis was not back at six o'clock Annie was angry. This was happening too often. She had already sent Hughie and Tammy out to look for him.

'I'm not going to them Mairs,' Hughie protested. He had already scoured the streets on his bike with Jura in tow.

'Nor me,' Tammy echoed. She had already searched the park and the school playground.

By seven in an agony of anxiety, Annie had run down the street to Greenyards and rung the bell urgently. Mr Bertie would know what to do. When after a while he appeared hastily swallowing his supper, she stumbled over the words. 'It's Elvis. I canna find him. He's no' been home all day and I'm worried sick.'

'Come in, Annie. Tell me exactly what's happened.' Bertie sounded so kind that the tears spurted out of her eyes. He listened patiently to her broken explanations.

'He can't have gone far. Have you checked with his school chums? He'll probably be playing somewhere and forgotten the time.'

'Maybe Mr Gordon's seen him - ye ken? Over the fence with them Mairs?'

Bertie was quiet for a moment, then he said, 'I'll go and ask him. We're in the middle of dinner.'

She would have followed him into the dining room but he stopped her firmly. 'You wait here, Annie. I won't be long.'

She could not keep still. As soon as he'd gone she ran up the stairs and into the spare room, where Mr Gordon had once said he could see into the Mairs' back garden. She peered anxiously out of the window, but the next door backyard was empty except for the little dog which was chasing a passing insect in a pool of late summer sunshine.

She was down before Mr Bertie returned. 'Seemingly all has been quiet today next door. What makes you think Elvis might be there?'

'Mr Mair has a guitar, and Elvis is daft on pop music. Tammy says he goes there to learn to play. I've tellt him he's no' allowed but when does he ever listen to me? I might as well be speaking to the birds,' she said wretchedly.

Mr Bertie put a firm hand on her shoulder. 'Have you spoken to the Mairs yet, Annie?'

She shook her head. 'Likely they'd tell me,' she said bitterly. 'Will I get the polis?'

'I'm sure there's a perfectly reasonable explanation. Let's go and ask the Mairs first.' He reached for his jacket in the lobby. 'I'll come with you and if Elvis is not there we can call the police.'

'Thanks, thank you Mr Bertie, sir,' she said, the tears starting afresh at such kindness. The truth was that she had been scared to go there herself, scared for what she might hear but not find.

They hurried down the drive and into the front garden of the bungalow. The bell chimed its usual chirpy tune. After a while Mrs Mair came to the door.

'Sorry to trouble you, Mrs Mair,' Mr Bertie said, all politeness. 'Might we have a word with your son?'

Mrs Mair looked surprised. 'My Colin?' She spoke to Mr Bertie, ignoring Annie. 'He's out. Can I take a message?'

Mr Bertie was not ready to give up yet. 'Are you expecting him back soon?'

She shook her head. 'He's due to go to one of those writers' dinners in Edinburgh. I don't expect him back till late.' Suddenly she smiled coyly and took a step closer to them. 'I know I'm not supposed to say anything but I have to tell someone or bust. My Colin's up for an award for his latest book. It's being presented tonight.'

'Really?' said Mr Bertie coolly. 'You must be very proud.' He paused. 'You haven't by any chance seen Elvis, Mrs Miller's son, have you?'

Mrs Mair turned her head to look briefly at Annie for the first time. 'Have you lost him?' she asked coldly. 'Why does that not surprise me? You should keep your children in better control, Mrs Miller.'

193

Annie felt her face warm up both with anger and shame. Before she could think of a suitable retort, Mr Bertie replied, 'Does that mean you have - or haven't seen the boy?'

'No, I have not,' she replied firmly.

'Then we'll trouble you no further.' He took Annie's arm and turned away from the door. 'Come along, Annie. It's time we contacted the police.'

He was as good as his word. As soon as they got back to Greenyards he rang the police who asked to speak to Annie. Their advice was to go straight home and wait for them there.

Mr Bertie had to take her arm, she was that shaky. 'I'll need to look for him. He's maybe fallen or been run over. He never looks to cross the street. He'll be lying hurt somewhere or mebbe he's in hospital, unconscious - .' She could not go on. She would have fallen but for Mr Bertie's strong arm. 'I canna just go home.'

'You heard what the police said, Annie. It's best you be there when Elvis comes back. Maybe he's there already and hungry for his tea.'

Maybe he was. The thought quickened her step, but he was not there. Tammy clutching her kitten and Hughie with Jura were waiting for her by the door, but no Elvis.

A thought occurred to her. 'Maybe he's at the shop. I'll just run down and check.' Why hadn't she thought of that sooner? 'Sunshine is awful fond of the laddie. Likely he'll be there.'

Mr Bertie held fast to her arm. 'Now Annie, you know what the police said. You need to be here.'

'I checked the shop, Ma,' said Hughie in a small voice.

'Aye but he might be there the noo. I need to speak to Sunshine. Mebbe she kens.'

'She's no' there,' Hughie said. 'The shop was shut.'

'And it'll still be shut,' said Mr Bertie firmly. 'It's nearly eight o' clock.'

Reluctantly she allowed Mr Bertie to take her inside and settle her on the settee. Her body clenched and she rocked back and forth, moaning. Tammy came and sat beside her. She was only dimly aware of her daughter. All she could think of was Elvis lying on the roadside struck dead by a careless car.

Minutes later the police car drew up and two officers, a man and a young woman both in full uniform knocked, opened the door and came into the sitting room. They showed their badges, and told their names, Constable Turner and Constable Shirley. They were very kind. Constable Shirley sent Tammy off to make her mam a cup of tea and took her place on the settee.

They asked a lot of questions, wrote a lot of notes, asked for photos - fortunately there was that school photo taken last year - and listened very carefully to everything she told them. No she had not seen Elvis since breakfast. Yes he had slept in his bed last night. Yes he had eaten cornflakes for his breakfast. No he had not come home for his dinner, or so Hughie confirmed. She had been out working over the dinner hour. Questions, questions, more questions. They questioned the children too. Who were his mates, where did he play, how did he get on at school, was he ever bullied?

It was Tammy who first mentioned the Mairs. 'He's learning the guitar off him,' she said a little defiantly. 'He got Hughie his dog, Jura.'

At the mention of her name, the dog who was lurking close to Hughie lifted her head and wagged her tail.

Both the officers were listening intently. Constable Turner paused, his pencil raised. 'And you are happy with this arrangement, Mrs Miller?'

'No,' she said miserably. 'But once Elvis' mind's made up there's no stopping him.'

'I hate him,' said Hughie suddenly.

'Why is that, then?' Constable Thom asked. 'Seems a nice dog you've got there.'

Hughie was silent while they all waited. Then he shrugged. 'I just do,' was all he said.

Mr Bertie interrupted at this moment. 'Elvis is not there. Mrs Miller and I called at the house about half an hour ago and Mrs Mair told us that her son is attending a dinner in Edinburgh tonight.'

Annie sat there in an agony of impatience. 'Why are you no' oot looking for him?' she cried. 'Sitting in here'll no' find him.'

Part of her was amazed at herself ticking off the polis but they were not bothered. The lass was nice. 'We need to know everything you can tell us about Elvis so that we can find him. Try not to worry, Mrs Miller. We need you to stay here.'

Mr Bertie saw them to the door. They were questioning him too but she never heard what they were saying. Waves of worry washed over her anew. She could not touch the tea that Tammy had brought in. It sat there the milk congealing on the surface. All she could see was her wee Elvis lying in a gutter, crying for her like he did when he was a baby, and she was not there to hold him.

Bertie

His first thought was that maybe Gordon had been right all along. It was obvious that the two police officers had also remembered his outburst on their previous visit to Greenyards.

When he had escorted them to Annie's door, Constable Turner had asked if his brother was at home. 'Perhaps we could have a word?'

'Of course. Let me just say goodbye to Mrs Miller.'

'As quick as you can, sir.' His tone had altered from reassuring, as they had both been to Annie, to official.

Annie had been reluctant to let him go.

'The sooner we all start looking the quicker Elvis will be back where he belongs,' he told her kindly and wished he could believe it. 'I'll be back.'

The officers insisted that he accompany them in their car though the walk down Church Street was barely two minutes.

Gordon having finished his meal was washing up. 'Where did you disappear to? Your chop's back in the oven.' He turned to find the two police officers standing there with Bertie. His mouth opened and his hand holding the tea-towel trembled. Bertie knew exactly what he was thinking. Gordon may have lost the plot in many ways and much of his short term memory but that accident so long ago was indelibly printed on his brain. He hastened to reassure him.

'You remember Constable Turner and Constable Shirley?' he said slowly, 'they're wondering if you've seen or heard anything of Elvis - you remember Annie's son?'

'Annie's son?' he repeated vaguely and then he brightened. 'That boy who delivers the papers, what's his name - the one with the dog?'

Constable Shirley took over the conversation. 'Perhaps we could sit down somewhere and you can tell us all you remember, sir?'

'Of course,' said Bertie and let them through to the sitting room. 'You too, Gordon,' he added as Gordon had turned back to his dishes. Reluctantly he folded the tea towel on its rail and followed.

Gordon was in one of his vaguer moods. He could not remember having seen or heard Elvis over the hedge next door because he had completely forgotten who Elvis was. He remembered the boy drowned in the loch however and the whole story came out again about how Colin Mair had kept him in a shed on the shore and taken him out in a boat and drowned him. The two officers were very patient considering they had heard it all before. 'He has boys next door, you know,' he told them confidingly. 'I see them and I hear them. The paper boy. He was there with his dog.'

'When was the last time you saw or heard Mr and Mrs Mair entertaining anyone in their garden, sir?'

'Not her,' he said quickly. 'I never see her.'

'Mr Mair then,' she pressed. 'Was it today maybe or perhaps yesterday?'

He looked vague, then turned to Bertie. 'You told me you could hear someone playing a guitar,' Bertie reminded him encouragingly.

'A guitar,' Gordon said vaguely. 'Did I? It can't have been much good or I would have remembered.'

After a few more questions which only revealed the extent of Gordon's memory loss, the officers rose to go. Bertie escorted them to the door. Constable Turner thanked him. 'You've been a great help, sir. We'll be in touch.'

From the hall behind them Gordon had the last word. 'That man, what's his name next door, is a paedophile.'

If they heard him, the two officers paid no attention. Bertie watched them walk down the drive and waited. Sure enough a moment or two later they reappeared outside the Mairs' bungalow ringing that ridiculous doorbell.

He ate his remaining chop now somewhat dried up, but he could not touch the sago pudding, 'frogspawn' as Gordon called it and normally one of his favourite desserts. 'I'm going out,' he told his brother who was back in the living room seated in his favourite chair shuffling through the already crumpled Telegraph.

Gordon looked up through his spectacles. 'Out? At this time of night? Where?'

'I need to see Annie.' No point in saying why.

'Annie?' Gordon said vaguely. 'Who's she?' But he wasn't really interested.

'I won't be long.'

Outside in the dusky street there were three police cars. Already, he thought with a stab of anxiety. He remembered that the poor lad had been missing since breakfast. He was stopped and questioned as he approached Annie's door. After explaining his business and giving his name he was allowed in.

Annie was sitting in the same position as when he had last seen her, the tea beside her stone cold by now. The whey-faced children had not yet eaten so he took them both back into the kitchenette. He could have questioned them about Elvis but he knew they needed to let a little normality back into their lives so he kept the conversation bland. 'Beans on toast do you?' he asked cheerfully. The cupboards were not exactly overflowing with choice. 'What about French toast?'

That drew a smidgeon of interest from Tammy. 'What's French toast?' she asked, clutching her wriggling kitten.

'Next door to heaven,' he told her as he cracked two eggs, whisked them with some milk, found three slices of white bread, soaked them and heated the unwashed frying pan which was already coated with a layer of bacon fat While they sizzled he ran out of platitudes so he turned his attention to Jura who was watching the procedure with interest. 'Is she after her share of the beans do you think?' It was meant to be a joke.

'I'll feed her,' Hughie said defensively. 'No one gets to feed her but me.'

'Of course,' said Bertie calmly. 'She's your dog.'

'Aye she is,' said Hughie. 'She was poisoned once. I'll no' let it happen again.'

'Poisoned?' Bertie, surprised but glad of a conversational lead. 'How did that happen?'

'It was something she ate,' he said. 'Poisonous stuff. She nearly died.'

'What sort of poisonous stuff?' Bertie asked.

'Seed things the vet said. Lab - something.'

'Laburnum?'

'Aye,' said Hughie, 'that was it. Laburnum' He pronounced it carefully, syllable by syllable.

Bertie whistled. 'When did that happen?'

'A week or two past. So nobody gets to feed my Jura but me.'

There were laburnum trees in practically every garden in the street. Some of them overhung the pavement. The yellow flowers had been spectacularly good that year. Bertie supposed the seeds must be ripening by now. A dog could, he supposed, pick up a seed in the street though it sounded unlikely.

'Poor Jura,' he said.

'Somebody did it and I want to know who,' he said truculently.

'It wasna me,' Tammy piped up quickly. She was still clutching her kitten in her arms.

'I never said it was,' Hughie snapped.

Before the argument could turn into a row, it was time to change the subject. 'Food's ready,' he told them. 'Can you find me three plates, Hugh?'

He forked the three fragrant slices on to the plates, added the beans and said to the little girl, 'It's your job to get your mother to eat something. Do you think you can do that, Tammy?'

She put down the cat, picked up the two plates and carried them carefully through to the living room. Once started, the children devoured their food and even Annie managed a mouthful or two.

Suddenly she put down her knife and fork and pushed her plate away. 'Does Sunshine ken?'

'Maryam?' he asked. 'I don't know, Annie.'

'Sunshine'll mebbe know where my wee boy is gone. I'll need to tell her.' She got to her feet a bit shakily. 'I'll no' be long,' she told the children.

Remembering just how helpful Maryam had been that first time when Gordon had gone AWOL Bertie realised that this was not a bad idea. Maryam would know better than he how to help the poor woman. 'No, Annie. You need to stay here. Remember what the police said? I'll go and find Maryam.'

The street lights had come on as he crossed the road and walked the few metres to the Old Rectory. He noted that the laburnum tree that overhung the drive was indeed beginning to seed but quite how the contents of one of the pods had found its way to the dog's gut was somewhat of a mystery. However he had no time to think of the dog. The building was in darkness except for a light in one of the upstairs windows. He found his way to the back entrance to the top flat; peered at the two names above the two bells found the right one and pressed it.

The young woman who answered was wearing a blue uniform and he remembered that Maryam's flat mate was a nurse. 'I'm afraid she's not here,' she told him politely.' I don't suppose she'll be long. Can I help?'

Bertie, who only knew Sheena Macleod by sight, explained somewhat incoherently what had happened, how devastated Annie was, how there was nothing much in the kitchen for the children to eat and that she had asked for Maryam, why he dared not leave his brother for too long on his own.

'I know Annie and I know the children. I'll go over if you like. Just give me a sec to find my keys.'

A minute or two later she was as good as her word. She was carrying a plastic bag containing a tub of Walls ice cream, biscuits and a hand of bananas.

'I've left a note for Maryam. Let's go.' she said briskly.

He could have kissed her.

Mo

He woke with a start. He could hear a roaring sound and thought it a low aeroplane. The open window sash was rattling. A photograph frame containing a picture of his mother as a young girl which had stood on the dressing table for as long as he could remember crashed to the floor. 'What the devil!' he exclaimed aloud as he realised that a gale was blowing hard. He struggled out of bed to close the window, peered at his alarm clock and saw that it was nearly two o'clock in the morning.

He padded barefoot into the kitchen to make himself a cup of tea. A crash outside warned him that a roof tile had been blown on to the pavement outside. He peered out of the window. The trees in the street were thrashing and the wind howling. A dustbin lid had blown off and was rolling down the pavement.

Then he remembered little Elvis. He hoped to God he was not out in this. When the police had called to ask if he had seen the lad, he had spent the rest of the evening scouring the streets with Geordie and several other concerned neighbours and it had been perfectly calm then. At eleven pm the police cars had left the street and he had gone to bed.

For a moment he considered going out again. The loch would be a sight in this wind. He hoped that no one was out late fishing. As he lay awake listening to the wind, he thought of Maryam, visualised her the last time he had seen her in the shop with that disturbed kid, how she had calmed him down and taken him behind the counter. The meeting had gone on for longer than usual and afterwards he had gone to the pub with a couple of mates and had got home to find the shop closed and locked. He had glanced at his watch and saw that right enough it was just after six. Maryam must have shut up sharp. He hoped that the Old Rectory trees were safe in this wind... A few minutes later, or so it seemed, the alarm clock had woken him and it was morning. The wind had gone.

Although Maryam was scheduled for the morning shift, he decided to get up early and go down, open up and suss out the damage from the night squall. The street was a mess of scattered leaves and broken branches. He swept up the remains of three of his roof tiles and made a mental note to ring the local building contractor at around eight o'clock.

He was still outside at the back when he noticed the Menzies van drawn up on the High Street. The driver gave Mo a wave. 'I just left the papers on the counter. What happened here?'

Mo went over to speak to him. 'What are the roads like? There'll likely be a lot of trees down after all that wind.'

'What wind?' the guy asked. 'There was no wind in Kirkcaldy.'

'I've lost three tiles and a dustbin lid and just look at the street.'

The guy whistled. 'Right enough,' he said.' Must have been a freak storm. Where's Maryam this morning? Slept in maybe?'

Sure enough the shop was still empty. The counter too was surprisingly untidy. Maryam was usually so punctilious about tidying up last thing. With a vague feeling of anxiety he found the paper bundles and began sort them. By eight o'clock he was distinctly worried. He had not been expecting Hughie this morning with all that upset at home but it was unlike Maryam to be so late. Something must have happened. Before opening he decided to ring her. There was no answer. The line was dead. That nurse she lived with, Sheena, would be at work. Maryam was probably on her way.

His attention was distracted by the various delivery vans and early customers so that for the next hour he had not a moment to worry about Maryam. All the craic was about the lost child and the wind damage. There was talk about getting up a search party when the door opened and Hughie stood there grinning at them. To a man, they turned to stare at him.

'Elvis is back,' he declared proudly. 'The polis brought him in a car wi' flashin' lights.'

After a wee moment of stunned silence the questions came. 'Whaur was he?' 'How is he?' 'That's guid news!' 'Wait till I tell the wife.' Some of them clapped him on the shoulder.

'He's fine,' he replied to them, or 'I dinna ken,' as he worked his way to the counter. 'Will I do the papers, then?' he asked Mo who was as curious as the others.

When the last of the early rush was over, Mo helped him fill the satchel. 'Are you sure you're not needed at home?'

'Elvis is just fine,' he repeated. Then Mo remembered; it was pay day for Hughie and he had a wee smile to himself.

'So are you going to tell me what really happened, Hughie?' he asked as the lad shouldered the satchel.

'A lady found him in Kirkcaldy. He was in her shed so she took him in and gave him bacon and twa eggs and phoned the polis. That's all I ken.'

'How did he get to Kirkcaldy?' Mo asked.

'By bus,' Hughie told him. It was hard work this questioning. Had he run away? 'Ah dinna ken,' and maybe he was speaking the truth.

Mo usually put his wages into an envelope but with all that had happened overnight he had forgotten. Instead he went to the till and took out a five pound note. 'A wee bit extra, laddie, because you didn't have to work today.' The boy looked so surprised and grateful that Mo went to the freezer cabinet and took out two boxes of fish fingers.' Give these to your mother and be sure to tell her we're happy Elvis is home and safe.'

Hughie thanked him. 'Whaur's Sunshine?' he asked before he left.

Yes indeed, where was Sunshine? It was past nine o'clock. Rachel and her stroller backed into the shop to be joined by a couple of other young mums and several customers. He was glad to be able to share the good news of Elvis and then it was all talk of the damage done by the wind.

They all had spoken at once. 'We've a tree down at the back and that new bit of paling's gone,' Rachel told him. 'I wonder what it's like at the Old Rectory. They've got so many trees.'

As soon as they'd gone off to nursery school and the other customers had been served, he went through to the office to ring Maryam again. The line was still dead. It would likely be a tree, Mo thought, but he was distinctly worried. His next phone call was to Rhoda. After he had told her about Elvis and she had reassured him that, apart from a couple of broken panes in her small but productive greenhouse, she had suffered no serious damage, he asked her if she could forward her afternoon shift to this morning. 'Maryam hasn't turned up and the Old Rectory telephone line must be down. I need to check up that she's okay.'

'Give me ten till I put my face on,' Rhoda had said obligingly.

Half an hour later she turned up looking smart and fresh already clad in her overall and a drench of perfume to take over the counter. He hurried up the street passing the time of day with Geordie who was out there clearing the debris, cheerful and busy.

As he had thought, there were two trees down at the back of the Old Rectory. The branches of a third had caught on to the telephone line. The grounds were a devastation of broken branches and leaves.

He rang the bell to the top flat but there was no answer. He was about to try the lower flat bell when the door opened and an elderly man with a very white, very even set of dentures stood there.

'That was quick work,' he said. 'I only rang BT about an hour ago. Our line's down.'

When Mo explained he was not from BT, the man interrupted him. 'I know who you are!' He exclaimed. 'It's Mr Bruden from the corner shop, am I right?' He held out his hand. 'I've been meaning to introduce myself. I was in the retail business myself, a newsagent in Corstorphine. Name's Peter MacGregor. Moved here just under a month ago. I know one of your employees, the young lassie who lives in the top flat.'

Of course. Maryam had mentioned that incomers recently retired from Edinburgh had leased the lower flat. After they had shaken hands, Mo explained his reason for calling, Macgregor was helpful. 'I certainly haven't seen Maryam this morning or yesterday either come to think of it. I know Sheena is at work. I keep a key for them. Give me a moment to find it for you and we'll check she's okay.'

At the foot of the stairs he handed the key to Mo. 'My knee's giving me gip this morning. Would you mind going up on your own?'

He inserted the key in the lock of the door at the top of the staircase. 'Maryam?' he called out tentatively. 'Sheena?' but the house was silent. He would have liked to leave rather than poke into these rooms feeling like an intruder but knew that he would not rest easy until he had checked the flat properly.

The sitting room was a comfortable clutter of magazines, cushions, a half-finished embroidered owl in an oval wooden frame with a work basket spilling out wool on the sofa, the furnishings sparse but adequate with a large framed mirror above the mantelpiece which was a adorned with half a dozen porcelain or brass owls and a litter of postcards and photographs.

Sheena's bedroom was easily distinguishable by the freshly ironed uniform that hung from a coat-hanger on the back of the door. This was a girlie room, the double bed strewn with cuddly toys, including a large plush owl. Clothes hung on a rail or were draped over the chairs, a rack of shoes protruded from an open cupboard door. Mo glanced round for long enough to satisfy himself that there was no one there.

Maryam's bedroom was reflection of herself, smaller, tidier, a back bedroom which faced north and thus should have been darker but which seemed, like herself, suffused with light. One thing made him smile. The single bed, neatly made up, was covered with a garish counterpane depicting images of the four Beatles in cheerful poses sporting guitars and wide grins. Mo reckoned it was probably a leftover from her teenage years. He noticed a small porcelain owl on the dressing table together with a scented candle and a few pots and jars of cosmetics. Both girls, it seemed, were into owls.

Lastly he looked into the kitchen. There was a note on the small table propped up against a fancy pepper pot.

7 30 am Sorry to have missed you. Spent the night with poor Annie. Hope to God they find Elvis soon. Won't disturb your beauty sleep! Back at the usual time. Love S.

Now he was really worried. Where was Sunshine? He thought of ringing the police but first he had better check with Miss Anderson. Perhaps the old lady had taken a turn and she was looking after her. Then he would ring Sheena.

Macgregor was waiting for him at the foot of the stairs. 'No joy?' he asked.

Mo shook his head and refused the offer of coffee. 'Miss Anderson may know something,' he told him and, as soon as he could get away, hurried down the street.

Lettie summoned him inside. Geordie was already there. Neither of them had seen Maryam since yesterday afternoon. Then Lettie said, 'I've been meaning to have a word with you, Mr Bruden. Now seems the right time.'

Mo, worried and itching to escape, was not prepared for the ticking off that was to follow. 'Have you not noticed how tired and down Maryam has been lately? Don't you ever give her time off? She's clearly exhausted. She needs a rest and a good holiday. I can't think how you haven't noticed.'

Before he could answer Geordie stuck his oar in. 'Mebbe you don't know how she managed when you were off sick. I ken Rhoda was there but it was Sunshine who ran the show. She's no' been hersel' lately.'

Of course Mo had noticed. Now he realised that he should have insisted that she have a proper fully paid-up holiday but he had not wanted to let her go even for a week. That was the truth of it. He felt ashamed.

'She only had to ask,' he replied as if to excuse himself.

'You only had to offer,' Lettie replied tartly.

'Now we need to find her,' Geordie said sensibly.

Mo left as quickly as he could escape. As soon as he got back to the office he rang Ninewells Hospital. Staff Nurse Macleod was busy. 'This is important,' Mo told the recipient. 'Can you get a message to her to ring this number?'

As soon as Rhoda was free he told her what Lettie had said and asked her what she thought he should do. She was immediately supportive, more so than he could have hoped. 'Ring the police,' she advised. 'I expect she's fine but old Lettie's quite right, she's not been herself lately and it can't hurt to alert the authorities. She needs finding.'

Rachel

She had not had the chance to talk properly to Maryam since their lunch together in the Cosy Café. Indeed she had hardly seen her apart from brief exchanges over the counter before nursery school or on errands for her mother-in-law when the shop had other customers. Maryam was always so busy. The last time she had seen her was when she had Elvis in tow. Elvis...thank God the little boy was home and safe. What wonderful news. She too had been involved to a small extent in the search for him. Even Al had taken the car and driven up into the Ochils at his mother's suggestion. Rachel had been a little surprised at the strength of Agnes' concern. She had obviously grown genuinely fond of Annie. She herself had searched the tool-shed and checked the leaf-strewn shrubbery. Her favourite ceanothus bush had been upturned by that sudden gale in the night.

But Elvis was safely home, according to Hughie. She knew that Maryam was expected in the shop. Leaving Jayjay at nursery, she called into Bruden's again hoping she had by now turned up so that they could arrange to have lunch together and have that chat. But Maryam was still not there. Rhoda told her that Mo had gone up to the Old Rectory to find out what had happened. 'He tried phoning but the telephone line's down...Was that all?' she added as Rachel deposited a bag of chocolate eclairs on the counter.

'My mother-in-law's favourite,' she explained. She would try to catch Maryam later.

The street was busier than usual with neighbours clearing their gardens or gossiping at their gates. Everyone had a word to say about the return of the boy and the sudden squawl in the night. For the unpteeenth time her thoughts returned to Al, the incredible change in his behaviour and her surprise when he told her he had made an appointment with Doctor Jack. She had first tried questioning him in Peebles on one of their walks down by the river Tweed but either he wasn't going to tell her or he had genuinely forgotten. It turned out to be the latter.

'It was all very strange. I think I was asleep,' he told her, his forehead creased as he tried to remember. 'Then Maryam was there.'

'Where?' she asked. 'I rang and rang you. Were you in bed?'

'No,' he said. 'I was the kitchen. I must have had the radio on. I never heard a thing. All I remember was sitting in a chair and Maryam standing there. Oh and the window was open and the wind had risen. I suppose I must have fallen asleep.'

She explained that she had rung Maryam in desperation. 'I was so worried about your mother. Maryam was the only person I could think of to find you and tell you what had happened.'

'She did. Then she made me tea. I can't honestly remember much of what she said but either it was her conversation or else she put something in my tea.'

'Maryam would never do that,' she began a little indignantly.

'I was joking,' he said dryly. Al joking? That hadn't happened for as long as she could remember. 'In spite of Mother's fall I felt so much better when she left.'

'I'm glad,' she told him taking his arm. 'I've been so worried about you lately, and so has Mother.'

He was quiet for a while. A moorhen rose up quickly from the river reeds with a splatter of wings. Then he said, 'Sorry Rach. I know I've been a bit down lately. I think maybe I should make an appointment with Doctor Jack. What do you think?'

'Sounds like a good idea.' Not for the first time Rachel remembered the hypnotist.

Since their return from Peebles he had been the old Alastair she had fallen in love with. Now she needed to tell Maryam, find out what really happened that night and there was no time like the present.

205

She was surprised by the amount of wind damage in the Old Rectory garden. Mr Macgregor, the new owner of one of the two ground floor flats, and Geordie Burns were both out clearing the front garden. The laburnum was leaning at a dangerous angle over the drive.

'Your garden is even worse than ours,' she called out to them.

'You should see the back, 'said Mr Macgregor.

When she said she was looking for Maryam, he told her that she was not there. 'Mr Bruden checked about an hour ago. We would have noticed if she'd come back.'

'And she's no' with Miss A,' Geordie added. 'Likely she's away shopping in Dundee wi' her chum,' he suggested helpfully.

Unlikely, Rachel thought, with a stab of anxiety.

Mother was delighted with the sweets and even more so at the news about Elvis. 'Do you think he ran away?' she asked.

Rachel shrugged. 'I suppose he must have done. Why else would he be in Kirkcaldy?'

'Unless he was abducted.'

'I imagine we'll hear in due course.'

They were both silent for a moment no doubt thinking the same thing. Annie had not been exactly quiet about her dislike of Elvis' visits to the Mairs. She had also heard that Hughie refused to deliver their papers. Smoke and fire.

'At least he's home,' Al's mother said eventually. 'Thank God for that.'

Actually, Rachel thought, I'm more worried about Maryam.

Annie

As soon as she had seen his small familiar figure on the doorstep Annie was possessed by a clutch of emotions; joy, relief, and rage. Of these the greatest was anger. Adrenalin wakened every part of her tired body. There he stood between two strange police officers as if butter wouldn't melt. She sprang into action. Seizing him by his upper arm she skelped him hard on his bottom three times. 'Whaur hiv' ye been, ye tinker? Did ye no' ken we were sick with worry? Did ye no' spare a thocht for yer family? No' you. Ye're bad, so you are!'

Before the police could interfere he was in her arms and she was squeezing the life out of him. Her tears were flowing and she was murmuring inarticulate endearments into his unbrushed, red hair. Inside the house with an arm still round his shoulders she was able eventually to thank the two officers and belatedly offer them a cup of tea. They refused politely and left

206

after explaining that two local colleagues would be round directly to question the lad.

As soon as they had gone she let rip all over again alternately hugging and berating him. Hughie with Jura and Tammy clutching her kitten stood by, open-mouthed and silent. Holding him away from her she had a good look at him. He was grubby and there were dark splodges under his green eyes. He looked small and pale and frightened. Finally she gave him a chance to speak. 'So are ye gonna tell us what happened, pet?'

Two large tears tumbled down his cheeks. At which moment Jura went up to him climbed on to the settee and licked his face. Clutching the dog he spoke through his tears. 'I'm sorry, Mammy. I'm right sorry.'

'So you bloody well should be.' Relief softened the harsh words. 'What happened? Did someone take you? Was it thon man?' She could not bring herself to give him a name.

He shook his head vigorously. 'I jist took the bus.'

'Why?'

'Jist because.'

'Because what?' Hughie interrupted curiously.

Before he could answer the police were at the door again. This time it was that nice woman, called Shirley. She had already forgotten the other officer's name. Poor wee Elvis looked scared. She was immediately protective of him.

'Let's all sit down,' said the lassie. Her blonde hair escaped in wisps from under her uniform cap. 'We're all so glad you're home safe and sound, Elvis. Is it all right if we ask you a few questions?'

He nodded still crouching under the protection of Annie's arm as she sat in a corner of the settee. The two police officers took the remaining chairs.

To begin with the questioning was kind. What was the tool-shed like? Had it been cold? How had he got there. Had he been frightened? Then they got harder. She listened as eagerly as they did for as yet she had no idea why wee Elvis had ended up in a garden shed for that's all he had told them. He had taken the bus and paid for it with his own money. Then in Kirkcaldy he had got lost.

'You're a big boy Elvis, eleven is it? You've got a tongue in your head. Could you not have asked the way to the bus stop?'

He looked down at his trainers and muttered something that turned out to be that he had spent all his change from that pound note on ice-cream and chips. There were a lot of gaps in his story that needed filling. She wanted to scream at them, 'It's that Mair man you should be asking.'

Eventually Constable Turner changed his tone and asked in a stern voice, 'Where did you get the pound note from Elvis?'

'I didna steal it,' he said defensively. 'I earned it proper.'

'How did you earn it, laddie?' the constable continued kindly enough but there was steel in his tone.

'I did some jobs for people.'

'Who were those people?'

'Sunshine in the shop.'

'Did you do any wee jobs for anyone else, Elvis?' When he didn't answer Constable Shirley continued, 'Mrs Mair? Maybe Mr Mair?'

'Aye her,' he said with a quick upward glance and then at his feet again.

'You see, Elvis, what we're wondering is this. Who were you running away from?'

'Naebody,' he replied quickly.

Too quickly, Annie thought and before either of the officers could continue she interrupted. 'Tell them about them Mairs, Elvis. You're never away from them folk.'

'It wasna they. He was learning me guitar. He got me a guitar of my own. He was gonna give it me when I'd learned. A proper guitar,' he added with a brief look at his mother.

'That was very generous of him,' Constable Shirley remarked. 'What did you have to do, Elvis, in return?'

'Naething,' he replied.

'Nothing at all?' Constable Turner pressed him.

He was silent for a moment then he said, 'Sometimes she'd get me to take the wee doggie oot the back and play wi' him.'

Annie could keep silent no longer. 'So it was me ye were running away frae, was it?'

He could not look at her. After a while he told them, 'Ah jist wanted to see Kirkcaldy.'

And that was it. Though the two policeman asked him what bus he had taken, (the 3 50 from Queich bus station, he still had the ticket in his pocket to prove it} who sat beside him (nobody) and what was the name of the chip shop (he couldn't remember) he had nothing new to add. They all guessed there was more he could have told them but that was all he was saying.

Eventually the officers stood up. 'That'll be all for the present, Mrs Miller.' Then he turned to Elvis and read the riot act. 'You have behaved very badly, lad, not only have you caused your mother and your brother and sister a great deal of grief, you have wasted police time. Next time you have a mind to run away, think on this. It'll not be a night in a shed; it'll be a night in a cell. Do you understand?'

Too overcome to speak, Elvis nodded and the officers took their leave.

As soon as they had gone, Annie took Elvis by the arm. 'Now I want the truth. What really happened?'

'The wummin was nice. She gied me twa eggs and twa bits o' bacon.'

That was all he ever said.

Bertie

It was Hughie delivering the paper a good hour later than usual that told him Elvis was back. 'The polis brought him in a car wi' flashin' lights.'

'Is he all right?' Bertie asked.

Hughie explained briefly where he had been found and that he was fine. 'I'll need to be away,' he said. 'Me and Jura's late already.'

'Off you go then. I'll shut the gate.'

'Thanks Mr Maclardy.'

Bertie watched him mount his bike; go peddling up the street with the dog at his wheels. Some good news at last. Several of the neighbours were still out clearing the pavements by their gates, all of them eager to talk about the freak storm and hear about Elvis.

After walking round his own garden and estimating the damage, nothing serious, he went indoors to find Gordon. Often these days he didn't appear until around eleven o'clock and Bertie did not rouse him. At least he was safe in his bed.

He had still not come downstairs. Bertie glanced at his watch. Just after eleven. He'd give him another hour. At the same time he felt uneasy. The house seemed unusually quiet - empty - so somewhat resentfully he stumped upstairs.

Gordon was not in his room, nor was he anywhere in the house. Bertie sighed impatiently. What a day to go walkabout. Where was he this time? Last time he had been picked up three miles down the Perth road. He could be anywhere. With a heavy sigh he phoned the police station. The duty officer who knew him well these days promised to alert the traffic team.

He decided to begin his search in the High Street starting at Bruden's where Rhoda assured him she had not seen him that morning. Glancing in every shop including the unlikely florist on the near side of the road, he eventually reached the loch and turned left. Though Gordon had not visited the hut lately as far as Bertie knew, he could well have gone there.

Negotiating the loch-side, he stepped over branches and fallen trees and other debris scattered on the shore by the gale. It was an unnaturally calm morning, cloudy and windless, and the air by the water was humid and thick with midges. Bertie swatted them impatiently in his anxiety. He was also mildly angry with Elvis. If he had run away from home on a whim, he deserved some sort of punishment for causing Annie such anguish. Remembering his days as a schoolmaster, the boy's behaviour would have merited a beating. He suspected however that there was more to it than Hughie had told him and his thoughts returned with increasing impatience to Gordon.

He was there, of course, sitting on a boulder staring at something in his hand. At the same time Bertie exclaimed, 'What the dickens!' The ramshackle hut had gone.

'What's happened here?' he said somewhat needlessly for it was fairly obvious. Indeed he could see wooden staves floating on the calm surface of the loch. 'It must have been the wind,' he remarked somewhat unnecessarily

'What?' said Gordon looking up curiously. 'Oh hello, Bertie. There used to be a shed here. Someone's removed it. Good job too. It was a bad place. Bad things happened here.'

'Nobody took it away, Gordon.' Bertie tried to keep the irritation out of his voice. 'It was that gale last night. Look you can see bits of it floating in the water.'

Gordon looked up briefly then turned back to what he held in his hand.

'What have you got there?'

Gordon held out his hand. 'I found it there.' He pointed to the scuffed and dirty wooden planks that had formed the floor of the hut.

Bertie took the small silver ornament and turned it over in his hands. It was a Celtic equal-armed cross with the sun circle linking its shafts on a thin silver chain. He recognised it at once. Maryam wore it, or one very like it. He knew about the hijab on Fridays and the silver cross worn permanently but prominently on Sundays in memory of her mother for Mo had told him. The clasp of the chain was broken. 'This belongs to Maryam,' he said.' We need to find her to return it to her.'

'I will.' Gordon held out his hand but instead Bertie pushed it into his own pocket. He was afraid Gordon might lose it in the same way as he lost himself.

'Let's go and look for her,' he said wondering what on earth had happened and why he felt so alarmed. What had she been doing here? That chain, surely it could not have broken of its own accord?

Sheena

She had been busy with a patient when an auxiliary had murmured that the ward sister wanted a word as soon as she was free. Ten minutes later she found Wilma at the nurses' station. 'What is it now?' she wanted to say. The ward was busy as usual and she had three more patients to deal with soonest. She was tired having slept fitfully on Annie's uncomfortable settee, disturbed by the storm. 'A Mr Maurice Bruden called. He left his number. Seemingly it's urgent,' she said briskly. Wilma, always brisk and to the point with never a wasted word, picked up the scribble she had made during the phone call. 'Something to do with a Maryam Patel. Your flat mate, isn't she?'

Maryam, mo charaidh, she thought as she dialled the shop number, what has happened to you now, a' ghraidh Rhoda answered. 'Mr Bruden's out.' She explained briefly what had happened. 'He's already rung the police.'

The police? But why? Could it be something to do with the missing child? 'What about the wee boy?' she asked.

Rhoda was blunt as always. 'He's back safe and sound. Seemingly he ran away from home, the wee rascal.'

Thank God for that at least. 'So where's Maryam then?'

'Mo thinks she's maybe had an accident. Something to do with the storm last night.'

'Tell him I'll be back as soon as I can get away.'

An hour later she was driving up the A92. Her mind buzzed with possibilities; that tree down in the garden, the littered lawn. Why hadn't she checked after leaving Annie? Quite possibly Maryam was lying there unnoticed and injured. Thank God Mo had had the sense to ring the police. When she had rung Shamus to tell him what had happened he had promised to come over as soon as he could get away. He tried to tell her that together they would find Maryam which comforted her but did not reassure. She thought of the Maryam she had known since they were five years old, always a little strange with her shadows and prescience. Her grandmother had called it second sight – 'the gift that is an affliction' – she had said with a pitying shake of her head. Celtic to her core, Sheena too believed in the second sight. What had her friend 'seen' lately to make her so distant, preoccupied, nervy, almost as if she were afraid, but afraid of what? The child's disappearance? Then it occurred to her who - apart from herself and Mo of course who cared a little too much in her opinion - who would give a kelpie's mane about her? No parents, some relatives in Pakistan, she supposed. Her - Sheena's - whole life and thoughts were centred around her boy-friend and their forthcoming wedding. Maryam had promised to be her bridesmaid. The sudden pressure of tears blurred her ceanothus eyes at the pathos of the situation. She could have been a better friend. Taking her hand off the wheel for a moment she groped for a tissue.

She went straight to the Old Rectory. Perhaps by some miracle Maryam had come home and she would find her there in the kitchen putting together one of her brilliant curries, all smiles and warmth.

It was Peter who saw her car draw up in the small communal car-park on the far side of the flats. Obviously he had been looking out of her. Peter was always looking out for one or other of them while his wife stayed firmly indoors. After a long day on the ward it could be slightly irritating. On this occasion she was glad to see him.

'No,' he told her. 'She's not back' He explained he had let Mo take their key to look for her. 'I do hope I did the right thing. Mr Bruden was really worried.' She was half inclined to be annoyed, but he was so apologetic that she forgave him.

The moment she had changed out of her uniform the police arrived.

Elvis

'Go straight home,' Sunshine had told him in the sort of voice you obeyed. 'Leave Mr Mair to me. I'll sort it. Run!' So he ran and he had kept on running. But how could he go home knowing what he had done? Not even Sunshine knew what he had done. She might not speak to him again if she knew. Mam might put him out of the house. Waiting to cross a side road off the High Street road he noticed the sign 'Bus Station' and the idea came to him in a flash. He would go away before he could be put out.

There were bus platforms to Perth and Dundee and Inverness and Edinburgh. He had a pound note and a handful of pennies so he couldn't go too far away. He noticed a bus draw in on the nearest stand. He waited and watched. People tumbled out of it and almost immediately more people from the small waiting queue started to climb aboard. Kirkcaldy was good. Kirkcaldy was near but not too near. He could afford it with a bit left over for chips. He joined it.

'Single or return?' the driver asked giving him a quick once-over.

'Single,' he said firmly. How could he ever come back? When he failed to show up that weirdie - he always thought of him as 'that weirdie' - would be round at Mam's to clype on him. He swallowed hard to quell the anguish roused by that one word 'single' and all it implied.

The bus was not that full. He had got a seat by himself. His heart was beating so fast that he thought people might notice. He wished he had brought his navy top with the hood. No one would notice him then. All he had on was his tiger tea shirt with 'Grrr' written on it and his jeans with the grass stains on the knees.

Thirty minutes later after a load of stops the bus drew into a big station where everyone started to leave. He reckoned this must be Kirkcaldy. He got off last. Not knowing what to do or where to go he decided to follow a woman with a bairn who looked a bit like Tammy. She was a right moaning minnie demanding her mam take her to the swings. 'A-richt,' her mam told her wearily, 'but mind only for ten minutes, hen.'

The swing park would do fine for him. Then he would get some chips.

It was a braw place right enough. Lots of swings and two shoots and a maypole and a slidy thing that you clung on to and it took you flying across the ground to the other end. Magic. There were a lot of bairns waiting to get a go. He queued and flew and queued and flew until after a while the other kids all went home and he was the only bairn left. Suddenly he was hungry. Mam would be looking for him. She would send Hughie and Tammy out to find him and she would get cross.

The woman with the lassie had gone long ago. He could see no one to follow so he just walked. Then he smelt it. Fish and chips and his mouth watered. He knew to a penny how much money he had in change from the bus. 30p off a pound note. Plenty left for a fish supper. Maybe tomorrow he could find a wee job.

There was a queue at the chip shop. While he waited he studied the notice board. It was like a school blackboard with the words written in white chalk. A child's portion of fish and chips would cost him 50p. But he was hungry. He could eat a horse and he was thirsty too but that would cost too much. When it was his turn he found himself ordering a large portion of sausage and chips, a can of ginger and a Mars Bar for afters. He thought he was not going to have enough to pay for it, but in the end he got five pence change. Taking the food outside, he stuffed his face and for about ten minutes he was happy. Then of course it hit him. Here he was stuck in Kirkcaldy with no money, no place to sleep, no jacket and no Mam and he was still hungry.

He tried begging. He stood on a street corner and stuck his hand out but he could see two uniformed bobbies on the pavement across the road, so he ran.

After a while he slowed down and just kept walking. No shops now, no tenements and not much traffic. This was a posh area. He noticed the street name - Townend Terrace. If this was the town end he'd better go back. He needed to stay in the town to get a job. He also badly needed to pee.

It was getting dark and he was getting cold. He hugged his arms and looked at the big houses set back in their leafy policies. A gate was open. The house behind it had no lights on and the windows were all shut. He slunk in and had a long pee in the shrubbery.

Still no lights. The house looked empty. He crept down a gravel path at the side of the posh building into the back garden. There was a shed. He hesitated. It looked a bit like thon shed on the loch, but newer. Sheds were bad but he was desperate. Then he noticed this was a brown shed. Bad sheds were green. He crept up close. It had a padlock right enough but the link was not closed. In seconds he slipped it off and opened the door. It was still light enough to see how neat it was. Tools dangled from nails, packets and bottles of gardening stuff were arranged on a surrounding shelf. A mowing machine stood in one corner and a wheel barrow in the other. Several folded deck chairs were stacked just inside the door. He glanced back at the house. No signs of life. He reckoned the owners were away on holiday. If he took out the wheelbarrow he could put up one of the deck chairs in the space. So he did. There were a couple of dusty old sacks folded on the shelf which he wrapped round his shoulders. It would have to do.

Then it hit him; a yearning agony that sent the tears rushing to his eyes. As he thought of his mother and his siblings the tears became sobs. Eventually he slept.

It was the wheelbarrow that gave him away. The woman who was a doctor had got back when it was dark and rose early, seen the wheelbarrow from her kitchen window and found him. She was dead nice. She had taken him into the house, she had held his wrist for a wee while and felt his head and allowed him to use her lavvy. Dead posh it was with a shower and all. While he was in the bathroom, she cooked him two eggs and two bits of bacon and a slice of toast. She had also rung the polis. They were dead nice and all, showed him how to do the nee-naw.

Mam had been cross but she would have been far crosser if she knew what he had really done. Those two local polis, the man and the woman had come round and all of them had been at him with their questions but how could he tell them? If he told them, then the weirdie would tell on him and he'd end up in jail.

So here he was alone at last lying in his bunk bed with Hughie's Beano unread on the pillow. Mam had gone to work, Tammy with her blooming cat was out with her mates and Hughie had gone to the farm with Jura. Two tears filled his eyes and spilled over down his cheeks. More tears came and then there were more sobs but no one to hear him.

As the tears fell so the memories returned. Those guitar lessons. He had kept going because of that new guitar, the one the weirdie had bought in Perth. The weirdie had made it sing. He loved the guitar and he was getting the hang of it but it had cost him. Sometimes the weirdie could be dead nice and the guitar was brilliant but he had had to pay.

'Have you ever been out in a boat, Elvis?' he had asked, nice as pie.

He had shaken his head.

'You're back at school next week, am I right?'

This time he had nodded.

'Well then tomorrow, what say you? Instead of guitar practice, I'll take you out on the loch in a boat and we'll go to the Castle Island for a picnic. Would you like that?'

After a long moment he had nodded again.

'Speak to me, boy.' His voice was all soft and breathy. 'You've got a tongue in your head. Answer me properly.'

But all Elvis' thoughts were focussed on the man's hand. He could see those strong narrow fingers massaging his thigh, squeezing it softly. He watched it move higher.

'Answer.'

'Okay,' he had whispered.

'It speaks! There's a good boy.'

Elvis knew he was not talking about his voice. The hand moved and the breathing grew louder.

'Right then,' he said afterwards. 'Be here by two.'

He nodded.

'This will be out little secret. We wouldn't want anyone to find out what a bad boy you've been, would we? Could be Borstal for you.'

But he hadn't gone, had he? Maryam had stopped him. Told him to run home. Instead he had run all the way to Kirkcaldy and now he was for it.

Every minute he expected the knock to come. That weirdie with his story to tell. Maybe he would just walk in. Maybe he'd come upstairs and... He slipped off his bunk bed and ran down the stairs and snibbed the front door lock. Then on a gasp of terror he ran through to the kitchen and turned the key in the back door.

He hurried back upstairs and pulling the blanket over his head he lay there and hid.

Suddenly he thought of Maryam. Maybe he'd go and see her in the shop later when Mam got back. He felt safe with Maryam.

Chapter Eight

Mo

She'd been gone over a fortnight now. Rumours were rife. Endless discussions, endless interviews with the police, endless searching of every back yard, every shrubbery for miles out of the village, into the barns and and mounds and valleys of the Ochils. Posters everywhere. He himself had organised evening searches but apart from her silver cross found by the Maclardy brothers there was no sign of her anywhere. Off the record, Jimmy Turner reckoned she had ended up in the loch, that the freak storm had blown her away with the shed and deposited her in the water. Divers were still searching. Another theory put her in Pakistan. Somehow she had been captured, shut up in the shed, her cross torn off by irate Muslim relatives and herself secreted back to Pakistan to be forced into an unwanted marriage. Daft. Her step-mother who had been quizzed by the Pakistani police was as upset and concerned as the customers. But what other explanation could there be? A loss of memory perhaps? Wandering the streets of Glasgow - possibly London - alone and unrecognised?

No one had been more diligent in searching than Colin Mair. Mo had never liked the guy but you had to hand it to him. He had done his bit. The Courier had had a field day with him. He had just won some prestigious award for his latest book and there were excerpts and interviews. The Evil Other it was called. Not Queich's cup of tea but, seemingly, it had been rocketing off the shelves. On the prize money and proceeds of excellent sales he and his mother had decided to up sticks and move elsewhere. The bungalow was already on the market. He had heard that they never stayed anywhere longer than two or three years. No real loss to the community, but credit where credit was due, he had signed up for every search.

Now here Mo was sitting in Rhoda's leather armchair, his stomach comfortably distended, an empty glass of beer by his side, once again going over and over the various possibilities.

'You have to admit,' said Rhoda seated opposite him in the twin chintzy chair, 'she was a little strange.'

'How?' he asked sharply. He did not like to hear any criticism of Maryam, nor did he like the way she used the past tense.

'You must know what I mean,' said Rhoda, undeterred. 'It was the way she looked - pardon - looks at you, not at you but sort of behind you almost as if she was seeing someone or something else.'

No use being annoyed with Rhoda because it was true. 'Aye,' he said with a sigh, 'I know what you mean.'

'That nurse friend of hers reckons she had - has - the second sight,' Rhoda speculated.

He nodded, remembering that strange incident with the cows and the Pictish stone. He had always meant to take her to the Queich Stone. He hoped it was not too late. 'Aye,' he agreed 'something like that.'

They were both quiet for a moment then she said, 'What about the shop? We'll manage just the two of us for a wee while, but mebbe you should be thinking of getting someone in. We don't want you ill again.'

It was too soon. 'Surely she'll turn up,' he said but he knew as well as she did that it might never happen.

'There's a local woman I know working at Safeway in Perth that would come at the drop of a hat if the hours were right. Would you like me to sound her out?'

He sighed. 'Mebbe,' he said reluctantly. 'I'll think about it.'

But it would not be the same. Already the shop was duller, the work harder and becoming a bit of a chore.

He should go. It was getting late and he had to get up early but it was comfortable here. It occurred to him it would be nice not to have to go home ever.

'I'll make us a fresh cup of tea,' she said rising to her feet. 'A wee bit of shortbread to go with it?'

'Go on, then,' he said weakly.

Eventually he left. His own house felt stuffy and there was a distinct odour of the bacon butty he had made for his lunch.

Next morning he let Annie in as usual. 'No word?' she asked as she asked every morning. He would shake his head.

'How're the bairns?' he would ask while he was sorting the papers for Hughie and she would say 'fine' and get on with her work. This morning he was more specific. 'How's Elvis doing?'

She propped the mop up in the bucket and turned to answer him. 'He's right quiet these days. Good as gold. Never needs a second telling. I reckon that night in Kirkcaldy brought him to his senses and the polis scared the daylights oot o' him,' she told him but there was no pride in her tone and no joy in her eyes.

'At least he's home and safe.'

'Aye,' she agreed,' but it's no' natural. Elvis was aye a naughty, noisy laddie. Now it's like he's turned into a wee angel.'

'Maybe he's missing Maryam.' He noticed he had stopped calling her Sunshine.

'Aye,' she agreed vaguely, 'mebbe... but there's something he's no' telling us.'

He looked up from the papers. 'Something to do with Maryam?'

She took a step closer. 'I thought it was that Mister Mair, but he's been as nice as pie. Gave Elvis a braw guitar. Jist left it on the door step wi' a yellow ribbon tied round it and a wee note.'

'That's nice,' he said perfunctorily. It was hard to get too worked up about a kid who had caused so much trouble, not with Maryam gone.

'Aye it was. I read it when I found the guitar. Just one line. 'For Elvis, a quick learner. Keep it up.'

'Elvis must have been pleased.'

She shrugged. 'There's no tellin' wi' Elvis these days.'

'I see the Mair bungalow is up for sale.'

'Aye,' she said. 'Good riddance if you ask me,' she added under her breath.

Though inclined to agree, he kept his opinion to himself.

Annie left. Hughie came in for the papers. Deliveries arrived. The busy morning routine continued. The early birds all had their comments and questions regarding Maryam but maybe not so many as yesterday. Colin Mair's success and removal from the village took equal place. 'A dark horse, thon.' 'Aye, who'd ever ken the wee mannie'd hit the jackpot.' 'Och well, good luck to him, I say.' Familiar faces, familiar cracks, but somehow the pleasure had gone out of it all.

Rachel Mackenzie summed it up for him and indeed for all the other young mums on their way to nursery. 'The street's not the same without Maryam.' Then she added half turning to include her friends, 'We were thinking that maybe we should have a little ceremony to think of her, sort of to say thank you?'

Eva took over. 'In the church hall or maybe here in the shop. What do you think?'

He did not know what to think. In some ways the idea appalled him. Had she really gone? It had not yet properly sunk in. 'Do you not think it's a wee bit soon to be planning a memorial?'

Rachel said quickly, 'We weren't thinking of it as a memorial, more of a well-wishing party. We would all hold candles and think of her and have some cake and hope that she was safe.'

It was a nice idea. 'I tell you what,' he said, 'I'll ask the customers. See what they think and of course you can have it here.' But oh - the finality of it.

The morning seemed endless. During a lull he made himself a cup of coffee in the office and brought it through to the counter. Usually he resisted the temptation to bite into one one of the Lomond Bakery iced doughnuts, but today somehow the sweet smell sent the saliva rushing to his mouth.

The door clacked and Bertie Maclardy came in. 'Nothing new I suppose?' He picked up a bottle of milk.

'How's your brother?' Mo asked at the same time. Gordon's illness was evident to all these days.

Bertie sighed. 'Still convinced Mair is mixed up with Maryam's disappearance.'

'The police considered his alibi to be watertight.' Mo laughed a little bitterly. 'No disputing it, is there, with his face all over the press at that dinner.'

Bertie reached in his shopping bag. 'I picked up a copy of his book in Perth yesterday. Thought you'd be interested.'

He was. Wiping his hands on his overall - the doughnut had been sticky - he took the hardback from Bertie. The cover was black with the author's name and title in shiny silver writing. The small image of a man, head bowed and turned away as he strode across the black paper was followed by his mirror image staring straight out at the reader, half-smiling, sinister. 'Any good?' Mo asked turning it over in his hands to look at the blurb.

'It's a page-turner for sure. Been done before, though. Reminded me a bit of Jekyll and Hyde but nastier. Reckons that evil is a separate entity that can take over any of us, a shadowy image that can attach or detach itself at will. Far-fetched but well-written. I can see how it won that award.'

Mo returned it. 'Don't much care for thrillers, but thanks all the same.' He rarely read anything other than Pictish journals and related themes. 'I hear the Mairs are leaving.'

'He's already left on some book tour. The furniture van is there right now. I had a brief word with his mother at the door.'

'Where are they going?' It all seemed mighty suspicious to Mo.

'Seemingly the move's been planned awhile. She mentioned Edinburgh, a flat in the New Town.'

'Weird folk.'

'Takes all sorts.'

He remembered Rachel Mackenzie's suggestion and put it to Bertie.

'I'm in favour,' he agreed immediately. 'She was a very special lass.'

'Aye,' he said, 'she was.' Everyone including himself said 'was' now, he noticed.

The morning passed. Just before twelve, Lettie came in.

'No Geordie this morning?' Mo asked when she came to the counter.

'He's still tidying his gardens of all that storm debris.' Both Geordie and Lettie referred to the gardens whose grass he mowed and whose weeds he plucked as if they belonged to him.

'That'll keep him out of mischief.'

'I thought I'd get him a treat for his afternoon tea,' she said eyeing the bakery gondola.' What would you recommend?'

'No contest,' he said moving round from the counter to serve her. 'Iced doughnuts any day of the week.'

She thanked him. Once again he marvelled at the change in Miss Anderson. Gone was the querulous old woman who constantly complained or derided.

'By the way, Miss Anderson,' he said as she prepared to leave. 'What would you say to a wee ceremony to remember Maryam?' It had turned into a memorial already in his mind. 'Mrs Mackenzie junior thought the customers might like it.'

'A splendid idea,' said Lettie. 'I wouldn't miss it for the world.' At the door she turned. 'Maryam's all right you know.'

He didn't know but he heard her out.

'She has a very strong faith. She is one of the special people in this world.'

He was touched. 'She is, isn't she,' he agreed, emphasising the verb.

Rhoda was there at two sharp. They discussed shop business for a few moments then he remembered. If they were to have a 'do' for Sunshine he needed her on board.

Like himself she wondered if it were too soon but in the end she had become almost enthusiastic. 'We'll have it here of course,' she said. 'It'll be a crush and we'll have to borrow some chairs for the oldies but we'll manage fine.'

''That's me for offsksi then,' he told her a few minutes later having removed his apron and checked the office.

Then the idea came to him. 'I was thinking,' he said (The idea had just come to him) 'Would you care to come out for your dinner with me this evening? Queich Hotel maybe?'

She pretended to think about it but he could see she was pleased. What on earth had made him do that, he wondered, but as he climbed the stair to his flat he found he was smiling. He had the feeling that Sunshine - she was Sunshine again - would approve.

PART TWO

2018

October

Hughie

He strode down the steep brae, two dogs bounding ahead of him. The air was cool and still, the bracken withering, the heather browned, and there was a faint smell of wood smoke rising from a distant cottage. The neighbours were having a bonfire. His flock was doing nicely; he had lost only two lambs this season and the rest were doing fine, fattening up well. Should fetch a decent price. The dogs had discovered a new rabbit hole and were sniffing round it excitedly but rabbits were not much of a problem these days. He remembered how in the old days Rob used to go mad at the sight of them. A curlew rose from a thicket of blaeberry, its warning call echoing and re-echoing through the hill behind him just at it had done then. His saviour. Once again he remembered. The dogs were at the very place he would not go. Though the hill was his, the sheep were his and the dogs were his, there was still one place on his land that he avoided, one place that he would never own, still recognisable after all these years. He called the dogs in a voice they had learned to obey.

Almost immediately he saw the car; a massive beast taking up the whole of the narrow rutted track that led from the main road to the farm - he would have to do something about the lane soon - a silver Merc. Trust Elvis, he thought with the glint of a smile. Always the best for Elvis. But who was he to complain? He would not be here striding his hill with a wife, sons and old Chrissie snug in the extended cottage a field below him, if it were not for Elvis.

A small surge of excitement quickened his step. Mostly birthdays raised little emotion in Hughie, especially his own, but tomorrow he would be fifty and Elvis and Tammy with Queich friends would all be at the farm - Foulis Farm as it was officially called these days to old Chrissie's pride - to celebrate.

Shona had arranged it with the help of his sons, their partners and his wee grandson - or maybe the hindrance of the wee laddie - who was a terrible two year old. Funny old world it was these days. Only the older of his two lads was married; the other called his girl friend his partner. 'Bidie-in' Mam would have said disapprovingly. Fleetingly he thought of Annie who had died of cancer a few years back. He wished she could have been coming as well.

He left his boots at the back door. Shona came into the kitchen all smiles. 'That's your brother arrived,' she said a little breathlessly. She was still in awe of Elvis. Not that he called himself Elvis these days. You couldn't be a top recording guitarist with your own world-famous number one band and call yourself Elvis. To the world he was the creator of 'Fergus and The Fifers', which was a bit odd considering he was the only Fife man among them. The Fifers were in fact from Australia where Elvis also had a home and a ranch called Queich in the hands of a manager where he usually spent his scant free time between gigs.

'Get a move on,' said Shona as he eased on his house slippers. There were still jobs that needed doing outside but they would have to wait.

Elvis looked tired. He got to his feet and held out his hand, 'Great to see you, mate. How're you doing, old man?' clapping his brother on the shoulder.

'Me too,' cried the wee laddie pushing his way between the brothers.

Hughie bent to pick him up. 'This is wee Bobby,' he said with pride. 'Meet your Uncle Elvis. Are you going to behave yourself, laddie?'

'No I'm no'.' The wee boy wriggled in his arms so he let him go. Shona and the lassies were passing round cups of tea. His younger son, who had just arrived from Perth where he worked in a distillery, came in the door with a bottle of malt. 'Put that stuff away and have a proper dram,' he insisted, but Elvis waved the whisky away with a joke and Hughie remembered. His brother had spent a year of his life in some posh rehab centre in Sydney for addiction. Hughie too refused the whisky. 'Maybe later,' he told his son.

So an hour passed of laughter and banter. Hughie for the most part kept quiet as he watched his brother charm his wife, flatter the girls, intrigue his sons and produce presents for them all, bottles of Ozzy wine for the boys and perfume for the girls and a pretty pashmina for Chrissie who was loud in her appreciation.

Once again he wondered how the green-eyed, whey-faced, cheeky, wee, ginger laddie, the withdrawn, driven teenager who left home as soon as he could get out and who had finally triumphed in a world Hughie knew nothing about, had turned into this confident, wealthy and now ageing pop star. Surprisingly ageing. While his figure was as slim as his nephews, his hair now golden and more plentiful than Hughie remembered and, unlike his own, without a hint of grey; his check shirt and jeans immaculate while his crocodile slip-on shoes must have cost a packet, he looked older than his forty-eight years. His face was already a network of fine lines. Hughie called to mind a school project where the teacher had beaten a sycamore leaf with a hair brush until all that remained was a skeleton of tiny threads. Elvis' success had cost him.

After a while Hughie slipped out murmuring he had the beasts to see to while the womenfolk prepared the evening meal. At the back door he was changing back into his boots when Elvis joined him.

Though the hill farm concentrated on sheep Hughie kept half a dozen cows for the milk products and Shona a couple of chicken runs because she loved them. The cows needed to be brought in from the lower field these nights and would soon be in the byre for the winter.

Hughie looked doubtfully at his brother's shoes. 'It's right mucky round the back. There's wellies if you're coming.'

The craic between them was mostly farm business. Elvis questioned and inspected and commented. 'You could do with a new byre, mate, that's for sure and Shona needs some decent chicken runs. Those were old when Chrissie ran the yard.' Hughie listened, demurred and for the umpteenth time wondered why. Elvis' generous financial contributions had made it possible for them to stay on in the hill farm. Without his brother's support, the small farm would not have been viable these days in spite of Shona's teaching job at St Serf's Primary. Elvis had also made it possible for the boys to be properly educated, Joe at the Edinburgh University where he had studied law, was presently working in Dunfermline but hoped to be taken on as a partner at Mackenzie and Macintyre (Foote was only a distant memory) and Robert, who worked at the Perth distillery, a degree in Business Studies from Glasgow. Without Elvis' support, their careers would have been unthinkable. Tammy too was set up in a nice wee bungalow in Kirkcaldy which was just as well as her man had lost his job as a rooster in the North Sea. Though Hughie had often questioned Elvis as to why he had been and continued to be so generous, he would laugh and reply evasively,' What else would I do with my ill-gotten gains?'

True he had no family and apart from some well-publicised flings not even a bidie-in. In the privacy of their marriage bed Shona would whisper, 'Do you think he's gay?'

'Don't ask me,' Hughie would reply honestly for truthfully he did not know any more than she did.

'Not that it matters,' Shona would add hastily to which there was no real reply.

That night round the laden tea table when the girls were all questioned out and Elvis to their joy had spilled the beans about the other celebrities he knew and wee Bobby was safely tucked up in his cot, the craic turned inevitably to Annie and the old days. Shona and the kids listened with interest as the brothers talked of life in Queich as they had known it as children, the houses where Annie had worked.

Queich had grown since those days with two new private housing estates on the periphery of the village. The corner shop had gone. It now housed a vet and his partner whom Hughie had got to know well over the past decade.

'What happened to Mo Bruden?' Elvis asked. Shona told him that he had married Rhoda. 'He passed on; it would be about five years ago.' His had been one of the largest funerals Hughie could remember. Rhoda, now into her nineties, had moved into a care home where he or Shona tried to visit her at least once a month.

The Maclardy brothers too had long gone. Rumour had it they were not brothers but lovers which had scandalised some at the time. 'Greenyards is now a posh B and B,' Shona added, 'run by incomers.'

'Your mam worked for the Mackenzies at Lochview, didn't she?' his daughter-in-law, Sylvie remarked.

'Aye, the old lady,' Hughie answered. 'She left her two hundred quid in her will.'

'Heard any more about the partnership?' Shona asked Joe.

He shook his head. 'I really hope he gets it,' his wife, Sylvie added. 'We like Jayjay and Janet Mackenzie a lot.'

Inevitably the conversation turned to Maryam. It was still a mystery in Queich that had entered the land of legend, the tale of the storm that had blown away the shop girl.

All the old theories were brought out, re-examined and rejected yet again. Shona nudged Hughie in the ribs.' This one was in love with her,' she teased him.

That old chestnut. 'I've never loved anyone but you, sweetheart,' he replied, as he always replied.

'Sunshine, he called her. You are my Sunshine...'she began to sing.

He shook his head good-temperedly.

'Come off it, Dad, of course you were in love with her,' his eldest teased.

'I reckon the whole village was in love with her, eh Elvis?'

'I guess so,' was all he contributed and the subject was changed.

'Colin Mair lived in Queich didn't he?' Sylvie, who was an incomer, asked.

'Aye,' Hughie replied when no-one else spoke, 'for a wee while.' Colin had gone on to become a popular writer of fantasy/crime fiction. His books had all been serialised on the box and his name was famous worldwide.

'I just love his books.'

No one spoke. I wouldna gie them house room, Hughie thought.

Elvis got to his feet. 'Well, if you folks will excuse me I'm for bed. Big day tomorrow, eh bro?'

Hughie's birthday passed in a blur of chatter, laughter and food, with intermittent breaks to see to the beasts. 'I told you,' Shona whispered to him as the cottage heaved with family and neighbours,' we should have taken St Serf's Hall.'

'Aye well, it's too late now,' he shouted back to her a decibel louder than the chatter around him. He had deliberately decided against a public hall because of Elvis. If a rumour had got out that Fergus of the Fifers was around, the village would have been mobbed. As it was, he was kept busy with selfies and signatures.

Tammy found him on one of his escapes mucking out the night's ordure from the byre. 'I need to speak to you, Hughie,' she called out.

'I'm coming back,' he replied. 'You'd better no' come in here in those posh shoes.'

'Privately,' she told him ominously.

He had a wee smile to himself as he remembered that Tammy, who had become remarkably like his mam, usually got her own way. He had almost finished his work any road. 'At your service, Tamsin.'

'It's Elvis. What's wrong with him?' she demanded as he opened the doors of the byre wide to let in the good fresh air. When he didn't immediately reply she added.' Surely you've noticed?'

'Noticed what?'

'Och Hughie, you're useless. You never did notice anything except your dogs and the farm.'

It was a common theme of hers. He had not noticed her when she fell pregnant aged fifteen and had the baby adopted by the local authority and he had been no help at all when Elvis had left home for good. He had done nothing to stop him. 'What am I supposed to have missed this time?' he asked a little huffily because there was a certain truth in her complaints. Shona said much the same.

So she stood outside the byre door, a little, fiery woman a bit too plump for her flowery dress, on heels that were a bit too high for her short legs, with hair that was too blonde to be natural, and make-up that was way too heavy for the countryside. Watching her and waiting for her to speak, the rancour left him and he realised he loved her. She was his little sister and he had always loved her. 'Go on, hen, 'he said,' tell me the worst.'

She saw his contrition and instantly forgave him. 'It's Elvis,' she said. 'He looks like death warmed up. There's something far the matter.'

'He's looking a bit tired I'll give you that. No wonder, the stuff he has to do, the career he's had.'

'I reckon it's more than that.'

'Have you asked him?'

'Of course I have, but you know Elvis. He's a right clam when he wants to be which, come to think of it; he's been for most of his life. Remember him as a bairn shut up in that wee room up the stair playing that bloody guitar from morning to night. Never spoke hardly. Never told us he was leaving home. I reckon he broke Mam's heart.'

Did he? All he could remember was that Elvis was just like any other teenager, moody, silent, secretive, and, right enough, obsessed with his guitar.

'You need to find out what's wrong, Hughie. It could be serious.'

'Yes ma'am,' he saluted mockingly, but he wondered if maybe she could be right.

'Come on,' she said,' we'd best go back. Shona'll be sending out a search party.'

No more mention was made of Elvis but he remembered what she had said. He watched him seated in the same easy chair that he had taken last night, surrounded by Tammy's three lassies, Jayjay and Janet's two teenagers, the vet's kids and he was joshing them, charming them, posing for selfies, this celebrity pop star who happened to be his wee brother and he loved him too.

The cake was cut, a toast given by his son, Robert, a lot of Prosecco and whisky drunk, a host of cell phones flashed and gallons of tea consumed with slices of Shona's home-made birthday cake. He even managed to make a wee speech himself, though afterwards he couldn't remember a word he had said. He hoped he had thanked everyone properly.

By seven most of the guests had left. Tammy was the last to go. Elvis joined him to see her and her kids off. As she hugged him, Hughie felt the wetness of tears on her cheeks. 'I reckon it's goodbye for good,' she whispered.

'Wheesht your nonsense, woman,' he murmured in her ear, deliberately misunderstanding. 'I'll see you next week.'

'Ye ken who I mean,' she told him and of course he did.

Time to bring the beasts in. It would be pitch dark soon. He changed into his boots, called to the dogs and found his stick. The cattle settled, he decided to take a dander up the hill. It was still light enough to take a look at the sheep.

In the glimmer of twilight the dogs started to bark and bounded off down the hill. The intruder was only Elvis. He was panting. 'For God's sake, mate, give us a break. This is some hill.'

They both sat down on tussocks of heather. The sky was black to the east, pin-pricked with stars and fading to midnight blue above which blended to azure and ended in a strip of fiery gold on the horizon for the sun had set. This was his chance, Hughie thought, but he could not take it for he did not want to know what Tammy feared. After a while they both spoke at the same time. 'This is a bonny place sure enough, bro,' Elvis began while Hughie said, 'There'll be frost in it later.'

They sat in silence for a while then Elvis said, 'I saw her, you know.'

'Saw who?'

'Sunshine - Maryam.'

He was instantly curious. 'You saw her? You never said. Where? How was she?'

He was silent for a moment. 'At least I think I saw her, but maybe I didn't. Maybe I dreamed it all.'

Hughie listened carefully. Seemingly Elvis had gone into a supermarket on the outskirts of Manchester after a gig late one evening a couple of weeks back to get some fags. 'I don't to this day know why I didn't get Zack - my driver - to get them. He usually does stuff like that but something made me go.' There had been only two pay check-out kiosks open at that hour so he took the one with the shortest line. While waiting he noticed there was a hold-up in the adjacent queue. Some old biddy obviously troubled, possibly drunk, was taking an age to go through the check-out, so long in fact that the short queue of impatient customers had drifted off to join the only other lane open which happened to be his. The girl on the other till was helping the old soul pack her bag and sort out her money. Tired though he had been, he noticed the care she was giving the old biddy. Suddenly or so it seemed to him the store seemed brighter, as if an extra light had been switched on. Then he noticed that the check-out girl was wearing a headscarf. He was just about to be served when she looked up and caught his eye. 'It was Maryam. I swear to you I thought it was Maryam... I remembered it was a Friday. Maryam always wore a headscarf on Fridays, didn't she?'

Hughie could hardly believe it. 'How did you recognise her? After all it was - what? Thirty five years ago.'

'That's the problem. She looked exactly the same. The same dark eyes, the same slightly hooked nose, the same brown, flawless skin. I'd forgotten just how pretty she was.'

Hughie was astonished. 'Did you speak to her?'

'Of course. After I paid for the fags I went over to her kiosk and I said her name.'

'So?' Hugh urged impatiently.

'She was still busy with the old woman but she stopped what she was doing and she looked up at me in that weird way of hers but all she said was, "Can I help you, sir?"'

Hughie listened avidly. Elvis had then told her his name, but it had obviously meant nothing to her so he had hastily apologised. 'I'm sorry,' he had said, 'I thought you were someone I used to know.'

He had turned to leave but then with his back turned she had spoken. 'Or maybe I imagined she had spoken. I'd just done a gig and I was a bit spaced out.' He paused.

'Go on then. What did she say?'

'Just two words. Tell Hughie.'

'Tell me what?' he asked but Elvis did not immediately answer. 'I turned round but she was busy with her next customer, so I left. I got back in the car with Zack and he drove straight to the hotel.'

Elvis had gone back to the supermarket the next day but there was no sign of her. He had found the manager who told him he had several staff who wore a hijab but no-one of that name. He even looked up to see who had been on the night shift. Several had Asian names but none of them was called Maryam.'

Hughie was quiet for a moment. It was a weird tale right enough and he was inclined to believe that Elvis had been hallucinating. Now was his chance to speak. 'I reckon I know what you need to tell us, Elvis.'

He was obviously startled. 'You know? You're telling me you've known all along?'

'Tammy guessed. You're no' weel, laddie,' he told him reverting to his childhood Scots.

'Aye, there is that, right enough.'

'Ye were aye peely-wally. Whit's wrang wi' ye, laddie?'

'My own fault, I guess. Too much booze and too many fags. When was I ever right?' He laughed, a little joyless bark.

'Was it yon Mair? Did he meddle wi' ye?'

'Aye, of course he did. Wi' you too, I reckon.'

Hughie felt his whole body flush with the memory. Thank God it was too dark to see each other's faces. He had never spoken of what had happened here on this very hill. 'I legged it in time.'

'Aye - and you had Jura.'

228

It was not said with bitterness, but as a matter of fact. And indeed it was true. Jura had saved him. Who had been there for Elvis? 'You got the guitar.'

'Aye and I reckon I paid for it.'

'Would you no' tell the polis? It's never too late, so they say.'

'Believe me, I've thought of it.'

'Why the no?'

He explained that it had been a transaction. He got the lessons and he paid the asking price. The guitar, however, was for something different. 'How different?' Hughie asked curiously.

What Elvis told him next shocked him into silence. 'It was me,' he told him abruptly. 'Me that poisoned your dog.'

Hughie listened appalled to the sorry tale. Mair had given him a bit of the steak he had got at the Safeway supermarket for his mother's wee dog. He had cut off a small piece as a treat for Jura and wrapped it in greaseproof paper. All Elvis had to do was feed it to the dog. 'Best keep quiet about where it came from, though,' Mair had told him. 'Hugh's not exactly enamoured of me.' Those were his exact words, so Elvis had slipped it to Jura when she was out peeing in the back yard.

'Were you not suspicious? Why would he want to give anything to my dog? He hated me,' Hughie asked.

'At the time I thought it was dead nice of him,' Elvis explained.

Afterwards when Jura was so sick the weirdie started the blackmail. 'Told me he'd tell Mam it was me that had pushed the laburnum seed into the meat and fed it to him out of sheer spite unless I did everything he told me. Who would believe a snotty-nosed little liar like me?'

So Elvis had done everything that was asked of him until that last day when he had run away. 'He was taking me out in a boat to the Castle Island for a picnic. A back-to-school treat for being a good boy,' he told me. 'He had a boat ordered at the pier for two o'clock that afternoon.'

'Was that why you ran away?'

'I was scared. I remembered the boy who was mysteriously drowned in the loch. I overheard Mr Maclardy, the daft one, telling Mam it was Mr Mair that did it. I thought he might push me off the boat too. I was finished whatever I did. If I went with him he'd drown me and if I didn't go with him, he'd tell Mam about Jura, and the police would put me to Borstal and you'd never speak to me again.' He paused. 'It was Maryam that stopped me. She told me to run home. How could I go home? Mair would go straight round to Mam, so I ran. I got the bus to Kirkcaldy. I was going to get a job.'

Pity and bewilderment silenced Hughie. He did not know what to think. Had Maryam confronted Mair? Was it Mair, then, who had got rid of her?

229

Was she still lying out there somewhere in the private woodlands behind the shed, her body undiscovered after all these years? Had he killed her and gone off to that dinner in Edinburgh? It was, after all, the perfect alibi. When he asked his brother, he had no answers either.

'How could you keep quiet all these years, Elvis? How come you never said?'

Elvis turned to him. It was now dark but a moon had risen. His face was in its shadow. 'I've tried to make amends,' was all he said.

Right enough. He had indeed made amends. 'Aye, you surely have,' he said as he remembered his brother's seemingly reckless generosity. 'Over and over.'

'Do you think it could have been Maryam I saw?' Elvis asked.

Hughie shook his head. 'How would I know, bro? But if it was, I guess she knew that I would aye forgive you.'

They were both silent for a while.

'Historic abuse,' Hughie said suddenly. 'That's what they call it these days. You need to go to the police, Elvis. It's not too late.'

His brother shook his head. 'I've written a letter. My lawyer has instructions to hand it over to the police in due course. Meanwhile I'm flying back to Australia tomorrow. I won't be visiting Scotland again. I'm finished, mate. In more ways than one.'

'How?' he made himself ask but he was dreading the answer. 'Tammy thinks you're sick.'

'Liver cancer. Too late for a transplant... I never meant to tell any of you.'

Hughie put his arm around his brother and pulled him close. 'You daft nut,' he said gently. 'I would have forgiven you even back then,' he said. Tears had gathered in his eyes.

Maryam

In the Tesco canteen on the outskirts of Manchester the women crowded round Dotty eager to see the photograph. 'I got some copies printed off my phone. See for yourselves. It's him. It's Fergus from Fergus and the Fifers, like I told you.'

Several women were keen to see. It was not everyday a celebrity stopped by. 'I never thought he wore specs. Are you certain it's him?'

'It's him all right. My mum'll be over the moon. She's a fan,' said another.

'He looks so fuckin' old,' said the youngest, a bit bored.

'Got one for you special, Rana, seeing you're in it.' Dotty handed it to her.

The brown girl who was called Rana thanked her and glanced at the photo. All it showed was the back of her head scarf. His body was half turned but his face was full on, looking down at her over his shoulder as he walked away. She tucked it into her purse.

'Did you speak to him, Rana? What did he say?'

She shrugged. 'Nothing much.'

'How could you not recognise him? He's dead famous,' said Dotty.

'Perhaps her folks don't bother with pop,' said Ruby who was old enough to be their granny. 'Maybe they listen to proper music. You're a lot of savages,' she added without rancour.

But Rana had recognised him, sort of. As the tea break was almost over there was a rush for the toilets. Safely locked in a cubicle she took out the photo and gazed at it but still she could not place him. She knew of Fergus and the Fifers of course. Who didn't? She'd seen photos in the papers but she had never looked at them for long enough to remember them. The glasses, wrap-around and tinted, obviously changed his appearance, probably on purpose. But it was not, of course, the face that she had recognised, it was the shadow. She had glimpsed it only for a moment as he had turned away to leave the supermarket. That exhausted, sad shadow was instantly memorable, but from where?

Though it had happened a few weeks past, the memory was still distinct and fresh, mainly because of what the photograph had not revealed. She had been helping Mrs O'Brian with her groceries. The old lady lived by herself and needed not just her help but also her company for she stayed alone in the tenth floor of Springfields, a high-rise building, surrounded by people but known to none of them, though, thanks largely to Rana and Dotty who lived in the adjacent tower block, she was now not entirely friendless. She had looked up by chance and seen the stranger as he was being served by Dotty but had not looked for his shadow. Then he had stopped by her kiosk and called her by a strange name; 'Maryam'. At first she thought he had mistaken her for someone else so then she had looked for his shadow, that precious reflection of Our Mother, and realised that indeed she had once known him. It was her shadow that had spoken to him though the words had been involuntary and, at the time meaningless to her. 'Tell Hughie.'

Who was Hughie? She knew no Hughie and who was Maryam? Whether or not he had heard her she had no means of telling for he had already gone.

For the next two hours she had been too busy to think of the customer who, according to Dotty, had turned out to be a celebrity, but, walking home to her apartment her mind was pricked with distant stars of memory which as the days passed had begun to grow into moons.

231

Rana lived in Summerleas, a three-apartment flat on the fifth floor which she shared with Beth, who had been in hospital with her after the accident. The hospital social worker had found it for them and it had worked out well. It was on the face of it, a strange friendship. They had met in the hospital café where Beth, frail and menopausal, was learning to walk again after a bad car accident and Rana was recovering from amnesia. She had been found by the traffic police on the hard shoulder of a six-lane motorway and taken straight to the nearest hospital. Unhurt in body, she could remember nothing and no one except for the wind; her amnesia was total.

The supermarket job had also been found for her by the social worker but sharing the flat with Beth had been their own idea. Almost her own idea. It was Beth's shadow that had drawn her, for it had a strength and humour that belied the brokenness of her body. She knew that she needed that strength but she could not remember why. She guessed there had been other shadows in her life, many of them, and all of them reflections of Our Mother. She knew too that the great and joyous wind that had brought her here had come from Our Mother, that somehow she had been saved by the wind that had at the same time blown away her memory. With her body? How did she know that? Because she could remember Our Mother gathering her up in a whirlwind of love and beauty and joy and telling her to listen. All she could remember for certain was the joy.

Before Our Mother and the wind, however, she could remember nothing, at least nothing but those little moons pricking the dark depths of her mind until the celebrity called Fergus had called her Maryam.

'Do you want to remember?' Beth asked her. 'Sometimes it's better to forget the past.' Beth had memories that she would rather forget; a cold mother, a profligate and philandering husband who was now in jail. 'Perhaps the good Lord, or the Mother you speak of, also gave you the gift of amnesia.'

She had taken comfort from that advice and had grown to love the disparate community where she worked at a check-out counter in a Tesco superstore on the outskirts of Manchester. There she befriended and was quickly caught up in the lives and problems of her colleagues and customers, watched over their often conflicted shadows and listened to Our Mother. She was too busy to be other than content. At least until that night… The photograph now rested against the stem of the lamp by the side of her bed.

It was the day after she had come off night shift. Sleep evaded her as it always did on the nights she changed shifts. She got up quietly so as not to disturb Beth next door - the walls of their small apartment on the fifteenth floor were paper thin - made herself a cup of chocolate that usually sent her straight off 'to Bedfordshire' as old Mr Hogg on the seventh floor would say, and almost immediately fell into a strange state of hallucination.

Rana knew she dreamed. Her nights were as busy as her days but apart from brief moments of realisation that she had had busy dreams, the memory of them vanished on waking. Beth often told her of her own vivid dreams, but Rana could remember nothing of her own until the night after she had changed shifts...

She was in the High Street in Queich and between the shoppers and other passers-by she had caught glimpses of Elvis, the little boy with the ginger hair, pallid skin and pure green eyes. His shadow immediately alerted her, so she had caught up with him and called out his name.

He looked scared and she knew that he was right to be so for at that moment she could see lurking in a shop doorway behind him that other shadow, the Evil Other that walked alone, that had haunted her from time to time ever since she had started work at Bruden's.

'You need to go home, Elvis, 'she had told him and because that other shadow had moved out of the doorway, she had added urgently. 'Run. You need to run.'

So he had run. His feet in grubby trainers wove between the strollers and browsers heedless of everyone. Several heads turned to watch, several mouths muttered disapproval.

The lone shadow too had gone. For the child's sake, it was time to confront the reality. Our Mother help me now.

Church Street was quiet. She had seen no one, not even a dog. A couple of sparrows flitted across her path but today she had no time to speak to them. It was warm and windless. Somewhere distant a dog barked. She opened the Mairs' gate and forced herself to walk up to the front door. The bell jangled its usual tune. After a moment or two Mrs Mair answered. Her shadow cowered quietly behind her. Mayam knew before she asked that her son was out.

'Well?' she said without grace or enthusiasm as was her way. 'What do you want?'

Maryam had never got to know the little woman with the frizzy perm and the yappy little dog, not because she hadn't tried. Her shadow revealed so little as to be sometimes barely visible. Though she had no craic on the occasions she visited the shop, she could be sharp and critical.

'Would it be possible to have a word with Mr Mair?' she asked politely.

'He's out,' she answered shortly. The little dog, recognizing her, pushed past his mistress to welcome Maryam.

'Hi, Tina.' As she bent down to fondle its ruff, the little creature leapt up into her arms.

Immediately Mrs Mairs attitude softened. 'She likes you,' she remembered, surprised.

'She's a precious little soul.'

Mrs Mair took a step closer to relieve her of the dog but Tina was in no hurry to leave her friend. Then she said surprisingly, 'I was just about to make a cup of tea. Would you care to join me? Maybe you're too busy?' she asked tentatively.

Still holding the vibrant little creature who was attempting to lick her face, Maryam thanked her and followed her into the sitting room.

'Make yourself comfortable. I won't be a minute.' Mrs Mair disappeared so she looked round her. It was a strangely featureless room; no photographs, no cards propped up on the mantelpiece, no books, magazines, potted plants or flowers. No pictures on the wall apart from a large rectangular print above the mantelpiece of mountain scenery which might have been anywhere in Europe but was certainly not Scotland. The obligatory sofa, two easy chairs and a couple of occasional tables with coasters were conventionally arranged on a beige carpet. The windows were shrouded in net curtains. It reminded Maryam of a hotel lounge. She sat down on one of the chairs with Tina now a fixture on her lap.

Mrs Mair came back with a tray, two mugs of tea and a plate of ginger snaps. 'I must apologise for the mugs. I prefer china cups and saucers but' - she placed Maryam's mug carefully on the nearest coaster - 'I suppose I'd better tell you the news. We're leaving Queich and my china is already packed.'

An enormous feeling of relief silenced Maryam for a moment. 'I hadn't heard,' she said eventually as Tina climbed down from her lap at the prospect of a biscuit.

'You're the first person I've told.' She leaned forward in her chair and added, confidentially, 'I suppose I might as well tell you the whole story. It'll be all over the papers tomorrow, I imagine.'

Her shadow took shape and emerged and Maryam could see that it was trembling with anticipation. 'What has happened?' she asked.

'It's my Colin,' she said. 'The reason he's not here. He's in Edinburgh. He's one of a short list of five to receive the Duncan award for Fantasy Fiction.'

'That's wonderful,' she said with genuine relief. Had she perhaps got him wrong?

'The results are to be announced at a dinner in the university tonight. Of course he might not get it, but I'm hopeful. He's worked so hard at his writing over the years. He deserves a bit of recognition.'

'He'll get it,' she said for somehow she had no doubt that he would win.

'Thank you for that,' she replied graciously, 'but we won't know until much later. I expect I shall be in bed long before the celebrating is over.' Colin had seemingly received a generous advance. They could now afford to move from this bungalow to something a bit more upmarket, a flat on the outskirts of Edinburgh New Town, in fact. The peace and quiet of Queich had suited him well for his research but now they could afford to live in the city.

'I'm happy for you,' she said meaning it. This sad little woman was obviously proud of her son. She rose to go but Mrs Mair was not yet ready to let her leave.

'Maryam,' she said. It was possibly the first time she had used her name. 'Did you mean it when you called my wee Tina a precious soul?'

'Yes,' she said firmly, 'of course I meant it.'

'You see most people don't believe animals have souls, my Colin for one. I wasn't sure you really meant it.'

Maryam was quiet for a moment, then she said, 'I know it, Mrs Mair.'

'But how? How do you know it?'

'Because they are all creations of Our Mother. How can they not have souls?'

Mrs Mair paused as she digested what she had heard but 'thank you,' was all she said. 'I believe it too.'

At the door Maryam had a final question. 'I never asked,' she said. 'What is Mr Mair's book called?'

"The Evil Other,' I believe.'

Of course, she thought as she let herself out of the gate, and who knows better than he does. Had he perhaps created his own 'evil other' shadow? It was certainly not of Our Mother's making. Chilled, though the late afternoon was warm and humid, she saw Tammy on the far side of the street and waved. She came running across the road. 'Hi Sunshine!' she said. 'Was Elvis wi' they folk? It's tea time and he's got to come home.'

'He's not at the Mairs,' she told her. 'I saw him in the High Street about an hour ago. He should be home by now.'

'Well he's no' come back.' Tammy was disgruntled. 'I always get sent to find him. It's no' fair.'

Maryam looked at her watch. It was well over an hour since she had spoken to him. Where had he gone? Had that shadow, that 'Evil Other', somehow waylaid him? Run home, she had told him. You need to run, she had urged him and he had done what she had told him. She remembered those trainers weaving between the shoppers on the High Street.

'I'll find him, Tammy,' she said with more assurance than she felt. 'You run home and have your tea.' This time she watched as Tammy ran up Church Street and disappeared into her own door.

So for the next hour or so she had scoured the streets of Queich, the back lanes, the front gardens, the garages. 'Our Mother protect your child,' she prayed as she searched the woods and prickly undergrowth of briar and brambles in the hedges that lined the road out of the village. She needed to make sure he was not still running. At the back of her mind she knew she would have to search the shore of the loch. She did not like the loch. The incident of the drowned lad which had dominated her first month at Bruden's and Mr Gordon's conviction that his neighbour had been involved in his death still haunted her.

It was getting late by the time she reached the loch. She was tired and hungry but she could not let it go. At every turn and at any moment she expected to see not Colin Mair but his much more frightening detached shadow, his Evil Other. Shading her eyes against the late evening sun that turned the loch to a fiery gold, she could see no boat, no disturbance on the water, no sign of the child or indeed of the lone shadow. A few people out for an evening stroll shook their heads. No one had noticed Elvis.

It was dark by the time she reached the shed. Warped and stiff, the handle long gone, the door eventually scraped open. The place stank of cigarette smoke and something else that she could not recognise but suspected was pot. Still standing on the threshold for she was reluctant to go inside, she could see nothing for the one small Perspex window was thick with dust and cobwebs. A boat house it may once have been but now there were no boats to be seen. All she heard was the skitter and scatter of terrified insects. 'You have nothing to fear from me,' she said aloud. Her voice sounded loud and strange in the stuffy silence.

Something glimmered in the far right corner. 'Elvis?' she called, 'is that you?

The bundle was still. Without thinking, she let go of the side of the door and stepped into the darkness, Immediately the door behind her screeched shut and she was left in total darkness. A moment of sheer terror transfixed her. She turned to push it open but the door would not budge. She pushed and pulled and she wanted to scream. 'Our Mother help me now,' she shouted aloud but she could not reach that place in her head where her shadow lived. It was as if the door to her soul was barred not only to her own shadow but also to Our Mother. Then she remembered why she was here.

236

'Elvis?' she cried, but there was only silence. Groping her way over to where the bundle lay, she forced herself to touch it and could have wept with relief to feel nothing but old sacking and disintegrating newspapers. The smell was overpowering, no longer the stink of smoke and pot or even faeces. This was feral, evil. She covered her nose with one hand and with the other groped her way back to the door. It must have jammed. The wood was old and rotten, the lock like the handle long gone. Surely she should be strong enough to shift it. What she needed was an axe, a weapon of some sort to break her way out. Groping her way round the small enclosure she felt in the corners and over the dirty splintering floor but there was nothing. Desperate now, she began to shout for help, but without much hope. The shed was half a mile at least from the pier, the woodland behind it dense, overgrown and private. Who would hear her? Maybe a late fisherman in a boat out on the loch? 'Help - please,' she shouted again and again, battering the stubborn door at the same time.

After a while she gave up hope. 'Our Mother where are you?' she cried in despair. Crouched down on the heap of sacking, she clutched her knees and tried to breathe. What had happened to Our Mother? Where was her own shadow when she needed it? What if it were all a huge deception, worse that she was mad, that she had never seen any shadows, never heard Our Mother? Those voices in her head proved she was schizophrenic as indeed she knew from her schooldays onwards she had often been called, not only behind her back but sometimes face-to-face.

After a while - she could not tell how long, for her perception of time had ceased to exist - she got up again and groped her way back to the door. This time it opened to her touch. But the relief that flooded over her abruptly ceased. There standing in front of her was a darker form against the darkness of the night. The strength of its presence forced her back inside the shed.

And now she was truly afraid. She tried to push past it but it stood there, dark and icy-cold, impenetrable, blocking her exit whichever way she turned. It was too dark to see its features but she knew exactly how it looked. Then she heard it laugh that lone shadow, the Evil Other. Colin Mair did not have to be here in person. Indeed he would be exactly where his mother had told her he was going; some dinner and ceremony to applaud his book.

The blackness engulfed her in a freezing embrace forcing her backwards into the depths of the shed. The door closed behind him.

'Allah, Jesus, Our Mother, save me now,' she implored aloud.

The shadow seemed to tremble. That laugh again. Then his words, clearly spoken in her head, voiced her own fear. 'How can they help you? They do not exist?'

'You're wrong,' she cried, shrinking against the further wall as the shadow now threatened to engulf her. She needed a weapon. Shaking, her fingers fumbled for the silver cross around her neck, found it and yanked it off.

'Our Mother save me now,' she cried and flung it into the encroaching blackness.

Then she heard the wind, at last the wind, the miraculous, mighty wind. Roaring, powerful, indomitable, it shook the walls of the little shed. The door blew in, and with it the window, until suddenly she was there. Our Mother was there and Maryam was caught up in that wonderful whirlwind of love and joy. The Evil Other had gone.

....

Rana lay there, eyes closed, quietly remembering Maryam but not just Maryam. There had been many others over the centuries, but in that moment and just for a moment, she remembered them all. A wind touched her cheek and played with her hair. She opened her eyes and it was no longer a dream.

'My daughter listen... liss-ten...'

'I am listening,' she said, immediately alert.

'It is time.'

'Why me?' she asked.

The answer came though the words were barely changed. 'My daughter - you lisss...tened.'

Then Rana too was gone, caught up in that whirlwind of love that was Our Mother, just as Maryam and all the others had gone and the dream forgotten.

Yet they still remained, these Daughters of Our Mother, to be remembered in time and in eternity with love in the souls and minds and memories of those whose lives they had touched.